Laura Fitzgerald

Principled and talented, she must learn to be her own woman in a town that is her mother's turf . . .

Jessamyn Friday

Astonishingly beautiful . . . shockingly vain . . . the actress who is incapable of having anyone else, even her own daughter, shine in her presence . . .

Jake Turner

A man determined to escape his past. Rugged and handsome, his aura of confidence masks his confusion about happiness, success, and especially love . . .

Nel Simmons

Jessamyn's long-time personal secretary was the mother to Laura that Jessamyn could never be. Now she is struggling with her own private hell . . .

Eddie Brown

Nel Simmons was all he ever wanted, but he got sidetracked along the way. Now the only thing worth living for is her love . . .

FRIDAY'S DAUGHTER

Also by Mary Ruth Myers
Published by Ballantine Books:

A PRIVATE MATTER

INSIGHTS

FRIDAY'S DAUGHTER

Mary Ruth Myers

BALLANTINE BOOKS • NEW YORK

Library of Congress Catalog Card Number: 83-91246

ISBN 0-345-30448-9

Manufactured in the United States of America

First Edition: March 1984

For Aunt Flo
And in loving memory of Uncle Glen

Friday's child is loving and giving.

One 🦋

With a deep breath Laura Fitzgerald crossed the porch of the sprawling house in Beverly Hills and leaned on the bell. By the dozens of cars in the walled motor court and the babel of sounds from within, she knew she had timed her arrival badly.

A shaft of golden light from the opening door fell on her, making a haze of the wisps of black hair escaping confinement high on her head.

"Invitation please?" said the white-clad houseman blocking her way.

Her green-gray eyes danced with angry amusement.

"I don't think I need one. I'm Miss Friday's daughter."

Unmentioned, unexpected, and about to start a civil war by my return, she thought. She had not set foot in this house for seven years, not since she was eighteen and it was made clear to her she was not wanted here even on holidays. This houseman was new, hired in the interim. Laura saw him look skeptically at her slim, slightly tall form in which there was no resemblance to her famous mother.

"Actually it's Nel Simmons I've come to see," she said to put him at ease.

"I'll have to check," he said, and closed the door.

Laura curled her hands into the pockets of the open tweed jacket swinging above her slacks and waited. It was done. The ties with New York were severed. She had come back to do what she'd always known she must do. Her heart was pounding.

Stan Weisbecker, her mother's agent, returned with the houseman.

"Did Jessamyn know you were coming?" he asked as they walked through a marble hallway and into a paneled living room filled with people.

She shook her head. Now that she was here her throat felt suddenly choked with nervousness. In New York her simple

1

silk blouse and the threadlike gold chains shimmering at her soft throat would have won her compliments for an understated elegance. Here, in this room full of people wearing designer jeans and handmade boots and madly expensive Halston evening clothes she was out of place. She should never have shown up here unannounced.

Laura's searching gaze settled on an apricot-clad woman surrounded by men. As if some electrical impulse had traveled between them, the woman looked up. Even at twenty-five Laura felt the quickening of the old hope, the thought that perhaps this time there would be a smile, but across the width of the room she could see the tensing of her mother's body.

What an idiot you must be, Laura. Don't you know you've never been more than an item on the tax return of Jessamyn Friday?

Jessamyn began to walk toward her, slowly at first, then with steps that whipped the silk pants fluttering at her ankles. She was beautiful. The billowing waves of her hair glinted with the color of fire through amber, and that color and spark glowed in her eyes. Guileful, smoldering, half-closed eyes, the trademark of Jessamyn Friday. The cameras of a dozen box-office hits had filled screens with their magic. Magazines had tried to capture them. Laura, watching her, became a child again, enraptured, longing to touch, yet knowing it was forbidden.

Suddenly a radiant smile broke over Jessamyn's face. She extended creamy hands in a gesture of welcome. Laura felt her spirits snap free of some carefully tethered mooring and shoot heavenward. *Jessamyn was glad to see her! Jessamyn was going to acknowledge her in front of all these people!*

"Darling!" sang her mother's voice as Laura reached out eagerly for the welcome she'd never dared to hope for.

Jessamyn sailed past her, caught the hands of a short, gray-haired woman with a bulldog face, and kissed at the air.

"How good to see you, Susie!"

Laura struggled against the crushing feeling of naiveté that threatened to make her blush. She felt so foolish, so small.

Damn it, Jessamyn, why couldn't you at least pretend to be glad to see me? she thought bitterly. What is it that I've ever done?

Her mother's flawless face turned toward her now.

"What are you doing here?" Jessamyn's voice was throaty,

seductive to most, dangerous to those who could detect displeasure in it as Laura could now.

"I read about Nel collapsing. It scared me out of my mind. I decided to come."

The truth, but not the whole truth. I'm here to win your approval, Jessamyn. I've got what it takes to be a terrific screenwriter. Five years in New York has proved it to me, and I'm going to prove it to you and to everyone else. I could never follow in your footsteps in front of the camera, but I've got a gift of my own. I want to be in your city. I want to be in your business. The days of being Jess Friday's plain little no-talent are over now. Reading about Nel just moved my schedule up a little.

Laura heard her voice running on calmly, hiding her nervousness. "I'm sorry I didn't let you know that I was coming. I wasn't sure I'd get a flight. How is Nel? What—?"

"She's in her apartment."

The famous eyes had narrowed with a speculation used on enemies. Was she her mother's enemy? Jessamyn turned, taking a glass from a passing houseboy and slipping into the crowd again.

Laura shoved her hands into the pockets of her jacket. When would she ever learn? Invisible to the glittering partygoers intent on themselves and their knots of conversation, she moved toward the wing of the house where her mother's personal secretary, Nel Simmons, had her rooms. As she neared them, a warm joy burst inside her, filling her with the certainty that at last she was home.

The voices and the throbbing rock music from Jessamyn's party were lost on the attractive black woman lying on a chaise lounge. She stared into shadows. Her fluid saffron robe fell open to reveal slim legs the color of deep, rich walnut; lovely, perfectly proportioned dancer's legs that had brought her long ago to this city of dreams. Nel Simmons studied them with a strange detachment, recrossing them, looking for some change in them that would bring the reality home to her. One year, maybe two. That was how long the doctor said she would live.

There was a tap and a soft voice at her door.

"Nel? Are you awake?"

All other thoughts dissolved in joy, and Nel sat up.

"Is that you, kiddo?" she asked, incredulous.

They did a quick, laughing journey into each other's arms. Then Nel, in rapid question, drew back to see if Laura knew. Of course she didn't. Only Nel and the doctor knew. Something else had brought Laura here. She was beaming at Nel with that impish, uncertain smile, stray strands of hair curving as usual into curls, cheeks bright with color.

"Hey, it's great to see you, kiddo. *And* you look terrific! What're you doing back in the smog belt?"

Laura brushed aside the question. "How are you, Nel? I read about you getting sick. What happened?"

Nel made a face.

"Stan says it was indigestion. My punishment for not chewing every mouthful thirteen times."

They laughed as one at Jessamyn's agent, who cured his own ills by wearing a square of flannel around his throat and drinking warm milk.

"Actually I think it was my comeuppance for being a smart ass and eating a sour cream *chimi* I bought from a street vendor. Wouldn't you know it would hit me a day later in some fancy restaurant? Such a fuss over nothing. That's the price for tagging along with Jess, I guess—instant press coverage."

Nel curled sideways on the chaise lounge, lighting a cigarette. Sleek, striking, smart-looking, she was a woman who radiated life. She had lived with Jessamyn's whims and tantrums for twenty-six years, since before Laura's birth, when they were both younger than Laura was now. A relationship much deeper than employer-employee had grown up between them. But it was nothing compared with Nel's feelings for this sparkling girl with the wistful eyes and vulnerable heart. Both of them played tough; Laura, poor kid, had learned how too young, had learned it to protect herself. Still, with no words spoken, Nel knew they shared the warmth of this moment.

"So what are you doing here, kiddo? You're supposed to be making heat waves back in New York."

Laura laughed, lips as dewy as rose petals. Like a goddamn painting with that perfectly cut nose and those flyaway curls—only she doesn't know it, thought Nel.

"Some heat waves. Rewriting history for talking animals five days a week," Laura said. "But public TV's a lot more fun than educational video kits ever were. And that last docu-drama I freelanced came out better than I'd ever dreamed. It's been picked up by a half dozen other stations. Looks like it might even win me an area Emmy."

"The one about the lady who's raped and takes it to court?"

"Oh, Nel! You're fantastic to remember!" Laura's eyes misted as she regarded the woman who had kept track of her every venture, her every project, starting with a role as Chicken Little in a first grade play.

"Yes, that's the one. It shows the kind of work I'm capable of, I think, and so-o-o..." She walked across one of Nel's Persian rugs and collapsed in a chair, wondering if Nel, who had always supported her, would say she was crazy. Draping elbows across the chair, she gave a small smile.

"I've decided I'm going to try for the big time, Nellie. I want to write for the networks."

Oh, shit, thought Nel. Oh, Laura, don't say it. Don't tell me you're going to come back to this town and try to break in. Don't you know it would be hard enough without your mother?

"I don't believe it," she joked. "You escaped to the good life, and now you want to come back here? What's the attraction?"

Behind Laura's shell of poise, Nel saw relief.

"It's in my blood, I guess. It's funny, I thought I wanted to be as far away as possible—away from Hollywood, away from Jessamyn." She sat forward on her chair, and her words rushed out. "There's something I've got to prove, Nel. To Jess and to myself. I've got talent, and I want that talent recognized. Maybe I've always known that and ran away rather than be judged in a town where Jess was known.

"It's all silly, isn't it? Outside the business no one even knows screenwriters exist, and inside the business they're at the bottom of the heap. It's sure not fame I'm after. I don't know what it is. But I love the work, Nel. I love the challenge. I want to see if I'm good enough to run in the big race—and that means here."

Nel studied the eager face turned towards hers, the intensity of the eyes, the undefinable air of breeding and manners that lent a soft luminescence.

Nel had always wondered where that air of breeding came from.

"I expect you can do it, kiddo," she said gently.

Could I change her mind if I tried? Nel wondered. Do I have a right to? She's going to get hurt, and I'm sitting here like a fool telling her it's okay.

Maybe I'm worrying for nothing. Jessamyn won't touch TV with a ten-foot pole. The last time Stan tried to approach her about a TV movie she threw him out. She's only listening to Jake Turner's pitch about his vidpic because she wants to get Turner into the sack with her. I've been with Jess long enough to know when she's hunting. Well, maybe if she doesn't have anything to do with the territory, she'll cede it to Laura without a war. But my God, Laura, I wish you weren't going to be where your two orbits could collide!

"Frankly, kiddo, I don't like the thought of you working your tail off," she admitted. "Don't tell anyone what a sentimental slob I am, but I've always hoped Sir Gallahad would come along for you."

With a grin Laura settled back in her chair, this time to stay.

"Flat fannie, flat future, Nellie."

"Hell, if that's the problem, we'll buy you a padded girdle from Frederick's of Hollywood."

Laura suddenly turned serious. "No, that's not the whole problem, Nel. I'm no raving beauty, but I'm not so bad. It's just that I don't—I'm not like Jessamyn."

There was a silence filled with understanding. Sex was a drug to Jessamyn Friday. On screen she was an innocent, the chaste young goddess whose eyes seduced without knowing they did, whose ripe, trembling breasts were all the more provocative because they seemed shyly displayed and never exploited. Even in the fan magazines and gossip columns she was credited with no more than light romances. Only those who had lived in her household knew of the excesses, the nights when two and even three men shared her bed, the legions who had answered to her blunt invitation. Laura swallowed back rage and disgust at the memory of the time she had gone to her room to change and returned to find her date, a sixteen-year-old boy, astride her mother who lay giving cool instructions.

"Don't worry, I'm not telling you that I like girls," she said. "I'm just not a romantic."

Underneath, though, she knew she was. In fact she suspected that was part of her problem, that she was too much a romantic. Sex without caring did not appeal to her. Her only relationship had been with a young ad copywriter she'd lived with for several months. She'd known it was going nowhere, and in the end she had felt cheapened by the experience. How ridiculous. She who had grown up in swinging Hollywood, attending a private day school and teenage parties where sex and drugs were freely distributed, was not modern. She'd always been shyer than her peers, though she managed to hide it. There was at the center of her something that longed for a man who would value her, who would love her and accept her love.

From what she had seen of the world, the chances of encountering a man like that were slim. It might have been different if she had been born in some small town, she thought. But she was what she was, a product of this capital of hustle, a woman with her own ambitions. Allowing herself to fall in love might be a disaster.

Nel's eyes regarded her with cynicism.

"Funny, I thought you might like a home and family."

"I'd love it," she admitted, her throat tight. "Hey, I'm starving. Do you suppose an uninvited visitor can get fed around here?"

Nel grinned. "Let's see." Picking up a phone, she dialed the kitchen. "Maria? Tell Lupita to get her aged tail over here with some sandwiches. Yeah, her. Just because she's been made queen bee of the kitchen doesn't mean she shouldn't do a little trotting now and again. Tell her to lug along some coffee, too, and an extra cup."

She hung up, and her finely cut lips, with their almost imperious arch, twitched with humor.

"Poor Lupita! She'll be furious," Laura laughed.

"She'd be more furious if she didn't get to see you. Might as well have a little fun while we're at it."

Lupita, who had cooked in Jessamyn's kitchen since Laura was young, rolled into the room like a storm front. The storm broke in a shower of astonishment and pleasure at the sight of Laura. Now Lupita called the kitchen and admonished Maria to bring cake and pickled shrimp and some of that salad *Lauracita* always liked. While Laura ate, she conversed with Lupita in the racing Spanish learned in childhood hours spent with the cook and her husband, Roberto, the gardener.

"Phew! But you have found an accent!" Lupita complained.

"Puerto Rican," said Laura and took a mouthful of cake. "I decided to live in Spanish Harlem, Lupita. Spent a lot of my time trying restaurants there. But none of the cooking came anywhere near yours."

Lupita beamed. "You come out one night and have supper with Roberto and me, okay? How long are you here?"

Laura exchanged a look with Nel.

"A while. I'll come, Lupita. Give Roberto my love."

When Lupita had gone, Nel chuckled.

"You're sunshine, you know it?"

Laura stretched. "Don't need any more of that in California."

"Your kind cuts through the smog. Things come alive."

"Well, sorry to tell you, but Sunshine's short-circuiting. I just realized it's four AM where I came from, and I'm beat. Meet me for breakfast tomorrow?"

"Sure. The pancake house?"

"You know it. Glad to hear they haven't torn it down to make parking spaces."

Laura stood with her hands in her pockets. "Good to see you, Nel."

"Same here, kiddo."

As Laura was opening the door, Nel spoke again.

"I wish you'd think again about this TV business. It's a big plunge you're thinking of making."

Laura's elf-grin surfaced again. "I'll wear my water wings. I promise."

A delicious feeling of rightness about the directon of her life came over Laura as she walked down the hallway from Nel's apartment. She had expected Nel to be somewhat appalled at her plans; *she* was appalled! In LA more than anywhere else screenwriting was a cut-throat, competitive business. Her age was against her, but she knew she could do it. And Nel thought she could too. Wonderful, wonderful Nel!

She rounded a bend in the hallway and stopped. Ahead of her, oblivious to the party beyond and the rooms behind, a couple stood pressed against each other, already well into a little free-flowing sex. The man had the girl's skirt hiked up over her thighs, and she was fumbling with his zipper. Why they hadn't vanished into one of the bedrooms Laura couldn't guess, but she hadn't the nerve to blunder casually past. She turned into a door that led to the library. From the looks of things, the act in the hallway wouldn't take long.

Only after she was into the room did she realize it was occupied. A man was using the telephone there, gesturing angrily with a hand that held a cigarette.

"You'd sure as bloody hell better have them," he was saying with his back toward her. "I said rushes at nine and I meant at nine!"

A producer, Laura guessed. He was large with rust-red hair, and he wore his expensive pinstripe shirt rolled at the elbows. Having come up practically on top of him, she wondered who he was.

She was starting to leave when something from the other end of the phone apparently enraged him. He swore, and his outstretched arm whipped sideways, hurling the cigarette. His target was the fireplace in the wall behind him, but Laura was directly in the line of aim. He had stepped back as he swung, and midway through its course, even as she tried to dodge it, his fist struck her eye.

She heard him swear again and drop the telephone. Blinding yellow spots exploded with dizzying force before her eyes.

"Damn it, are you all right?" The stranger caught her arm, but she couldn't see him. She couldn't answer. The experience of being half-blind, and from such a freak accident, had left her frighteningly disoriented, short of breath.

"Did I burn you? Christ, will you *say* something?"

His face danced unsteadily in her vision. It was white and angry. But just for an instant she thought she glimpsed in it an almost youthful alarm.

"I'm okay." She gasped the words as a new thought hit her. "Oh, damn everything! The cigarette's lost in the carpet!"

She dropped to her knees and began to fumble clumsily in the spotless white plush.

"Forget the cigarette. Let's see your eye." The man who had struck her knelt too and spoke impatiently.

"You don't understand—" Laura twisted away.

"Lady, a hole in the rug's no goddamn big thing." He imprisoned her hand, then reached across her. "Okay. There, I've got it."

Laura squinted as he swept the smoldering stub into an ashtray. An ugly brown scar remained where it had been. Knowing that this minor disaster would be blamed on her arrival and blown out of scale, she was torn between vexation and ironic amusement.

"Oh, damn," she repeated, this time exasperated. "Jessamyn will have a fit."

The stranger's eyebrows had been drawn together like two rusty hooks. Now suddenly they relaxed, and he gave a wide grin.

"That all you've got to worry about? You don't have much imagination, do you, babe?" Reaching out a finger, he twitched a low table a few inches back to cover the blemish. "Now let's see where I clipped you."

As he spoke, he grasped her shoulder. His easy touch on her cheek was such a contrast to his curtness that her breath caught.

His grin grew wider. He sat back slowly, his hand lingering on her shoulder just a fraction more confidently than she was comfortable with. His brown eyes danced at her, and nothing in her years in Hollywood had prepared her for such undisguised humor. Men on the move in this town usually took themselves and everything around them much too seriously.

"I'm Jake Turner. And I don't usually go around slugging women—or straightening furniture," he said. He was in his middle thirties. A cliff of straight hair jutted over his forehead.

"Laura Fitzgerald," she said briefly, aware he had misinterpreted her reaction.

He had a quarrelsome chin, blunt and cleft at the end, and was obviously sure of his attractiveness to women. She tried to rise, but his hand on her shoulder restrained her. Perhaps he hadn't been so wrong about her reaction after all, she thought. She felt both intrigued by him and slightly threatened.

"You'd better get a piece of steak for that eye, Laura Fitzgerald." His voice was easy, as amused now as it had been impatient earlier.

"Does that really work? I've always wondered."

She'd been thrown off balance by that punch in the face—by his style maybe. She was chattering.

He helped her to her feet, and though he was not much taller than her own five-foot-eight, he seemed to dwarf her.

"I wouldn't know." His grin was lazy, and his gaze lingered on her face as she brushed back a stray strand of hair. "I haven't had a shiner since I was a kid, and I didn't know what a steak was way back then."

She laughed, mostly in relief of tension. His laughter joined hers. It had a rough edge, like his manner, Laura noted. Both deliberately cultivated? Whatever the case, it made him different, made him distracting. She began to think she'd only imagined that glimpse of exposed uncertainty when he knew he'd hit her.

A cool voice spoke from the doorway, interrupting.

"Ah, here you are, Jake. I see you've met my daughter."

Jessamyn's eyes were dangerously narrowed. The humor faded quickly from Turner's expression.

"Daughter!" He flashed a look at Laura that accused her of not telling him. "Well . . . I'm afraid I've just slugged her," he said slowly.

"Oh? You'll have to take care of that, Laura darling. You bruise so easily." Jessamyn crossed the room to link her arm through Turner's.

"Jessamyn?" Another voice was heard, this time a man's. A virile-looking Mexican with angular features was peering in. He held up a glass. "I thought I saw you come this way. Here's that tequila sunrise you were wanting."

Jessamyn, with a melting smile, blew him a kiss.

"Aren't you an angel, Enrique, but I've changed my mind. Maybe Laura would like it. Come on, Jake, there are some people here I want you to meet."

So the man she had thought so attractive was her mother's current plaything. Or one of them, Laura thought angrily as they left the room. She must be a lousy judge of character, for she would never have imagined Jake Turner in that part. She was annoyed with herself that she had even noticed him at all.

"No thanks," she said to the drink now offered her.

She went down the hall to a bathroom and soaked a guest towel in cold water for her eye. With towel in hand she slipped back through the noisy crowd and out of the house.

The car park boy had gone for her rented Chevy when someone called to her. She turned and to her surprise saw Jake Turner approaching.

"Let me drive you wherever you're going," he said.

She tried not to notice that definite cleft in his chin.

"Thanks, but I rented a car at the airport. I just got in, and I stopped to see Nel."

"You shouldn't be driving. Your vision's probably off."

A slight breeze teased at the ledge of hair above his forehead.

It made him look restless and somehow oblivious to the civilization that sprawled all around them.

But he was not oblivious to Jessamyn, she reminded herself.

"I'm fine," she said. "And anyway, aren't you on call?"

"On call?" His chin raised sharply.

Laura bit her tongue. What had made her say that? "Forget it."

Her car came around, and she got in. Turner leaned down to close the door.

"Good night then." His eyes dug into her, and he stepped back.

Laura felt shaky, conscious of the force of will behind those eyes. With skillful movement she shifted to drive and pulled away, aware of him watching.

As her maid brushed the gold-brown of her hair, Jessamyn sat gazing into a high oval mirror, searching for some evidence of the despised issue of flesh that had diminished her. There was none, not a line, not a wrinkle to betray she was old enough to have borne this creature whose very existence sucked away her own. She had almost—almost—forgotten Laura. Why had she come back here? She was grown. She ought to be out of Jessamyn's way forever.

The fat little lhasa apso on Jessamyn's lap nuzzled her for attention. She reached into a foil-wrapped box of chocolates on her dresser and took one out, holding it above the dog's eager mouth for a moment before dropping it in. The dog's red tongue covered her fingers with grateful kisses. Satisifed, Jessamyn smiled.

Rising abruptly, she flung off the rust silk wrap that had covered her and stood naked at the center of her mirrored bedroom. From three walls and the ceiling her body was reflected back in all its perfection, the mounding breasts, the small waist, the luxuriant fuzz the same rich color as her hair. Only on the fourth wall, behind the platform that held her heart-shaped bed, was her image lost to her.

"Deidre, do you think I'm losing my figure?" she asked, craving attention. In the mirror she watched the maid's cheeks color.

"Oh, no, ma'am."

She knew Deidre hadn't even looked at her, the little prude. She knew the maid felt uncomfortable when her employer chose to stroll naked in her presence. Well, that was what one paid servants for, to endure discomfort. To answer the needs at hand, thought Jessamyn, who tonight felt the need of being admired.

"What about the nipples?" she insisted.

Reluctantly Deidre raised her head. With malicious enjoyment of the power she held, Jessamyn pressed a finger under one pink tip and then the other to make them jut forward, commanding the maid's attention, demanding her awareness.

"You are . . . completely beautiful, Miss Friday."

Completely beautiful mocked Jessamyn silently. Firm, dull, sexless piece of furniture. Deidre was efficient and silent and no more noticeable than the other furnishings of the room. Beyond that Jessamyn could not remember why she had hired her. The woman was thirty and had probably never uncrossed her legs.

"That will be all," she said.

"Yes, Miss Friday."

Vaguely annoyed, Jessamy continued across the room and threw herself face down on the heart-shaped bed. She didn't need some virgin maid to tell her she was beautiful. Men's eyes told her all the time. Her own daughter, who was half her age, could not compare with her. There was not a single feature in Laura worthy of notice.

So why had Jake Turner been laughing with her there in the library? Jessamyn wondered angrily. Why had he gone out after Laura when she left?

Turner was a challenge. A nonconformist. Jessamyn sensed it. Those were the qualities that made him tantalizing. She liked the thought of controlling a man who had never been controlled. His only interest at the moment was in signing her for his insignificant made-for-television movie, but she would change that. Jessamyn had never wanted a man she couldn't have, and she wanted Jake Turner.

Two

If she could have chosen a daughter, Nel would have chosen Laura. Yet possibly not, Nel mused as she rode through morning traffic, for Laura was also all she looked for in a friend. Were the two things exclusive? She was not sure.

If she had had a daughter . . . Nel felt a strange pang of wistfulness at the thought. What would life have been like if she hadn't left Detroit, slipping away in the dead of night, running away to find the future she hungered for . . . running away from Eddie? The memory of Eddie filled her with longing just as the memory of what he had done to her even now produced an anger.

He had hurt her. Betrayed her without a qualm. Yet now, almost thirty years later, there still was scarcely a night she did not see his face. She was going to die, and Eddie would never know it. Men. They were the most fatal disease of all.

Her cab pulled into the parking lot of a nondescript franchise pancake house, a place frequented by families and travelers, people from a world more real than the one she occupied. She got out and twisted one of the fourteen-karat-gold hemispheres that adorned her ears, pausing just long enough to note her reflection in the taxi window—the high dramatic cheekbones, the arched brows, short hair sweeping back in smooth, well-tended waves. Life as Jessamyn's secretary had been good to her, she thought. Better than the four years she had struggled to make a name for herself, working at clubs where the pay was uncertain and finally landing some bit parts, all the time waiting for the big break that would make her another Katherine Dunham.

Last night had she thought of discouraging Laura from pursuing her dream? When she was an eighteen-year-old runaway, no one could have talked her out of pursuing hers. Year after year we're the same, women like us, she thought, half-smiling.

What makes us different? Why can't we be content with a home and family, with something as eternal as being a link between the generations?

We fool ourselves. We think that we'll be able to have it all, glory and some man's devotion. Well, Laura, I hope you do have it all, your bite of the apple and a man who can give you the kind of love you need. You deserve it, kiddo.

Laura sat in a booth beside a window, sipping coffee. Her black hair hung free in curls that reached her shoulders. She wore jeans and a turquoise turtleneck that emphasized the delicacy of her fine bones. Nel studied her with satisfaction. Laura was oblivious to her own attractiveness, unspoiled enough to enjoy the anonymity of this place so far removed from the giddiness of money and glamour.

"Hi there," Nel said. "Been waiting long?"

Laura looked up, mouth curving gently. Nel saw with a start that the flesh around one of her eyes was puffy and black.

"Just half a cup worth. Was traffic bad?"

"When isn't it bad? You're buying, I trust, to get me out and about at this hour?" Nel tried not to stare.

"I always buy breakfast for little old ladies. It's safer than helping them across the street in these parts."

"Watch it, watch it, or I'll get up and walk on my hands to prove that I'm neither old nor a lady."

Laura laughed in delight as Nel had known she would.

"Oh, Nel! Can you still really do that?"

"Catch my act. First Thursday of every month, just before lunch." She opened a menu. "What looks good?"

When they both were settled with coffee, Laura sat back.

"Okay, I filled you in about me last night. Now you tell me what's going on around the old homestead."

"Not much. Jess finished the film in Italy three months ago and is being very *grande dame* about what she does next. I have to say none of the scripts she's been reading excited me either."

"She's okay? Well?"

Laura's expression had a serious cast that made Nel sigh. How could a girl be as smart as Laura and still ask that, really caring, as though Jessamyn with all her coldness still meant something to her?

"She's fine. A little bored, but then that's usual when she's not working."

"Who's Jake Turner? I met him last night and gathered he was the current interest."

The question sounded too casual. Without quite knowing why, Nel was alert.

"Associate producer. TV. Why?"

Laura shrugged. "He just doesn't seem the type for Jessamyn, that's all."

"Jess has a type? I hadn't noticed." Nel's gold lighter snapped. She drew on a cigarette fitted into a tortoise-shell holder. "He works with an indy at one of the studios. Wants to break away and be top man himself—form a production company. He's optioned a novel and wants Jess to say she'll be part of the package."

"The star, you mean? In a TV movie? Don't tell me she's considering it!"

"Not really. At least that's my guess, based on her unchanged view of the tube as the minor leagues. I expect she's willing to string him along, though. He's damn good-looking, and she's between men just now. Maybe it's that and not the lack of work that's boring her."

Nel noticed that Laura had not picked up a fork for the plate of pancakes placed before her. It was unusual for her to ask so many questions. What was her interest in Jake Turner?

Laura began to drown her pancakes in maple syrup. "I take it she hasn't gotten him into bed yet, then. How come?"

Nel grinned. "Maybe she's met her match. Or maybe he's playing hard to get. He's ambitious. I've seen enough men hustling this deal and that to recognize one who's even more determined. Let's face it, there are actresses as good as Jess, but if he could sign her for her first TV role his score as a producer would go zooming. Who knows? Maybe he's hit on a way of bringing her around."

She must be going senile to react like this just because Laura asked a few questions, Nel decided. Laura wasn't crazy. Laura wouldn't get mixed up with some man Jessamyn had designs on.

"Now will you please put me out of my agony and tell me how you got that shiner?" she asked.

Ruefully Laura touched a finger tip to it.

"An accident. It's ugly, isn't it? I don't expect it'll help me much in the interviews I've got scheduled for this afternoon."

"You've got prospects already? How'd you manage that?"

"I've got an agent. Ben Webber. I met him in New York. I called and told him I was coming, and he set them up. I doubt they're really prospects—more like courtesies to him, I expect. But I have to start somewhere, right? This afternoon I'll be pitching a chance to write lines for a soap or to carry the head researcher's coffee on some animal special."

Nel was silent for a moment. "You using Jess's name?"

Indignation showed in the face looking back at her.

"Never have and never will! I'd think you'd know me better than to ask! Even if Jessamyn wanted it known she had a daughter—which she doesn't, I've always known it—even if she did, I'd hide the connection. Writing's my business, and I do it well, I think. I'm not going to give anyone a chance to say she helped me along!"

"Sorry. I didn't mean—"

"I know."

They passed another half-hour together before they parted. The mansion in Beverly Hills was still silent when Nel returned. Stay up half the night and sleep until noon, she thought with disgust. Some day it's going to catch up with you, Jess my friend. You're not a kid anymore. Is that why you hate Laura? Because she reminds you of that?

There was no malice in Nel's heart as she thought it. She had known Jessamyn too long, knew her too well. Walking into her office, Nel groaned at the pile of mail awaiting her on her desk. She opened the draperies and looked out on acres of olive trees, then continued toward her own suite to brush her teeth.

Her personal mail had been left on a silver tray, one of the fine antiques that furnished the room. Nel shuffled through bills from a shoe store and Sak's, then stopped, hands trembling. A heavy cream-colored envelope stared back at her.

The embossed black letters of the return address were eyes, eyes which somehow, incredibly, had searched her out. They challenged her to meet their gaze, and her heart raced painfully. L. E. Brown. Lawrence Edward Brown. Officer Eddie Brown. Eddie.

Laura sat well back in her chair, her crossed ankles and her carefully unmoving fingers betraying nothing of her inner nervousness. Black moygashel linen suit, tailored white silk blouse, a knotted rope of antique pearls—she'd tried to look as businesslike as possible for these interviews.

Roy Schindler, vice president of Apex Productions, was flipping through a copy of her rape script. She had no idea whether he was seriously considering her or not.

No, probably not. She'd prepared herself for the fact these first interviews would be good practice, nothing more, and already she'd gleaned one insight. You had to acquire the kind of calm that allowed you to sit quietly while telephones rang and prospective employers dropped your script to talk with someone else for the umpteenth time. You had to learn not to wonder how much of your work they were really digesting.

Schindler's feet were on his desk. He had a double chin. The production company he worked for was small, but it regularly packaged specials for two studios.

"Sorry," he said, closing the script and tossing it back to her. "Your work is too soft for us. We need writers whose work will appeal to more viewers. Both men and women."

She swallowed back her outrage at the put-down. Was the rape script an unwise choice to show to men? But it was well-structured, well-written, a piece of work that showed good craftsmanship whether one was in sympathy with its subject or not.

"I thought you were hunting a researcher, not a writer."

"Same problem. Your point of view's too discernibly female." He smiled the smile of one in power.

"I see. Well, thank you for taking the time to talk to me."

"Yeah, sure."

Ten minutes and any hope of a job with Apex was down the drain. Laura went into the hall and pressed an elevator button, watching people from the offices in this highrise building that housed half a dozen independent production companies and an editing studio. Earlier that afternoon she had been turned down as a soap writer. If her style was soft, why hadn't *they* liked it?

Stop it, or you'll make yourself silly, she cautioned herself. You didn't expect to land something the first day, or even the first couple weeks for that matter. You've got a good bankroll to see you through.

All the same, her agent hadn't come up with a single appointment for her the following day, and that was discouraging. She would have to nose around on her own and see if she could get wind of projects in the making.

A girl with an ad portfolio and a well-built man in a suit of Italian silk got on the elevator with her. They rode down in silence. After another stop, where they were joined by a woman in jewels and face-lifted skin, Laura felt the man staring at her in fascination. She glared at him defiantly, but he did not notice. All at once it struck her that he was looking at her eye.

He seemed about to explode with the need to speak. When the elevator doors opened on the lobby, Laura felt him press near. His face showed feverish excitement.

"Are you into S&M?" he asked hoarsely. "Look, my name's Al, and I could show you a wonderful time—"

Laura walked briskly past him and the potted palm trees and out to the street.

Into sadomasochism? Her? But definitely she was back in California! She started to laugh.

It was late afternoon, and she began to stroll along slowly, listening to the drone of traffic heading for the Ventura and Hollywood Freeways. She liked this tangle of cars speeding through wide streets that reflected the sun. She had missed it in the narrow canyons of New York. There was just as much hurry, just as much urgency, on one coast as the other, but in Los Angeles a crazy carnival atmosphere permeated it all. Sometimes she thought the whole city had secretly been designed by Walt Disney and populated by Mouseketeers who refused to grow up. Sniffing the gas fumes of her home, she felt satisfaction and set course for a drugstore that in her youth had still made cherry phosphates.

The remembered taste was fresh on her tongue by the time she returned to the residence hotel where she was staying. A man was leaning against the front desk, reading a paper. As she started on past, he looked up and folded it.

"Miss Fitzgerald?" he said extending a hand. "I'm sure you do not remember me, but we met at your mother's party last night. I'm Enrique Portero."

"We did? Oh, yes. The tequila sunrise."

He made a little bow, then smacked the folded paper smartly against his hand. "Well! What a coincidence we both are staying here!" With confidence he displayed a row of even white teeth.

"I was just about to head out for a drink and dinner. Why don't you join me?"

It was a strange time to be leaving for dinner, and stranger still that a man who wore handmade alligator shoes would be staying here instead of the Hyatt House or Chateau Marmont. Laura looked shrewdly at the spare, triangular jaw and the eyes bright with energy. Enrique Portero . . . she had heard that name. Didn't he make movies back in Mexico?

"You're not going to get to my mother by going through me," she said. "She'd be less than impressed, believe me."

The forceful contours of his face showed color.

"I am wounded you misjudge me," he protested, sounding genuinely injured.

Laura gave him marks for not being a half-bad actor, and for being rogue enough to try even now to bluff on through. Too many men in film, if they reached any status, took things too seriously. She rather liked Portero for being corny enough to try such a ploy.

"You need a better writer," she said with a grin. "Your lines are lousy. Try very hard, and I expect you'll survive without a broken heart."

She fished out her key and with a light, swinging stride crossed the lobby. Behind her she heard Portero give a low, typically Mexican whistle, one that expressed admiration not of her body but of her spirit. Looking back, she saw him laughing. He threw back his head in a salute. Whatever he wanted from Jess, Laura hoped he had luck.

The first thing she did when she reached her studio apartment was kick off her shoes. Wiggling her toes in the carpet, she headed for the kitchenette tucked into one corner. She dropped her purse on one end of a tiny breakfast bar and opened the refrigerator. The phone on one end of the breakfast bar began to ring.

"This is Jake Turner," said the voice on the other end. "How's your eye?"

She gripped the phone with both hands without knowing why. "Fine," she lied. "Just fine."

"You didn't stop for that piece of steak, did you? How about letting me buy you one tonight? Or whatever else sounds good for dinner."

How had he gotten her number? Her heart beat as though she had run up the six flights of stairs from the lobby. She was angry with him for trying the same ploy Portero had tried, angry with herself for responding like this. Was this what her life was going to be like, being sought out as Jessamyn Friday's daughter?

"I can't," she said briefly. "Thanks anyway."

"What about tomorrow then?"

"No. I'm . . . busy settling in."

"I see." The receiver clicked.

No, you don't see, she thought crossly. Damn. Why did Nel have to tell her about the project he was pitching Jessamyn? But for that she could have—would have—gone with him, blissfully ignorant. And maybe lost her head, she realized uneasily.

She had taken the right course. There was no sense going out with a man whose interest was not in her, but in pushing a project. Besides, had she forgotten Jessamyn had designs on him?

Jake Turner hung up the phone and lighted a cigarette. Wandering restlessly through his apartment, he watched the first lights of evening wink on in the Hollywood hills.

He was not accustomed to being turned down by a woman. It startled him. He felt more than a little annoyed.

It had been simple impulse that enticed him to call Jess Friday's daughter, but he had always done very well by following impulses. They had brought him from his threadbare existence as the son of a dry cleaner's helper to this rooftop oasis with burnt-orange carpets and Navaho wall hangings. They had brought him through jobs as gopher and production assistant and into the realms of power as associate producer. They told him when to move and in which direction, and Turner had come to rely on them, using them to move upward through jobs that had toughened him and taught him and prepared him for the solo flight he soon would make. He was not used to his impulses failing him.

There were other women he could take out tonight and on short notice, young actresses with pretty faces and willing bodies, or a researcher at the studio who wanted a shot at writing. Turner was aware of his attractiveness to the opposite sex. The turn-down by Laura Fitzgerald perplexed him.

He tried to picture her, but her image eluded him. Instead it was the air of quality that clung to her that he remembered.

Although he had grown up without it, Turner was quick to recognize quality. This girl had a loveliness that went deeper than beauty, a presence, an incorruptibility that somehow showed in the firm pink line of her mouth. Quality was something he prized, one of the few things he admired. He had rarely noticed it in a woman. Now his straight, reddish brows drew into a frown.

Turner studied a signed Picasso lithograph hanging on one wall. He was a poor loser, and Laura Fitzgerald had as much as admitted she had no other plans. Heading into the bedroom, he changed into a turtleneck and slacks. If traffic was with him, he could reach the address where she lived in twenty minutes.

It was. As Turner rang her doorbell, he was aware of adrenalin pumping through him, exactly as it did whenever he walked into a war with the studio brass about some project he cared for. He had to ring the bell a second time.

When the door opened, he remembered at once the features he had forgotten. Her hair escaped in silken wisps to lie against a face unspoiled by makeup. Her nose was perfectly formed and finely edged. And her eyes . . . he had never known green-gray eyes could be so appealing. They were at once shy and bold, uncertain and determined. Turner winced involuntarily as he saw the discolored skin around one of them.

"You didn't tell the truth about your eye," he said.

She had fallen back a step at the sight of him, and for an instant he glimpsed her without defenses, unsure and a little angry. Then her face became a mask of stubborn control.

"What are you doing here?" she asked.

He stepped in uninvited.

"Reissuing my invitation to dinner. You didn't give a very convincing reason for turning me down."

She was in her stocking feet, and it made her seem small. Her white silk shirt was rolled at the elbows, and she was wearing a narrow black suit skirt. It should look businesslike, Turner thought, but on her it was sexy. The way she dressed and her bristling stance only accentuated those soft black curls.

"I can't believe you!" she said, hands on her hips. "I came home to find one person camped on my doorstep hoping to catch Jessamyn's ear through me, and now you have the nerve to show up here after I've told you—"

Turner interrupted, his own temper rising. "Listen, I don't

get my jobs cozying up to anyone. I like to think the quality of my work makes it unnecessary!"

She stared at him, a long, thoughtful look. Her eyes were more green than gray now, and hidden deep in them Turner saw confusion.

"Well? How about it?" If he kept her on the defensive, he knew he could win.

She crossed her arms. "Are you sure you know what you're doing?" she asked unsteadily.

"What do you mean?"

She gave a slight shake of the head. A smile played at her lips.

"A man in an elevator saw my eye today and assumed I was into bedroom torture. If you want to risk getting that kind of reputation . . ."

Turner grinned.

"I'll take my chances."

"Sit down a minute then. I'll put on some shoes."

As she left the room, Turner studied her backside. It was flat. Incredibly, marvelously flat. He wanted to trace it. He wanted to take her to bed. This was ridiculous, he thought, amazed with himself. He wasn't used to losing control. He hadn't said fifty words to this woman and he wanted her.

In the bathroom Laura slumped against the door. Turner must be crazy, she thought. If he wasn't using her to get to Jessamyn, then couldn't he see what a very impolitic move this was?

No, you're the crazy one, she told her image in the mirror. Hastily she twisted her hair back into temporary submission. She readjusted the rope of pearls beneath her notched collar and rolled down her sleeves.

Turner's car was a twelve-year-old Mercedes. He seemed pleased when she knew it was one of the last of the handmade models. They drove to the coast, stopping at a restaurant well off the celebrity trail, where tables wore simple green cloths and the fish for the evening meal swam in a rock-walled tank.

"Well, do you suppose our addition to the carpet's been discovered yet?" he asked as they were seated.

Laura laughed. "That room's hardly ever used. It's just there for show. I'm sure the help vacuums around the furniture, so I suspect it will go unnoticed until spring cleaning."

"Maybe they'll write it off as moths."

She laughed again. It was fun, this childish conspiracy in doing something naughty and getting away with it. Turner seemed to be enjoying it too. His eyes danced with a mischief younger than his years.

"I understand you want to write for TV," he said.

She looked up, startled. "Who told you that?"

"Nobody, actually. I stopped to see Jessamyn this afternoon. She and her secretary were having what you might call a heated discussion about it."

A knot came up in Laura's stomach. So Jessamyn knew. She looked out toward a darkened ocean, wondering what had been said. "Jess doesn't approve." It was a statement, not a question.

"She's afraid you'll be hurt."

Always the honeyed lie, thought Laura. Jessamyn was a master of them. It annoyed her that Turner and Jessamyn had talked about her.

Their menus came. With scarcely a look at hers, Laura ordered abalone. The fresh taste of that particular shellfish was one of the things she had most missed about California.

"A real native daughter," Turner observed.

She liked his grin. It came so easily. She also liked the charged directness of his eyes. They approved of her looks; she felt it; she felt every inch a woman. Falling for someone like Turner would be a heady experience, but also dangerous.

And you're already halfway there, she told herself. But she wasn't one of those women who believed in being swept along by fate. She could stop any time she wanted to and never set foot across that dangerous halfway line.

Over dinner they talked about current books, and Laura was surprised to find Turner quite well read. She wondered how he found time to fit reading into his schedule.

"What's it like growing up the child of a famous actress?" he asked as they had coffee.

She turned toward the window again.

"No different from being the child of a doctor or a lawyer, I suppose. What's it like being a producer?"

"Hard. Exasperating. Sometimes rewarding. A lot like writing scripts, I expect."

"That's not how you started then, as a writer?"

"No."

"Family in the business?"

"No." Lighting a cigarette, he leaned back in his chair. "I just took an interest. Did the usual apprentice things, and now I have a hole in the wall with Bernie Goldman at Universal. No complaints, I suppose, but I'm getting restless. Two other fellows and I plan to launch our own production company soon. That's why I've been trying to interest Jessamyn in a property we've optioned. It's a challenging role. She'd be good in it. And if I could sign her for her first TV role, it would make my reputation sterling."

His candor intrigued her. It was odd in a business where almost everyone pretended to be more important than they were.

"Modest, aren't you?" she said.

"No."

They smiled together. His eyes held hers, and she felt the halfway line she had vowed not to step across growing less distinct.

"Let's go," he said. He held her chair.

As the warmth of his hand settled against her back, Laura felt the tips of her breasts swell in excitement. What was this, she thought in indignant surprise, her mother's genes surfacing in her? The casual contact had sensitized her entire body. She was taut. Aroused.

Turner's hand glided easily up across the thin silk of her blouse. It traced the line of her neck, and his fingers pressed lightly against her skin.

"How about stopping up at my place for a drink?" he said.

They both knew it was more than a drink he was suggesting. Her mind railed against the response of her body, so uncharacteristic . . . so intense.

"No thanks," she said, giving a smile that was bright and quick.

There. That was done. She was safe. But as Turner looked at her, his gaze darkening, Laura wondered if she was. She saw that the eyes that laughed so easily also had a hardness, a capacity to hurt.

Three

The phone in Nel's office rang, her private line. She reached absently across the clutter of mail to answer and appointments to be scheduled, the daily ordering of Jessamyn Friday's life.

Her copper-tipped finger punched at a phone button, and she lifted the receiver. "Yes?"

"Nel? Is that you, Nel?"

She looked up half-expecting to see the lean, tall man who belonged to that voice standing before her. After all these years, after all this time, it still had the same sound, vaguely arbitrary, vaguely coaxing. And gentle. Always gentle.

"Hello, Eddie. It's been a long time," she said, keeping her own words calm.

"Twenty-eight years, Nel. That's how long I've been hunting you."

That's what he had said in the letter that arrived three days ago. Nel rested her head in her hand. She felt herself shaking.

"Let me alone, Eddie. What happened back in Detroit was a long time ago. I'm not a dumb kid in need of protection anymore, and you're not a cop out for an easy make."

"That's not how it was, Nel—"

"No?" Her voice sharpened. "That's how it looked to me! You slept with me, and then you had me busted."

"You don't understand—".

"I don't want to understand. I don't want to talk about it. I have a good life here. I'm happy. Don't call me again."

"Nel, wait! I'm coming out to the coast next week. I'd like to see you—"

"No."

She hung up quickly. Her hand pushed against the telephone console as if to crush it. This was all because of that stupid damn news item. That insignificant little story identifying her as Jessamyn's personal secretary, "a one-time member of Katherine Dunham's troupe." How did it happen that Congressman Eddie Brown was reading *Daily Variety*?

After a minute Nel lit a cigarette and went to stand by the window. She smoked too much. It would kill her. She smiled at the irony of the thought. Closing her eyes she took deep, steadying drags of the burning tobacco. Maybe she should have seen Eddie again. Maybe it would have gotten him out of her system. She had been too damn young when she met him, too young and susceptible to the way a man could make you feel secure in the world in spite of all those lofty ideas about independence.

Laura was susceptible too. Nel frowned. She didn't like the fact that Laura was seeing Jake Turner. Only three days had passed since he called seeking Laura's number. She hoped to hell what she'd read this morning wasn't true.

It was time for her mid-morning coffeebreak. Nel decided to see if Jessamyn was stirring. Apparently Jess had made some commitment to a celebrity style show. That had to be straightened out. Besides, Nel felt the need for company this morning.

Before she even knocked at Jessamyn's sitting room, Nel knew she was up. Through the carved oak door she heard the actress's clear voice raised in abuse.

"This coffee's too strong again! Take it away. No, I don't want water in it. I said take it!"

There was a crash. Jess had knocked the tray being offered from Deidre's hands, Nel guessed. Quietly she opened the door and stepped inside.

Jessamyn was pacing. Her open robe flapped with her steps. Nel knew what had triggered her anger. There was a copy of the *Daily Reporter* folded in her hand, held like a club. She had read the gossip item about Jake and Laura, the comment that they had dined tête-à-tête at La Scala, both looking enraptured.

Nel grinned to herself. She could not imagine either one of them fitting that description.

"Well, well, I see we're in cheerful form today," she said.

Jessamyn looked up. "Go to hell."

"Sure thing. But first I have to sort out this schedule of yours. Cedars of Sinai has been bugging me all morning. Something about a benefit style show you promised to be in." Nel glanced at Deidre, who knelt frantically trying to retrieve the contents of a breakfast tray upended on the room's pale carpet.

"DeeDee love, would you bring me some coffee? Maria had a fresh pot on when I came in. Maybe you can catch a cup that's half-done for Princess Heartburn."

She raised her eyebrows. If Deidre didn't have sense enough to shoot some hot water into whatever coffee was left in the kitchen, then she deserved the abuse Jessamyn heaped on her.

Jessamyn picked up one of the fat white dogs whining at her feet and threw it at a couch where it fell with a yelp.

"Watch it, Nel. That smart mouth of yours could get you fired one day."

"Not likely. I know too many secrets. Now about this benefit—"

"To hell with the benefit." Lapsing into a chair, she waved the paper in her hand. "I see you haven't been telling me what's going on behind my back!"

"Behind your back? Oh, Jess, come on."

Unconsciously Nel's voice softened. Jessamyn was a child, a spoiled, selfish child, but they had been together too long for Nel not to feel some pity for her. The spectre of growing old must be a terror to one who has never grown up.

"So Turner took Laura out," she said. "So what? You know how things are blown out of size in print."

"It's unprofessional." Flying from her chair, Jess paced again. "I have business dealings with Jake. It's unprofessional for Laura to see him."

"Half of Hollywood has dealings with the other half. Be reasonable."

"She's trading on my name."

"Oh, hell! That item doesn't mention you at all."

"I introduced her to Turner, didn't I?"

This was going down every bit as badly as Nel had expected. She was glad when there was a timid knock and Deidre slipped back into the room. Poor creature must have run to the kitchen and back, Nel thought. She watched Jessamyn pick up a fresh glass of orange juice, which replaced the one somebody would have to clean from the carpet later.

"You might accuse Turner of being the unprofessional one," she suggested, ducking down for a sip of coffee, her eyes on Jessamyn. "He's the one who called here wanting to know where to reach her."

Nel had no qualms at all about seeing Turner's ass kicked around a bit. Not that she bore him any ill feelings, but he had probably done things along the way that deserved it, and he was toughened. Better him than Laura, that was the bottom line.

Jess had settled now, and her eyes held a look that Nel did not trust.

"Blame Jake?" She smiled slowly. "Why should I? He probably thought I'd be more sympathetic to that project of his if he asked Laura out. There's something about an unscrupulous man that's always attracted me. But I'll have to set him straight on what I like and don't like, won't I?"

Reaching into a nearby chocolate box, she dropped a dark morsel into the waiting mouth of the dog at her feet. The dog she had flung to the couch whined piteously, its head on its paws. A chocolate flew in its direction too. The little dog caught it and with silken hair dragging over the carpet, ran toward its mistress, yelping joyously, reprieved.

"The Sinai benefit's on the sixteenth," Jessamyn said. "That in the morning and Marty Lanz in the afternoon. Two hours between which should be adequate even if the benefit runs late—which they always do."

Nel shook her head, amazed as always at the organization of Jessamyn's mind. It was not simply looks or talent that had gotten Jessamyn where she was.

When her secretary had gone, Jessamyn stood looking at the white dogs at her feet. Kneeling, she gathered them to her and fed them each another chocolate. They loved her. They proved that she was a lovable person. When she sent them away from her, they whimpered and cried. They really didn't care for anyone but her.

Now she forgot about the two animals. Picking up the discarded newspaper, she stared at it for a long minute. The famous amber eyes grew lazy with shrewdness. She crossed to a desk of inlaid cherry and from the drawer took a slim book of telephone numbers.

She studied it. An index finger, tended twice weekly by a manicurist, flew over numbered buttons.

"This is Jessamyn Friday. Put me through to Sam Bernstein. I don't care if he *is* in conference, I want to talk to him!"

Inasmuch as the telephone cord would allow, she paced, more calmly now. It was how she got into a scene. When Bernstein's voice came on at the other end of the line, the performance was ready.

"Sammy? It's time to call in that little favor you owe me, and I'll put you at ease and tell you I don't want anyone's throat cut. Just a silly request from an overprotective mother actually." She laughed. "Yes, didn't you know I had a daughter? I've tried to shelter her from the public eye. Her name's Laura Fitzgerald, and she's taken it into her head that she wants to be a screenwriter. No, wait, Sammy! I don't *want* you to hire her. I want you *not* to hire her. I know what a rat race the business is, and I just don't want to see her hurt. If you could pass the word around a little . . . I don't want any of this to get back to her, of course. Thanks, Sammy."

She hung up, smiling at her own success. She couldn't close every door that might open to Laura, but she could reduce the odds.

Laura woke in the same knee-to-chest position in which she had gone to sleep. City sounds drifted around her, and she lay for several minutes listening to them, eyes closed, lips stirring gently in a smile of sleepy contentment. A thousand poets and writers had lauded awakening to the cock's crow. Perhaps no one but her enjoyed the music of garbage trucks clanging and sirens wailing. She liked the thought of a whole city stirring. She liked the sounds of shop doors opening and buildings being unlocked, of taxis screeching and buses lumbering along paved streets. This morning, though, she was not among the early risers.

Turning over, she clutched the sides of her pillow, trying to banish the thought of Jake Turner, which sprang immediately to her mind, and the pulsing between her thighs that it produced. She had wanted to go to bed with him last night. He had kissed her fiercely when he had brought her in, and she had known he wanted it too. Even now she was not sure what had stopped her. Perhaps it was only pride. She would not have been the first woman Turner slept with, nor the last, and their encounter would have meant nothing to him. All her life she had meant nothing. Not to Jessamyn, not to a father or any other sort of relative. And so last night she had resolved not to see Jake Turner again.

This morning it was harder to face that decision. She walked to the kitchenette and plugged in coffee. She could have instant in a quarter of the time, but without the smell, the hearty, deep aroma.

I'm crazy, she thought. About coffee and about men. I want some kind of solid, perfect little world, and that's not how things are.

Leaning on the counter, she closed her eyes and remembered the night before, the sound of Turner's laughter, the feel of his hand over her arm. He had laughed easily and often, his dark eyes looking into hers as though some secret lay hidden there, and from the moment he had reached across the table and taken her hand, Laura had known she was flirting with fire.

She did not want to be burned. That was the sum of it. And so when Turner had suggested going out tomorrow night, she'd said she was busy. Right now she hated herself.

Straightening, she walked quickly back across the room and shoved the hide-a-bed back into place. She threw the cushions on and made it a sofa once again. For the rest of today, she would think about nothing but her work.

That afternoon she was turned down for three jobs. When she returned at half past five, her phone was ringing. She stood in the doorway a minute, nerves tensing. But no, it would not be Turner. He was meeting with his soon-to-be new partners tonight. Giving the door a shove to close it, she answered the phone.

"Laura? Jess. I'm having a little buffet by the pool on Saturday for Nel's birthday. I know she'd love to have you. Can you make it?"

So this was how it was being invited to one of Jessamyn's flings, thought Laura. She didn't know what to feel. They were mother and daughter; they might as well have been strangers.

"Saturday? I wouldn't miss it," she said politely. "What time, and may I bring a present?"

"Eight o'clock. Suit yourself about the gift."

"Thanks, Jessamyn."

There was a slight hesitation. "How's the market for writers these days? Have you found anything?" asked Jessamyn.

Laura sat on a high stool, surprised by this interest. "Nothing definite, but I'm learning a lot just from the interviews."

What a stupid thing to say. She sounded like Pollyanna. And Jess could probably guess that "nothing definite" meant flat rejection.

"Yes, well, it takes time," said Jessamyn brightly. "Saturday at eight then."

After she hung up, Laura sat looking at the phone. When

had Jessamyn ever come so close to encouraging her before? When, for that matter, had she ever been invited into Jessamyn's presence?

Leaning elbows on the tiny breakfast bar, she thought of the photograph propped up in the kitchen cabinet, hidden from all eyes but hers, the only photograph she'd ever seen of herself and her mother. In it Jessamyn was holding her. Laura could not remember that. There were other things she could not remember doing with Jessamyn. She had never gone anywhere with her in public. She had never kissed her. She had never spent five minutes with her alone. She had never been allowed to call her Mother.

But that was simply part of being a star's child, wasn't it? Laura knew it was not. From grade school on, she had been acquainted with the children of other big names. In spite of aberrant lifestyles where they learned the ins and outs of deals, the weaknesses of nannies, and the whims of a revolving carrousel of step-parents, some had warm, even close relationships with their mothers and fathers. Others admittedly were afterthoughts. She alone had been rated a nuisance, not worth the effort of even a superficial hug or guilty compensation at Christmastime.

Who was her father? She had wondered it a thousand times, wondered what he was like and whether he cared for her as little as Jessamyn did. Once she had gathered her courage and asked his identity. Her only answer had been the icy flick of Jessamyn's lashes. Was he dead? Alive? Why had Jessamyn borne the product of her mating with him? Laura was sure even Nel didn't know those answers.

She was starting to hang up her jacket when someone knocked at the door. The same half-hopeful fear that had touched her when the phone rang gripped her again. She could say nothing, do nothing, just wait for whoever it was to go away. But certainty drew her on toward the door, and when she opened it on its guard chain, she saw Jake Turner.

"I was in the neighborhood," he said with a grin.

This was when she must make the break. She needed to keep her life uncomplicated. But for a moment she could not move. Then, wordlessly, she slipped off the chain and let him step in.

"Saul Finer got called to New York," he said. "We scrapped the meeting."

That was all. He stood looking at her. Laura felt the sudden running of a pulse in her throat.

"I see," she said. "Well. Would you like a drink?"

Did that sound impersonal enough? She couldn't come out and say she didn't want to see him again; she couldn't explain. She would get the message across in coolness, the very antithesis of what she was feeling.

Turner smiled. "I would indeed."

She quickly turned away from the lingering force of his eyes. To her consternation he followed her toward the kitchen.

"Jesus, it's a pain in the ass dealing with studios," he said, stretching. "You've got rocks in your head to want to do it."

Leaning on the short breakfast bar that separated them, he watched her. Her liquor supplies consisted of whiskey, gin, and tonic water. She mixed whiskey with tap water and handed one to him.

His gaze moved from the three fat cookbooks arranged on her counter and up to the soft colors of the flower garden quilt she had hung on one wall. They were her treasures, items she'd brought with her from New York to make her feel at home immediately instead of shipping them with her collected books and paintings. So although she'd been in this small apartment less than a week, she felt settled in.

"It's very nice," he said. "Very . . . Laura." And then with a shift of meaning, "You haven't seen my place yet."

"No."

She moved past him, carrying her drink.

"What about tonight? We could broil some steaks and fix a salad."

"I've got an interview with Weiss Productions first thing in the morning. I'm going to hole up and watch the shows they've got on tonight."

"Abe Weiss isn't going to give you the time of day."

Laura's head shot up. She was stung by his bluntness. Who the hell did he think he was to tell her that? What was the point?

"Maybe he won't. I'm going to watch them anyway." She grasped at anger, at anything to keep immune to him.

"I've got a TV." Turner's voice was low in his throat. He stepped closer and brought his fingers up against her shoulder, stroking it lightly.

She shrugged free of the contact. Heat spread from her

center, and she felt molten. Molten and weak. She moistened her lips.

"Look, Jake. I don't want to get too involved. Not with you, not with anyone. Okay?"

She could feel him behind her. She could feel the heat from his body as he closed the gap between them.

"What's too involved? I don't deal in exclusive contracts except in business."

He touched her again, this time at the side of her neck. His mouth moved against the softness of her hairline.

"I don't ask anything from a woman that I don't give. You're still free, and so am I. So why don't we enjoy each other, hmmm? I think we could."

Laura held herself rigid against the tremor beginning inside her. When she did not respond, his tone grew sharp.

"If you're thinking of playing hard to get, don't do it. I don't care for games."

She pivoted to face him with a bright, protective smile.

"I'm not playing hard to get. I'm just . . . not interested."

Please, please believe it, she begged inwardly.

His eyes stared back at her. For a second they seemed to reject what she was saying. Then they cracked with anger.

"I see. My mistake."

Without another word, he set down the glass in his hand and walked out the door. He had not touched his whiskey. Kneeling on the couch, Laura drank her own methodically, wanting it to last forever, wanting it to be next week, next year, her old age.

On Saturday Laura arrived at Jessamyn's with a bouquet of pansies, a foil-wrapped box, and a crashing headache. She had not slept in three days, and after a week in LA she still had not found a job. To top it off, today's interviews had been completely baffling. Just as she was learning to sift each word for meaning, there suddenly was nothing to sift. The men she had seen today had barely spoken to her and had only gone through the motions of looking over her sample scripts. In each case it had been as though she'd stepped into a freezer. She was puzzled and discouraged.

It was one of the reasons she had dressed with such care tonight, buying high-heeled red sandals with ankle straps to wear with the lace-trimmed white peasant dress that bared her shoulders. The dress was expensive. Even amid Jessamyn's friends, it should be at least adequate. At the last minute she'd decided to wear her hair down, sides caught back with a red ribbon, knowing its silken thickness exited envy in most women even if the straying curls were impossible to discipline.

Coming unsuccessful into Jessamyn's presence was a hard pill to swallow. Secretly she had hoped to land a job in record time. She had hoped to surprise even Nel.

Well, what the hell? She could lose herself in a party. Maybe she would get drunk. She would lick her wounds.

The same houseman who had almost turned her away on her previous visit showed her to the pool. On one side, under palm trees, a long table had been spread with a bright aqua cloth, and next to it gaily colored lounge chairs and padded gliders had been drawn up in a casual grouping, already well-populated. Nel sat lazily on one of the lounges, laughing with a sandy-haired man in a three-piece suit. Catching sight of Laura, she waved in delight.

"Hey, kiddo, how's it going?"

"Great. Just great." Laura dropped onto the foot of the lounge Nel occupied. "So how's it feel to be a hundred?"

"Just ninety, kiddo. I hope those goodies are for me?"

Nel arched an eyebrow at the pansies and the box, which Laura now presented with a flourish.

"Happy birthday, Nellie. I hope you're still crazy when you do hit ninety. Are pansies still your favorite?"

"You know it. Hey, Laura my love, do you know Van Greenberg? He's one of the boys who pulls the pursestrings at ABC."

The blond man who had been talking to Nel nodded to Laura. A few white hairs at his temples belied the youthful tone of his body. His eyes were icy blue.

"Hello," he said.

This greeting, in a town where people protected themselves with quick one-liners, was just short of stuffy. So were his clothes in this gathering of jeans and casual wear. Van Greenberg was unmistakably and unflinchingly the corporate executive. But then he smiled, and the effect was pleasant.

"ABC, huh?" said Laura. "Well! Don't tell me Jessamyn's finally jumped aboard?"

The reserved Mr. Greenberg broke into a laugh.

"No. As a matter of fact, I'm not sure she knows I've

switched jobs. I was with Columbia when she made her last picture."

"Hey, you've been squandering money on me and I love it!" grinned Nel, waving the antique pitcher from Laura, which she had just unwrapped. "If you two will excuse me, I think I'll put it inside before someone guzzles too many martinis and sticks a foot in it."

Still smiling, Greenberg watched her cross the patio.

"Great lady," he said. "How did you get to know her?"

Laura watched Nel's retreat across the patio.

"Oh, she's been my guardian angel for years."

She wondered if Greenberg was a romantic interest of Nel's. Instinct told her he wasn't quite right.

"Would you like a drink?" he asked.

"Yes, please." She looked around. "Where's Jessamyn?"

"Haven't seen her for a while. Inside, I expect."

When he had gone, Laura stood for a minute, feeling a breeze tug the flounce at the top of her dress. She was home. She belonged here. Not in this house, perhaps, but in this climate, around this kind of talk, amid these people. She closed her eyes and let the feeling spread through her. It would take more than the past week to discourage her. Just now she felt unbreakable.

She hardly heard the step behind her. Only the low, certain voice of Jake Turner.

"Hello, Laura."

She whirled, the unbreakable feeling shattering.

"Hello, Jake." She looked down quickly at the concrete.

He laughed softly. "You look like a kid when you're caught off guard, do you know that? How was Abe Weiss?"

Her pale face raised, and she faced him squarely. "He's a stinker."

"Most people aren't so kind when they describe him. I take it he turned you down. Any luck?"

"No."

It had never occurred to her that he might be here. Jessamyn had invited him naturally, and for herself, not Nel. Laura felt trapped. The lovely calm of a moment before was gone.

"What about you?" she asked. "Have you sold the role to Jessamyn yet?"

His dark eyes met hers with a hint of irony. "Nope. No

luck in any aspect of my life this week, it seems. Good thing my ego's made of sturdy stuff. Can I get you a drink?"

"No thanks, I—"

"Here you are, one gibson," said Van Greenberg, coming upon them. "Dry and with an extra onion. Yes?"

Beside her, Laura felt Jake stiffen. His eyes were angry.

"Thanks. Do you two know each other? Van Greenberg, Jake Turner."

Greenberg appeared unperturbed and only slightly interested. "I don't believe so."

"Well." Jake turned to leave, but there coming toward them was Jessamyn.

"Everyone having a good time?" she asked gaily. She leaned on Jake's shoulder, and his hand went accommodatingly to her waist. With a small gleam of triumph, her eyes sought Laura's.

"Nice party, Jessamyn." Laura was remembering the long-ago scene with Jessamyn and a teenage boy beside this pool. She was filled with disgust and an inexplicable anger.

"Your hair looks so sweet down, Laura. So girlish," Jessamyn was saying.

Now Laura didn't know quite what to think. She wasn't used to compliments from Jessamyn.

"Thanks," she said.

"Not very polished, of course. I do hope you do something with it when you go around hunting work." She turned a glowing smile to Jake. "I want to dance now. Come on, darling."

"Sure." Jake raised the glass in his hand toward Laura. "Here's to your uninvolvement," he said with sarcasm.

A trio of overweight men had started to play. Nel was doing the latest steps with a wasp-waisted song-and-dance man adored by the teen set. Laura sat down on a glider, Greenberg beside her. She drank the gibson he had brought her and two more. Her knotted nerves began to loosen. The party around her grew pleasantly fuzzy.

"You'd better slow down with those," Greenberg cautioned.

"Don't worry. I can handle the onions." Flinging back her head, she smiled her imp smile at him, aware that she was flying a little and not really caring. "You're too uptight, Mr. Greenberg. Relax a little."

His mouth was well-molded. It stirred as he leaned back, his blue eyes on her.

"If you're bored, why don't we go to my place?" he suggested.

The words were immediately sobering. She stopped smiling. Greenberg laughed.

"Am I too direct? That's the trouble with us corporate-types—no creativity. But then it's the bottom line that counts, after all. You're pretty, Laura. And you're ... different. Pleasantly so. Is there a man in your life? If not, you'll hook up with one sooner or later. Why not with me?" He held a gold lighter up to a cigarette and took a breath. He had not touched her. "You want a career? I can give you one. I can give you power."

"For something in return, of course." Laura did not try to keep contempt from her voice.

"Of course."

She started to rise.

Greenberg, with a light touch, stayed her. "You're disgusted. You're an idealist, and you wonder how I can make the offer I'm making." The words were calm. He gave a slight smile. "I don't very often." He brought the cigarette to his mouth and away again. "You haven't been hurt yet, Laura. When you have, see me again. I can make or break anyone here tonight—you, Turner, maybe even Jessamyn. When you have scores to settle, you'll understand that power's very nice. Keep my offer in mind."

Bending forward, he extinguished the cigarette in a ceramic tray. "Shall we see what's been put out for supper?"

More than anything else, his smoothness jarred her. It was all so casual, so matter-of-course. And with a sick feeling, Laura realized she was out of her league. Maybe she wasn't ready for the big time after all. Not for the maneuvering that went hand-in-hand with the business.

Greenberg's blue eyes rested on her kindly. She was sober and nervous, and her head hurt more than before.

"I have to go inside first," she said. She was frightened by the interest Greenberg was showing in her.

Why shouldn't she snap up his offer? she wondered as she retreated into the house. He was an attractive man, and she had a feeling there was much about life she could learn from him. Maybe she was an idealist. Maybe she would never make it on her own.

"What's wrong? King Midas come on too strong?" asked a

voice from a chair in the shadows just inside the house.

She did not turn at the sound of Turner's voice, only stopped back straightening, hands going automatically toward the pockets that didn't exist in her dress.

"As a matter of fact I have a headache. I'm going home."

"I'll drive you."

"No, I—" She stopped. If she said she would call a taxi, he'd think she was leaving with Greenberg. His tone was taunting, and his earlier dig about noninvolvement stung afresh. "All right. Thanks," she said with a shrug.

They drove in silence until Turner cut left at an intersection. Laura flashed a look at him.

"This isn't the way to my apartment."

"I have to take a leak, if you don't mind. Mine's closer." When they pulled into the underground garage, he opened her door. "Come on. I'll get you a couple of aspirin. If you have to get yourself drunk to go to bed with Greenberg, maybe you should forego the pleasure."

"I'm not drunk!"

He pushed her, not very gently, into an elevator. As it rose, an angry tension filled the space between them. He was jealous, Laura realized with satisfaction. Jake Turner, who talked about nonexclusive contracts, was jealous. She smiled.

"What the hell's so funny?" he asked under his breath.

Half-closing her eyes, she leaned against the elevator rail. "You are."

He swore and took her arm again. "Come on."

His apartment surrounded them like a desert cave, soft-hued, quiet, stretching endlessly. Laura stood just a few steps inside the door and heard it close. Suddenly the sound seemed very definite. She was aware of being in Turner's world.

She knew when he moved, though she did not hear him. He went into another room, and Laura felt a pressure easing. Why was she so keyed up? She certainly didn't believe a man of Turner's self-confidence, who could have his pick of beautiful women, would stoop to force. But being here had unlocked repsonses she hadn't counted on. Beneath the surface of her skin, her body was quivering.

She heard him return.

"Here," he said, handing her two aspirin and a glass of water. Then he disappeared while she stood staring at the soft folds of a Navaho rug spread on one wall.

A long time passed before she was aware of his presence in the room again. She was opening her mouth to make some comment about the rug when he spoke.

"What I said about you and Greenberg was out of line. I apologize."

"It's all right. I deserve some marks for bitchiness myself."

Her shoulder was to him. His hand settled on it, disturbing all her senses.

"You know what's the matter, don't you? With both of us?"

She was silent. Heat flooded her. She could say something, change the direction of this minute. He moved without warning, brushing the top of her dress down and kissing her bare flesh.

She tried to speak and couldn't. Desire pulsed inside her, hammering. Turner turned her toward him, pushed at the dress again as his mouth slid toward the soft inner curve of her breast.

Laura dug her fingers deep into his shirt. When he had said he would take her home, she had known this would happen, hadn't she? She had wanted it. They had both known his flimsy excuse for stopping here was a lie.

With unexpected gentleness he lifted her and carried her into the bedroom. In a moment they were both naked. He began to kiss her body, the soft brush of his lips tracing a trail of fire. Then, changing tempo abruptly, his tongue curled urgently around her nipples, first one, then the other, the faint, hard moistness shooting her into a galaxy where pleasure mixed with pain. Time had stopped. She felt nothing, not even the bed beneath her, only him. He turned her over and began to kiss every inch of her body again—her back, her narrow waist, the inside of her thighs—arousing her as she had never been aroused.

Unable to bear the delay, Laura twisted and brought them together. She tried to slow her own rush toward loss of control to prolong the pleasure. But he too had lost all restraint. His thrusts were hard, fast, and furious. The end came quickly for both of them.

Long minutes passed, and still they seemed to be revolving slowly on some planet, remote from everything but each other. Laura lay experiencing the sensation of naked flesh on naked flesh, of his body on top of hers.

Slowly Turner stirred, lifting himself on his elbows to peer into her face. He gave a wide grin.

"Lady, for someone who isn't interested, you give a good imitation." He kissed her temple, rubbing the backs of his fingers against the escaping tendrils of her hair.

She smiled in return, her eyes fluttering closed as he kissed them.

You don't understand, she thought. I don't understand myself. I'm so afraid, and I don't even know of what. Of tomorrow. Of when I don't have you. That's crazy because I know I don't have you now. This isn't how I planned my life to be. This is all wrong.

She wrapped her arms around the smoothness of his back, wanting to prolong the peaceful feeling of sharing with him. She felt him enlarging inside her.

"Let's try this when we're not at war," he whispered, and they began to make love.

Four

Jake Turner studied the face on the pillow next to his. It was soft, translucent, lovely. And innocent. Above all, innocent. Not necessarily in terms of sophistication, but in the absence of all inclination to hurt or deceive.

He did not like what he saw. Swinging out of bed, he slid into slacks and went to stand at the window, frowning in thought. He felt vaguely like a debaucher for having slept with this woman so different from himself.

Through half-drawn draperies he watched the sky brighten into a cloudless California day. A rustling of sheets told him Laura was awake. He listened for a moment, then turned. She was sitting up, her hair a tracery of fine black lace against the pillows. Her lips were smiling hesitantly, but her eyes were sober, and he saw tension in the line of her arms as they circled her knees. A tension that shouldn't be there, Turner thought.

She tried to give an impression of invincibility, but he could see through it.

"You're never going to make it writing for television," he said shortly.

He watched the line of her arms grow tighter. Her gray eyes stared at him, then suddenly kindled.

"You could tell that by sleeping with me? I didn't realize last night was an audition!"

Her bare shoulders set square and straight. Turner thought he had never seen such icy dignity. Her hand moved to the sheet to fling it back, but he stepped quickly to the bedside.

"Hey, babe, don't fly off the handle," he said half-surprised, half-angry. He hadn't expected her to spark like this, she was so soft. That was the trouble. She was too damn soft.

He reached out to touch her cheek, but she drew back. Turner shrugged.

"I'm honest, babe, whatever else I may be. Why take a bloodbath before somebody tells you the truth?" He sat casually on the edge of the bed, his gaze direct. "I like you, Laura. I don't especially want to see you in tears."

Laura regarded him with a fierce, private anger, still stunned by the way this day was starting. Was that the whole basis of his blunt assessment of her, his personal convenience? Of course it wasn't. He was in a position to gauge a writer's potential. Maybe she didn't have what it took.

Yes. Yes, she did. And anyway, Turner hadn't read anything she'd written.

"Look, you're intelligent and you've had some useful experience," he continued. "There are dozens of studio jobs you could have in a minute. In fact, I know of a reader's job that's just opening up."

Why did this remind her of the conversation with Van Greenberg the night before?

"With you, I suppose?"

He rolled back on one elbow, laughing, relaxed. "Oh, no. I wouldn't wish that on you. I'm hell to work with." He twisted, suddenly looking at the clock. "Speaking of which, I've got to take a meeting first thing this morning. There's coffee in the gadget there beside you. I've got to run."

Already he was in motion, opening a closet and snatching out a shirt. In the face of her silence he paused for a moment, looking back at her and frowning slightly. He didn't know what to say. She was the wrong sort of woman for him. She made him want to protect her.

"Look, I'll give you a call sometime," he said.

A drip splashed loudly in the bedside coffeemaker. The door to Turner's dressing room and the connecting bath beyond clicked shut. Laura crossed her arms on her knees and leaned her head against them, breathing deeply to keep the tears of angry self-rebuke from her eyes.

Everything with Turner had been exactly as she'd known it would be. She'd been nothing more than a one-night stand.

It was late afternoon. Turner crumpled an empty cigarette pack and tossed it at the wastebasket. He did not normally go through a pack a day. Damn it, why must he continue to think of Laura Fitzgerald?

It annoyed him that she wasn't tougher. He wanted to see her again, but he didn't want to be responsible for her feelings. And he couldn't stand the thought of a woman who'd suffer in silence as his mother had done.

He had a feeling Laura Fitzgerald would be that kind of woman. He'd seen the pain in her face that morning when he dropped the line about calling her. It hadn't been his fault. And it had been better to break things off then than it would have been later. Nevertheless he felt like a first-class bastard. Hell.

At least maybe he'd kept her from being torn limb-from-limb as he was sure she would be if she tried to write for television. She was vulnerable, truthful, all the things that ill-equipped her for his sort of business. Or his sort of life.

Sometimes she acted tough enough, resilient enough, but he knew it was exactly that—an act. In the very wideness of those gray-green eyes of hers you could read her integrity. She'd have to give that up, or this town would eat her.

He, on the other hand, had everything required for survival, he thought with irony. What he wasn't sure of was whether he had that gift—that genius—that would make him a god among producers.

Turner grinned at the immodest pipe dream. He was just reaching for the pink copy of a script he would have to defend in story conference the following morning when his door snapped open.

"That fag Petronelli couldn't run a honey wagon, let along a camera crew!" complained the white-haired, cigar-smoking man who came in.

Turned grinned more broadly. "Come on, Bernie. You know he'll be great when you reach the boonies. He's going to be the one who keeps the whole crew from mutiny."

Bernie Goldman stalked across the room bending and flexing his arms. "Damn these cramps. I think it's from suppressing the urge to strangle Petronelli. What do you think, Jake? We going to be able to lead this turkey into another season?" He was looking at the pink script on Turner's desk.

"Not on the basis of this script we won't."

The pink pages were an acknowledgment of his ability at crisis management, Turner thought. It was he who had sold the two-hour movie about to be filmed to NBC, putting together the creative package, overseeing the first draft of the script, and getting initial cost figures when Goldman, who had spawned the idea, got tied up elsewhere. Until midweek he had been scheduled as Goldman's assistant on the project. Now he was being left behind to rescue a sitcom that smelled worse than Limburger cheese.

"It's got to be redone," he said calmly. "But I think I can talk it through to them. Don't worry."

Goldman nodded and turned away. The phone on Turner's desk rang.

"Jake? Jessamyn. Look, I've been thinking about that project of yours. Maybe it's not so far-fetched after all. Why don't you stop over after work? We'll have a few drinks, and you can tell me about it."

It was an order, not an invitation, and Turner knew it. It was also the first good thing to happen all day.

"Sure thing," he said, agreeably surprised. What could have happened to change Jess Friday's mind?

Goldman, predictably ulcer-prone at the start of a shoot, was wearing a mournful face when he hung up. "I think Petronelli's just the tip of the iceberg," he lamented. "I can feel it in my bones—this project's jinxed." He left Turner's office, flexing his arms.

Turner was thinking of Goldman when he pulled into the circular drive at Jessamyn's. Would Petronelli prove to be a disaster after all? Among the cinematrographer's many virtues was the fact that compared to others of his caliber he came cheap. Goldman would have to humor him to get the best results, that was all.

He was ushered into the two-story-high entrance hall, and there coming toward him in a silky wrap-dress that made her look like a girl was Jessamyn herself.

Her hand was outstretched. "Hello," she said in husky tones. "I'll bet you're exhausted, aren't you? It was naughty of me to make you come straight from the office." She laughed and slipped a white hand through his arm, her head thrown back. "I'll make it up to you, I promise. Come in and relax."

She drew him into the opulent hush of her paneled living room, and for an instant he was once again Jake Turner whose father had worked at a dry cleaner's press, lost in this room of marble fireplaces and crystal lamps, overwhelmed that he had come so far. Every now and then he tripped, and the boy who had dressed in hand-me-downs looked out through the eyes of the calm young producer. He absorbed these surroundings now, the crystal bowls of pale coral roses that matched the hue of Jessamyn's dress and lent their light scent to the air, and he remembered his parents' two-room apartment smelling of potatoes and his father's whiskey.

A houseman offered him a martini on a silver tray.

"Thanks," he said, sitting back in a white velvet chair. The past receded.

Jessamyn sat across from him on a loveseat, her dress fluttering open at the knees. One of her ridiculous-looking white dogs lay watching her expectantly. She pulled it into her lap and smiled.

"Well. You've done something no other man has ever done to me," she said.

He looked at her—really looked at her for the first time since he'd known her—and marveled at her beauty. She was every man's fantasy, seductive in eye and gesture. Above the neckline of her dress he saw the deep cleft of her breasts. He wondered whether those breasts were as magnificent in real life as they were on camera.

"Oh? What's that?" he answered smoothly.

"You've tempted me to even consider considering television."

He laughed, nodding acknowledgement. "Good."

For the next two hours he told her about *Helen Somebody*, the disturbingly bittersweet story of a lonely wife's battle with schizophrenia. The houseman slipped in twice to refill their glasses.

"You know how to play an audience," said Jessamyn when he finished. "You'll have them weeping in their shirts."

"Does that mean you're interested?"

With a noncommital smile she tossed back her hair.

"Why aren't you going into theatrical films? You're wasting yourself on television."

"On the contrary. I can take more chances, be more creative. If I did a theatrical film, I'd be tied up for a year or more and tied to the gimmicks assuring a big box office. I'm where I can take on more projects, break new ground. I can deal with a smaller story, richer characterization, real art." He paused. "Characterization's what *Helen Somebody's* all about. You should appreciate that, Jess."

"Oh, I do."

She leaned forward, and he felt the full force of those famous eyes. He realized, slowly, that the action was deliberate, but that did not stop small tongues of excitement from licking him. She was turning him on. On purpose. And he liked it. Only why the hell was she expending this effort on him?

"But I think you're foolish not to go for the money," she said softly. She pointed to a small swelling in the carpet near where he sat. "Step on that buzzer and we'll have some dinner."

Turner's instincts told him not to rush her, to play all this as indifferently as she did. Of course she must know he was not indifferent. He had spent enough time making small talk with her about other things, dancing lightly around the subject, trying—as they both knew—for the chance to even get so far as to broach the plot.

He did not mention his film again until the dinner dishes, set between them on a low table draped in linen, were taken away.

"Well?" he said as the coffee was brought in. "What about it? The role's going to guarantee whoever plays it an Emmy."

Jessamyn laughed. "My, my. A guarantee! You're quite a salesman, Jake. But—" She rose and went to a side table where the coffee had been left. She poured two cups. "I don't need awards. I know I'm good. It doesn't take those little tin Oscars in my study to tell me that."

She walked toward him. Turner watched the subtle stir of her thighs beneath clinging silk, and in a flash he thought of

Laura's, long and smooth. Could this lush, compelling woman really have been a mother? He found it impossible to think of her in that way. Every inch of Jessamyn had the power to hypnotize. He knew that faculty had been carefully cultivated, and he admired it.

"I never make fast decisions," Jessamyn said.

She held a cup of coffee down to him, directly in front of her and a hand's span below her waist. As Turner reached for it, eyes traveling at close range up the contours concealed by her dress, he realized suddenly that she wore nothing beneath it. In that moment of recognition he glanced up, and her eyes met his.

Her laugh was low and rich.

"What's the matter, darling?"

Turner knew she had read his thoughts perfectly, in fact had planned them. He sat back with his coffee.

"You're a sexy woman, Jessamyn," he said easily. More easily than he felt. He saw her surprise at his bluntness and felt rewarded that she must have seen it as proof of nonchalance. The outer pose he'd constructed to hide uncertainty was pretty nigh impenetrable after all these years. Relaxing slightly, he took a sip of coffee.

Jessamyn sank onto the loveseat opposite him again, crossing her legs with a kick so that the folds of her dress slid well apart.

"Oh?" she said. "I wasn't sure you'd noticed."

"I'd noticed."

Turner felt his body reacting to her deliberate provocation.

"Good. I hate to be ignored," she said through lowered lashes.

The communication between them was open and complete, and Turner, looking at her, slowly identified what burned, what fascinated people in those amber eyes of Jessamyn Friday's. It was an invitation to gourmet sex. Seated across from her now, he could understand it. Her appearance was young and soft and innocent, but the glint in those eyes promised skill— and pleasure.

Why had she singled him out for this invitation? he wondered, blood coursing. A dark anger pricked him. Did she suppose she had only to signal interest in a man to bring him running? That was not his style. Yes, he thought, watching her lazy smile, she was aware of both her desirability and her power. Did she sense how far he had come from his origins, or suppose his interest in the project he was trying to sell her would make him so willing to come to her on her terms? He was seized by a fierce urge to throw her to the floor and take her without foreplay to see her expression as she realized she did not control him.

He drained his cup and set it beside him.

"There's not much chance of ignoring you," he said.

"More coffee?" she asked, her eyes demanding his. "I've sent the servants away for the rest of the night."

Turner grinned. The front door opened, and they both looked around.

"Well, well." Jessamyn's very attractive secretary strolled in wearing a smart belted suit. "Sorry to intrude."

"I thought you'd gone to a dance concert," said Jessamyn, and Turner thought he detected a dangerous note to her voice.

"Yeah, well, their choreographer ought to be changing tires for a living. That's how bad it was." Nel Simmons glanced at him, and Turner felt slightly annoyed at the wry shrewdness of her gaze. "Laura okay? I saw you leave with her last night."

"She had a headache. I expect she's just fine today."

He hadn't slipped up. He wondered how much Nel Simmons suspected and why it should matter. With a nod she continued on into another part of the house.

Turner stood. "Thanks for the dinner, Jess. I hope you will consider my project."

He saw her startled look.

"You're leaving?"

"I've got an early day tomorrow."

A few minutes later, as he slid into his car, Turner wondered whether he would have made the same decision if the Simmons woman had not intruded.

His apartment was quiet and sheltering when he returned. Turner liked the sense of privacy that he felt there. Collapsing on the couch, he tried to digest the fact that a woman millions of men dreamed about had just come on to him, and that he had declined. Instead he began to think about the night before.

It made him feel restless. He sat up, glancing at the headlines of the evening paper laid on the coffeetable. Why had he taken Laura to bed? There were other women who were more blatantly sexy. Her own mother was one of them. Yet now he found himself remembering the way she had trembled at first in his arms. He had liked what that told him about her. Damn it, why did he continue to have these conflicting emotions?

He stood up. It was not late. Maybe the way to get her out of his thoughts was to see her again. After all, it was not as though the lady had been unwilling, he thought with a grin. Another time or two and he would discover what it was that intrigued him about her. By then the interest she held for him would start to wane.

As he was picking up his keys, the phone rang. Turner looked back at it, undecided. Often when he was home, he simply let it ring, aware that it brought news of some crisis at work more often than not. Experience had taught him that most problems could be handled just as well the following morning. But now he turned back and picked up the receiver.

The voice on the other end spoke in rushes, punctuated by quick breaths.

"Jake, goddamn it . . . they're carting me out of here in an ambulance . . . Coronary . . . You've got to head up the shoot, do you understand? You . . . That fag Petronelli—"

"Jesus, Bernie, shut up!" Turner interrupted, finally breaking free of the shock of what he was hearing. "Shut up. Breathe. Lie down. I'll handle Petronelli and the shoot. I'll be right over."

In the background he could hear voices—paramedics, a night guard, someone. At least Bernie Goldman wasn't alone. But he had to get the fool off the phone. He hung up quickly.

Turner's own heart was racing. The fool, he thought again, calling in the midst of a heart attack about a lousy project. But he knew he would do the same. The movie about to be shot was not just *a* project, it was very good. If the script and Petronelli's cinematography were brought together well, it could be sensational—and now it was all his baby.

Good God, he was starting to think like everyone else in the business, not even pausing to wonder whether poor Bernie would live or die. He frowned, not completely liking what that told him about himself. His impulse to answer that phone had opened a door to him.

It also had freed him from further thoughts of Laura Fitzgerald.

"So how was Turner?"

Laura picked at her plate of chicken salad and avoided the

meaning of Nel's question, not because she supposed her friend
would be disillusioned by any moral laxness on her part, but
because she detected disapproval.

"He says I'm not going to cut it writing for TV."

Nel's eyebrows raised. "And are you?"

"Hell, yes." Laura brought her fork tines down into a seed-
less grape. "He may be just dandy as a producer, but he's
wrong about me. Maybe I'll get the kind of break he did one
of these days, and someone will keel over with a coronary to
accommodate me."

Nel's eyes held dry amusement. "From what I've seen of
him, I might suspect him of having engineered it if he hadn't
been with Jess when—" Abruptly Nel's words halted.

"He was with Jessamyn the night it happened?"

Laura admired the poise that kept Nel's gaze from wavering
as Nel pulled forth a cigarette, fitted it into a holder, and lighted it.

"Yes." She took a slow draw at the cigarette. "They'd had
dinner together by the looks of it when I came in. Just discussing
that project of his, I suspect."

Laura looked quickly at her plate again. "Don't worry, Nellie. Things are all over between Turner and me. But over."

She would never stoop to competing with Jessamyn for a
man, she thought above the anger coursing through her. Not
ever. The very idea made her feel filthy. More than that, however, was the fact that she knew it was something Jess would
like.

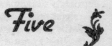

Five

Laura walked the perimeters of her small apartment, feeling
as light as the sunbeams that came in through the window and
almost as directionless. For two hours now she'd been expecting the phone call. It was almost noon.

Now that a job had nearly come to pass, it seemed a miracle.
A month of ghastly interviews and disappointment was over.

And the compliments that had been laid on her yesterday! She had grown light-headed as a principal story editor and his assistant continued her interview over lunch and began to talk with her about yet-to-be-written episodes eight weeks down the line, seeking her input, making her one of them. She sighed and stretched. Yesterday, despite assurances that getting her on the payroll as staff was only a formality, she had tried to tell herself that all manner of things could still go wrong. Today she could do nothing but wait in an ecstasy of anticipation for the phone to ring and Al Rosen to tell her when she should report for work.

When her nerves could not bear another second, she heard the jangling bell.

"Miss Fitzgerald? This is Mr. Rosen's secretary," a cool voice said.

Laura nodded, unable to stop the smile that was spreading across her face. "Yes?"

"Mr. Rosen asked me to call and say he's very sorry, but he's found someone who fills his staff writing job very nicely. He did appreciate the chance to see your work."

The world began to crumble like a buckling jigsaw puzzle.

"But—" Laura checked her protest. "I see." She didn't at all. "Well, thank you."

Could this be happening? Rosen and his assistant had been so explicit about the facts that she would get the job. No vague half-promises. "You're the one for us," they'd said. She felt numb. Cold. Unable to believe it, despite all those warnings to herself that something could go awry. There had been no explanation. Should she call back? Should she demand one? Or would that only serve to make her look foolish?

She still had two interviews scheduled for this afternoon, she remembered in a daze. By not canceling them, she had thought to insure the luck that this would go through. Now the scrambling would start all over again. Now after a month she was back to square one.

Pressing fingers against her eyes, she was fiercely determined not to cry. She couldn't cry at her age. Not if she hoped to be the poised and competent young career woman, she couldn't. To hell with a career, she thought savagely. What she really wanted was bedrock, a sense of no longer being adrift. That came from something very different. It came from having someone who came home to you every night, who shared the bruises of the day and made them seem inconsequential. Thousands of women—hundreds of thousands—enjoyed that. Why shouldn't she?

But damn it, she wanted this too! With an angry shake of the head she stood up, resolving to treat herself to lunch in Griffith Park and to come to the afternoon interviews ready to give a good accounting to herself.

Her first appointment was at four. She stayed amid the soothing chatter of the bird sanctuary till after three. As she drove back toward Columbia Studios, she recalled the conversation she'd had with Nel a month ago about wanting to write. She *had* to succeed at what she'd set out to do. If she didn't, she couldn't believe in herself, and what else was there, what anchor, what security other than that? She couldn't give up. She couldn't. She had to prove—to herself most of all—that she could do this.

In a folder under her arm she now carried, with the scripts of her docu-drama on rape and some of her talking animal shows, a film "treatment" for an original movie, which she had worked over in the last weeks. The treatment was the first step in a film project, an outline in narrative form. She had no expectation of arousing any real interest in it. It served only to show her understanding of the technique and to keep prospective employers studying her work for perhaps five minutes longer.

She waited in a chrome-and-glass waiting room that looked like many another chrome-and-glass waiting room to see a man named Archer. He was the producer of two currently popular series, one a police drama specializing in flashes of flesh and the other about a teacher in a ghetto school. Laura had found the latter especially well-written. She was curious to meet the man who had conceived the idea.

Archer was middle-aged. He wore white slacks and an open shirt, which emphasized his tan. He had a small goatee. As they talked, Laura was aware of him observing her closely. She tried to relax, but couldn't until he picked up her work and began to look at it, one foot resting casually on the open drawer of his desk, his chair turned toward her.

It seemed to Laura that he did not spend much time inspecting her work. After a few moments, he leaned back in his chair, his expression pleasant.

"You show promise," he said with a smile. "Of course you

do realize that getting a start in this business depends a good deal on luck."

"What do you mean?"

"There are a lot of promising young script writers. I'll be seeing several more this afternoon—some of them with credits. So a lot depends on having your name—and your work— remembered, doesn't it?" He paused. "Why don't we talk about your work over dinner?"

Disgusted comprehension spread through her. She had been offered auditions on the casting couch before, but never quite so smugly. And never after such a bitch of a day.

"Oh? Just dinner's necessary?" she asked coldly.

"And breakfast, I imagine. It would help to keep your name fresh in my mind."

He sat there unruffled, and suddenly Laura was reminded of Van Greenberg. It would be nice to have power. She would love to wipe the complacency off Archer's face.

"Such a kind offer—does it come with a guarantee?"

Surely he could recognize the sarcasm in her words, but he merely sat up and closed the desk drawer, still smiling.

"Nothing much in life is guaranteed now, is it?"

Laura stood up. "In that case I think I'll let another of those promising young writers jog your memory. Or whatever else it is you require."

She walked two blocks past the parking lot where she'd left her car before her temper cooled enough for her to realize where she was. God but she was sick of men like Archer, sick of the games of cat and mouse, sick of egos. She felt as though she were trying to claw her way into a cube that had no doors. Surely not every woman who wrote for film in Hollywood had hopped into the sack to get her chance.

Now she had no desire to cry. She wanted to clobber someone. She missed her New York friends with whom she could let off steam—Al Lopez, who edited confession magazines and could think up more original insults than anyone she'd ever met, Jean Willis, whose stockbroker father sometimes had met both of them for a drink and cheered them on. What would her own father have been like? Would he have boosted her spirits and sent her back to fight? She didn't have time to think about it. Her next appointment was in Century City, and she would be late.

Ben Lewis, the man she was to see, was thirty minutes

behind schedule. He was looking for a reader, not a writer, but there was the bare possibility that one job could lead to the other. Laura watched his bald head warily as he looked over her scripts.

"Say, you understand what's structure's about," he said flipping one closed. "The question is, can you think dirty? That's what prime-time's all about these days. Innu-endo . . . suggestion . . ."

"I know." Lewis specialized in sexy sitcoms. "I've seen your shows."

He pinched his lower lip and looked at her.

"The problem with you, sweetheart, is that you don't look like your mind runs that way."

Laura gave him a hard look. "It runs however it's paid to run. I was never especially a history buff, but I think I gave a good accounting of myself when I signed on with a show based on that concept."

Lewis chuckled. "There's history, and then there's what people watch, sweetheart." He glanced at his watch. "Look, I'll tell you what I'm going to do. Since I kept you waiting, I'm going to take you across the street and buy you a drink. I'll give you ten minutes to tell me what you think's wrong with my new show and how you'd fix it. We'll see if you have what it takes to weed out good scripts from bad."

She wondered if it was a test. Was this a come-on like the one before, or was Lewis trying to determine if she was a prude? He was obnoxious, she thought, watching light reflect from his nose to the crown of his head. But obnoxious wasn't the same thing as disgusting.

"Okay," she said and frantically tried to think about his show.

She didn't realize where they were going until an elevator opened and they were in the lobby of the Playboy Club. A wasp-waisted bunny with thighs bared to the hipbone ushered them in. When they were seated in well-cushioned swivel chairs, Lewis glanced around and grunted as though satisfied with a well-known scene.

"Ya see, this is what the male viewer wants, visions of this. How do you give him that, huh? Ya gotta do that and still keep the girls in dresses."

Laura surveyed the room full of bunnies in their high-heeled pumps and satin ears of assorted hues. She looked at the lighted nude above the bar, its expression seductive, none of its details airbrushed away. Was Lewis right? Was this what the male viewer wanted? And what about the female viewer? She opened her mouth to speak, but Lewis, leaning comfortably back, began to talk.

After twenty minutes and his second Chivas Regal, Laura began to suspect he wasn't interested in her ideas at all. Ben Lewis was obviously impressed with himself, with his shrewdness, with his own importance.

"Listen, I've had three hit series in a row," he was boasting as his eyes flitted in a desultory manner from one briefly attired bunny to another. "Not one of 'em depended on the cast. They were mostly crap. Give me any broad with the right equipment, and I can make her a sensation so long as she's got smarts enough to learn her lines."

Lewis was a bore, thought Laura, and she was less and less certain she could stand working for him even if he was considering her, which she thought unlikely. He paused and signaled their bunny, a blonde in lavender satin who said her name was Pete. Laura watched her adjust the silly little tuxedo collar above her bare and very well-rounded breasts and start toward them.

"It's all a matter of situation," Lewis was saying. "And script." He looked up at Pete, who stood by the table smiling. "Just take this little girlie here. Look at those knockers. That's all I need to make her a star."

Laura felt herself going hot with embarrassment. Even though the girls who worked here must know they were signing up to be ogled, Lewis's crudeness was beyond belief.

"Pay no attention to him. He's an ass," she said, meeting Pete's surprised eyes. Snatching up her purse, she walked out alone.

Nel sat in the room where Laura had first met Jake Turner. When Jessamyn was out for the evening, she often came to the library. She liked the fireplace, though a fire was never laid. She liked being able to eavesdrop on the servants in the kitchen, a pleasure she was too busy for during the day. Right now one of the housemen was trying to put the make on Maria, and Maria, with majestic scorn, was having none of it. Nel finished the coffee sitting beside her and turned the page of a book.

A few minutes later she was startled by a knock at the library door.

"You've got a visitor," Harry, the other houseman, announced.

"I do?"

She put her book aside. It must be Laura. The poor kid had called some time ago and told her about the episode with Ben Lewis. Laura had made light of it, but Nel had sensed she was more upset than she was letting on, and that possibly more had happened than she was revealing. The strain in her cheerfulness had been apparent.

"It's okay," she said. "I'm 'in' tonight."

She stood up and stretched, pleased that Laura had come by to talk with her. As the door swung open, she started to make a joke. She stopped. The words froze on her lips as the years slipped away. Suddenly she was frightened, terrified, her heart beating in her throat and choking her with joy as well as apprehension.

"Nel. You look just as I've always imagined you would," said Eddie.

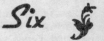

Six

"What I mean is that you're beautiful," he said, coming into the room. "You could go back on the stage tonight if you wanted to."

Nel could not bring her eyes away from his face, the familiar coffee-brown contours, strong yet smooth, traced, memorized by her fingers, never forgotten. His narrow moustache over an equally narrow yet sometimes coaxing mouth was just as she remembered. Stubborn shrewdness still burned in his eyes. Only his glossy hair, combed back simply, was different—longer.

"I don't want to go back." Her voice was the breathless

whisper of an eight-year-old kid, awed by the tough young cop whom everyone feared because he was incorruptible and who said he loved her. She cleared her throat. It seemed to give her back a measure of her present self. Why had she spent almost thirty years cultivating a reputation for being unflappable if it couldn't serve her now?

"Hey, I'm a private citizen these days, Eddie. But thanks for the compliment. You don't look in bad shape yourself."

In spite of the glibness she still felt awkward. She reached automatically for the cigarette holder lying next to her discarded book.

"Damn," she said. "I think I need a drink. Can I get you one, or are you on duty?"

They both laughed shyly at her reminder of the past.

"I don't think I've been on duty since I won my first election," said Eddie.

He made an easy gesture with the hat in his hand. When had she last seen a man wear a hat? Maybe it was a holdover from the old days, from the uniform.

"Okay if I sit down?" he asked.

"Why not. Since you're here."

She was trying to keep it light, but she gave up the attempt, at the same moment turning away all thought of fitting a cigarette into the holder for fear her hands might shake. Her voice grew low, and she looked away from him.

"I wish you hadn't come."

He took a step toward her. She could sense it. She could feel him there behind her about to touch her.

"Nellie—"

Harry, summoned by the buzzer she'd pressed, stepped into the doorway.

"Shall I get you something, Nel?"

She faced him with an equanimity she hadn't felt since Eddie's intrusion, groping her way back toward this safe mooring in the past.

"Sure, Harry. How about a couple of martinis?"

They both stood silently until he disappeared. Eddie started to speak, but she cut him off.

"Look, Eddie, I don't want to stir up the past, okay? I've got it cushy. I like the way my life's turned out. Let's have a drink and go our separate ways. What brings you here?"

She saw the hurt in his eyes. She couldn't have caused that

thirty years ago; he had been too sure of himself, too wise, and she had been too young. Or could she have?

"I had some business here," he said. "A little legislative snooping." He still had that quiet composure through and through. There was no trace of rancor in his voice.

"Say, you've become a pretty big gun in Congress. I've seen your pictures—" She broke off, wishing she could bite her tongue.

Eddie didn't comment, only looked at her, smiling slightly.

"How'd you find your way into politics anyway?" she asked.

His eyes dropped to his hands, smooth, well-manicured hands without any ornamentation.

"Started little, got bigger. The story's not very interesting."

There was a faint sound as Harry appeared with a tray. On it were two martinis and two small plates of caviar. The staff would have their turn to speculate about her tonight, Nel thought. Had it been so long since she'd entertained a man that it rated caviar?

"My, my, you do have it cushy," Eddie smiled when Harry was gone. "Big house, servants, the works. How'd you get where you are, Nel?"

"On a Greyhound bus." She could manage a cigarette now and did, looking into the flame of the lighter before she continued. "I always said I'd make the big time, Eddie. I suppose by some standards I did. Worked my tail off for a couple of years, got some good club engagements, some movie parts. I'd never appreciated what that struggle up the ladder takes out of you, though." She paused, thinking of Laura.

"When the green grew thin, I worked as a secretary. One day after a show I'd been in had closed the same night it opened, I heard Jess Friday was hunting someone to handle her personal affairs. I figured 'What the hell? I'll try it for a while and give myself a little rest.' I guess you could say I've been resting ever since."

A silence followed. They both sipped their martinis.

"Why did you run, Nel?" Eddie asked softly.

That easiness—that gentle tone he'd always used with her—was suddenly more than she could bear. She stood up, agitated, and walked toward the fireplace, elbows gripped tightly in opposite hands.

"You know why, Eddie!"

He hadn't moved. She knew that he was watching her.

"Had I ever lied to you, Nellie? I told you I'd always take care of you."

"You had one hell of a way of doing it! Seeing that the club where I was working was raided while I was on stage!"

"I didn't know you'd be on stage. Did you suppose I wouldn't get you out?"

His voice was controlled while hers was growing tighter. She felt uncertain again, as she had when she was a kid and he was seven whole years older.

"I got myself out—through a back door. Did you suppose I wouldn't be scared shitless? I'd heard about what happened to young girls in jail—especially young black girls. And that fat pig Warneke had already tried to come on to me several times—"

"I wouldn't have let you go to jail."

"You could have told me that. You could have warned me. Why did you have to pick that club anyway? There were others that were worse."

"That was the one where you were. I cared about you. You had no business being there in the first place. You were under age—"

"Yeah, yeah."

"And then I found out that one of the bartenders was dealing drugs. I had to get you out of there, Nellie, before you got mixed up in something. And you were too stubborn to leave. It was the only way."

Eyes closed, Nel felt as though the night they were talking about was happening again.

"You could have warned me," she repeated.

"And had you tell your friend Lucy? She was sleeping with the bartender. He got out of prison, you know. And he turned her into a junkie and a whore."

Eddie's voice softened. She heard him rising.

"Nellie—" He was coming toward her. "Nel, I never dreamed you'd run. You were so young—"

His hands caressed her rigid arms. Nel felt herself shrinking, trying to draw away from his touch, but an old familiar music began to play across her skin.

Eddie's breath stirred her hair. "I want you, Nel. After all this time I've finally found you, and I want you."

Nel's mouth was dry, but she had grown far beyond that frightened girl in Detroit.

"Eddie, don't be a fool."

"Why not? I still love you. And I think maybe you still love me, or you wouldn't have made such a fuss about not seeing me."

Always so steady, always so sure of what he wanted, she thought. Maybe that was why, when they first met, he had seemed almost a hero to her.

Nel's eyes stung with sudden tears. She had forgotten something. Feeling the security of him there, holding her, she had forgotten the illness that would still her hands, her legs, finally her breath.

Laura forced down another swallow of the fragrant herb tea she'd brewed to relax herself. Her mood was leaden. How could she have been so stupid as to leave her folder of scripts there with Lewis when she stormed out? Now she'd have to face him to get them back. Or maybe he'd simply leave them there and they'd be lost for good.

Here's to Lewis. Here's to Archer, she thought, downing the tea. This round was yours, but maybe one of these days our paths will crisscross again and I'll be the one who can make you squirm. I doubt it, but it's a nice thing to contemplate. Holding the whip hand, as Van Greenberg had suggested, could have its moments.

The phone rang. She walked toward it listlessly. It was probably Nel calling to see if she'd slit her wrists.

"Hello," she said without much energy.

"Laura? This is Van Greenberg. I hope you remember me."

She gave a short laugh he couldn't hear and decided to pass on telling him she had been thinking of him.

"Come on, I wasn't in that bad shape," she said.

"Look, I realize it's late, but I'm suddenly free for the evening and I wondered if you'd have dinner with me."

Laura drew a breath, summoning all her thoughts about the direction of her life. Greenberg was pleasant, and he had interested her more than most men did. If she had met him first, she might never have lost her head over Jake Turner. If she went with him now, she might blot out that memory.

"All right," she said. "On one condition. You must understand that it's not because I want any favors in return."

He laughed. "I see you do remember the night at Jessamyn's. I agree to your condition, and I'm doubly flattered. Put on something beautiful. We're going to The Bistro."

The name sounded so modest, almost homey, Laura thought. It hardly suggested a place where Hollywood's biggest celebrities sometimes waited for tables. She had not been there before, though among the very wealthy girls at the private day school she'd attended the thought of dinner at the Bistro had been a favorite fantasy, the symbol of true indulgence and of passage into womanhood. Now she looked with interest and a slight uneasiness at the elegant mirrored walls, the black Bentwood chairs, at a *belle époque* dream of starched white linen, silver, and a profusion of fresh roses arranged in baskets and pots. This was not the place for a casual dinner date. She began to wonder what Greenberg would expect in trade.

"Gibson?" he inquired as the cocktail waiter appeared.

Ruefully she shook her head, smoothing the sleeves of the sliver of fluid black jersey that was her dress. It was cut out just above her breasts and deep between them, the fabric licking up in firelike tongues beneath an overlay of beaded chiffon. She wore no jewelry with it. She needed none.

"No thanks," she said. "I'm not usually as intemperate as I was the night we met."

He smiled and ended up ordering a frightfully expensive wine.

"Such serious eyes," he said after it had been served. "What are you thinking?"

"That I'm a little nervous about such lavish treatment."

"Don't be. You'll think me vain for saying it, but I rarely crave companionship beyond my own. Tonight I did. You answered that need—and very charmingly. You were forthright with me; I shall be with you. Neither of us expects anything of the other."

Laura didn't know what to say. She looked at her wineglass. Greenberg sat back, relaxed, regarding her.

"Your candor on the phone intrigued me," he said. "My two attempts at marriage—and other liaisons—have pretty much convinced me most people value the element of uncertainty in personal relations. While I expect that's highly reasonable, I find it bothersome." He looked out over the room now, the silver flecks at his temples glinting attractively. "All in all I find business more to my taste. It's much less complicated."

"But also uncertain," Laura said, thinking of the sums of money a network gambled away on shows that folded.

"Mine isn't."

He smiled, his cool blue gaze returning to her. What lay behind it? Laura wondered. At Jessamyn's she had thought she saw a flash of kindness and now humor. Or was it icy to the core?

She could not decide. Throughout dinner, ordered from a blackboard brought tableside, she studied him. She discovered only that she felt comfortable with him and that if he was reserved, he was also engaging. He was polite. He was self-assured. He was a far cry from the sort of men she had been meeting. As they talked, he ceased to be a man with power to wield and became instead simply an interesting companion.

They were about to leave when she noticed Archer sitting at a nearby table, no doubt giving the cute redhead across from him the same chance to imprint herself on his memory that he had offered Laura that afternoon.

"Something the matter?" asked Greenberg, though she did not think she had let her expression alter in the least. He looked around. "That's Hugh Archer."

"Yes, I know."

"Ah. Have you had a run-in?"

"No."

As soon as she'd said it, Laura realized that she had done so too quickly, prompted by the memory of Greenberg's mentioning his own clout. Not that she thought he would do anything, but she was still wary of having him know anything about her battles.

To her surprise he laughed.

"I hope you're not worried that I keep some sort of enemies list. Be practical, Laura! I mentioned what I did the other night simply because I wanted to initiate a merger, and I wanted all cards on the table. I don't traffic in grudges. Yes, I occasionally pull a string, but not very often. Certainly not as often as most of the people in this town. And never over trifles. I promise I won't taint you."

She was blushing for the first time she could remember. Greenberg took her arm. At that moment Archer happened to look in their direction, and Laura, although still struggling with her embarrassment, found the look of uneasy surprise that came to his face worth it all.

"Now we have established that you and Archer have crossed paths and probably swords," Greenberg continued as he steered her from the galaxy of mirrors, china, and famous faces. "From his constant supply of young women I would guess that he propositions. Am I correct?"

"Yes."

"Not too unusual."

"No."

As they left the restaurant, she found herself telling him about Hugh Archer.

When they reached her apartment, Greenberg unlocked the door and returned the key to her. He hesitated a moment, then put an arm around her and kissed her. It was not a passionate kiss, but it was warm and pleasurable, and Laura liked the firmness in the arm encircling her.

She looked at him directly, deciding not about the offer but about the present, about how easily they got along, about her need to eradicate all memory of Jake Turner.

"I hope you'll reconsider that offer of mine some day," he said, releasing her.

"No," she said and waited until there was no chance of misunderstanding. "But will you come in for a drink?"

She saw his eyebrows raise and then he nodded.

"Yes, I'd like that."

She wondered, as she got down glasses, what he thought of the invitation. It was exactly what he had said he didn't like. It was an invitation to uncertainty. She intended to sleep with Greenberg, and yes, in return for something—only not for what he had offered, not for anything he would understand. Strangely she almost thought he would understand if she told him she wanted to go to bed with him to forget someone else, but her pride forbade it. She filled her own glass to give her courage and went into the living room.

They talked, but she didn't know of what. She drained her glass. Van Greenberg had barely touched his drink, and he hadn't touched her at all. She wished he would. She wasn't sure that she could make the first move.

Her heart beat harder as she returned to the small kitchenette for a refill. Her hand shook. Eyes closed, she took a quick

drink, telling herself the nervousness would pass, that everything would be all right.

"I seem to make you drink those things very quickly."

Greenberg spoke from beside her elbow, and she jumped.

"It's . . . just been a bad day," she faltered.

"Has it?" Taking the glass from her, he set it on the breakfast
bar. His hands rested easily on her shoulders, and his eyes
swept hers. "I think you invited me in intending to sleep with
me. Only now you need something to help you go through
with it."

"No! I— Oh, damn!" She pulled away from him and leaned
against the kitchen wall, one arm above her head, her face
averted. "I'm sorry. I honestly am." She couldn't think of
anything else to say. On top of all this she recalled Turner
hurling the same accusation at her, taunting her. She was
ashamed of herself. Van didn't deserve this.

"I'm sorry too," he said. "I was flattered. Still am, a little.
It's been a while since a woman showed an interest in me
without wanting something."

He paused, and she heard the snap of his cigarette lighter.
There was silence.

"If you had really wanted to fall into bed with me, there
wouldn't have been the need for even a cup of coffee, though,
would there?" he inquired. "What is it, Laura? Were you trying
to prove something to yourself? Or to forget someone perhaps?"

She wondered how much he guessed.

Greenberg took her gently by the hand and turned her to
face him.

"You haven't been used enough to be comfortable using
someone else. In a way I'm glad." He brought her hand up to
his lips and kissed it. "I hope some day we'll be able to have
an agreement between us without the booze."

A moment later she heard the door of her apartment click
closed.

Jessamyn slid back into bed with a cup of coffee, the day's
trades, and a contemptuous look for the man still sleeping beside her. She did not expect any man to lie there unaware of her
after she'd awakened. He would not even be mentioned in the
diary of her love affairs, which no eyes but her own had ever seen.
And he would not be invited back into her bed again.

Altogether he had a lot of deficiencies, she thought with

narrowed eyes. He projected the image of a young stud, but he had proved too bland, too young to be satisfactorily skilled as a lover.

Not that he was that much younger than she was. How old was she anyway? Thirty felt about right. A woman reached her peak at thirty. She was beautiful, firm, supple, no longer a child. At thirty she began to appreciate the endless variations of getting and giving pleasure. Yes, she was thirty.

In an unwelcome flash she remembered a younger Jessamyn, no more beautiful, less wise. That was the Jessamyn who had allowed herself to become pregnant, had planned and wanted it, she thought scornfully. That was the idiot who had let herself— But no. She wouldn't think of that. The first time the photographers had trained their cameras on a drooling toddler and excluded her, the radiant young mother, she had known she had made a wrong choice. Letting her perfect body be used to produce a child had been the single colossal mistake of her career.

With a crack she opened the paper on her lap. The man asleep beside her had put her in a terrible mood. When an item on the second page caught her attention, she moved almost by reflex to shove him onto the floor.

The act made her feel better.

"Wha-what?" He floundered in the sheet he had taken with him, looking sleepily up at her, hardly the dandy he'd been in the recent movie that made him a name.

"Get out," she said and straightened her paper.

He sat up staring, expression indignant.

"What the hell do you mean, pulling something like that?"

"I mean you're boring and the sight of you annoys me. So get out."

She poured more coffee from the silver pot beside the bed, ignoring him. He watched her for a moment, then she heard him stir. Picking up his Gucci shoes and shirt and custom-made pants, he crept away.

With satisfaction Jessamyn spread the glossy pages of the paper and read the article inside again. Jake Turner was back in town, and from the sounds of it the film he had produced when Goldman keeled over was going to be a triumph. She reached for the phone. There was no answer at his apartment. She dialed the studio. Jake Turner apparently was not a man to rest on his laurels. That didn't mean he wouldn't lap up praise, though. He had an ego. Everyone who dipped a spoon into the caldron of the film world did. Well, she would feed it.

"Darling, I've just been reading wonderful things about you and your film," she said when he came on. "How does it feel to be a genius?"

He laughed, but with great satisfaction.

"Come on, Jessamyn. No one's called me that yet."

"'A fresh modern view of the West's hard morality . . . Harsh but, compelling.' That comes pretty close. So I want to get my bid in before your head's turned. I have to show up at a dreary party tonight. Will you take me and save me from absolute boredom?"

"I don't know how entertaining I'll be after three weeks in the wide open spaces. I may moo."

"Bulls don't moo, darling. Pick me up at eight."

She hung up smiling. They would have a drink together before they left. She would see to it Turner made some useful contacts at the party. He was going to be in a fine mood tonight, and so was she.

And little Laura was going to learn a lesson, she decided slowly. It vexed her that she had thought of Laura just now, but she had, and when something annoyed her, she always got it out of her line of vision. Firmly, carefully, she began to dial another number.

"Michael," she said when there was an answer on the other end. "This is Jessamyn Friday. Listen, I have a little favor to ask of you."

She stretched, savoring the morning, savoring the knowledge that Michael would comply. There were very few people in Hollywood she could not manipulate. There was only one man whom she feared.

Actually she did not fear him either after all these years. They both had changed. Their paths seldom crossed. Yes, she was every bit as powerful as he was now. And he had no idea that he had a daughter.

Seven

Michael Townes was a homosexual. The ultimate proof of his
skill as an actor was that he played some of the most sizzling
love scenes ever captured on celluloid with Hollywood's current crop of leading ladies. Casting him as a film's romantic
lead guaranteed waiting lines snaking around the block when it
was released, and the lines were equally long in college towns
and suburban shopping centers. He showed up at parties with
pretty women, and his fans never suspected that his true tastes
ran toward thin blond men.

Laura had met him ten years before when he was a young
actor with a minor role in a picture Jessamyn was making. He
had driven to Tiajuana with her and Nel a time or two, sharing
their passion for Mexican food. They had been friends of a
casual sort. Still Laura was surprised to hear from him after
all this time.

"Hey, listen," he said when his phone call had aroused her.
"I just found out that you were in town, and I've got a favor
to ask you."

Laura looked at the clock on the coffee table and saw it was
almost eleven. She had been trying to avoid the day, the headache left by the gin she had drunk too fast, and the memory
of what a fool she had made of herself with Van Greenberg.

"Sure, Michael," she said, forcing cheer into the words.
"What do you need?"

"I've got to show at this party tonight—studio boss's birthday. My date just called to say she's sick. Would you fill in?"

Laura brushed her hair back out of her eyes and leaned on
the breakfast bar.

"You want me to fill in for some gorgeous babe who'd get
you photographed for *Women's Wear Daily*? Thanks for the
compliment, but I really think you'd be better off with someone

else. You haven't seen me since I was a kid, and I'm definitely not the Beautiful People-type."

"You are the right gender, and frankly that's all I care about at the moment. For God's sake, you can hide behind the potted cacti if you like, just say you'll go. I am clearly desperate, there aren't that many women I'm comfortable with, and I figure you owe me something for taking care of you when you got sick coming back from the border that time."

She gave a weak laugh. "That was your fault—yours and Nel's—letting me drink beer after all those *enchiladas*. But all right, since you're appealing to my sense of fair play, I suppose I can do it for you. What must I wear? Long dress?"

"And slinky, preferably."

"You'll have to settle for something less."

"Okay, okay."

When he hung up, Laura looked at the clock again. She had to hurry and shower. She had almost forgotten that she was to meet Nel for lunch.

Nel already was in place when she arrived. A hefty Manhattan sat on the checkered tablecloth in front of her.

"Hi," said Laura, eyeing it in surprise as she slid into a wooden booth. Except when they were vacationing—something she and Nel had done as a twosome for years—she could not remember Nel ever having a drink at lunch.

"How's it going, kiddo? The world look any better today?" Nel's greeting was as robust as usual, but Laura thought she detected a hollowness underlying it. There was a drained look in the area around Nel's eyes, and it alarmed her. The marvelous contours of her cheeks seemed a little too pronounced.

"Oh, Nellie, don't ask me," she sighed, her thoughts deflected now by the memory of her own folly. "Yes. No. I don't want to talk about it."

She turned her face away, toward the anonymity of the crowded restaurant, drawing solace from the simple fact of Nel's presence. If yesterday had been different, would she even have considered what she had tried with Van Greenberg? This morning she was disgusted with herself. She didn't want to tell Nel what she had almost done. Nel would understand and would tell her it wasn't anything so terrible. It wasn't. All the same, she was ashamed to confess her weakness.

"Some days are a bitch," Nel agreed in a strange voice.

She picked up her glass. Laura glanced at her, curious, and

once again almost instinctively uneasy. It wasn't like Nel to be this quiet, or this low on humor.

Laura's expression was gentle. "You sound like you're having one of them yourself. What's wrong?"

Nel shook her head. "Nothing. Oh, hell. All right. It's a man."

In spite of herself Laura grinned. Nel's face relaxed.

"Okay, okay, don't kill yourself laughing."

"I didn't know you had anything on, Nel." She felt enormously relieved.

"I don't. It's just someone I knew a long time ago. He turned up last night, and I guess it shook me. All these years supposing he'd get fat and bald and be overrun by a dozen ungrateful kids, and he had the gall not to."

Underneath the joking Laura heard an unfamiliar note. She watched Nel fit a cigarette into her holder. What was wrong?

"It doesn't matter," Nel continued. "I think I got across to him that I don't intend to pick things up. Thanks for letting me mention it. It's gotten me out from under, somehow."

Laura knew she was lying. On the surface Nel seemed to be her old self again, but the set of her mouth said she was still deeply disturbed. Who was this man? What had he done to Nel?

Laura had seen Nel drift through a few casual interludes with men in their years together. In fact, in Laura's younger days she'd often found herself included on Nel's dates, wafted to the park or to Disneyland by Nel and some disgruntled suitor, or sneaked into risqué reviews when Nel was more favorably disposed toward the man in question.

This was different. Nel was in pain. That alone made it unfair. Laura wanted to help.

"Nellie . . ."

"Dog One died." Nel cut her off. "They haven't been able to find a replacement in LA. May have to have one flown in from Frisco."

All right, Nel wanted to nurse whatever wounds she had in private. Laura would respect that and not intrude.

"Such tragedy."

She didn't try to keep the sarcasm from her voice. Dog One and Dog Two were the joke of Jessamyn's household, though Laura doubted Jessamyn herself was aware of it. To Jessamyn they were Po and Ying-Ying, two fixed personalities regardless of the fact that a dozen dogs had answered to those names in Laura's memory. Because of her constant dole of chocolates, Jessamyn's pets had criminally short life spans, and when one died, she expected it to be replaced within the day without any fanfare. Then she ignored the fact that her dog had shrunk to the size of a puppy once again. To Laura the whole thing bordered on the ghoulish. To the household it led simply to snickers about their employer's disposable pets.

"Hey, who are you mad at?" asked Nel as Laura twisted apart a roll from the basket sitting between them.

Laura shook her head, thinking that Jessamyn's household had been somehow corrupted, made cynical about the pudgy yet pathetic little dogs whose lives came and went.

"So what's on for the afternoon? More interviews?" Nel asked.

She seemed less tense. Maybe diversion was the thing she needed just now.

"Um-um. Just shopping." Laura knew the news she had to share would amuse Nel. "I'm going to a party with Michael Townes."

"Laura!"

Michael planted a quick little kiss on her cheek and then stepped back to admire her black chiffon skirt and sheer white blouse. The combination was as simple and as striking as the contrast of Laura's dark hair swept into a pompadour against the perfect whiteness of her skin. The blouse, its finger-thin pleats spreading into winglike sleeves, draped open to the waist in back. As she turned, Michael whistled.

"Hey, you're a lot better looking than that skinny kid who used to stuff herself with tacos. I do like the rags. Who's your tailor?"

Laura laughed. "Strictly off the rack, I'm afraid. Glad you approve."

"Yes, yes. Now tell me what you've been up to since the last time I saw you."

By the time she had finished, they were entering the gate of the estate where they were headed. As a child Laura had viewed the Hollywood great from a distance, from the kitchen with Lupita or from the margins of a room as she crept through. Occasionally, grudgingly, she was introduced. Then she had felt invisible, and though that was sometimes painful, it was mostly comforting. Now she was aware of being not only visible, but a complete unknown in the gathering at hand. She still could not fathom why it had occurred to Michael to ask her.

He was gallant in his attentions to her, seeing that she immediately had champagne and introducing her to everyone they met.

"Do you know Dan Katz?" he asked as a man in the near uniform of open shirt and gold medallion spoke in greeting.

Katz was shorter than Laura and slightly comic-looking with a fringe of white hair curling wildly above his ears. His face had a kindly look, and before he could continue through the crowd, on Michael rattled.

"This is Laura, Dan, and I have more reasons to love her than I could name. Just have a look at her. Isn't she great?"

Laura saw curiosity fill Dan Katz's gray eyes, and she wanted to laugh. If Michael kept this act up, would she find herself publicized as his newest interest? The thought made her merry. A lot of women had been cheated by Michael's preferences of the flesh. He was perfectly gorgeous with those toughened muscles and the wealth of black hair exposed by his satin shirt.

"How do you two know each other?" Katz asked politely.

"Oh, we go back a long way." Michael squeezed Laura's shoulder and gave a conspiratorial wink. "Dan's big network brass," he whispered, propelling her onward. "Swell fellow, but awfully straight. I'd just as soon he thought you were my honeybun."

The party around them swallowed them up, and Laura found herself once again floating anonymously through a sea of faces. She recognized one at the very instant Enrique Portero spotted her.

Flashing his wide grin, Portero came toward them with hand outstretched.

"I have not yet recovered from my broken heart," he said in greeting.

Laura laughed and, flinging herself into the absurdity of the evening, spoke in rapid Spanish. "Have you tried fasting? Meditation? Writing morbid poetry? If all else fails, a monastery is an excellent solution, so I'm told."

His grin grew wider. "I will bear my suffering before I go that far, I think. But what is this? Is part of the blood in those delicate veins of yours Mexican?"

"You'll have to ask Jessamyn," she answered, lightly because everything was light at parties like these. Light, witty, and very carefully edited lest it betray any real concern. Old press clippings told a romantic tale of Jessamyn's brief, secret marriage to a French explorer who had died in the Amazon, leaving her with child. That, Laura thought, was fabrication—probably Stan's work. Had her mother ever been married?

Portero looked at her with interest. "And how are you, Michael my friend?" he asked, returning to English.

"Just fine, Hank. You're spending a lot of time in town these days. What gives?"

"I'm trying to nail down the last bit of a new project. It's a disaster at the moment. Tell me, how did you persuade this shy young lady to be seen with a glittering fellow like yourself?"

Michael gave his wink and squeeze. "We go back a long way. Laura's recently back from New York. She did scripts for some local stations, and now she's trying to land something here. We're just catching up on old times."

"Ah. How interesting."

The three of them talked at length while the party went on around them. At last Portero excused himself to make a phonecall.

A little ripple of excitement started through the room, and Laura looked up, wondering who was arriving.

"Well, well! Look who's here," said Michael.

On the far side of the room a couple was making a royal progress through the other guests. It was Jessamyn—and with her Jake Turner. Laura felt a trap door drop open in her stomach, and all the heat drained from her. Her mother and Jake. She could not take her eyes from them. All the hints had been there, but she hadn't believed them—hadn't wanted to. Disgust spread through her, and something else that hurt.

Jessamyn, a hundred carats worth of diamonds glimmering at her neck, was exchanging little kisses with people, and everyone was interrupting Jake to shake his hand. He must have brought off some sort of triumph. The film he'd been shooting? The deal with Jessamyn? Or maybe it was only his appearance here with her.

"Want to go over and say hello?" asked Michael.

"No thanks. I'm going to try some of the Oysters Rockefeller." With cold waves churning inside her, she moved away.

This was too much, this chance encounter with the two of them, she thought bitterly. When had Jake returned to town anyway? She realized two days had passed since she'd read a paper.

With a dark flash of humor she noticed there really were potted cacti in the room, great majestic specimens that must have flourished for years in the desert before being transplanted here for a chic decor. However, she had no intention of hiding behind them as Michael had suggested. She did not care to come face-to-face with Jake or her mother, but she wouldn't slink through shadows to avoid it either. She wasn't the weakling both of them thought her.

She found herself in the thick of things, sitting on a couch, listening to a woman she didn't know give a lengthy account of the trials of finding monogrammed black velour bath towels. Was it her hostess? No, her hostess would be mingling. Her hostess's mother perhaps. Or a neighbor. Someone invited for some obscure reason, as she had been. Where had Michael disappeared to after all his earlier hovering?

At last she was forced to excuse herself to find the bathroom. She moved through the room with grim resolve, encountering no one. On her return she threaded her way around a noisy quartet, high on cocaine and singing discordantly while a girl in a gauze dress with bracelets around her ankles swayed to their rhythm. As she plunged through people, some impulse made her suddenly glance over her shoulder. She stopped, her senses stumbling, as her eyes were trapped by the brown intensity of Jake Turner's.

He was standing not ten feet distant. Calmly, carelessly, she averted her face.

"Laura!"

He called to her, but she pretended not to hear. She started to walk, her pace increasing, gripped by an unsteadying anger. True, Turner had not seduced her or been deceitful, yet she smarted beneath the knowledge of how easily she had been dropped. Her pride clamored for her to make him regret that choice.

"Hey." A hand fell on her shoulder, impatient, startling. "Remember me?"

She tensed at his touch and was vexed that it should affect her. Turner seemed not to notice. He was grinning, in fine spirits, the cliff of rusty hair hanging over his forehead.

"What are you doing here?" he asked. "Land a job with the studio?"

"No. I came with Michael Townes."

"Townes!" His eyes laughed at her. "Come on, Laura, don't you know he's—"

"Is he?" She raised her eyebrows in challenge, goaded by some inner voice. "I've known Michael for a long time."

Turner's jaw slackened slightly. He started to speak. But before he could, a cornsilk blonde with hair to her waist spilled from a nearby group to catch his sleeve.

"Jake, honey, do you remember me? I understand some big congratulations are in order!"

"Karen—how are you?"

Laura watched him maneuvering to keep both of them, flashing an automatic grin for the blonde even as his attention, slightly strained now, swung back to her. Being the much-sought-after Jake Turner must require quite a balancing act. She felt a remote and chilly amusement at his predicament. Lips curving with disdain, she let herself look through him, telling him their night together mattered as little to her as it had to him.

She set a course for the farthest part of the room, searching the crowd around her for some trace of Michael. Damn Turner. Her emotions were out of control. Damn Jessamyn too.

There was no sign of Michael, so she pretended to be interested in a long buffet table and picked up a plate. Spread before her were pots of shrimp paste and platters of salmon mousse; small red cherry tomatoes, seeded and stuffed, as well as the requisite caviar. A separate table held the birthday cake, three feet by five feet and shaped like a biplane. Laura could not begin to guess its significance.

She dabbed things onto her plate without enthusiasm until an arm reached across her own, sleeve brushing it, toward a cheese board.

"Do you always fade out in the middle of conversations?" asked Turner.

She did not look up. Why had he sought her out again?

"I didn't realize we were having a conversation."

"About Michael Townes. Remember?" He took the plate from her hand and set it beside the biplane along with his own, forcing her to look at him. For a dozen long beats of her heart, they faced each other. Strange patterns played over the depths

of Turner's eyes, lightening them, darkening them. They flickered toward the bare whiteness of her back. Finally he spoke.
"I've had enough of the party," he said in a low voice. "Let's
leave."

She was jarred by his blatant conceit.

"You came with Jessamyn!"

"So? Half the people here tonight will go home with someone else, not the person they came with."

"Then you have a dandy choice of finding someone to amuse
you, don't you?" She started past him.

His hand caught her arm, fingers biting her flesh.

"Grow up, Laura. What the hell difference does it make if
you came with Townes and I came with Jessamyn? What out-
moded set of rules do you think we all ought to live by?"

Her mouth had gone dry at his touch. She looked at him
furiously, unable to speak.

Cruelty spread slowly across his lips. "Oh, I understand.
You're jealous of your mother, aren't you?"

She wanted to hit him. Her whole body crackled with an
energy she couldn't explain.

"I'm not! However you might consider what Jessamyn would
have to say about that arrangement. I'm surprised you have
the poor taste to suggest it."

She tried to break away and failed. He moved closer, his
body above hers, reminding her of the feel of it merged with
his own.

"I'm not much concerned with taste, babe. Or hadn't you
noticed?" His hand moved upward, laying claim to the soft
flesh of her arm. "And don't play that game of saying you're
not interested. The night we spent together proved that was a
lie."

Laura fought the sensations inside her. Wounded once, she
longed to wound in kind. She raised her chin, her eyes defiant.

"What did it prove? That two people can be in heat at the
same time?"

She struck his arm aside and began to walk, and as she did,
she spotted Jessamyn halfway across the room and lazy-eyed
as a purring cat, watching the two of them.

At the sight of her the truth about the night flashed home
to Laura. Jessamyn had arranged to have her brought here
tonight. Jessamyn was flaunting her power. Except that Jessamyn couldn't possibly realize what Jake had just been sug-

gesting, Laura thought with angry satisfaction.

Well, to hell with all of them. They could play their ridiculous games. Laura doubted that anyone—male or female—had ever walked out on Michael. It gave her great pleasure to think she'd be the first.

As though tempting her to collision or retreat, Jessamyn began to saunter toward her path. With jaw set Laura continued, pace never slackening.

"Laura, darling, what a nice surprise to see you here." Jessamyn's voice was velvety, her eyes flickering with pleasure. Her mouth moved in an innocent smile. "Why, darling, you look out of sorts. Aren't you enjoying yourself?"

Laura halted momentarily, fueled by a contempt that made her unafraid of any scene.

"Never mind the nastiness, Jessamyn. If you want Jake, you may certainly have him. You didn't need to have Michael drag me here to show me how clever you were."

Surprise rippled briefly through Jessamyn's eyes, banished at once by a laugh that was droll and poised.

"Surely you don't suppose he was ever yours to dispose of? Don't be naive."

"Naive? I gave up being naive when I was a baby, Jessamyn. I had to survive around you. But you know what? That's exactly what's going to help me get what I want."

She could feel her mother's fury billowing out in thick clouds as she walked away.

"Get me a cab, please," she said to the houseman as she neared the door.

"Ah, Miss Fizgerald, I'm leaving now myself. Please allow me."

Whirling, Laura saw Enrique Portero. He was smoking a cigarillo, and his manner betrayed not the least curiosity.

"All right," she said shortly. Had he overheard the clash with Jessamyn? She did not care.

Portero chatted lightly as he slid into his white Ferrari and pointed it through the night with ferocious speed. Then after a space he fell silent, his thin cigar jutting up sharply between his teeth.

"So you want work as a writer, eh? I have an offer that I think might interest you." His smile was dazzling.

Laura's gaze swept over him.

"I've had a lot of 'interesting offers' lately. If there's a bed involved in this one, save your breath."

"Ha!" He threw his chin up as he laughed. The cigarillo was squashed unceremoniously in the ashtray. "I wouldn't dream of trying that with you. Not at the outset, anyway. We'll start by dealing strictly in business. Later on I might try to negotiate something else—who knows? I am no saint, and you are delightful. But business, first, eh? Here's the pitch."

"I need another writer for a new series of mine. It's partly soap and partly family drama. It airs two nights a week. I came here hoping to steal a young Latino scriptwriter of my acquaintance, but he was too big on ethics to break a contract. Do you want to have a go at it?"

Now Laura stared at him.

"I would pay you only slave wages naturally," he continued. If he looked like something of a wheeler dealer in the streaks of light flashing in through the windows, he was also intriguing—both in his style and in his affront. "The advantage is that you get some experience," he said. "And a contract that allows you to leave any time you want to, if you like. I got the feeling tonight that you might welcome some arrangement that took you out of town for a while."

He offered no apology for his bluntness, no explanation, and Laura's face felt hot. Had he overheard her scene with Jessamyn? she wondered again. Or the one with Jake? Her brain raced, trying to decide whether this offer of his was on the up and up. Leaving town was running, wasn't it? It was exactly what Jessamyn wanted. Yet if it helped her, if she looked upon it as strategy. . . .

"How do you know I can handle it?" she asked.

"I don't." He gave another smile. "I have a reputation in the business as a gambler. But from our first exchange tonight I gather you're reasonably proficient in the language you would be working in, and you would be working with two other writers. I made some calls this evening and learned something of your work in New York. All in all, I believe you're a safe bet. What do you say?"

She let her breath out, playing for time. For all his charm she suspected Portero could be deadly to deal with. Then perhaps she would do well to learn from him, in that respect as well as others.

"When would I start working?" she asked as the front of her residence hotel came into view.

With a steady glide Portero's car came to a halt.

"There's a Mexicana flight tomorrow evening. I'll be on it."

Laura nodded, recognizing the edge of challenge. "All right. So will I."

Eight

"*Ai, Lauracita! You* are one hell of a worker, do you know that? What do you say we round up Avilas and have some tequila?"

Portero clapped her affectionately on the shoulder as they walked through the gate of the set where they had been filming since five that morning. Once, in the early days of their working alliance, he had aimed a similar gesture at Laura's fanny. She had set him straight quickly on what she thought of that. Now, after three months together, she was used to the friendly hand on her shoulder, and their relationship was that of comrades.

"Sounds good to me," she said, though they both knew that after a scorching day like this one her tastes ran strictly toward beer.

"Pile into the car," Portero said. He turned back to find the director, Avilas.

Laura walked slowly along a narrow street in a rundown suburb of Mexico City. She felt drained yet fulfilled. With two shows a week to air, a schedule like today's was not uncommon. She, or one of the other writers, had to be on the set adjusting bits of dialogue while camera shots were still being set up by the cinematographer, Avilas was coaxing his actors to make each take count, and Portero, like a wave of endless energy, was everywhere.

Portero's accolade made it all worth while. That was why

his shows were so damn good, she thought in amusement. Everyone gave their max for him because he made them feel important.

She slid into Portero's Lincoln and kicked off her sandals. They were the most important part of what had become her working uniform, a blouse of the gauziest possible material, a cotton skirt, and the wedge-heeled sandals that kept her cool but more or less businesslike, an important consideration in this city of indisputable male dominance. Maybe that was why Portero and Avilas included her in their after-work tequila sessions so often, because she was the only female on the production end of the show, a curiosity. Lucky neither of them had decided to get too friendly and ruin things. Lucky she had this chance to witness the thought processes of a superb producer and director. She wiggled her toes luxuriantly. Just plain lucky.

It was after six when she left the two men. On Reforma the evening rush hour was in full swing, and the air was filled with the din of buses, Volkswagen taxis, and collectivos all jostling for space with private cars. Laura felt relaxed as she stood watching the scene. When the light changed, she made her way to the safety island, waited for another light to change, and continued toward the quiet neighborhood where she had been living.

True to his word, Portero was committing absolute piracy with the wages he paid her. Still, she liked the small hotel she had finally found nestled between a maternity hospital and a hairdresser's. At the desk she found a letter from a New York friend. She continued to her room and kicked off her shoes.

Down in a grassy courtyard people were gathered at wrought-iron tables, ending the work day with a drink—soft or hard. Their voices floated up to her as she swung open a window. She stretched out on her bed to enjoy her letter, but before she had even unfolded it, the telephone emitted its watery ring.

The line crackled when she answered—a long distance call. "Laura? Laura, are you there?"

It was Ben, her agent, calling from Los Angeles. The connection made him sound more distant than he was.

"How fast could you turn a couple of those scripts you've been writing for Portero into English?" he inquired without preliminaries.

"As fast as I have to, I suppose. Why? What's up?"

"*Twenty-two Wentworth* needs a writer. I think you'd stand a chance at it, but you have to see them day after tomorrow."

Excitement began to pour through her. *Wentworth* was a family show, new, highly rated. It was a jewel.

On the heels of the thought, hesitation crept in. She frowned, perplexed. Slowly she realized that her uncertainty had to do with Jake Turner, and with Jessamyn. Perhaps she had been fleeing when she came here after all. Her existence with Portero was tranquil, sheltered from conflict. She was loath to once again think about unpleasant things. And she was learning from Portero. . . .

"I don't know, Ben," she said.

The silence on his end expressed his amazement.

"Your choice, of course. There's bound to be a lot of competition for the job."

He sounded as confused as she herself felt. Was she going to let this opportunity slip away?

"Look, I'll call you if I change my mind," she said. She hung up to lie on the bed rigid with frustration. What was she afraid of?

After all these months she still felt a bitterness toward Jake Turner, a bitterness because he was controlled by Jessamyn. While that might not spoil his charms for other women, it did for her. And Jessamyn knew that. Jessamyn had planned that. For the first time in her life she hated her mother.

Then why not fight her? she asked herself wearily. Why not go after this job and show them both how little they affected her?

Something from her childhood cried out against it. An inner voice reminded her that in spite of brave pretenses, it hurt to be a cipher. If she stuck with Portero a while longer, she was bound to grow stronger.

Outside her door a scrubwoman's clattering shoes and the slam of a bucket announced the late afternoon washing of floors.

Jake Turner watched a plump, brown-skinned woman in ill-fitting shoes survey the freshly mopped linoleum stretching behind her. As she prepared to depart, he moved to one side of the corner where he stood to let her pass. Laura had picked one hell of a place to live, he thought. Behind him there stood an enormous, ugly blue glass container of purified water.

He drew on the last of a cigarette, tired from his plane trip. He still could not decide why he had made it. She had a damn screwy set of ideas, Laura did, unrealistic. When he remembered the ice queen she'd been the last time they met, his anger choked him.

Yet here he was. Why this annoying fascination with a woman who had given him the brush-off?

Maybe precisely because of that, he thought wryly. He wasn't used to indifference from a woman. Turner mocked himself. Yeah, that was why he had come here—to prove to himself he hadn't lost his touch.

Except he knew that wasn't the reason. Other women had shared his bed these past three months. Lots. And willingly. But the sex hadn't been as good as it had been with Laura— or as he remembered it had been. Maybe that was only some trick of his mind. He was going to find out.

He walked down the hall and knocked at her door. Inside there were vague sounds he impatiently tried to identify. Then he was looking at her, at the Victorian loveliness of her face, her small soft mouth, those fly-away curls.

"You certainly hide yourself away when you decide to split," he said, his spirits rising at sight of her. "How the hell did you find this place?"

Maybe she'd just been out of sorts the night of that damned party. Maybe she'd just been miffed that he'd shown up with Jessamyn. Whatever it was, he was glad he'd given into the crazy instinct that kept nudging him to see her again.

"Jake," she said mechanically. "What are you doing here?"

She closed the door behind her, and they were there face-to-face in the dimly lit hall.

She looked dazed, uncomfortably wary, her face frozen in an expression he couldn't quite read. Turner struck a pose of immense relaxation, one elbow propped on the wall, one thumb in his belt.

"Oh, just between projects with some time on my hands. Figured I'd fly down and take you to bed." He grinned, seeking refuge in humor. Christ, what would she think of him if he'd blurted out that he'd missed her? Everything was going to be okay.

She gave him a long withering look before she began to turn back toward her door.

"Hey—" he said with a quick laugh. "I meant to buy you dinner first."

Surely she would recognize he'd been half-joking. Her green-gray eyes cut through him as though he were some gauche barbarian, too substandard for consideration.

"I can buy my own dinner," she said sharply.

Turner felt his own temper rising. Without realizing it, he caught her arm.

"What's the matter? Got something on with Portero?"

"If I do, it's nobody's business but mine!"

She writhed in his grasp, and he shook her.

"Look, baby, I flew down here to see you, so how about being civil?"

"Let go of me!"

Maybe she really was involved with Portero. The thought enraged him.

"Sure thing, Laura, my love. If you want to play games, we can."

He released her and saw her surprise, and in the next instant sezied her face between his hands, imprisoning her arms with the angle of his as he kissed her.

The movement of his mouth on hers was more brutal than he'd intended. He wanted to hurt her, to awaken the response he knew must be inside her. But there was no response. After initial resistance to his superior strength, she went rigid, merely enduring. He raised his head to stare at her. The contempt in her white face jarred him.

Turner wanted her to want him. There had been hundreds of nights with dozens of girls where it hadn't mattered, but with Laura it did. He needed her, with that shy refinement of hers, to want him. It would affirm him. It would assure him somehow he had value. It would make him decent.

She raised her hand and drew it carefully across her mouth.

"Will you go now? Or are you going to rape me so you can go on telling yourself you're irresistible? People like you are sick. You're pathetic."

Like a surgeon's knife, her words sliced through carefully hardened layers of confidence. Turner found himself defenseless and confused. He didn't believe she was like this. She was not the sort to wound. Her eyes were unflinching, but slowly, almost desperately, he became aware of the pulse beating in her throat. It was out of control, as frenzied as his own, and it gave him hope.

"No, by God, I'm not going to have to rape you," he said.

He tangled a hand in the dark mass of her hair, loosening one side of it, and saw her wince. Her eyes fluttered closed. Turner smiled, grimly satisfied. With the back of his hand he rubbed the hair against her neck, feeling the coolness of her soft flesh beneath its strands.

Her breath caught. Slowly, very slowly, Turner let his hand move down. The nail of his index finger trailed over her skin, scraping gently. The tautness in her body had changed now. He saw her teeth catch at her lower lip.

"Had enough?"

She did not answer.

When he bent to kiss her again, a small sound, a sound of despair, escaped her. He opened the door to her room and shoved her inside.

Her mouth had parted to his. Now he became the tormented instead of the tormentor, fumbling with her blouse, ripping a button off in his haste. She wanted him now, he thought thickly, but he had proved nothing except the urgency of his own need. She had been aroused by the right touch at the right spots, not by him.

His hands shook as he stripped down her skirt. He was crazy to have come here. He was crazy to have exposed his weakness like this. But he was going to make this go as he wanted it. He was going to make her want him and no one else. His hands moved hungrily, in circles. There was something in this cool, fragile woman that he must have.

He lifted her easily, his own excitement mounting as her nails dug into him like small needles. The wooden bedstead creaked beneath their weight. She held tightly to him, and Turner was aware of little else. They made violent love, hard, bruising, exhausting for both of them.

When the tempo of his body returned to something approaching normal, Turner rolled away from her. It was all right, he told himself with relief. He felt ashamed of the way he had treated her out in the hall and of the cavalier way he'd mentioned going to bed. But everything had turned out all right. Here in this bed she had held him close, and they had moved and experienced as a single being. They were day and night, oil and water. He did not understand. But he never questioned luck and neither would he question the pleasure they brought each other. Now, he thought, she would not either.

He looked at her, at the slightly old-fashioned freshness of her face. She opened her eyes. They were strange, distant, troubled, fixed on him.

"I hate you," she said in a low, tight voice. "Go away."

The words stunned Turner. He felt like a gangly youth again, caught off guard when he least expected it and uncertain where to turn.

He rose to one arm, counterattacking, though he did not understand the battle.

"What the hell do you mean? You loved every minute of what just happened."

She looked at him a moment, then turned her head away.

"Yes. You made your point. You can turn me on like . . . like some animal. Now please—"

Her words stopped abruptly. Turner guessed they had been on the verge of breaking. He stared at her, aghast, needled by guilt and angry with her that she should make him feel it.

"Damn it, Laura, what's wrong with you? I don't understand. I hopped a plane to find you down here because you turn me on. Because I've had you on my mind for weeks and weeks. What's the matter with that?"

She didn't answer.

He retrieved his shirt from the bedside and lighted a cigarette, studying her. He felt the pull of a frown across his forehead. He didn't know why he should give a damn, but he was puzzled. Laura had just admitted she liked sleeping with him, so what was the problem?

Smoking made him feel calmer. He was in control of the situation, and he began to think more clearly. Laura was a little bit behind the times. Unrealistic. Maybe that was what gave her that untouched quality. It was also a damned nuisance.

"It's the casualness that bothers you, isn't it?" he asked coldly. "You can't accept a good time at face value. What is it you want? For a session in bed to lead automatically to some sort of long-term faithfulness?"

Her face turned toward him again. Its contours were set.

"Yes. That's exactly what I want."

"Well, you've picked the wrong business. You've picked the wrong man."

"Yes. I know."

She did not turn away again, merely closed her eyes. Frustrated, feeling he had lost without knowing how or what, Turner watched her. He felt effectively banished. That movement of an eyelash had cut him off from her as effectively as a wall. At last he got up and put on the clothes he had discarded. Opening the door, he looked back at the silent figure on the bed.

The scrubwoman he had watched earlier came out of a hall closet, carrying linens, and Turner, passing her, found he could not meet her gaze.

Laura heard his footsteps reach the elevator, and she listened as its ancient trellised doors clattered closed. Thoughts wove themselves through her mind, but she could not sort them. Did she really hate the man who had just left her? She did not know.

She hurt. An agony of loneliness devoured her. Why did he have to come here? Why had she, in spite of all her resolve, responded? She felt used and discarded. Why did she have to feel?

Long after the room had grown dark around her, she still had not moved. A fire was growing inside her. She fed it with reminders of her own past foolishness and of how the weak were hurt. In its flames she forged a new resolve not to be hurt again—not by Turner or by anyone else. She would learn to strike first. She would learn to be hard. She would build a shell around herself so strong that no one could see beneath to her vulnerability.

Picking up the phone, she called Ben Webber. She could be on a plane to Los Angeles in the morning, and en route she would translate the scripts for her next interview.

There were two things she wanted: A career that would make her Jessamyn's equal and a man who would be a constant in her life. Jake Turner had said she couldn't have either. She was going to have both, no matter what the cost.

Nine

The trembling in her arm had plagued her all morning. Nel lit another cigarette.

"Shit," she said aloud to the empty office. She looked at the pile of unfinished correspondence stacked neatly to one side of her desk.

Unfinished.

The word danced through her mind with an increasing tempo.

Unfinished.

The paperwork waiting there.

Unfinished.

Her goddamn life.

So this was what it was like, she thought, still staving off the panic that wanted to claim her. She was too tough to panic. And maybe this was as bad as it would get.

"To hell with it," she muttered. She'd make a mess of any attempt at typing, and everyone she needed to talk to on the phone was out. Squashing out her cigarette, she walked onto the patio.

"Mornin', Nel. You look very beautiful today," said Roberto, looking up from the flowering shrubs whose spent blooms he was carefully removing. He straightened on his knees.

"Come on now. I look beautiful every day," Nel said, striking a pose.

He chuckled, wagging his head. "You are a crazy woman, you know it?"

"But lovable." She flopped down with mock exhaustion in a lounge chair. "Let's see, what shall I have Lupita fix me for lunch? That's about the level of decision making I'm up to today."

Roberto chuckled again and moved off with his pickings wrapped in a dropcloth.

This was, unofficially, Nel's chair. Reaching out to the table beside it, she picked up a pair of sunglasses. When they were in place, she looked at the sky and sighed. She had exaggerated to Roberto, but she did feel tired today—or maybe not so much tired as low in spirits. That damn shaking of her hand had darkened her mood. Or maybe she had borrowed a page from Jessamyn's book and was bored.

What could she do to amuse herself? She meant to exit her days on earth kicking and laughing. She had money, more than she could possibly spend. Did she want to travel? Go back to the Riviera where she had spent some fine times with Jess? There didn't seem much point in making the effort. She could laze in the sun as easily here as there.

"Excuse me, Nel . . ." Harry spoke from the terrace.

Nel cast half a glance at him, wondering what he wanted, then sat up sharply. Eddie, hat in hand, stood just behind Harry, and he was grinning.

"Well, I've got to say you don't look too overworked," he said. "Never again will I feel guilty about the good-label scotch I drank on taxpayers' money."

Harry was already disappearing. After Eddie's earlier visit, the houseman must have assumed it was all right to show him in without Nel's clearance.

The shock of seeing him was not so great this time. Still she was at a loss for words. And exasperated. How many times must she tell this man she didn't want to see him?

"Damn you, Eddie, you're so damn *persistent*," she said.

He laughed. "Going to give me the bum's rush again?"

She sighed and let her eyes fall closed. "No, not today." It was pleasant to feel the years slipping back for a minute. She had led a lusty life, in a way very different from Jessamyn's, and even the bad times had given it a gloss that made the good times better. She opened her eyes again. "Well, since you're here you might as well sit down."

Eddie pulled up a chair.

"What cockamamie excuse do you have for being out here this time?" Nel said.

He lounged back comfortably and grinned, his moustache stirring softly. "I've got a woman here I wanted to see."

With a feeling of being outclassed—and shamelessly so— she shook her head.

"You are the limit, Eddie Brown."

"Don't you forget it, Nel. Join me for lunch?"

"Okay. I have a feeling it wouldn't do much good to tell you no. And as a matter of fact, I feel like playing hooky today."

A short silence edged between them. "Pretty necklace," Eddie said.

Nel touched the enameled gold pansy hanging at her throat. That's me, a pansy, she wanted to say, but the joke wouldn't come. "It's from Laura," she said instead.

"Laura? Who's she?"

"Jessamyn's daughter. Terriffic kid. I guess I feel she's my creation, vain witch that I am. I've watched her grow up. Right now she's trying to break into TV, which I tell you is taking years off my life."

"A hard business, is it?"

"Oh, no worse than the streets of Detroit."

They both grinned.

"Ever sorry you got mixed up with it?" Eddie asked.

"Not for a minute. I found my pond; I love it. Can you imagine me keeping house six days a week and whooping it up in a church choir on the seventh?"

"No." Eddie's grin grew broader. "During all those years I was trying to find you, sometimes I figured you must be married. But I never quite pictured you baking cakes. I figured you'd be teaching dancing, working out steps for some big show, something like that."

Before Nel knew it, they were talking easily, talking of a thousand things. When the telephone rang beside her, she was vexed at the interruption.

"Yes?" she said into the receiver.

Laura's voice came to her, light and happy.

"I got it, Nellie! I have a job!"

Nel felt her own face glowing with pleasure. "Hey, kiddo, that's terrific! Congratulations. When do you start? Will you get to do some episodes solo?"

"Yes, that's the promise. I start tomorrow. Do I sound giddy? I didn't get any sleep last night. I was too wound up. And I know I can't now—oh, God, what if I get there tomorrow and crash—"

"Hang on now, kiddo. It's only the big time." Glancing up, Nel mouthed the name Laura to Eddie.

"Oh, Nellie, you don't know how great I feel!" Laura was saying. "I'd started to wonder—"

Nel felt the receiver slide suddenly out of her hand and into Eddie's.

"Hello, Laura. I'm Eddie, an old friend of Nel's. If you'd let me take you two ladies out to celebrate, it would be a big favor. I've been courting the lady for years, but she's hard to get on with. What do you say?"

Nel stared at him, completely speechless.

"Wonderful! We'll pick you up at one," said Eddie into the phone. He hung up and smiled.

"You're the limit," Nel repeated for the second time that morning.

Laura liked the face of the man offering his hand to her. It was warm and kind.

"Laura," Nel said, "this is Eddie."

They were standing in the lobby of her hotel, which looked plush after her stint in Mexico. People were milling all around them. Was this the man who had come into Nel's life some months back? Laura hoped so. His handshake was as nice as his face. As nice as his voice had been on the phone just a few hours ago. And he and Nel looked perfect together.

"We've got a table waiting. Shall we go?" he said.

The table was in the softly lit main dining room at La Scala, a place where deals were made and more deals broached, and waiters occasionally brought a telephone tableside for an Important Call. Laura walked through the crowded room with a sense of belonging. Amid flowers-stuffed brandy snifters and a grandly displayed wine collection, she recognized faces— faces from behind the cameras. They wouldn't recognize hers, but she was one of them now. She had joined the fraternity.

"Now *this* is what I call a celebration!" Nel said with approval.

A bottle of champagne was waiting on ice. The cork popped. Nel and Eddie were toasting her. It was Christmas and a birthday all rolled into one, and Laura laughed. She was only a working girl now, but she felt like a celebrity. Across a blurring table her eyes reached out to Nel's with a silent message: *Thanks, Nellie. Thanks for supporting me. Thanks for caring.*

Nel was grinning, fitting a cigarette into her holder.

"So, kiddo, tell us all about the interview."

Laura laughed. "I love you, Nel. I really do!"

"That's champagne talking. Get to the good part."

Only as she began to go over the morning's events with them did she herself finally believe that they were real.

"The series' ratings are slipping," she concluded much later. "That part makes me nervous."

Nel tracked down a last bite of lobster from her cannelloni La Scala. "Ah-hah. It's that seamy new sitcom they've put on opposite it. My God, what some people will watch while the kiddies are still up and around."

"What would you do, Nel? Change the channel?" teased Eddie.

"Not let them watch at all on a school night if you want the hard-ass truth."

"Good grief! You're putting me out of a job already!" Laura moaned.

At tableside a waiter cleared his throat as if to admonish such ribaldry.

"Laura Fitzerald?" he inquired. He carried a telephone.

"Yes..."

He was placing the telephone in front of her. She looked from Nel to Eddie, but they both seemed as surprised as she was. She had told Ben Webber she was going to lunch with Nel, but she hadn't said where. She hadn't known where. All at once she was apprehensive, and she didn't know why.

She gripped the phone as if it had been a hot dish from the oven.

"This is Laura Fitzgerald."

"Ah, *Lauracita*! Finally I've found you!" Portero's voice sang to her cheerfully across the miles.

"Enrique! What—how—?" She was incredulous.

"I called that no-good agent of yours to see if you'd gotten the job. He told me you were off somewhere celebrating with Nel. Congratulations, Laura. Avilas is with me, and he says congratulations too."

"Thanks. Thanks to both of you. But how did you find me?"

"Kept calling likely places and describing you. I figure this call will give you a lot of prestige at La Scala. From now on you can do your big business there, and they'll remember you. Much better for your career than if I sent you roses, eh?"

By now she was laughing again, but she realized that what he was saying was true. She was aware—just barely—of several waiters watching her and someone at a nearby table. She had become one of those Important People with a phone.

"Frankly I hope they fire you tomorrow," Portero told her. "I'm going to miss ogling your sweet little tail."

She smiled at his joking—she thought it was joking, although with Portero she was never quite sure.

"How flattering!" she said, and at least that part of the conversation sounded professional.

"So good luck," he said. "I'll buy you a beer next time I'm in town."

She hung up smiling and looked up into the dark gaze of Jake Turner.

He was half the distance of the room away from her, holding the chair for a well-stacked blonde. As their glances met, he did not look away. In an instant the cozy cocoon of success and jubilation slipped from her. She was naked, looking at a man who two nights before had torn her pride from her there in that distant hotel.

A voice inside her told her to go on. The wounded walked. Motion was the ultimate victory. Pouring energy into her smile, she let her eyes glide on, and with triumphant smoothness passed the phone back to the waiter.

"Can you believe that? It was Portero," she said. Had the lilt gone from her voice? Would Nel notice?

"Good man," said her friend. "Hell, yes, I'm going to have dessert. I plan on getting so fat today that I won't be able to get out of this dress."

Euphoria gone, Laura listened to the conversation pass back and forth between Nel and Eddie. After a time she no longer felt the need to steel herself against all stimuli and began to see things. Nel's hand rested languidly on her champagne glass. Eddie's lay inches away. Laura knew those two hands wanted to touch. Why didn't they? She looked at Nel with affection. She was going to have to give Nel the same kind of talking to that Nel gave her.

"You starting to crash, kiddo? You're mighty quiet," Nel said.

"I guess I am, a little bit. But then I was thinking too that I got all the attention when we came in. The two of you hadn't had much chance to talk. After all, I did allow myself to be wined and dined this way just to help out Eddie."

Eddie, hand to his chest, gave a little bow. "So nice to have someone in my corner."

"Awfully noble of you to make such a sacrifice," Nel said drily.

Laura laced her fingers together and rested one elbow on the upholstery. "Well, *I* appreciate being spoiled with lunches like this, Eddie, even if old hard-heart doesn't. If she ever turns down an invitation, call me instead. Even if it's just for hamburgers."

"I can't take any more of this mutual admiration," Nel groaned, rising. "I'm leaving—not that you'll notice."

Eddie escorted both of them. Outside the restaurant Laura turned to smile at him.

"It really was lovely, Eddie. I'll never forget it. You and Nel made me feel very special today."

"You are special, kiddo," Nel said. "So aren't you going to let us take you back?"

"Not today, thanks. I hate to be so prosaic, but I have to look at apartments. I'll get a cab."

Nel looked so relaxed, she thought, and so happy. Whatever had happened in the past, Eddie was good for Nel. Laura was glad she'd had the chance to meet him, and she hoped he'd be unwavering in his pursuit.

On impulse she looked back at him. Rising on tiptoe, she kissed his cheek.

"See you, Eddie. You take good care of her, you hear?"

Catching sight of a cab, she flagged it and ran, turning to the window for a final departing wave.

"Nice girl," said Eddie.

"The greatest." Nel felt Eddie's hand rest lightly against her shoulder.

"It's a fine day, Nel. What say we take a drive along the coast?"

The pansy necklace felt tight around Nel's throat. She saw Eddie's patient smile, the warmth in his eyes.

"It won't lead anywhere," she said.

"I'll take my chances."

Ten

"No! Get away from me! No!"

The cries came through the sleeping house, and Nel awakened. For a moment she thought she had only dreamed them. They were part of the landscape of her life with Jessamyn. Then she heard them again, the wails of a child, the pitiful soundtrack of Jessamyn's nightmares.

Flinging aside the sheets, she ran to the hallway, moving through darkness until a light flooded the base of the U which separated her rooms from Jessamyn's. Deidre stared at her, eyes large with horror. One hand still touched the light switch and the other clutched her robe.

"Do something!" she gasped.

Nel brushed past her without answering. Ten years in this household and DeeDee still didn't know how to deal with these midnight terrors. Not that she expected DeeDee to *do* anything. She herself was the only one who could handle Jessamyn. But it did seem to Nel that DeeDee should be able to take it all in stride by now.

"Hey, Jess. It's me," she said as she opened the door. She knew she wouldn't reach Jessamyn's subconscious just yet. Or whatever it was she talked to and tamed on nights like this.

She left the door open behind her for gentle light. At the head of the bed Jessamyn sat crouching wide-eyed. She put out a threatening hand at Nel's approach.

"I won't wear it," she said in that strange girl's voice. "It's ugly, and I won't wear it. You think you can make me, but you can't. I won't be ugly like you! I won't! I won't!"

It was always like this. Nel had long ago pieced the ramblings together, or thought she had. She switched on a small china lamp on Jessamyn's dresser.

"It's been a long time since anyone made you wear something you didn't want to wear, hasn't it?" she said mildly. "I remember that brandy-colored thing you wore when you got your last Oscar. God, but you stole the show . . . all those people just gawking . . ."

There was a whimper; and Jessamyn pulled the sheet up to her cheek. "Nel?" said the child's voice. "Nel?" And then, though still frightened, it became imperious. "Nel!"

"I'm here, Jess," Nel said.

The woman on the bed blinked. Her hair was disheveled. "Where are my dogs?" she asked in a tight voice, looking around. "Damn it, I want my dogs!"

Nel stepped to the door. "DeeDee— Oh, good."

Maybe Deidre was learning after all. She was waiting, the dogs in her arms, the obese Dog Two and the smaller puppy that had become the current Dog One. They sat sleepily on the edge of the bed where Nel deposited them.

"Here, doggies. Come say you love me." Jessamyn reached for chocolates, her hand shaking worse than Nel's had the morning before.

"I'll have Harry make us a drink," Nel said. She sat down in a chair and waited.

She was tired tonight. She didn't want to go through the slow movements of this ritual. But she knew Jess counted on her. Funny how Jess trusted her and no one else. Nel knew these journeys into the past were hard on the actress who now had everything. She didn't know precisely what Jess saw there, but she knew there was no adulation, no pampering, no being beautiful. Not for the first time she wondered if the lovers Jess filled her bed with were talismans against the past, for the nightmares only came when she was alone.

Jessamyn had pushed the dogs away and sat sipping her drink. She gave a casual toss of her hair, regaining control.

"I think I'll sleep in in the morning," she said. "Call Stan and cancel my lunch date with that damn English producer he wants me to talk to, will you?"

Nel murmured an answer, but she was thinking of Eddie. He was getting to her. Little by little, he was getting to her. The lunch with Laura . . . the drive afterward . . . and tonight he had taken her dancing . . . She wasn't sure she could hold out against him. She wasn't sure she wanted to. But there was no future for them, and she was too big a coward to say the words out loud. As long as she didn't say them, they didn't have to come true.

"I was talking, wasn't I?" asked Jessamyn. "What was I saying?"

"Nothing worth jotting down for blackmail. If I'm going to trot in here to wake you up, I wish you'd at least make it juicy enough to be worth my time. But no, clothes horse that you are, you just mumble something about a dress."

Nel lit a cigarette and waited, but Jessamyn seemed satisfied by her answer. Did she believe it, or did she merely pretend to? Nel had never repeated any of her midnight ramblings.

"Well done, kids. These next few weeks look good."

Maxy, the story editor for *Twenty-two Wentworth*, gave a parting wave as the Friday morning story conference broke up. Popping one of her ever present sugarless mints into her mouth, she headed for her office. Laura, accompanied by the other two writers, turned into the room where they each had a cubicle. She had made it through her first four days on the job, she thought with elation. Today her name had appeared in the trades with the announcement of her association with the *Wentworth* series.

The secretary who occupied the fourth corner of the divided room looked up.

"Call for you on line two, Laura. Also the cleaners called. Said you told them to call here for your address when you dropped off your clothes, so I complied."

"What? I don't know what you're talking about."

"Oh, Jeeze," said the secretary, and Laura knew they both were seeing visions of some maniac staking out her apartment.

"Never mind. Thanks," she said. In two steps she was in her cubicle and picking up the phone.

"Hello and congratulations," said Van Greenberg. "I'd say you landed a pretty impressive spot after all your waiting."

"Thanks, Van. I do feel pretty lucky."

"How's it going? Are you swimming for your life?"

"Not just yet. I've had a pretty hard taskmaster putting me through hoops these last three months."

"That's good. Listen, I want you to have dinner with me tonight."

No 'Would you like?'—this was a definite statement. Laura hesitated.

"No strings attached, no expectations," he said. "I won't take no for an answer. There's something I have to warn you about. A snake in the garden."

She felt a queer little surge of adrenalin.

"All right. But please, I'm not up to a restaurant. I'll cook. No seduction scenes this time, I promise. I have no talent for them, as you may have noticed."

They agreed on a time, and Laura hung up. A snake. What did Van mean?

The Westwood bars already were filling with students welcoming in the weekend by the time she climbed the steps to the white stucco house with yellow shutters where she had found an apartment just two days before. Only fifteen minutes west of the affluent homes of Beverly Hills where she had grown up, and separated from them by little more than the Los Angeles Country Club, it was nonetheless a mixed neighborhood of university people, aspiring writers, workers, and professional people.

Once her building had been a grand private house with a pool in the back. The pool was still there, but the building had been divided into six units. Laura's was in front. She set down her sack of groceries to unlock the door and almost tripped over the fat package propped at her door.

As soon as she picked it up, she guessed that the silver wrapping and yellow ribbon hid a book, but from whom? There was no card. Nudging the groceries inside, she fastened the security chain. Then kicking off her shoes, she opened the package.

It was a cookbook, large, beautiful, and frightfully expensive. A white slip fluttered out from inside the cover. *Good luck on the new job. J. Turner.* The words left her damp from her hands to her neck.

Damn, she thought sitting back on the couch. Her mind could get no further. Just damn.

She was conscious of anger—that he knew where she lived, that he had nerve enough to breach her privacy again after what he had done to her. Yet she was aware, too, of confusion. He had noted and remembered those cookbooks on her counter. He had left this oddly personal gift when he might more easily have sent flowers. Why had he sent anything at all? Why had he communicated? Surely he did not believe that she would ever welcome it! She felt angry all over again.

She wanted to throw the book in the trash, but she could not. It was too beautiful. In some mysterious way, it seemed to belong with her. Where was her new resolve, where was her hardness, that she could not annex a gift and forget the giver?

In the end, she set it on the kitchen counter alongside her other three volumes, telling herself it had been a guilt offering, a trite gesture that she would take revenge on by enjoying. An hour later, not without a sense of irony, she found herself preparing a dessert for one man from a book given by another.

"Well! I thought maybe I'd gotten the address wrong," said Van when she opened the door. "Hiding out or something, are you?"

Laura laughed. "Not really. Come in."

He did and handed her an armful of roses wrapped in green tissue. "A little something to celebrate the job."

"How lovely. Umm, they smell good too. Sit down, and try to overlook the mess. I'm still moving in."

Unbuttoning his white linen jacket, Van sank into a chair. He looked around the room. "It's pleasant, but unless they're pulling some shenanigans with your salary, surely you could afford to be more in the stream of things."

Laura looked up from the glass vase she was getting for the roses. She found the roomy apartment with its unusable old fireplace far more charming than the efficient sameness of some highrise. It was a letdown to have her first visitor imply that he thought otherwise.

"I'm in the stream of things all day," she said. "And it's only minutes from here to anywhere else I'm likely to work. I like the neighborhood, I like the mix of people."

"Of course." He gave a slight smile. "Very attractive."

"Thank you."

She had the distressing feeling that they were now mouthing parts.

"What can I get you to drink?" she asked.

"Ah! I brought some wine." He produced a bottle.

Laura murmured thanks and went into the kitchen for an opener and glasses.

They lounged over wine while the noodles cooked for fettucine Alfredo. Van watched her when she got up to bring plates of salad to a makeshift table covered with a bright floral cloth.

"You're murdering my waistline," he said as she brought in the steaming pasta. "Remind me to find out what the menu is the next time you ask me here."

He was teasing, but Laura found herself wondering if he
didn't hide a grain of seriousness behind his words.

"Now tell me all about *Wentworth*," he said.

She was surprised to see how long it took. Already she had
come to admire Maxy's sharply honed instincts for a script's
potential audience appeal. She also liked her fellow writers,
one a morose homosexual named Adam and the other a slightly
egocentric dynamo whom everyone called Fritz. They were
good at their craft, both of them, and gave more than a day's
work for each day's pay.

"Heavens! Let me get coffee," she said at last, realizing that
it had been some time since either of them touched their plates.
When she came back with coffee and fruit steeped in kirsch,
Van had returned to a comfortable chair in front of the fireplace.

"Well," she said, settling herself across from him. "You
said you needed to talk to me about something."

He put his fruit aside and balanced the coffee cup. "What's
Jessamyn Friday got against you?" he asked.

"I beg your pardon?"

"Perhaps you thought you had trouble finding a writing job
because you weren't good enough. Or experienced enough. Or
because you weren't popping into bed with roaches like Hugh
Archer. I think you ought to know that none of that is true.
After you'd gone, I found out you'd been blacklisted with a
lot of people. By Jessamyn. She called in a lot of favors."

Van Greenberg picked up his cup and drank, his cool blue
eyes regarding her steadily.

"I see."

She felt like a fool with nothing more to say. Why hadn't
she considered Jessamyn's hand in her constant turndowns?
Had she wanted to be blind? She crossed her arms and warmed
her shoulders. Something inside her was—not sick perhaps,
but sad. Ineffably sad.

"I'm Jessamyn's daughter," she said in a toneless voice.

She saw his pupils flare. His cup connected abruptly with
the saucer.

"Ah."

He made it sound as though he understood. Laura didn't
see how he could. She didn't. She was twenty-six years old
now, and she still didn't understand her mother's hate of her.

A heavy mood was settling over her. She envisioned a future
in which there would always be this warfare, always Jessamyn

moving against her. She had thought it was only Jake Turner Jessamyn wanted. Was it everything, her complete annihilation?

"If she's done that, I wouldn't put it past her to try something else." Van's words reflected the course of her own thoughts.

She managed a smile. "No, neither would I. Thanks for telling me, Van. How did you find out?"

"I have my ways." He put his cup aside and looked at her thoughtfully. "There's a new show opening at a club I like next weekend. How about coming to see it with me?"

"I'd like that."

"And for now I expect you'd just as soon I left."

She nodded.

"Thanks for . . . the warning, I guess," she said at the door. "And for the roses."

"My pleasure." He studied her for a minute, then kissed her lightly. "I'd forgotten how unusual you were. How very appealing. See you next week."

As soon as the door closed behind him, she turned away from it, moving, groping her way toward action, not listening for his footsteps or the sound of his car. In the mere mechanics of living, it was not necessary to think. In clearing up dishes and emptying coffee cups, soul-searching could be postponed until the busy-work was done, when the truths and questions waiting to be faced had grown a little stale and lost their tartness.

She cleared. She turned off lights. She went into the bedroom, feeling weary, thinking she would sleep as late as possible tomorrow morning and then do laundry. The news about Jessamyn had hurt her, and she knew it shouldn't. She pushed it down inside. It wasn't her fault that Jessamyn was her enemy.

She went to the dresser and picked up her cherished photograph, the one of an amber-haired woman and a dark-haired toddler. Funny, she thought, you read about mothers hating their daughters, but you never think it'll happen to you. Fighting emotions she didn't want to acknowledge, she stared at the images.

The restaurant where Jessamyn sat with her agent was not the most expensive in Hollywood, but it was one of them, suitable for a working luncheon and financially out of the reach of gawking tourists. She was not listening, however, to what

Stan Weisbecker said. Her eyes were watching him, but the rest of her was smiling over a delicious morsel of news. That morning she'd heard that *Twenty-two Wentworth* was floundering.

Goodbye, little Laura, she said silently over her Perrier water. It was all so beautiful. In spite of her efforts Laura had landed a job. Now, if the rumors she'd heard were true, that job might be over in less than a month.

That was the problem with television, she thought with satisfaction. The people who cast themselves on that medium were fools, living forever in the shadow of the axe. Not her. She could pick and choose. And she chose not only money but security. Let Stan bitch all he wanted. She knew what she was doing.

"Frankly, I think the whole thing stinks," she said as his voice fell silent. He stared at her, and she knew he was aghast that she was turning down what he thought was a very good project. "The script is weak, and the choice of cinematographers is all wrong," she ticked off calmly. "And by the skinniness of the advertising budget, I think they already know they've got a bomb on their hands. They're hoping for a few big names to save it. I wouldn't touch it if they were offering twice the points."

Stan cleared his throat—he was always coming down with a cold, or thought he was—and glared at her.

"Is that what the real problem is? The money?"

"Oh, stuff it up your ass, Stan. Do you think I'm some insipid little starlet? I'm telling you it's going to be a very forgettable film, that's all. And I won't do it."

The agent waved impatiently for another scotch and soda. "It's been a year since you did a picture. Stay out of things much longer and you'll be forgotten."

Jessamyn wondered sometimes if he was a bluffer or actually stupid. She gave him a chilly look.

"The longer I stay out, the bigger the fuss will be when I go back, and you know it."

He was silent. They'd had this conversation before, and she'd been right. Supply and demand. Couldn't Stan get the concept through his head? People would realize she'd taken her time and waited for a picture worth seeing. They'd see it too. They'd love it.

"Well, what the hell are you going to do then?" he snapped. "You've turned down everything on the horizon for the next six months. And let me tell you, honey, some of those films are going to win Oscars for someone."

"I doubt it." She sipped her Perrier. "I might do something that's good for publicity. I might do that TV movie for Jake Turner."

Stan choked on his drink. "Jeezus. *Jeezus*! I've brought you TV parts that would make you millions. I've begged you on my hands and knees to do them. You called me every filthy name under the sun and threatened to fire me. Now you're telling me you want to do something for some third-rate new production company that can't pay its bills?"

"It's a good property. And the critics loved the screenings of that coup he pulled off when Goldman's heart played out."

"So he launched a company of his own, and how many packages has he sold since then? One, maybe two." Stan Weisbecker's puffy eyes narrowed. "Is it the property you're eyeing, or what's inside Turner's pants?"

Jessamyn smacked her glass onto the table.

"Go to hell!"

Stan was hotter under the collar than she had expected or else he would never have dared say such a thing to her. To her amazement he continued, gathering steam.

"Go right on being a sex-crazed chippy in your personal life since that seems to suit you. It's not my affair. But for God's sake, don't be such a fool that you trade career considerations for a lay. When that starts to happen, honey, you're finished!"

"Shut up!" Jessamyn's manicured fingers gripped the table of edge. She managed to keep her voice low enough not to be heard by people around them, but it was full of venom. Stan shouldn't be treating her like this. She was his meal ticket. "How dare you talk to me like that!" she hissed.

"How dare I?" The agent stubbed a fat cigar in her direction. "I dare because I *made* you! Don't forget that, honey. I picked you up when you were Jessamyn Fitzgerald, just another pretty girl in a nightclub act. Oh sure, you had talent, but it wasn't the talent men came to see, it was your body. And you played right into it, didn't you, sweetheart? Whispering that breathy little come-to-climax line of yours: 'I'm your girl Friday. I'll do *anything* to bring you pleasure.'"

"Shut up! Shut up!" Jessamyn was leaning forward, weaving slightly.

"You can't stand looking back, can you, Jessamyn? The only thing you got out of that sultry little act of yours was a new last name—and me. And I've stood by you, sweetheart. I didn't walk out when you decided to get yourself pregnant because you thought a baby would be a cute trick, a way of getting even more attention, a wind-up toy for when you were bored. That one went sour mighty quick, didn't it, Jessamyn?"

"You son-of-a-bitch!"

She stood up without seeing him or the tables around her, and with head held up grandly sailed out of the restaurant. The gossip columns would get wind of it, of course, but that was all right. They wouldn't know what the tiff was about. It would make good reading.

Eleven

"*I can't believe* it. Laura's first show." Nel felt misty-eyed as she curled on the couch in Eddie's hotel suite. She looked at her watch. Fifteen minutes to go. Eddie had put the picture on without the sound. She wondered if he thought she were soft in the head to feel so satisfied and yet so close to weepiness this evening.

"Think I should have them send up some champagne?" he smiled.

"Nah. I'll let you take me downstairs afterwards to buy me a real drink."

At the back of her mind she was also wondering, as she had several times in past weeks, how much longer Eddie planned to stay in Los Angeles. It was over a month now, and he must be spending a bundle at this hotel. Surely he wasn't crazy enough to still be hanging around just because of her. Whenever she'd tried to raise questions, he'd turned them lightly aside.

This evening, however, something else had happened that made her curious.

"Eddie, how come you're registered here under another name? Tonight was the second time someone at the desk's called you Mr. Lacouture."

He laughed and leaned back comfortably, his hands behind his head.

"That's privileged information, Nel. Don't worry about it." Turning on one arm, he smiled at her. "You're excited about tonight, aren't you? About Laura."

"Yeah. She's my kid, I guess. At least as close as I'll ever get to having one."

Eddie touched her cheek lightly. "I wish we'd had a child, Nel. You and me. I've thought about it sometimes. A lot. Have you ever thought how it would have been?"

His directness caught her off guard. She had no place to hide.

"Yeah," she said. "Sometimes."

His hand squeezed her shoulder, and something inside her broke apart. He kissed her, and some gate she long had barricaded was left undefended. She had been so controlled, so careful, but now she reached out to him in hunger. The years slipped away. Their bodies were those that had met nearly thirty years ago, quivering, hard, filled with passion that belonged to youth yet driven by the knowledge of the decades that had intervened. They did not have breath for words, or even sound. They simply moved together there on the couch, resuming the possession of each other that was broken off one dark night in Detroit.

Nel felt dizzy after they had finished. Eddie lay beside her, holding her, cradling her, the two of them wedged together on the narrow confines of the couch. Marveling at the intensity of the storm that had passed over them, she lay semiconscious, reluctant to spoil her sense of satiety by rousing herself.

"Hellsfire." Eddie's voice came to her from a distance. "Nel." He sat up, touching her shoulder urgently. "Nel. We've gone and missed the whole damn show."

She opened her eyes. The first thing they saw were the silent colors flickering on the television screen. The credits. More than half an hour had passed.

"Oh, shit," she whispered. Then noticing his worried

expression, she reached out and caressed his cheek. "Well, don't the two of us have egg on our face, cutting up like a couple of kids!" Her humor was hollow, but she didn't think Eddie would hear that. "Hey now, don't worry," she said gently. "Jessamyn's probably got her taping machine on for this one. I'll see it in the morning."

But of course that was a lie. Jess was neither watching nor taping. She was throwing a dinner for friends at La Bella Fontan. Deliberately, Nel felt sure.

As Laura neared the writers' room, she heard laughter. Maxy, wearing a jolting red dress as she always did after a show, was leaning against the secretary's desk. Adam and Fritz were gathered around.

"Hey, here she comes now," said Fritz, catching sight of her.

Maxy pivoted on a needle-heeled shoe and eyed her without expression.

"Well, Miss F., your first overnights are in," she said.

Laura felt her heart leap. Was that a grin Fritz was supressing? Or was she only hoping that, hoping the first ratings in from a few key cities were good ones?

"How were they?" she asked, almost afraid to speak and spoil the afterglow of seeing her own story, her own dialogue, on a prime-time series.

Maxy's face broke into a grin. "Way up there, honey. The highest they've been in two months. People didn't flip to another channel halfway through. Looks like we might even have edged out the competition."

Suddenly everyone was laughing again, and talking and congratulating her. Only Adam's enthusiasm seemed a little forced, and she could not tell whether that was envy or his usual moroseness. When Maxy left, she fled into her cubicle and punched the phone.

"Nellie?" she sang when it was picked up on the other end.

"Hi, kiddo. Congratulations!"

"Hey, Nellie, my overnights are in and they're good. The best the show's pulled in two months, I'm told."

"That's great, Laura, really great. Gee, but I'm proud of you."

Delirious with happiness Laura smiled at the air.

"Well, seeing as how I'm a working girl and a neophyte, I

can't get away for lunch, but I thought we should have a drink together to celebrate. Want to meet me at six? Van's picking me up for a play at eight, so I can't offer dinner."

There was a short pause on the phone.

"Of course. I wouldn't miss it. What about Macho's?"

Laura hung up smiling. The console buzzed.

"Jake Turner on line two," said the secretary.

The high of the morning started to slip. She caught it back to her.

"Tell him I'm out," she said.

She turned from the console and concentrated fiercely on Van. Of late they had seen each other perhaps once a week, sometimes for dinner, sometimes for nightclub acts, which he seemed to prefer to other types of entertainment. It was hard to synchronize schedules, and she was not vain enough to suppose he didn't go out with other women. She shrugged and sighed and wondered whether she would ever feel completely at ease with Van.

By late morning, in spite of the promising start, it had evolved into what Maxy termed a glue-pot day. Everything that could had fallen apart, and it all needed pasting back together. At four she found herself down on the production lot, delivering script revisions for Adam, with several hours' work still waiting upstairs.

Her hair was coming loose in a dozen places. Holding a pin between her teeth, she attempted to smooth back the fly-away curls as she walked. Her head ached; that was a common occurrence of late. She must remember to make an appointment to have her eyes tested. But not today. There was still too much to do today.

"Hello there," said a voice.

She looked up, almost colliding with Jake Turner. The composure she had been cultivating came quickly now.

"Hello," she said briefly.

She started past him.

"Laura, please wait." He caught her sleeve. "I'm sorry about what happened in Mexico. I want you to know that. I've been trying to reach you so I could say it. I—"

He stopped and swallowed. His face was strained. She stood poised on uncertainty, aware of two stage hands arguing in the background, aware of something tormented in the depths of the eyes seeking hers.

"Forget it," she said.

As he opened his mouth to speak again, she walked away.

It was twenty past six when she made her way through the plants and macramé hangings at Macho's and spotted Nel.

"Sorry I'm late. I got called in to do another script in two weeks' time."

She was triumphant. This kind of overwork she was glad to take.

"No problem. I've been working on my share of the margueritas."

Laura filled her glass from the pitcher Nel indicated and took a long drink. "Ummm. Tastes good." Sighing blissfully and folding her arms on the table, she looked at Nel. "So tell me, what did *you* think of my solo flight?"

Nel's smile was quick. "I think you've got a lot of talent, Laura—but then I could have told you that before. I also think you should forget that nonsense I gave you when you left New York about thinking twice about television. You've proved me wrong about that. You seem pretty happy."

"Yes." She laughed, then asked with an indifference she didn't feel, "Did Jess watch?"

Nel hunted her cigarettes. "I don't know. I went to Eddie's place to watch with him."

Though skillfully hidden, there was a sheepish look about Nel's face. It amused Laura, and it filled her with affection. Nel seemed rather flustered. Did she suppose it would surprise Laura to know the romance with Eddie had progressed to a full-blown affair?

Laura laid her fingers on Nel's arm. "I think he's wonderful. I think you should shack up with him and quit working. He's good for you—good *to* you too. I love him."

"Oh, shit. Any more talk like that and I'll drink the rest of the margueritas."

"Okay, okay, we'll talk about me again then. I'm on an ego trip today anyway, as you can see. You've always been good at critiquing scripts with Jessamyn. How about doing mine? What do you think my weak points are?"

Nel fiddled with her lighter, frowning slightly. "Oh, I can shoot off my mouth about what I think makes a good piece for Jess, but I don't know a damn thing about scripts in general. Look, if you've got a date at eight, you'd better get some food in you. What say we order a couple of *enchiladas*?"

The familiar eyes avoided Laura's.

"Sure thing."

Laura picked up the menu and stared at lines of print that made no sense. Her chest felt hollow. Nel had acted strangely ever since they met. Was she trying to skirt the fact she hadn't liked the show?

Then, as surely as though the words had been spoken aloud, Laura knew. Nel hadn't even watched the night before.

Nel moved toward the window, her back to her desk.

"Damn it, Eddie, I wish you hadn't come here."

"I got worried when you called and cancelled out on dinner."

"I told you, some things have come up here that I've got to deal with."

"I got scared, Nel. I lost you once. I didn't want to lose you again. I had to come to see you."

She could hear him come closer behind her. She tried to think. It had never occurred to her to run away again. Not at her age. Yet in a way she was running—trying to—if only she'd had the space to figure out how to go about it.

"What is it, Nel?" Eddie's voice was gentle. "Is it these last two nights? Have they seemed wrong to you?"

Nel held her breath and let it out slowly. How did it happen that of all the men in the world she had found this one, who almost read her moods better than she did herself? He was way off base about this one, though. While she felt guilt over missing Laura's show, her blood still sang with the memory of that long-delayed reunion on Eddie's couch. Last night, with a whole long evening ahead and a bed beneath them, had been even better.

It didn't matter. Eddie knew something was amiss. There was no point delaying.

She turned and eyed him ruthlessly. "Yeah," she said. "I guess that's it."

She saw the pain in his face, watched the words stab into him.

"But, Nellie, you don't understand. I love you. I want to marry you."

The knife she had tried to turn against him twisted inside her. She moved away from the magnet of his presence. Her voice was shaking.

"I wasn't asking for a proposal, Eddie. What do you think,

that I'm some sort of little puritan? I can't handle things the
way they are, that's all. It's too much. I knew from the start
it would be. I asked you to leave me alone, but you wouldn't.
It would have been easier then; it's harder now. I'm sorry,
Eddie. I just can't go on."

The silence was sharp. Then the quiet voice she was used
to rose with an anger she'd never heard before.

"Are you crazy, woman? Do you really suppose I'm going
to just take a walk? I've thought of you and wanted you for
thirty years, and now that I've found you, I'm not going to
budge. I love you, damn it! Tell me you've got cold feet, tell
me you like the life you lead, tell me there's been someone
else in between Detroit and here, but don't try to put me off
with some vague crap about things not working. I love you,
Nel! *I love you!*"

Tears were squeezing out of her eyes. It had been years
since she cried. In anger she caught his arms, shaking him,
holding him.

"Damn it, if you care about me, go away! Let me have
some peace! I don't want to love you. I don't want you to love
me!" The bitterness she'd tried to hide from spilled out in shrill,
screaming words. "It's too late, Eddie! Can't you understand?
I'm going to die!"

Twelve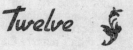

"*Jessamyn, you look* more gorgeous each time I see you!"

Jessamyn bestowed a wide smile on the chief advertising
man for a cosmetics empire.

"Well, Thatcher, I see you know the proper way to start a
business lunch." She shook back her hair.

Thatcher Kirby reached across to steer her carefully, as
gently as though she were fine porcelain, around the narrow
table to a velvet banquette.

"Believe me, if I knew how to start any other sort of meeting with you, I would," he said, voice lowering.

She looked at him from heavy-lidded eyes. Her lips parted slightly.

"Let's talk about it sometime, shall we?" They sat down as one, their gazes intertwined, and Jessamyn knew she had him, though she also knew that Thatcher would rise to the occasion and keep business foremost in his mind for as long as necessary. "Right now," she said, "I want to see the pictures."

He motioned for a waiter to bring them drinks, then drew a padded envelope toward him.

"The only thing lacking in them is that they're not alive, believe me," he said. "The company's more than satisfied. If these don't sell mascara, then the women of this country are a bunch of dykes."

As he spoke, he drew out a series of glossy photographs, rich with color. Jessamyn's famous eyes stared seductively from each of them. They would run full-size in every women's magazine from *Vogue* to *Family Circle*, promoting a new line of mascara, shadow, and eyeliner under the company's already prestigious label.

"Well?" he said, unmistakably pleased. "What do you think of them?"

Jessamyn calmly ripped one in half. "Not this one." Not the slightest imperfection showed in it, but the line of the cheekbone was wrong. It made her look less than young. A waiter set a dish of caviar before her. Kirby's company was going all out to keep her happy. She knew she would get what she wanted.

"I think the gold earrings come across the best," she said.

"Yes, that was our verdict. We're out to conjure up images of sex appeal, not snobbery, and gold still seems more attainable than diamonds."

She smiled, aware of the fine, flawless stones that adorned her own ears.

"There's just one thing," she said, returning the pictures.

"Sure, Jessamyn. What is it?"

She locked her hands loosely around her drink. "I can't let you use them if you don't pull your ads on *Twenty-two Wentworth*."

The glass in his hand twitched slightly. Its contents splashed on the table.

"Jesus! I hope that's a joke."

"I'm perfectly serious."

"You want us to pull—why the hell should we?"

"I just told you. Because you'll lose me if you don't."
Raising her glass, she toasted him.

Kirby sat with jaw slightly slack while she sipped her drink.

"It's a very bad show," she said. "Or haven't you noticed?
It's losing out in ratings to the sitcom that's on opposite it, and
I don't like any association with losers."

"But—"

"It's the writing. It's gotten bad of late." She sipped again
and seemed to think. "You might mention that when you pull
the account."

Thatcher Kirby straightened his cuff links.

"Look, Jessamyn, if the ratings are going down, maybe we
should look into it, but I can't promise—"

"You'd better."

"You signed a contract."

"So sue me. It's going to be your neck if this falls through."
She paused. "I'd hate to see that, Thatcher. I really would."

He drained his martini glass quickly, not stopping for breath.

"Be reasonable, Jessamyn. I can't just take it into my hands
to do something like that. I have to answer to the board."

"Then do a study. Fake one. Do it fast. I haven't signed
your precious model release form yet."

"Jake Turner on line one. Are you out?"

"You got it."

Laura made a temple of her fingers and leaned her forehead
against them. There was a rustle of sound at the door to her
cubicle, and she looked up. Tracy, the secretary, lounged there,
grinning.

"I wish you'd give him the time of day so he'd come around,"
she said. "I'd like to see him. He used to take out some pretty
hot names. Guess he's pretty hot himself these days for a new
producer."

Laura saw no need to answer.

"Have you been out with him?" Tracy persisted.

Laura gave her a steely glance, surprised at such forward-
ness. "Yes. He's quite forgettable."

The secretary turned and left. Laura struck the top drawer
of her desk with the heel of her hand and slammed it shut.

She was in the third draft of a difficult script and wondering whether she should slit her throat and end the agony when Tracy buzzed her.

"A Mr. Lacouture to see you."

"Who? Oh, heavens! Send him in." She rose, still frowning at the page in front of her, and rounded the desk to meet Eddie.

"Hi," she laughed. "What a nice surprise. Where's Nel?"

"Nel's not with me. I came to collect you for that lunch you said you'd have with me one day."

"Oh, Eddie, I'm swamped. I can't—" She stopped. "Is something the matter?"

Eddie saw the quick concern in her expression. He liked that. So many of the faces he passed on the street and in buildings weren't really faces. They were only the bright, painted armor of the upwardly mobile. Laura was genuine and quick to feel. No wonder Nel was fond of her.

"Oh, well, Nel's still giving me a hard time, but it's nothing I can't handle." He smiled, wanting to reassure her. He had reassured himself. He had found a measure of peace, though only two days had passed since Nel told him about her illness, and vestiges of the shock remained with him. "As a matter of fact I wanted to do a little shopping for her. I was hoping you might help me."

"Oh . . ."

He saw her glance back at her typewriter. She made a sound of exhaustion and stretched, hands in her pockets.

"Actually it will probably save me from an early death. If I don't get away for a while, my brain's going to turn into pudding. But please," she said, catching up her jacket, "don't make it any place fancy."

They found a lunchroom that served thick sandwiches and homemade coconut cream pie. Eddie relaxed, certain that Laura had bought his story of all being well with Nel. He'd have known without being told that Nel didn't want Laura to know her secret. "Don't tell anyone," she'd said at the end of that emotionally exhausting evening two nights past. "Especially not Laura. I don't want anyone worrying. I don't want pity."

Lou Gehrig's disease. He couldn't remember the fancy name Nel had given it. The whole thing seemed impossible. She had even made a joke about having it when it so rarely afflicted women. His beautiful, beautiful Nel.

He hadn't told her yet that it didn't matter. Or rather he had, but only in the sense that it didn't matter to him. He hadn't explained to her that his life, too, was running out. He hadn't told her what he had done, why he was hiding, using another name, fooling himself when all the time he knew that one night he would step out onto the street and it would end. At first he had worried about that part. Now all he worried about was Nel.

"Now tell me about this shopping." Laura said.

"I want you to help me pick out a ring for Nel." He laughed. "Don't jump the gun, I didn't mean that kind of ring. I have hopes, you understand, but I'm in this game to win. Nel's skittish enough. She might slip through my fingers altogether if I tried to pin her down. So I'm going to butter her up instead."

"Why, Eddie? Won't she be pinned down, I mean? Is it because of whatever happened between you way back when?"

It startled him to know the girl knew something of their past relationship. Then he was glad she knew.

"Oh, mostly it's just because of the way Nel is," he said. "She goes her own way. She always did. Are you ready?"

After half an hour in a jewelry store, they agreed on a handsome topaz edged with small diamonds. It would remind Nel of the yellow of pansies, Laura thought, and would glow becomingly against her dark fingers. In spite of Eddie's disclaimers, she knew the ring had special meaning to him. Maybe it would to Nel as well. Maybe it would allow her to preserve some air of independence in a way a diamond wouldn't.

Laura felt a warm sense of belonging as they walked out of the jewelry store. It must be like this having a father who asked your opinion on a shopping trip, she thought. Nel had taken her shopping at Christmas and other times, always praising her selection of gifts and making her feel like the smartest child ever—a child any adult, even Jessamyn, would love to spend time with if only they had a schedule as free as Nel's. But Nel, with her impeccable taste, had never needed any imput about her own purchases.

"Do you know no one has ever asked me to help them pick out a gift before?" she said to Eddie.

He seemed lost in thought, studying the crowd on the other side of the street as if to commit it to memory.

"What are you watching?" Laura asked curiously.

"What? Oh . . . just the passing scene. A hobby of mine." He smiled at her. "Well, I'm glad I asked," he said, patting his pocket. "And I think Nel's going to like what we got her."

He insisted on walking her back to the door of her office. To her surprise Van Greenberg was waiting. He had never visited her in her working environment, and he looked startled as the two of them came through the door.

"Well," he said, "hello."

"Hi, Van." Laura turned to introduce Eddie, but he was already turning back toward the hallway with a wave. "Good luck," she called after him. She smiled at Van. "What are you doing here?"

He lighted a cigarette.

"I had busines in the area." Repocketing his lighter, he regarded her with piercing blue eyes. "Someone you work with?"

"Eddie? No, he's a friend. We had lunch together."

"Ah." He stood up from the corner of the desk where he had been sitting. "You're such a conventional girl, I suppose I'm surprised to see your choice of companions."

Was there a tinge of disapproval to the words? Perhaps not. Yet Laura found herself drawing up.

"I stopped to see if I could take you to lunch," Van said. "Apparently I need to get a bid in early, don't I?"

"By God, but you're a good writer, Laura! You're all good writers," Maxy gloated. Her nails were painted brilliant red today to match her dress. "The ratings are starting to look halfway presentable again," she said. "I do believe we may keep this bloody show afloat."

Laura basked in the morning-after glow that lately had followed each episode of *Twenty-two Wentworth*. This morning it felt especially warming. The night before had seen the airing of her second script, and it had been mentioned in the trades with favorable comments.

The console rang. "Top dog wants to see you," Tracy told the story editor.

Maxy popped a sugarless mint into her mouth.

"See, kids? Even that bastard producer's going to give us compliments today. Grudging, I'm sure." She sauntered out.

"Laura, Nel Simmons on line two," said Tracy as the phone rang again.

Laura left the love-fest and slipped into her private domain.

"Hey, kiddo, it was just great!" said Nel. "I cried all over my shoes over that damn spineless woman."

This time Laura knew Nel had seen the show. As the knowledge spread through her, she realized this was the accolade she'd been awaiting. Only now could she admit to herself how hurt she had been about the first show. Would she ever know why Nel had missed it?

"Eddie said to tell you he loved it too," Nel continued. "He thinks you should buy a yacht for all of us when you get rich and famous."

"Sure, and be seasick the whole time," Laura laughed. "Have you forgotten that I get queasy watching swimming pools?" She paused, then asked, "How is Eddie?"

"Fine. He's settling into an apartment. Guess I'll have to buy him a plant or something."

Laura treaded lightly, relying on humor. She and Nel were so close, yet even they had to have their pretenses.

"Ah-hah!" she said. "And here I thought that ring he bought was just a payoff of some sort!"

"The man's impossible to discourage," Nel said cheerfully.

"Well, don't try. I need someone around to buy me another nice lunch. Listen, Nellie, I'd better go now. We're always behind."

She was starting to feel the need for her mid-morning coffee when Tracy appeared in the doorway. The secretary's face was grim.

"Maxy wants to see you out here right away," she said.

Switching off her typewriter, Laura followed Tracy out. The door to the hallway was closed. Adam sat on the edge of Tracy's desk. Maxy was standing. Fritz was nowhere to be seen. Maxy bit a mint in two with a crack that filled the room. Laura felt the story editor's eyes fixed on her.

"The eye glop people have pulled their commercials," she said. "They're going with the sitcom."

Laura's heart began to swell and shrink. Maxy still was eyeing her.

"I wasn't called upstairs to receive any compliments after all," Maxy said. "I was called so they could tell me they're cutting the budget. I'm afraid they spell that letting one writer go."

As she labored to breathe, Laura tried to look philosophical. Last hired, first fired. It hadn't lasted long, but at least *Wentworth* had given her a start.

"I had to break the nasty news to Fritz," said Maxy. "He'll be in after lunch to get his stuff."

Laura stopped on the downside of breath, certain she had somehow misunderstood. Maxy picked up a manila folder and tossed it toward her.

"Here. This script he was working on stinks. You've got to fix it. Get your butt upstairs to see Veta. He wants to hear your ideas."

Heels clicking in the silence, she left the room. Laura looked down at the envelope with Fritz's script.

"Baby, you are lucky," Adam said softly. "We both are." He slid from the desk and started for his cubicle. "Guess I'd better get busy and pull off some minor masterpiece or I'll be next."

"I don't understand," said Laura, finding her voice. "I'm the newest. Why wasn't it me?"

Fritz was a hard worker, she thought. He was a good person. He didn't cheat on his wife—or at least not openly. He talked about his kids.

Adam gave her a cynical glance.

"Never question," he said. "Just be damn glad. Maybe you've got talent, whatever that is."

Clutching the folder to her, Laura stepped out into the hall. She felt harried instead of safe. Instead of relief, she felt desperation. What would she say to Veta? She had no ideas.

Suddenly another thought slammed into her. Cosmetics. Nel had made some recent reference to Jessamyn being photographed for mascara ads. Surely this loss of a sponsor couldn't be Jessamyn's doing. Yet the dull feeling spreading through her told her it was.

Then I should have been the one who was fired, she thought thickly, not Fritz. Not an innocent man. I'm the one to blame!

She whirled and saw Maxy still in the hallway.

"Maxy! I've got to talk to you!" she called.

The story editor halted, expression wary, as Laura caught up.

"Listen, Maxy, it's me who should have been fired. Jessamyn Friday's my mother, and she's working with the cosmetics people. It's my job she wants, not Fritz's. Tell Fritz it was all a mistake. Let me quit instead!"

Maxy listened to her stumbling words with a jaundiced eye.

"Nasty game. But Fritz isn't coming back no matter what you do. My tushy goes if this show folds, and I'm not about to take chances on someone I see going stale. Save the martyrdom for that sweet little family we write about and get the hell upstairs."

Laura did not see her surroundings as she began to walk again. She was aware of moving, but in a trance. Then a familiar figure loomed in front of her and spoke without her hearing, and as one who broke suddenly from the heavy depths of water into too light an atmosphere, she surfaced into total consciousness.

"Hello, Jake. How are you these days?" she asked almost gaily.

He looked at her strangely. She wondered if her hair was coming apart and twisted at it automatically. Had to have it looking right for Veta.

"Are you all right?" Jake asked.

"Oh, yes," she said glibly. "In very good shape, in fact. The word just came down to fire one writer, but they picked Fritz instead of me..." All at once she could hear herself talking, rattling on, except she didn't know what she was talking about. The colors in the hall looked very bright. Her eyes searched unsteadily for the women's room a few steps away.

"Excuse me," she murmured, subdued now. "I think I'm going to be ill."

She wasn't, though for ten reeling minutes she stood bent over a wash basin. The fingers clutching the manila folder were icy. She was cold, trembling, shaking. After a long time the room stopped moving around her. She sat down on a couch and closed her eyes.

Everything had happened so swiftly. She had known people in her business were fired at the drop of a hat—that was why executives demanded and got such astromonical salaries, because they knew they might not be around long to enjoy them. She knew, too, that the bottom line in TV was save your own skin. But knowing was not the same as the horror of seeing. She was shocked by the brutality, shocked by Maxy's attitude, shocked by the ugliness.

It might not have happened except for me, she thought. Yet the rational part of her accepted the fact that apart from Jessamyn, apart from any meddling that might have happened this time, incidents such as the one she'd just witnessed took place in every studio every week. Maybe Jake Turner had been right, and she was too soft to survive.

She stepped out of the women's room and drew up in surprise. Turner himself still stood there.

"It happens all the time," he said with a level look.

"I know. I suppose I have to get used to it, don't I?" She tilted the folder. "I have to get upstairs with this."

"No, you don't. Not right now." Turner took her elbow. "You never want to see the powers that be when your nerves aren't steady. Or when you don't at least look like they are. Sorry, but right now you don't pass the test. Let's get out of the building. I'll buy you some coffee."

As she resisted, his mouth hardened into a comprehending line.

"I like to think there's a little bit of decency left in me," he said. "You need someone to talk to."

Laura nodded, feeling weary. Jake Turner had hurt her. She thought she despised him. But maybe there was, as he'd said, a decent side to him. It helped, believing that. It kept her from feeling like such an idiot for ever having fallen for him. Right now she was grateful for the company of someone who understood.

Across the street there was a coffee shop with vinyl booths and Formica tables.

"Bring us each an English muffin, too," Turner told the waitress who poured their coffee. Laura opened her mouth to say she couldn't eat, but the waitress was leaving. "You need it," said Turner. "It steadies the stomach or blood-sugar level or some damn thing."

She smiled, and it took every ounce of energy in her. The elbows propping her on the table felt ready to collapse at any minute.

"Thanks."

Laura wrapped her hands around the coffee mug, drawing warmth from it. There was just a slight chance she'd been wrong about Jessamyn's part in what had happened. Then she wondered dismally when she'd ever stop pretending.

"It's the callousness of everyone that gets to me," she said at last. "The business-as-usual air. The unflinching joy of everyone who didn't get pitched. It's shameless."

"It's a pose. Voodoo to ward off the fear that you might be next. In this business you have to live with the fear, but you don't have to look at it. If you stop and think about someone else getting screwed, you start to panic, so you just learn not to think."

"I suppose. I'm not sure I ever want to be like that."

The shell she had resolved to build around herself was slipping. She struggled to pull it back. When the English muffin came, she ate half of it without tasting, and after a bit she had to admit she was feeling steadier.

"I suppose this isn't the best day to ask you how you like the job," Turner said. His mouth held the hint of a smile, but it was a compassionate one.

"No," she agreed, "but I can tell you anyway. I like it, basically. No—more than basically—more than like. You know." She shrugged. "I'm not sure how long it will last. One of the big advertisers pulled out today. That's why Fritz was fired. I think the network's going to throw something else on against that sitcom."

"I'm surprised it's lasted as long as it has. It's a good show. Too good. Too sensitive. Viewers don't want to think that hard on a weekly basis. Which is why I prefer to do movies. It's the only chance left to rise above the triteness. One shot now and then, and the audience likes something to chew on, but only in between big doses of earthquake, sharks, and plague-infested jumbo jets or jiggles and giggles."

Laura regarded him with surprise. For a second his face was open to her, and she saw his passion for what he was saying. He sounded so much more serious than she'd ever supposed him that she wondered if he too had erected a shell.

"Well, even if we're cancelled tomorrow, I still have a job to do today," she said, looking down at the table. "I do feel better. Thank you."

"You're welcome." He stood and left the money to cover the check.

As they left the coffee shop, the silence between them grew awkward.

"Did you like the cookbook?" he asked, looking straight ahead.

Laura held the manila folder against her like a shield.

"Yes. It's lovely. Very nice."

"I'm glad."

They crossed the street to the studio. Turner reached past

her to open the door, but stopped when it was ajar no more than a crack.

"Laura, if I give you a call some time, at home or at your office, will you talk to me? I'd like to see you. Please."

She fixed her mind on the meeting ahead of her, on the script she must doctor, on anything that would remove the intensity of the present moment. If you stopped to think, you panicked, Jake had said.

"I don't know. I don't think so," she said.

She opened the door.

Thirteen

Jake Turner finished one cigarette and lighted another, shoulders cramped from a morning hunched over the Movieola in the editing room. A week had passed since he'd had coffee with Laura. Another moment of indecision elapsed, and he reached for the phone.

Perhaps he should simply accept the fact he had a case for her, he thought ruefully. That was the only explanation for this obsession with her all these months. He had not gone through an adolescent crush at the time when one would have been normal. All his time and energy had been invested in the future he planned to make for himself, in the part-time jobs that would make further schooling possible, in hanging around location shootings in hopes of piecing together how they worked, in reading. He supposed it was fair, in an ironic sort of way, that he should suffer a grand passion now.

Whether he stood a chance of doing anything more than suffering in silence, he wasn't quite sure. After how he had behaved in Mexico, he didn't deserve to. He had gone a little crazy at such coolness from a woman, especially since she was the first woman he had wanted so fiercely. Could he make Laura understand that? He shouldn't try.

"Jake Turner for Miss Fitzgerald," he said as the phone was answered. He pictured a smirk on the unknown secretary's face, certain she must be amused by how often his calls had been turned away.

"Yes, Jake?"

He clutched the receiver. He had forgotten how her voice sounded on the telephone. It was cautious, though.

"How's it going?" he asked. "Have things settled down?"

"A little."

He took a breath. "Laura, I realize there's not much chance of picking up the pieces between us, but I'd like to try. I'd like to see you again. I'd like to have dinner with you. That's all. I swear. I'll let you out at your door when the evening's over. Will you think about it a minute before you say no?"

There was a silence. He ground his cigarette out in an ashtray. Another button on his phone began to blink at him, but he ignored it.

"Laura?"

"I'm here. And I'll go out with you. But understand that it's on my terms, Jake. I'm not available for casual sex. Or any other kind. So if that's what you're angling for in the long run, forget it. Nor do I expect you to turn up, ever, at my place uninvited. I like my privacy. I like my work. I don't like—as you put it—'exclusive contracts,' though I once thought I did. I've come to see what a fine philosophy looking out for Number One is. If you understand that and still want to take me to dinner, fine. Why not?"

It sounded as though it might have been a speech she'd been rehearsing. Turner found himself caught off guard by the force of it. Something in Laura had changed, and he wasn't sure he liked it.

"Okay," he said, unsure now what it was he had expected. "I understand. How about Friday night?"

When he hung up, he ran a hand through his hair and sat frowning. He'd remembered her as softer, less outspoken. He punched the button blinking on his phone and heard his old boss Bernie Goldman.

"Jake, you lucky son-of-a-bitch! It's bad enough that you're getting pats on the head for that western that should have been mine, but now I hear you're up for an award for it too. I think the least you can do to make amends is buy me lunch."

"Amends for what? I deserve all the frosting I can get from

that one. Don't forget, I'm the one who was saddled with Petronelli." Turner enjoyed this sparring. He missed it now that he had an office of his own. "But I'll kick in for lunch anyway," he said. "How are you feeling?"

Goldman strung together assorted obscenities. "What I'm allowed to eat these days, I can count on one hand. And I'm supposed to walk yet!"

Turner laughed. "Louise will see to it you do that. She's a mighty fine lady."

Actually she was a bit of a nag. She no doubt enjoyed this new chance to manage Bernie's health, Turner thought as he hung up.

"What's new with Bernie?"

Saul Finer lounged in the doorway. Turner sat back and propped his feet on his desk, preparing to chat. Finer was a working partner in the new production company, a writer with a sure touch that Turner admired and a pleasant absence of inflated ego.

"Walking and dieting."

Finer chuckled.

"He thinks I should buy him lunch to smooth his feathers over the Montana project," Turner said. "I think I'll buy him a jogging suit instead."

A cat-in-the-cream expression was coming over Finer's face.

"What the hell, buy him shoes too. We can afford it. While you were tied up with him, I fielded another call for you. I do believe your hard-to-get act's paid off, old buddy. Jessamyn wants to see you at four. She says bring the script."

"Does she now."

Turner tried to keep annoyance from his voice. He did not like being told to show up like a schoolboy. He'd declined an invitation into her bed the night of the party for much the same reason. Gut wisdom told him it would not do to let a woman like Jessamyn gain the upper hand in things. Not if he hoped to work with her.

Reluctantly he had to admit her body held a strong attraction for his, one that he was not certain he could resist. And was he forgetting she was the mother of the woman he'd just asked out? Christ, he was perverted.

"I think we'll get her then," he said aloud. "It's a damn good script, Saul."

At four o'clock he rang the bell at Jessamyn's place. A

houseman showed him out to the patio. Jessamyn lay on her side by the pool, her silken breasts rubbing together beneath the confines of a loosely tied swim top. For a moment he almost abandoned his plan.

"My, but you're an elusive man these days," she said, sitting up.

Her eyes held seductive amusement. Twice since the party he'd taken her to, she'd asked him over, but he'd pleaded business. They both knew he'd been avoiding her.

"Yes, I'm afraid so," he said with a laugh. "And all the pleasanter parts of life are eluding me." He knelt and handed her the script, still smiling. "Sorry I can't stay and go over this with you. I've got a meeting with CBS East Coast on the schedule. Saul should have mentioned it. I know you're going to like this script. Give me a call and we'll get together when you've read it."

For the first time in his life Turner found that he had consumed a meal and tasted nothing. His senses had been occupied in registering every nuance of Laura's words and expression. He watched the soft line of her mouth and wanted to trace it, knowing he couldn't. She had changed, she was more cautious as well as more sure of herself. They would help her survive in her work, those changes, and yet he found they left him vaguely depressed.

"I see your co-worker Fritz found another slot," he said.

In spite of her new-found composure, her face still lit up.

"Yes. I was so pleased to read it. It's bad enough for anyone to get the sack, but when you've got little kids to think of, it must be pure hell. He's so crazy about them. Goes home from work and coaches a soccer team, can you believe it?"

Turner motioned for the waiter to bring more coffee. "I guess I don't think of the people I see from day to day as having kids."

"I know. They clutter up the aura of the businessplace, I guess."

"Did you? Clutter, I mean. I have had to endure a few of those spoiled little brats whose parents are stars. No bouncing them from location."

"I was never on location with Jessamyn. I never went anywhere with her. She felt about me then exactly as she does now."

"And your father? I don't even know who he was or what he did."

"Neither do I."

She looked quickly at something on the other side of the room, and Turner had the uneasy feeling of having blundered.

"I'm afraid it's one of those things I have a terrible hang-up about," she said at length. "I've always wished I could meet him just once, or see what he looked like anyway. I expect I've just romanticized it. It doesn't matter."

Turner knew by the way she said it that it did matter to her.

"Thank God we're not influenced by heredity," he said.

She looked at him with interest. "No?"

"I hope not. My father was a foul-tempered slug whose only ambition in life was a bottle of whiskey. Drank up his paycheck every Friday and then beat my mother. Not that she was that much better, I guess, since she never left him. She died of old age before she was fifty."

He stopped, wondering if he'd shocked her and why he'd told her in any case. It was something he was ashamed of. Something he'd taken great pains to keep secret. Now he cursed himself for sounding like some self-pitying weakling.

"How sad for you." Laura's eyes were bright with sympathy.

For the first time all evening Turner allowed himself to hope that the softness in her nature that had frustrated him—that still did perhaps—was nonetheless intact. He waited two days before he called her.

"Guess what? I have tickets to that sold-out performance of the philharmonic you wanted to see," he announced.

After a brief silence he heard her laugh.

"Now just how did you manage that?"

"Conned a tuba player. I'll give him a little spot in a film one day. Would you like to go?"

"How can I refuse?"

He hung up, smiling. It would never have occurred to him to go to an orchestra concert any more than it would have a bingo game. As far as he knew, he enjoyed all kinds of music, but it was something in the background of his life and little explored. Too damn much of his life was unexplored, he thought sometimes. If Laura hadn't mentioned over dinner that she'd waited too long to get tickets for the upcoming concert, he would never have considered it as something to do with a woman.

On the night he was to pick her up, he stopped by a department store. He had ordered the jogging suit and shoes for Bernie Goldman, but he wanted to deliver them in person. As the escalator took him past the floor with cookwares, Turner noticed a display of wineglasses and thought of Laura.

Impulse told him she would like them. He debated buying a set for her. But he didn't want her to think he was trying to buy *her*. And it wasn't as if he wanted to marry her, after all. In the back of his mind he wanted to go to bed with her, but to his amazement that wasn't what he wanted most of all. He had agreed to her terms in order simply to see her. He sensed he was walking a narrow line. She was unyielding. If ever there was a move toward intimacy, it would have to be by her. Turner was afraid she'd never make it.

"I'm not sure I should applaud whatever questionable deal you made with your tuba player," she said when he called for her. "But I will anyway. This is far and away the most relaxing way to spend an evening that I can imagine."

"I'm ready for that. What about you?"

"Betsy's having a nervous breakdown soon, and it's hard on me."

Turner laughed. Betsy was the sweet young wife on *Twenty-two Wentworth*.

As they entered the building, he did not so much as attempt to take her elbow. When they reached their seats, she was equally careful to see that her legs did not touch his. Did that mean she felt susceptible to him? Turner wondered. It was producing a curious strain on him, sitting here so close beside her in the hushed and crowded openness of Chandler Pavilion.

Or perhaps it was the unfamiliar setting. He felt anonymous. In the row upon row of people around them, he recognized not a single face, no one from the studios, no one from the networks. It was slightly awesome. Then he decided he liked the feeling.

"You're right. It is relaxing," he said.

She looked up from her program with a smile suggesting puzzlement. No doubt it seemed an odd statement. The concert had not yet started.

When it did, at first he was acutely aware of Laura sitting beside him in the dark. He wanted to take her hand and dared not. The scent of her perfume teased him. He could almost feel the vibrating of the atoms in the body so near his own, as though energy given off by the particles jumped a gap between them. He tried to concentrate on the stage, and at last, to his relief, he succeeded. At some point that he was not even aware of, he became a captive of the music, and his mind, freed from all concerns, simply drifted.

"It was lovely," Laura sighed afterward.

"Ummm," he agreed. "I didn't realize what I'd been missing."

The crowd pouring out of the Music Center jostled them against each other. She looked up at him in surprise.

"You mean you've never been before?"

Aware that he'd been caught out, he did not answer immediately.

"No," he said at last. "I'm afraid I haven't."

He suggested a drink, but she declined, and when they reached her apartment house, she got out quickly, making clear her intention of avoiding all contact between them. When he reached a bar district, he pulled to the curb, angry yet not angry, confused about what it was that he was feeling. He started to get out of the car, then stopped. The thought of setting foot inside some noisy bar after the concert hall repelled him. He felt above it.

Lips twisting humorlessly, he laughed at himself. Was it possible he felt purified by Laura? The thought was so bizarre that it annoyed him. Being with her tonight had affected him. The need for her consumed him, sweeping over him in a flood of physical sickness. Bending over the steering wheel, he pressed his eyes.

Turner found himself scowling as he waited on Jess Friday's doorstep. At last his project might be in the bag, yet he was edgy. All day he had found himself remembering the invitation Jessamyn's body had sent his and he felt restless, like a caged lion, wanting to strike at something without knowing why.

The door swung open, and as he followed the houseman through to the patio, he met Nel Simmons. Turner wondered why she didn't like him. He felt a twinge of discomfort as he saw the irony in her eyes as she nodded to him. She made him feel inferior, as Laura sometimes did.

Laura. Damn. Laura.

"Nice afternoon," he said to Nel.

"Not bad."

"Fine job that Laura's doing on *Wentworth*, don't you agree?"

"I'm biased."

"I hope she goes on to movies one of these days. I'd like to work with her."

Nel's look was cynical. What the hell was wrong with him this afternoon? He wasn't handling things with his usual smoothness. He had noticed uncharacteristic tension in himself these last few days—ever since that concert. Christ, he felt like he had as a kid, scared, no one to talk to. Only now he had the outer Jake Turner, a man who was always confident, almost always right. Turner smoothed his hair.

Jessamyn was standing at the far side of the patio. At the sound of the glass door closing, she turned and came toward him, her slim hips encased in expensive slacks, her blouse a cloud of transparent whiteness. Laura's blouses always drew his attention to her throat, to the softness of her skin. This one held his interest somewhat lower.

"Ah, you did come," she said, her smile not an altogether pleasant one. "I'm never quite sure when I ask for a meeting with you these days."

Her eyebrows raised. A reprimand. She held his gaze with a look of challenge, and Turner found himself responding to the seething bitchiness more than he ever had to her out-and-out overtures. She was the imperious queen, thwarted and annoyed by it.

"I hope you have time to stay and discuss this little script you dropped off," she was saying.

"For you, Jessamyn, all the time in the world."

Turner was hard pressed to keep amusement from his voice.

Jessamyn's magnificent eyes narrowed slightly. She did not know what to make of him, he thought with satisfaction. Good. That was what he wanted. He knew instinctively that was how she must be handled.

"Let's go into the study then. Harry, bring us some wine."

She sailed past the houseman without a glance for him or Turner, who followed after her, and led the way into the room where he had met Laura.

The script lay on the table he'd repositioned that night. Jessamyn curled up in a chair beside it and threw him a look tinged with malice.

"Is your company going to be in business long enough to make this film?"

"Yes, I think so."

Without rising to the bait, Turner relaxed in a chair across from her. He waited, unruffled, watching her face. There was cunning in her eyes, and it was electric. Her whole body seemed to pulsate. Her willfulness, her dangerous slyness was much more intriguing than her unmistakable sexuality, and all at once Turner began to wonder if she was aware of it.

The door opened. Harry brought in a tray with wine and glasses.

"That's all. See that we're not disturbed."

Jessamyn's eyes were golden embers, burning, daring Turner to ignore them. He realized he had not looked away since entering the room.

"Are we celebrating a deal then?" he asked, his calm voice betraying nothing of what he was feeling.

"I haven't decided yet." Slowly, lazily, she reached for the bottle of wine and filled the glasses. "It's not a bad little script. It has its appeal. But if I did it, I'd want three million off the top."

Bitch, thought Turner. Scheming, vindictive bitch. You know that's outrageous. I didn't jump when you whistled, and you want the satisfaction of seeing me pay for it. Right now you're sitting there waiting for me to explode.

Instead he tipped his head back, laughing softly.

"You're hell to handle, aren't you, Jessamyn?"

He saw the startled look cross her face. Her eyes grew hard.

"Yes." She spit the answer in warning.

"Well, so am I." Picking up the glass of wine she had not offered him, he toasted her.

He rose and walked casually to the fireplace, puzzled to find the anger in him changing to excitement. Christ, there'd be fireworks in bed if a man ever tried to get the upper hand with her. He wondered if a man ever had.

The air in the room was brittle with tension. He leaned an elbow on the mantel and sipped his wine, aware of danger in the course his thoughts were taking. He didn't want to go to bed with Jessamyn. He could see her ruthlessness too clearly.

"You know three million's out of the question for television," he said mildly. "I'll give you one, plus a part of the package. Take it or leave it. You're my first choice for the project, Jessamyn, but you're not my only choice."

Her eyes had almost disappeared behind her lashes, and he could not see what turn her mind was taking. Nevertheless he could sense it working. After a moment, head set to one side, she rose and walked toward him. She stopped directly in front of him, hands on her hips. Her tongue ran stealthily along the upper curve of her parted lips, heightening his awareness of their moistness. Parting further, those lips curved over words that were seductive in their huskiness.

"Are you sure you know what you're doing, Jake? Have you thought about what's in this deal for you?"

Those lips were teasing him. Tempting him. Reminding him he had not touched a woman in weeks. Turner felt the stirring of urges controlled for too long, suppressed while he'd sought the company of a woman he could not have. Damn it, he knew he'd never find satisfaction with Laura. And with Laura he'd have to change, be better than he wanted to be to keep from crushing her. Yet he thought of the integrity visible in every line of her small pink mouth. She'd never give even an inch of herself just to get what she wanted.

He looked at Jessamyn, and a sense of potency flared in him. He seized her angrily.

"What's in it for you, don't you mean?"

Conscious of her sharp intake of breath, he crushed her mouth beneath his, ramming one hand down the inviting openness of her blouse. He caught her breast crudely, experiencing both desire and a will to control. Jessamyn leaned into it, allowing her creamy flesh to spill over his fingers.

Eyes burning with satisfaction, Turner released her. Let her try her grand act with him now. She'd just proved how eager she was for anything he offered. Aware of the pitfalls of conscience, he blocked out the thought of Laura that tried to nudge in.

Jessamyn laughed wantonly, her head thrown back.

"I was starting to think you liked boys, Jake. But you don't, do you, hmmm? I can see we both will like working on this project. I think we ought to get started right now, don't you?"

Her fingers moved restlessly down his chest. Her arousal was apparent, and Turner felt it infecting him. He caught her hands, imprisoning them against his waist.

"We'll get started as soon as we have our names on a contract."

He was not sure himself what that promise meant.

The expression on her upturned face became incredulous. She pushed away from him, fingers curling.

"You son-of-a-bitch!" she shrieked, voice rising. "You son-of-a-bitch!" Turner laughed and walked toward the door.

Fourteen

"*I really can't*, Jake. I've got to patch up a script, and I may be here till midnight by the looks of it. Thanks anyway."

Laura slid the receiver back into place and sighed before releasing it. The dinner invitation from Jake Turner was better turned down, and she knew it.

She'd agreed to see him again to punish him. It had seemed a perfect avenue for venting the bitter anger she felt. On that day when he'd given her coffee after Fritz had been fired, she'd begun to realize that Turner was strangely vulnerable to her, that he wanted her perhaps. So she'd seized the chance to show she was as little affected by the claims of a few hours in bed as he had been. She'd wanted to inflict on him, hour after hour, the knowledge she had no real interest in him.

The only trouble was she had failed to reckon with the treachery of her own body. The first time they had brushed together accidently, a part of her had ignited. Since then she'd scrupulously avoided the most casual touch, barely acknowledging the fear that physical contact might lead to sexual involvement.

The sex was a manifestation of some other capitulation, she thought slowly, but she put that idea out of her mind. Cranking paper into her typewriter, she began to peck: Establishing shot. Poor neighborhood. Ethnic mix.

She would see Turner once, maybe twice more, and then drop him. She might tell him she'd give him a call sometime.

At eight that night she pulled her last sheet from the platen and sat back. The wastebasket by her desk was filled with discards, but she was finally satisfied with her rewrite. Slowly she became aware of the stiffness permeating her from waist to shoulders. The rooms beyond her cubicle were empty. She was alone.

She was too tired to stretch, too lethargic to move for another cup of coffee to revive her. She closed her eyes.

"Hey," said a voice.

She jerked, wondering if she'd dozed, and blinked at the sight of Turner standing in the doorway.

"How's the rewrite coming?" he asked. His eyes were warm, friendly, slightly amused as they had been that first time they met.

She tried to pull herself erect.

"I think I've licked it. How did you get in here?"

"Told the guard I was meeting you."

Anticipating what would come next, she started to speak. He held up his hand.

"I can see by the looks of you that a long dinner where you have to sit up straight's the last thing you need. But I suspect you could do with some nourishment and a chance to unwind."

"Thanks, but—"

"Wait. You haven't heard my offer yet. I think you need a hot dog followed by the second show at some sleazy neighborhood theatre. Popcorn included."

In spite of the weariness pervading her and the war she was waging against him, she laughed. There had been some subtle change in Turner since she'd started to see him again. It was hard not to like him.

"Popcorn too? I'm not used to that much glamour. But I honestly don't think I'm up to any of it. I'm beat."

"Small wonder. Your shoulders are probably calcified in position. Here." He crossed the small room swiftly, and as their eyes met in a split instant of uncertainty, he began to rub her back so briskly and impersonally that she yelped.

"Say, do you mind not killing me?" she gasped through rattling teeth.

"Sorry." He eased off, but the kneading of his fingers still brought tears to her eyes.

A welcome suppleness seeped back into her muscles. Her body started to relax. She became aware of his hands, still brisk and businesslike but gradually slowing. Just for an instant they rested against her, against the soft skin of her neck, which they had been bruising, and sensations flooded her that had nothing to do with pain or relaxation.

Almost as if he felt it too, Turner stepped away from her.

"How about the first part of my gala evening anyway?" he said. "I'm starving. If you don't feel up to anything after that, I'll take you home."

Laura caught back her composure. Perhaps she'd only imagined that instant. His words, his manner, were that of a friend. The pleasures he was proposing were so safely unromantic. Besides, she was tired.

"All right," she said. "And I hope I never have to wrangle with you over business. You're awfully persuasive."

They ate in a stuffy little diner, seated on stools. Their footlong hot dogs came smothered with onions and relish, dripping their juices over the edge of the small plates that held them. To Laura the atmosphere was a delicious change of pace, a vacation from the sleekness that sometimes seemed to stretch around her like a desert. This was the world apart from Hollywood, which she herself sought out from time to time. Glancing at Turner with his perfectly tended hair and custom-made shirt, she marveled at the thought that he did the same. She certainly could not picture Van Greenberg seated at a lunch counter.

"All right," Turner announced, consulting his watch. "We have time for a dish of ice cream or to make the movie. Which will it be?"

"What's the movie?"

"An old Woody Allen. Umpteenth rerun."

"If you're still good for popcorn, I'll take that."

It had been years since Laura set foot in the kind of theatre he had selected. Tucked between a bakery and a clothing store, it had only one screen and only one feature. The seats folded down, but nothing more. There was even an usher. At the nine-fifteen show, it was two-thirds full, with couples young and old, singles, even a few school children.

Turner caught her wandering gaze and grinned.

"My version of the symphony," he said. "To tell the truth, I don't always care that much about what's playing. It's the place itself I come for."

Laura found herself feeling more light-headed than she should. There were so many facets to him. Seeing this side of him, she could almost forget the man who had forced himself on her in Mexico, or at least she could forgive him. He had been less swaggering these last weeks, less sure of himself, and it moved her. She closed her eyes. She was being an idiot. It would be insane to let herself be charmed by him again. Tomorrow she would harden herself against him. She was too tired tonight.

The show had started long ago. She opened her eyes, turning to study the man beside her in sheltering darkness. His head had fallen to one side. He was breathing deeply. He was asleep.

Laura's own breath caught. There could be but one reason why he'd brought her here tonight. He wanted to be with her. Even asleep. Even in a crowded theatre. She weakened with the knowledge.

Much later, when the houselights came on, she touched his sleeve. He roused slowly at first, then blinked in alertness.

"Did I nod off?" he asked with a laugh that was patently embarrassed. "Now that's what I call the power of suggestion. You yawn, and I fall asleep!"

They followed the tail of the crowd out into an alley. Turner breathed deeply as if to clear his head.

"You're right," said Laura. "It is like the symphony in a way. You can get lost in it."

He nodded slowly. "There's never anyone I know. I like that."

They got into his car in silence.

"Does it strike you that maybe we're a little crazy then? To be doing the work we do if we feel such a need to get away?" she asked.

"No, not at all. Doctors play golf. Business tycoons take trips around the world. I like some of the people I work with, too. But when I get away—completely away—I get recharged. Make any sense?"

"Yes. It's one of the reasons I chose to live where I'm living."

How odd, she thought. Turner seemed so content in his environment, enjoying the big deals, thriving on praise. Everyone liked praise, of course. Maybe there was a contradiction deep in his character that even he didn't recognize.

When they reached the huge old house where she was living, she struggled with impulse. It had been a pleasant evening.

There was an openness between them. And she really was safely indifferent to him.

"Would you like to come in for coffee and cake?" she asked. "Seeing as how we had to pass up ice cream?"

Thoughts shot through Turner's mind. Uppermost among them was the desire to prove his control, to show her he was not the animal she must think him. He deserved the label. Now he wanted to deserve her trust.

"That sounds nice," he said, inclining his head. "This place of yours always looks so interesting from the outside. I'd like to see what the rest of it's like."

She laughed a little breathlessly and slid from the car before he could come around to open the door. He took care to keep sufficient space between them. He had no intention of making her regret this lowering of her guard. With a shock he wondered if he was willing to wait forever for her to come to him. He clamped his mind shut on such thoughts.

"A fireplace," he said as she switched on the lights in the domain that was so distinctively hers. The room was welcoming. Unpretentious. His attention swept the quilt on the wall, which he remembered, and the dining alcove, but his steps continued toward the fireplace with its handsome carved mantel. "Does it work?"

"No, just decoration, I'm afraid."

"Gives the room a spectacular feeling, all the same. You've got lots of room here."

Her eyes looked surprised as he turned to smile at her. They met his for a moment, and he froze, unable to look away. The desire to stay here in this room with her in his arms almost crushed him. He felt safe with Laura—safe even if he dropped the pretense of being always in control. She stirred, moving toward the kitchen.

"It won't take a minute for the coffee to heat," she said. "Make yourself at home."

He pretended to study bric-a-brac and leafy green plants. Coming in here was more of a strain than he had expected. He was mesmerized by the sound of her moving, by the two of them isolated from the world.

Her kitchen was small. He stood in the doorway and watched her move efficiently, taking cups from a cupboard, opening the refrigerator.

"If you don't like the cake, you'll have to blame your very own cookbook," she said. Her voice sounded a shade self-conscious. She was as tense as he was, Turner realized.

"I'm afraid I'll have to take off as soon as I've sampled it," he said in hopes of reassuring her. "Long day for me tomorrow—and you had one today. May I help carry?"

The coffee light had come on. She was filling cups.

"Sure."

She handed him some coffee and a plate of cake in which there was the aroma of raspberry preserves. In the living room they settled in chairs on opposite sides of the fireplace.

All at once there was nothing to say. Turner was painfully aware of her presence and of the silence of the room in which he heard the distant ticking of a clock. She sat so rigidly. He wanted to reach out and touch her and tell her it was all right, that he wouldn't bother her, though his head was growing thick and his mouth felt dry. He wanted to confess his anguish over what he had done and could never expunge. Most of all he wanted to take her in his arms.

Instead he told her that the cake was very good, and she thanked him with a smile that was half-frightened. Her eyes were large, filled with confusion. Was she remembering?

He recalled how her body had felt the first time they made love, and how she had held him, held him as no other woman ever had, seeking, it seemed now, more than mere physical pleasure, striving to touch some part of him that he could not name. The memory of it made him want to cry out. Abruptly he set his empty plate aside and leaned forward, catching her hand.

"Laura . . . I'm so sorry. So sorry for ever hurting you—"

She jerked free of his touch as though it brought contamination. Her breath came quickly. Turner felt his own senses reeling, out of control, sick with the certainty that in that moment of contact he must have revealed to her the desire blazing through him. He bowed his head, unable to speak.

"I'll . . . I'll get more coffee, shall I?" she said. She got up, but he did not see. He sat shaken by the depths of his own incredible blundering.

After some moments she spoke to him, her voice almost a whisper and strangely shy.

"Jake?"

Feeling ancient and clumsy, he looked up. She stood in a

half-open door beyond the fireplace, one arm crossed in front of her as if to draw strength from the solid door frame that it gripped. Slowly Turner absorbed the reality of what he saw. Behind the refuge of that arm, she stood completely naked, her body a soft white column being offered to him with dazzling clarity.

His leg struck a low table as he rose, moving toward her. He did not notice the pain. He did not notice anything. He embraced her with a sense of wonder, shaken by a startling feeling of unworthiness.

"Laura!" he said hoarsely. "Oh, Laura, *Laura*!"

As he spoke her name, Laura knew she had made the right decision. There might be pain, there might be danger, but somehow it had been right.

There had been tenderness in those words. There was tenderness now in his arms as they wrapped around her, sheltering her. This was a different man, a different Jake than the one who had come to Mexico.

"Oh, sweetheart—Laura—" He was covering her hair with kisses. His fingers were shaking. They traced the planes of her face, the curve of her neck with wonder.

"I've missed you so, I've wanted you so—" Suddenly his hands held her face as though he would never let her go, and he kissed her fiercely.

Laura felt months of denied desires flooding her. She opened her mouth to him. Their tongues wound around each other until they were lost in the vortex of some whirlpool spinning them toward another world.

The bed. The feel of her quilted spread, not even thrown back. She clung to Jake even as he slid from his clothes. They rubbed against each other. They gasped with mutual need. He bowed his rust-red head between her legs and kissed her.

But it was not the sharp caresses of his tongue she hungered for. She urged his head up gently, fingers tangling in his hair. Their mouths met again, bringing her to the brink of orgasm. She writhed between him, wild with the feel, the wonderful pressure of bone and flesh. He entered her so slowly it drove her mad. She was lost, her body pitching upward to receive him, and as the world spun and he cried her name, she was drunk with the wondrous knowledge that he was equally lost in her.

They lay, and Laura could feel their two hearts beating. It

made her think of something primitive. It made her feel free
of all restraints, of all practicality.

"Did I hurt you?" he whispered, smoothing back her hair,
which she only now realized was damp at the temples.

She shook her head.

"No."

This was a different man. Concern showed in his face, even
in this room whose darkness was relieved only by a faint ray
from the distant living room. She felt welded to him, as though
this coupling had made them a part of each other no matter
how much time and space might come between them.

As though feeling it too, he bent his head reverently to the
soft outer curve of her breast, kissing it over and over, each
time with infinite gentleness, until she moaned.

"Eddie, you know the answer."

Nel's voice sounded tired. That was how Eddie meant to
get his way with her, by wearing her down. She was the stub-
bornest woman he'd ever known, but he'd win yet.

They were lounging on the king-sized bed in his new apartment, Nel at the head and him at the foot. They were both
fully clothed, just in from the early show at a supper club, and
Nel looked in fine spirits. She enjoyed this continual jousting,
Eddie thought.

Leaning on one elbow, she tried to look fierce.

"I've already told you I'm not going to marry you," she
said.

The topaz ring glittered against her finger. Eddie saw her
eyes slide to it, and he smiled inwardly at the way she waved
it about like a duchess.

"But that was last week," he argued affably. "This is this
week. Now listen, we could be on a plane to Reno tomorrow
and have the whole weekend. Why not say yes?"

Her eyes had filled with tears.

"You know why, Eddie."

"No, I don't. None of the reasons you've given me make
any sense."

Her palms struck the bed beneath her, and she sat up.

"Then you haven't been listening! What's the point in marrying you when I may not be alive next year, even next month?
What's the point in it?"

Yes, what was the point? Eddie wondered. In spite of her illness, Nel might outlive him—no, probably would. So was it fair of him to hound her? He'd turned the question over in his mind a thousand times and still knew only that marrying her was what he wanted. If her illness was long, there would be bills to pay, and he didn't know what sort of savings she'd accumulated. His insurance might as well care for Nel as fatten some church he hadn't been to in years. He wanted to take care of her, and by joining them together now, he wanted to make up for all those years when they'd been estranged.

With his eyes, he nestled her against him. He thought he understood her fear.

"Life's frigging uncertain for all of us, Nellie. I don't figure that's any reason for not living it." Reaching out, he took her hand between his own. "The point is, Nel, it would mean a lot to me. Nothing else has to change if you don't want it to. You can go ahead living with Jessamyn, working if you like. We don't have to tell anyone. We can be the only ones who know about it if that's your style. But I want this, Nel. I want to know that you and I are . . . something special."

Nel spoke with her usual gruffness, but her hand lingered in his.

"Come on, Eddie. You and I are something special anyway, aren't we? We don't need to prove it by going to Reno."

One slender leg was tucked beneath her. Her legs had always been so sexy.

"Don't we?" He let his fingers trace the long, sleek contour he was admiring. "What if you get me so worked up I have a stroke here in this bed and die first? Look a lot better if we were husband and wife."

She slanted him a look.

"Think there's much danger of that, do you?"

Eddie smiled. "Yeah." He slid his hand on up, tracing her thigh. "So what about it, Nel? You going to marry me?"

She closed her eyes and leaned back on the bed. Shamelessly, wickedly, she enjoyed his overtures.

"Maybe," she teased.

He watched her face, but it gave him no clue.

"Does that mean yes?"

"It means maybe, Eddie."

* * *

Laura wakened reluctantly, suffused with an extraordinary sense of well-being. Her back was sheltered by the solidness of Jake's chest.

"Awake at last," he said.

She twisted onto her back and looked at him. He was propped on one elbow, watching her. For how long? she wondered.

"Is it very late?" she asked.

"Not very."

He smoothed her hair and kissed her forehead lightly. She turned her face against the warmth of him. For moments they lay merely holding each other.

It's different this time, Laura thought. Has Jake changed? Have I?

All the protection she had sought to build for herself she had now destroyed. She could be hurt, but she did not care. Nothing worth having came without risks.

"I don't deserve this," he said against her hair. "I'm not a very admirable person—you know that. I want to tell you I'll never hurt you again, Laura, but I can't. I don't know. I can't promise. I know myself well enough to realize there are ugly sides to me."

His humility touched her. She pressed a hand against his cheek.

"No expectations," she whispered.

He raised his mouth and kissed her. Like a single bolt of lightning, she felt desire strike them both. In a frenzy of movement they joined themselves, touching, exploring, and her thoughts grew disjointed, ceased to exist, as the seminal river crashed into her.

At length Jake stirred and moved gently away.

"We'd better get up, or we're likely to lose a whole day," he said. "If you want to shower, I'll get some coffee going."

When she came out of the bedroom, bathed and dressed, Jake was in the kitchen. He leaned against the counter, reading the morning paper. There was fresh coffee on the counter as well as orange juice, and he had made toast.

"Want to share?" he asked, passing her the front page of the paper. "I figure we can spare about five minutes before we take off."

"You don't need to drive me. You'll be late yourself."

"Not very. Besides, I'm the boss in my little piece of turf, and I never schedule appointments until the people I deal with have been up long enough to feel friendly."

She looked at the paper, sipping her coffee. It's too perfect, she thought, savoring the quiet of the kitchen, the easy companionship of them standing there together. Four minutes later she brushed her teeth, and they left.

As they drew to a stop in front of the studio, Jake reached across the seat, detaining her.

"Am I invited back tonight?"

She swallowed. No expectations. She must remember.

"I'll fix dinner," she said. "You've never tried my cooking."

"Good. I'll be there when I can."

They parted like two people in a car pool.

It was a grim day at the studio. Maxy was called to the producer's office twice to confer about upcoming episodes of *Twenty-two Wentworth*—episodes that Maxy, Laura, and Adam, and the secretary thought were sure to grab an audience. Now word was filtering down from the top that those episodes needed more "life."

"Whatever the hell that is," Maxy grumbled.

They sat without looking at one another. The prognosis was not good. *Wentworth* had regained some of the ratings lost to the sitcom, and in the last week three important critics had praised the show, particularly the writing. But inside the industry, gallows humor held that critical praise was the kiss of death. Those aware of dramatic excellence—or lack of it— were not the people who plopped in their easy chairs and, with remote-control button in hand, flipped through the channels until some flash of action grabbed them. Against her will Laura began to share Adam's view that the show would be cancelled. She was glad, at the end of the day, to put all thought of it behind her, steeping herself in the joy of picking up groceries for the evening ahead.

She had changed into slacks, and the table was set before she heard Jake's knock.

"Ummm, am I glad to see you!" he said, encircling her waist with one arm and kissing her. "Christ, I didn't even think to stop for a bottle of wine or anything.

"No problem, I'm well supplied. But would you like to relax for a few minutes first?"

"I would, as a matter of fact."

He threw himself down on the sofa and stretched out his legs, his head dropping back wearily against the cushions.

Laura sat beside him in silence. The hand holding hers was tense. He was so tightly wound, she thought with a frown. Was that the price of success? Was he like this every day?

It occurred to her how little she knew about him. She sat quietly watching his face, wondering what Jake Turner was really like. After a few minutes she realized he was asleep. Gently she freed her hand from his and picked up the parts of the paper she'd not had time for that morning.

After half an hour she woke him. While he went into the bathroom to wash his face, she poured two goblets of wine and left them in front of the couch, returning to the kitchen to turn on the stove.

"What are we having? I'm starved," he said from the doorway.

He was sipping wine and holding her glass out to her, content to keep her company as she worked, it seemed.

"Fettucine Alfredo." She gave a small smile. "It's sort of a test."

"Test?" His eyes were questioning, but he grinned. "Sounds wonderful."

He took two plates of salad from her hands and carried them to the table. They sipped wine in the kitchen while the pasta cooked, talking about their respective days.

"What will you do if *Wentworth* folds?" he asked.

"Worry about it when it happens. I'm getting looser."

She looked at him impishly, and he saluted her with his wine.

"I hope so. Say, are you torturing me? I'm going to die on the spot if you don't slip me a taste of that."

They took more than an hour over dinner, with Jake telling her all about Bernie Goldman and the recent presentation of his jogging suit. In the course of it he finished two more help-ings of fettucine. Afterward they continued to talk until Laura rose to get coffee, declining his offer of help.

"Do you know," he said, catching her by the waist on her return and pulling her down into his lap, "I can't think why it was I ever took you to restaurants." His eyes were teasing. His lips sought hers and lingered. "This is much better in every way."

Laura felt the pressure of his body against her own, of his blunt hands pressing her waist.

"Is it?"

"Mmmm."

They kissed again, tasting each other.

"You're likely to get cold coffee this way."

His forefinger traced the line of her jaw and then her neck.

"I can do without. And you?"

She nodded.

He kissed her violently, urging her deeper into the recesses of his lap, closer against him. Later she could not even remember how they reached the bedroom.

The satisfaction of their lovemaking filled her and wound around her like a luxurious comforter, spoiling her senses for anything else. She felt Jake leave the bed and wondered, not very energetically, how much time had passed. It must have been hours. It must be in the middle of the night. She had never been so happy. She had never felt so much a part of another person.

The bedside lamp went on.

"Sit up, babe, or you're going to slop this all over you."

Jake stood before her, completely naked, adroitly balancing a bowl in each hand. She recognized the macerated fruit she'd prepared for dessert.

"What are you, crazy?" she asked with a laugh. She scooted to a sitting position.

He came around and slid beneath the sheets again, a grin on his face.

"The soul of thoughtfulness, I'd say." He licked juice from a finger tip. "This was for dinner, I presume? My impoverished childhood makes me loath to waste good food."

"I can't believe you!" She leaned forward over her bowl, trying to curtail her merriment.

"You can't get service like this in a restaurant. I'll bet you've never eaten without a stitch on before this, now have you?"

"No." She laughed again, blood rising to her cheeks. She wanted to ask if he had, but didn't. She preferred to think that this, at least, he'd done with no one but her.

"Do you know that so far it appears you're wonderful at everything you try?" he said. "Of course I can only judge you on writing, cooking, and one other thing."

She set her empty dish on the night stand.

"That's good. That means if *Wentworth* folds and I can't get another writing job, I have a chance at catering or one other thing."

"Don't even say that." He kissed her temple, lips lingering on the pulse that beat beneath her skin. "Oh, Christ, but I love you, Laura!"

Fifteen 🦚

At eleven o'clock on a Friday morning, the axe fell on *Twenty-two Wentworth*. The producer came down in person to announce the show had been cancelled. Only two more episodes, already on film, would be aired.

"Sons of bitches," said Maxy. "The whole bloody network's run by sons of bitches. I wouldn't mind that if they weren't all stupid to boot."

Laura thought of the spate of reviews complimenting the show in the last month. Two of them had even singled out different scripts of hers for praise. That and a dollar would get her a cup of coffee. The big question was, would it get her another job, or would she be faced with those dreary offers of the casting couch again?

She watched Adam packing the contents of his desk, slowly, methodically.

"Hey, Adam, let's go somewhere and get smashed," she said.

He looked up with his usual sour expression.

"No thanks. I intend to get my ass cracking after another job this afternoon. If you've got any sense, you'll do the same."

Turning her back on him, she made a face. *Cram it, Adam.* She walked into her cubicle and opened a desk drawer. Out of sight, but not out of earshot, Tracy the secretary was tapping at her IBM Selectric. Shows came and shows went, but she was a cog in the studio typing pool.

Laura listened to her clicking keys and looked through the open door at Adam, still packing precisely. She herself felt the urge to dump the contents of her desk into a box and be done with it. An episode in her life was finished. Over. She longed for the action that would symbolize it. Instead she reached into the drawer and started to pack item by item.

Nel yawned and stretched, feeling warm inside from Eddie's loving, gloating over the pile of letters she'd typed that morning. The phone beside her rang. She answered smiling.

"Miss Friday's residence."

At first she thought she had gotten a breather. Then a man's voice spoke with a briskness that attempted to mask uncertainty.

"This is Jake Turner. Is Laura there?"

"Laura?" She was so startled that she betrayed herself. "No, why?"

"There's no answer at her apartment. I thought she might be with you." He seemed to weigh further comment and then said heavily, "Her show's been cancelled."

"Oh, no," she said. "Oh, shit!" Damn it, *damn it*, she thought bitterly. "Well, I'm glad I know," she said. "If she does turn up, is there a message?"

"No. Just that I'm sorry. Thanks."

Nel hung up. The fineness of her morning had been spoiled. The news of Laura's loss was enough of a blow, but Nel was just as upset to learn that Laura was seeing Turner again. Didn't the girl have any sense? Couldn't she see that he wasn't the sort to take his involvement with a woman seriously? True, he had seemed concerned about her just now, Nel acknowledged grudgingly, but she had seen enough of men to know that he and Laura operated on two different wavelengths.

If that wasn't enough, there was the fact that he actually seemed about to embark on this project with Jess. Nel knew the sort of tricks of which Jess was capable. She didn't like the direction of this at all.

"What are you shaking your head about?"

Jessamyn breezed into the room, a dog in one arm. She always came in without knocking. It was her house; it was her right. This time, though, Nel had to struggle to keep from scowling.

"Just thinking." Nel knew she would find it hard to like Jess if she watched her savor the news about *Wentworth* folding. Instead she waved at the neat stack of letters. "You in the mood to sign these, or you want me to forge?"

Jessamyn sank into a chair, one leg tucked under her. She laughed and shook back her hair.

"When was the last time you knew of me signing letters, Nel?"

Nel shrugged. "Just wondered."

Bored by him now, Jessamyn dropped the dog in her arms onto the floor where he yelped and after a moment of piteous hopefulness waddled away.

"Since you're so efficient today, how about doing one more letter? I think it's about time I answered poor sweet Giorgio, don't you? And I don't want to phone."

Nel snorted. "Poor sweet Giorgio" was a sloe-eyed Italian count whose physical appetites were as excessive as Jessamyn's. They had met the last time Jessamyn was working in Italy, and he and Jess had kept each other well-amused.

"So are you going to join him for a peek at his new little villa?" Nel asked.

"No . . . no, I don't think so. I've got things to see to here that interest me more."

Some subtlety in her tone made Nel uneasy. Taking sides between Jess and Laura was something she'd always sworn she'd never do, but it was time to end this shadow boxing. If Jess intended to be a stinker, she wanted to know it.

"I hope those interests don't include Jake Turner," she said clearly.

With studied slowness, Jessamyn turned her head. The eyes famed for their lazy softness were open now and endlessly hard, and Nel knew Jessamyn was surprised by this intrusion.

"And if they do?"

Nel heard the warning to back off, but she ignored it. For once in her life she was going to meddle.

"If it's just his project, no problem—though I do doubt it was worth giving Stan the pitch," she said. "If it's Turner himself, use some common decency, Jess. You're forty-six years old. He's seeing your *daughter*!"

There was silence, profound and frozen. In slow, regal anger, Jessamyn rose.

"I'll forget that, Nel, because we've been together a long time. But don't ever presume to lecture me again. And don't stick your nose in my personal concerns unless I ask you to!"

Her voice was huskier than Nel had ever heard it, almost hoarse. Seconds squeezed past, and Nel felt the straining of some fragile thread between them. If she ever raised this subject again—if she ever crossed Jess in any way—that thread would snap. Oddly, Nel found herself hoping that wouldn't happen.

At first Laura contemplated merely letting the telephone ring. She sat watching as it filled her quiet apartment with its voice. She wanted to be alone now, to regroup, to gather strength for once again starting the struggle of finding a job. It hurt being told your show wasn't good enough to go on with. Even knowing how quickly the good shows died and that high network execs were given the pitch just as easily hurt. Sighing, she stood up and answered the phone on the twelfth ring.

"Laura?" It was Jake. "I just heard," he said. "Are you okay?"

"Oh, sure. Trying to wax philosophical about it all." The words came tightly from her chest despite her efforts.

"I'm sorry. You deserved to have your first show last a little longer."

"Ummm. Well, hopefully it won't be as hard to find something else this time around."

"Of course not. Look, there's someone here to see me. I'm going to get away as soon as I can. I can be at your place by five, I should think. We'll drive up the coast and have dinner somewhere. Meanwhile remember, the first time's the hardest."

"I suppose so. Bye."

She had hardly returned to her chair when Nel called.

"I'm sorry, kiddo. Tough luck."

"Oh, well, I got my foot in the door anyway. How did you find out?"

"Jake Turner called hunting you."

Laura could hear the unspoken question coming at her through the phone. Nel wanted to know what the hell was going on in her private life.

Instinctively Laura knew Nel must be thinking she was taking a risk with Jake. Nel was probably right. But she was not going to think about that now. She was going to cling, for the moment, to what she had.

"He just found me," she said. "He's going to take me for a drive up the coast so I'll get through the crisis as painlessly as possible. I'm not super depressed, I promise. I know the facts of life out here."

"Okay, but if you need a shoulder to cry on, come on over."

"Thanks, Nellie. It makes me feel better just knowing you're rooting for me."

"Hell, yes. I expect to be well taken care of when you hit it rich."

Laura hung up smiling. How could she feel blue when she had two people who cared for her? Nel she had always been able to count on, but Jake's thoughtfulness in the week since they had become lovers filled her with a disbelieving happiness. She had seen a gentle side of him, a private side she hadn't known existed.

Drifting to the bathroom, she turned on the tub. She sat on the edge and thought of the pleased look on Jake's face when he'd brought her the set of wineglasses two nights ago. He had told her he'd make no promises, but she did not believe he'd ever intentionally hurt her. He was pragmatic, but he was not cruel. Did Jake really know himself at all?

Yes, maybe. Laura lay back in an extravagant depth of water and faced the fact that there was perhaps a dark side to him as well as a light. Only time would tell which side predominated.

The doorbell rang at a quarter past four. Laura got down two of the wineglasses Jake had brought her and set them on the low table by the fireplace before she answered.

"It's a perfect day for a drive—" she began, stopping as she saw Van Greenberg standing there.

"I was hoping I'd find you here," he said. "I heard the bad news. May I come in?"

He did so with no apparent intention of seating himself. The jacket of his three-piece suit was thrust back as he stood with hands on hips, looking toward the window. He never really seemed at ease here, Laura thought.

"Laura, I've been doing some thinking," he said. "Jobs are a little hard to come by just now. It may take a while before you find something else. I want you to consider moving in with me until you do. Or if you'd rather, I'll provide a separate place for you."

He stopped, and for the first time ever, Laura saw the edges of his mouth draw together and then relax, as though he felt the need to swallow.

"I realize we've not been intimate," he said. "But then we don't get on that badly, do we? Perhaps this is as good a time as any to move ahead."

"Are you out of your mind?" she asked, tact failing her.

"Yes, perhaps I am." He gave a tight smile. "As you know, I make it a practice to avoid emotion in my alliances. I find that growing difficult with you."

"Van . . . I'm seeing someone else."

His blue eyes flickered with an emotion she could not read.

"Yes, I thought so. As you must have gathered by now, I'm not too easily intimidated. I want to take care of you, Laura. Whoever this other man is, I'm confident I can manage that better than he can."

The doorbell rang. She turned her head.

"Think about it," Van said, and touched her hand.

For a moment she felt confusion. He showed precious little confidence in her ability—in herself in general—to suppose she'd take the easy way out, which he was offering. Yet his refusal to waver, even after having his ego bruised, was hard to ignore.

As she opened the door, Jake's arms reached for her, then stopped. His gaze passed over her shoulder to settle on Van.

"I'm early. Obviously," he said stiffly.

Hostile currents flashed between the two men.

"I think you know each other . . ." she commenced and stopped as Jake's eyes shifted to something else in the room. Turning, she saw the two glasses she had set out to welcome him, and with sick perception knew he must think they had been emptied and left there by her and Van.

Jake's face was drained of color.

"I didn't realize you'd be busy," he said. "I'll stop some other time." Without another word he spun back toward the hall.

Laura ran after him.

"Jake! Wait!"

"What for?" He faced her savagely. "You told me you didn't expect me to stop by uninvited. I guess I forgot."

The front door slammed.

With anguish ripping her, Laura turned slowly back to the apartment. Van stood in the same spot, smiling slightly.

"Well, I gather I've upset the balance of things," he said.

Sixteen

"*I lost my* temper, didn't I?"

Jake Turner felt awkwardness flood him as Laura stepped back from the door and let him enter. She was wearing a silky robe, not quite secured at the waist, and she looked bemused. It was ten in the morning, but he knew he had awakened her.

"I . . . Christ, Laura." He stopped to swallow the lump that was blocking his throat, and he was afraid. He searched the vast depths of her green-gray eyes and saw the pain there. Uncertainly he put his arms around her, his whole body breathing with relief when she did not pull away. They stood pressed against each other. He savored the coolness of her cheek. "I guess I've never suffered from jealousy before," he said thickly. "I saw him here and I—"

"Van stopped by because he'd heard the news about *Wentworth*, Jake. That's all. When he rang, I thought it was you."

He smothered his face against her hair. "I'm sorry I got you out of bed. I wanted to see you. Are you all right?"

Moving slightly away, she drew him into the living room with a wan smile.

"A little hung over, but otherwise fine. I could do with some coffee if you'd be nice enough to bring it."

He went to the kitchen where the full pot sat waiting on its electric timer.

"I tried to call last night," he said. "It didn't take me long to realize I'd been an ass."

"I went out with Adam." Cautiously she shook her head. "Can you beat that? He was his usual nasty self when I suggested having a few belts right after the word came. And then last night the doorbell rang and there he was—him and his lover. They took me to a gay bar, and we all got smashed. What time is it?"

"Late. That's why I stopped by. I'm leaving town for a few

148

days, and I wanted to see you first. Jessamyn's agreed to do that picture for me, and I'm off to find a location."

"Oh."

Turner could hear the sudden tightness in her voice and was half-amused. Catching her hand, he kissed the fingers.

"Don't you think there's been about enough jealousy for both of us?"

"It's different with Jessamyn?"

"Different? How? My God, Laura, you don't suppose I'd have anything to do with Jessamyn now, except in business, do you? I'm not that dissolute."

Wincing inwardly, Turner recalled that he had kissed both mother and daughter. In fact he had desired both. Well, they were both desirable women. He'd keep his interest in Jessamyn strictly professional now, though. He was no saint, but he didn't want to hurt Laura—didn't even want, he thought with surprise, to do anything that might offend her.

Across her coffee her gaze was penetrating. It made him feel uncomfortable, as though she could see his secrets. As though there was a stain on him that he didn't want to acknowledge.

"You don't know what Jessamyn's capable of," she said.

The stubbornness of her words gave him a moment of uneasiness. Averting his eyes, he lighted a cigarette. Perhaps she knew Jessamyn better than he did; he was starting to believe so. By Hollywood's fecund grapevine, Turner had heard that the loss of several big advertisers had been a major factor in the network's decision to cancel *Wentworth*. He also knew that one of them, a big cosmetics firm, had recently signed Jessamyn for a series of ads. Was there a connection? He suspected so.

Damn her, he thought bitterly. How could anyone deliberately hurt Laura? He felt a surge of something akin to hate.

But he couldn't afford to hate Jessamyn. He needed her to realize his dream. With her as the star of *Helen Somebody*, he had no doubt that he would establish himself as a producer of top quality. Only then would he have completely slain the ghosts of the past. Only when he had made it to the top.

For a moment guilt nagged him because of Laura. She deserved more loyalty than he was giving her. It was incredible that her gentleness had survived what Jessamyn had condemned her to—a life of no warmth, no one to call her own, no one to cling to. Sometimes he wanted to let her cling to him, only he was afraid of it, too. What if he wasn't strong enough for them both? What if he couldn't be all that a woman like Laura wanted a man to be?

Taking her in his arms, he kissed her, bringing the long, unhappy silence between them to an end.

"I love you," he said gently. He was thinking. Perhaps there was something he could do to make things up to Laura.

Eddie nodded his thanks and drew the tickets across the counter at the travel bureau. He'd given his name as Paul Tully, and he'd paid cash. He'd purchased two tickets just in case he could talk Nel into going with him. Now, as he pocketed them, he sighed, looked out at the rush-hour crowds passing just beyond the plate-glass window.

It was deliberate, his choosing to take care of business at a time when the sidewalks were mobbed. He didn't think they'd try to get to him then, with people around. The chances were too great. Whoever they'd hired could be caught or traced easily. So he felt safe, yet still uneasy. He'd been in LA for some time now, with no hint of anyone watching him. Logic told Eddie Brown that was too good to buy.

He knew he'd broken the rules by coming here. In Detroit they'd urged him to go to Atlanta, Harlem, somewhere where he'd be just another black face. Eddie's mouth stiffened with the stupid bigotry of that assumption. Do you tell a redhead all redheads look alike? It was there, among his own people, that he'd most likely be recognized.

In the Hollywood environs, he'd rationalized, every face on the street looked excitingly familiar, mostly because they were expected to by the starstruck populace of LA. Maybe there was some truth in his reasoning, but mostly he suspected it had been an excuse to be with Nel. Once he'd caught track of her after all those years, nothing on earth would have kept him away.

Eddie smiled as he thought of her, then froze. A largely built woman who might be a man—blond hair, white shell knit sweater and skirt never meant to contain a figure like hers—was watching him, her gaze not flickering. The changing light gave her passage. Eddie turned on the ball of his foot and started back up the street, trying to move with no show of concern, making his way toward an arcade. Once inside he could duck into one of the shops or out on the other side. From there he could continue to the parking garage where he'd left his car.

He paused and looked in a store window. The woman behind him was closing in. He began to walk again, more rapidly. Ten steps... six... he swung toward the arcade. From the corner of his eyes he caught the flash of blond hair as a body jostled his.

"Excuse me," said a voice. "Aren't you Richard Pryor?"

The woman who blocked his way peered up at him with undisguised excitement.

Eddie felt his whole body go limp. Still geared to a threat, which now proved nonexistent, he opened his mouth to tell this woman he was a good six inches taller than the man she thought he was. But suddenly the irony of the situation touched him. Relief made him lighthearted.

"Sure am," he said. "Would you like my autograph?"

Fumbling, she produced a tourist brochure, and Eddie signed it with a flourish. He hoped this moment was never spoiled for her by seeing the actor's real signature. Then for good measure, and because he was still alive, he kissed her cheek.

"There you go, dear. Have a very nice evening."

"Where's Eddie?"

Nel waved a breezy hand. "He couldn't make it. Gee, but you know how to make a friend feel important."

Laura laughed and sank onto a lounge chair by Jessamyn's pool. Not half an hour before she'd called from downtown to see if Nel could meet her for dinner, but Nel, explaining that Jessamyn was about to depart for the evening with some count named Giorgio, had suggested she come here instead.

"I'm exhausted and I'm famished," she said, hanging her tongue out. "I don't know which is worse, working or hunting work."

"I can answer that one," Nel said cheerfully. "The hunting is. Once you find something you can slack off shamelessly. Just witness me."

They both laughed then, and Laura looked affectionately at Nel. They hadn't seen much of each lately. Too busy with our respective men, she thought.

"So have some of Lupita's goodies," Nel said, waving. "You know she'll be insulted if you don't stuff yourself."

But Laura found that all thoughts of food had vanished. She stared in amazement at Nel's forearm. No, she could not be imagining it. The smooth brown skin was rippling in small waves.

"Good grief, Nellie! What's wrong?" she gasped.

Nel looked down quickly and clamped her free hand over it.

"Just a little muscle spasm. I'm getting too damn old."

"Are you sure? It doesn't look like any muscle spasm I've ever seen. I think you'd better have a doctor check it. Really, Nel."

"Check what? Is something wrong, Nel?" Jessamyn's voice was unexpectedly intrusive. And, Laura realized as she turned to look at the woman poised by the patio door, it held an anxiety that was unmistakably genuine.

"Thought you'd be long gone with Giorgio," Nel drawled, avoiding the question.

"He's late—as usual. Probably knocking a piece off with some young boy in the back of his Rolls." Coming to the bar, Jessamyn popped open a split of champagne. "What should you have a doctor check, Nel?"

With a snort, Nel hunted for her cigarette holder. "All right, all right, if you both insist on knowing my darkest secrets, I'll tell you. I thought I could try a new twist to my walking-on-hands routine. I tried going down the steps. Looks like I'm too old a dog for that trick. I must've pulled something."

Laura struggled to suppress a chuckle. Jessamyn looked vexed.

"For heaven's sake, Nel, can't you act your age?"

"Starting today," Nel promised serenely.

For a moment there was no sound but the faint drone of the air conditioning. Laura watched her mother's eyes flit toward her and saw that the displeasure in them was more blatant than in days gone by. She felt like an annoying insect, intruding where she was not wanted, and before she could stop it, her age began to roll backwards. Twenty-five... twenty-four... twenty-three... twenty-two....

"So you're going to do Jake's movie," she said, ending the regression before she became a child again, unequal to Jessamyn.

Jessamyn gave a careless laugh, a laugh that dismissed her. "So he tells me. He asked me to go with him scouting locations, but poor Giorgio had just flown in to see me, so I said no."

Her smile was secretive, and Laura found herself sitting straighter, her breath choked from her. Then she realized that Jessamyn was faking. Of course she was. Laura had no doubts that Jake's interest in her mother was and would be confined to business. Still, she began to see what easy prey she could be to such doubts, with Jessamyn taking every chance to fuel them, and Jake and Jessamyn working together.

She mustn't fall into the trap. She had to stay calm. Yet she now viewed the weeks just ahead as a walk on a tightrope.

Jake Turner grinned down at Laura. She looked perfect today, like an exquisite painting, that breathtaking air of quality enhanced by the simplicity of her white silk blouse and the long rope of pearls knotted low beneath its collar. She made him feel so good—not because he was smart or successful, but because she loved him. The sun seemed to bounce from the brick floor of the restaurant patio ahead of them, firing the outlines of her hair with glints of red.

"Hey," he said. "I've just decided this is a waste of time. We could be back in bed right now."

He watched with enjoyment as embarrassed pleasure washed her cheeks.

"Not a chance," she said. "You're the one who suggested lunch. Besides, here comes the headwaiter."

Turner laughed. He was in fine spirits. He'd found a wonderful spot for shooting his film, and in the forty-eight hours since his return, he'd also accomplished the next major item on his list, the one for Laura. That is, he had if his hunch was right.

His eyes moved quickly across the tables gathered beneath a huge Brazilian pepper tree. He spotted several people he knew before his gaze came to rest on a man whose wiry fringe of hair stuck out like wings behind his ears.

"How about something over there in the shade," said Turner to the headwaiter. As he'd expected, the man with the wings of hair looked up and recognized him as they came near.

"Jake!" he said, breaking into a smile. "How are you?"

"Just fine, Dan. I'd forgotten this was one of your favorite watering holes."

From the front as well as the back, the man at the table

looked like a stereotype of a mad scientist, except that his eyes were lucid and very alert.

"I just got here," he said. "Why don't you join me? Or are you here to talk business?"

Turner raised an eyebrow at Laura, who nodded acquiescence.

"We'd like that. Thanks." So far his luck was amazing.

When they were seated, Turner made introductions. Dan Katz's smile took on a quizzical look as he peered at Laura.

"I've met you once before," he said. "You were with Michael Townes."

Turner chuckled at Laura's chagrin.

"Yes, he needed a date on the spur of the moment, and I was drafted." The tight compression of her lips showed her embarrassment.

Katz sat back, his smile broadening slightly.

"Well, I'm relieved to know that's how it was," he said. "Nothing against Michael, you understand, but I've always heard he doesn't like girls." He winked at Laura. "I trust Jake does, and I must say I envy him. Despite the white hair I can still remember what fun was."

Laura looked as amused as she did delighted. She sought Turner's eyes, and he knew she was thinking that here was a rare man indeed to have retired so gracefully from the chase. Katz was probably no more than sixty, and there were men far older than that who still made fools of themselves. Their aversion to hedonism was something Katz and Laura had in common.

"Laura's a writer, Dan," he said. "Most recently for *Twenty-two Wentworth*."

"That's too bad, my dear. Although I confess I never saw the show, from all I've heard it was quite good." He turned to Jake. "And what are you up to these days? I just got back from Paris, and I've heard a rumor that you may be doing something with Jessamyn Friday."

Turner inclined his head to light a cigarette.

"That's right."

Over lunch they talked about residuals and satellite piracy, a matter to which Katz was devoting a great deal of study. Katz asked Laura about her work before *Wentworth*, so he was at least mildly interested in her, Turner thought.

He'd never known exactly what to make of Katz. The man

was a loner, though Turner had always found him pleasant company. It was true he never chased after girls half his age, but on occasion he turned up with a woman of his own vintage. He had a reputation in the business for being uncomfortably ethical.

That part would work in Laura's favor, he decided. Maybe they were two of a kind.

At last Katz looked at his digital Rollex.

"Well, I've got to be on my way," he said with a sigh.

Tossing his napkin onto the table, he stood up. "Look, I'm having a little party Saturday—cold cuts beside the pool. I'd like the two of you to come if you can make it. Why don't you bring some of your scripts for me to look at, Laura? Or leave them by my office if you'd rather. I'd like to see your work, in case I hear of an opening before you do."

"He's nice," said Laura as he walked out of the patio.

"Very."

Turner grinned, wondering what she'd say if she knew how he'd planned this.

Seventeen

Nel recognized the lilt in Laura's voice the moment she said hello.

"Well, Nellie," she continued on the same happy note. "Guess who's going to write a movie!"

Thank God, thought Nel as she sat back in her chair. When the series folded, she had been more worried than she wanted Laura to know. With each passing day the agony of wondering whether Laura would find something else had increased until Nel had almost been driven to biting her well-tended nails.

"High class," she said.

Laura laughed. "Low security. They can cancel out any time they want. But it's something at the moment, and at the moment I'm awfully pleased with myself."

"So tell me all about it. How did you land it?"

"Jake introduced me to Daniel Katz. Ever hear of him?"

"No."

"He's really a sweetheart, a veep for programming, but ultra nice. He referred me to someone at Peppridge Productions about the *Gauntley* series.

"They couldn't use me—or didn't want to—but they're also packaging this movie, and they offered to give me a crack at it. It's sort of a clinker, to tell you the truth. The book they want to adapt has a wonderful situation but zero plot. I won't be surprised if it doesn't go beyond treatment. It's a chance, though, and it keeps me from pounding the streets, so I intend to keep my fingers crossed while I'm typing.

"Now. What's new with you?"

"Not much." Nel watched a pencil seesaw on one outstretched finger. "A few minutes later and you might have missed me. I'm running out early, heading up to Solvang with Eddie."

"Ah, to have such a leisurely life! Think of me and feel guilty when you're eating ableskivers."

Nel chuckled. "Might even bring you back a couple if Eddie's buying."

They said goodbye, and she looked impatiently at her watch. Damn him, the man was keeping her waiting!

Probably doubling back down an alley somewhere. She didn't know why he was always doing it; he didn't even use the same route to his apartment twice in a row. She'd teased him about it, and he'd said it was just habit, the cop in him. Smiling fondly, she shook her head.

Nel went to the window, and while she waited for Eddie she gave herself over to a curiosity that had nibbled at her all morning. She hadn't seen fit to share it with Laura, but she was nosy beyond endurance over yesterday's unexplained visit by Stan Weisbecker. It had shocked her when Jessamyn fired her agent of long-standing, and Nel had never really learned what caused the parting. Now, after two months, he turned up. "Jess wanted to see me," he'd said sourly, so she'd known Jessamyn had called him herself. An hour later, when he'd left, Stan had still looked out of sorts while Jessamyn looked positively smug.

Nel scented something afoot, some plot of Jessamyn's. Maybe that was what had kept her in Jess's employ all these years, she reflected. The pay was good, she was treated well, and it was so damn interesting. Day-to-day she witnessed more intrigues than in all the soaps put together.

A car engine purred outside as Eddie arrived. Nel walked out filled with pleasure at being alive.

"Say there, Nel, I missed you last night."

Eddie's voice was low as he came around the car to help her in. His hands touched her waist, caressing her as though she were naked, making her suddenly regret the night apart.

"Shoulder better?" she asked.

"Yeah, fine."

It had hurt like sin just yesterday, her shoulder and her neck along with it. She had insisted on the privacy of her own bed, and he had agreed. Rheumatism, she thought. Or the other.

Inside the car Eddie made no move to start the engine.

"Hey," he said. "Let's forget this Norwegian place and go to Las Vegas."

Nel yawned. "Thought we'd agreed not to talk about that anymore."

"You agreed. I never did. But okay, if I can't sell you on Las Vegas, what about Washington? It takes a few days longer, but they still do weddings."

"Washington!" Nel sat up, dropping her pretense of boredom. Her eyes grew shrewd. "Oh, let me get the picture! Congress starts again next week. You've got to get back. That line you were giving about how nobody'd have to know we were married, how I could go on living my own life and working for Jessamyn, that was a come-on! You thought you could transplant me all along!"

Eddie's expression was sober. "I never planned to transplant you, Nel. I'm quitting Congress. I'm flying back next week to make the announcement. That's why I figured you might as well come along."

For once she was too flabbergasted for a comeback.

"What?"

"I'm resigning. Getting out. I'm tired of the rat race."

Nel stared at him, at the man who had brought Detroit's poor blacks a high roll of housing projects, work training programs, clinics, and other aid.

"You can't be serious, Eddie!" Another thought chilled her, leaving its mark on her voice. "You're not going back to police work, are you? Not after all this time!"

He laughed, a tender sound, and Nel felt sheepish.

"No, Nellie, I figured I'd do just what you're doing—loaf."

"Hah." She tried to cover up the soft spot she'd betrayed. "Can't do that in much style on government retirement, can you? Or have you been playing the ponies with taxpayers' money?"

"I've managed to put away enough to keep me comfortable." A smile that was strange and fleeting crossed his face. It puzzled Nel. "In fact I can live like a rich man till I die," he said.

Nel snorted. "Well, then, you don't need to marry me for my money. Now let's quit talking this nonsense and get to Solvang. I promised Laura we'd bring her back some able-skivers."

Jessamyn struck the dress being offered her out of Deidre's hands and onto the floor.

"No, you stupid little twit, not that one! I said the green *Trigère*. Don't you ever listen?"

Her eyes mere slits of satisfaction, she watched as the maid scuttled back toward the closet. She could always judge how strongly in control of things she was by the extent of Deidre's cravenness, and for this meeting with Jake Turner, she would settle for nothing less than undisputed control.

He had not been pleased by her insistence on seeing him. That was fine, she thought, fastening a flawless emerald through her ear. She had waited for weeks to teach him a lesson, to even the score for that evening in her study when he'd walked out on her. He was about to be schooled in the perils of trying to get the upper hand with Jessamyn Friday.

All the smoldering softness had gone from her eyes. They were clear and hard. Enjoyment bathed her face as she fastened another green stone the size of a robin's egg at her throat. Turner was planning to announce her part in his movie to-morrow. The press conference was set for half-past-three.

A white dog stirred at her feet, and she dropped it a chocolate, smiling lazily. The only things worth having were power and sex, and she had both.

Half an hour later she stepped from her car at the small club she'd selected for this rendezvous. A doorman hurried down to escort her inside. In the vestibule Turner was waiting, looking impatiently at his watch. Jessamyn allowed herself a gluttonous moment of anticipation, then walked toward him.

"Jessamyn." He was frowning slightly as he came to meet her. Squeezing her hand perfunctorily, he tucked it through his arm. "Now what's all this about? What couldn't wait until our meeting tomorrow?"

She laughed at him. She knew her eyelids were teasing.

"You'll see in due time, darling. Let's just get settled with our drinks first."

He'd made the right gestures to charm her, Jessamyn noted. A bottle of champagne was waiting on ice at a corner table, and as they sat down, he told her she looked stunning and flashed her a grin. But they were just that—gestures. Nothing more. He thought he was smart, he thought he could have his own way, the arrogant son-of-a-bitch. He thought if he went through the motions, she'd overlook the fact he'd tried to play her for a fool, and for that miscalculation he would pay dearly.

"To your first Emmy, Jessamyn," he said, stretching his glass toward hers.

She smiled, enjoying the moment, enjoying the cocktail crowd that was filling the club. Turner would be afraid to make a scene with so many eyes watching. That was why she had chosen this place.

"That's what I need to talk to you about," she said.

She could see the wariness touch his face. That jutting shock of hair made him look as hard as it did attractive, but she had never picked a battle she couldn't win.

"There's not going to be any Emmy. I'm not going to do your movie." She paused and took a delicate sip of champagne. "Stan's lined me up a theatrical film. I start next month."

Across from her, Turner's face had gone ashen.

"Jessamyn, what the hell—"

"Stan won't let me. We're back together now, and he says I can't. You do see the bind I'm in, don't you, darling? I'm sorry."

She shrugged, aware the words were falling on him like a crumbling wall. It was worth the humble pie act she'd done to get Stan back. It was worth agreeing to do a movie that might turn out to be less than a quality piece, and at a rate considerably beneath her. A long time had passed since she'd made compromises, but these had bought her what she desired. Turner was speechless.

He hunched toward her, and there was steel in his voice.

"Do you realize what it would do to me if you backed out?

And that I'd sue you for breach of contract?"

"Oh, yes, I realize." Slowly, fearlessly, she smiled. "But you won't do that, will you, Jake? You're far too clever. If we part amicably, you lose one project, maybe some face with the network too, but you'll regain that. If you sue me . . . if you take me to court . . ." Her eyes met his, and her satisfaction deepened. ". . . If you try that, I'm afraid the expense and the publicity just might wreck your little company, new as it is. I'd hate to see that."

Unexpectedly he moved, seizing her wrists so harshly that she gasped. Her glass careened over the table, spilling its contents.

"You bitch! You never had any intention of doing my project."

The words, barely audible, ground through his teeth. They excited her; his bruising grip excited her. She was going to have Turner some day, and on her terms.

"I might have, but I didn't get what I wanted," she said. "See that I do, and I might do your project yet—next year— as soon as I've done the one Stan's lined up for me to pacify him."

Turner stood up with such violence that the table rocked. People nearby turned to stare.

"You mean fuck you, Jessamyn? No thanks. Sign a contract with someone else if that's part of it. I like to pick my projects— and my women!"

He strode from the room, and Jessamyn could see the tight curve of his fists. She could not keep her tongue from flicking over her lips. Reaching across the table, she claimed his glass for her own and sat back, rolling the stem between her hands, eyes bright. Some men were aroused by seduction, some by innocence, and some only when they were forced to crawl. Turner was one of the latter, too determined for his own good. He was too angry now to know it, but this very clash was going to bring him back to her.

In his darkened apartment, Turner stood drinking blindly. He had come to the liquor cabinet for a refill, and now there seemed to be no point in even returning to the couch. The Scotch in his glass was going down quickly. He poured from the bottle again.

How had Jessamyn put him so neatly in a corner? His mind

still staggered beneath the question. He'd had her signature on
a contract, damn it. Yet he knew that trying to sue her would
be as futile as she'd suggested. Somehow she'd patched things
up with her agent so he would stand by her. They'd claim she'd
been unrepresented, hadn't understood what she was signing,
might even contend she'd been under mental stress, on pills—
Christ, who knew what Jessamyn might do?

He thought of her amber eyes, laughing at him, and drank
again. It was there in her eyes, what she was when she wasn't
acting. Now he recognized in their glitter the same fascination
he'd found in those of snakes at the zoo. It was a sleek and
deadly challenge to all comers. He'd crossed the copper-haired
viper, and she'd struck him.

Turner laughed aloud to the empty apartment. A copper-
head. That was what she was. And she might just have ruined
him. All along he'd half-promised her to the network to sell
his film. Now they knew he had her name on the dotted line,
or was supposed to. Christ, how would he explain her backing
out? He'd be the one who'd be sued. Or more likely they'd
just blacklist him. Jake Turner, the inept, the con man, too
careless to be trusted with anyone's project.

He up-ended the bottle again, raging at his own naiveté, at
the stupidity that had allowed him to be so thoroughly deci-
mated by this woman. The bottle was empty. Furious at its
betrayal, he hurled it against the wall.

It shattered with an ugly pop in the silence. The dregs marred
the wall beneath a Navaho wall-hanging.

Like the old man he'd hated, he thought; drunk, violent,
lashing out at the world for his own failures. He'd vowed not
to follow the pattern, but here he was. He'd scorned his father
for being self-pitying and self-indulgent, yet here he stood, and
for one bitter moment Turner wondered whether this was what
his father had felt, this rending, ripping sense of being pow-
erless.

Well, what the hell, he decided. What the hell. There were
other bottles with liquor still in them—bourbon, rye, gin. He
selected one and carried it with him toward the couch.

As he sat down, he looked around the apartment, realizing
how few nights he'd spent here of late. Once it had soothed
him, its spaciousness and expensive furnishings tangible assurances of his success. Now those trappings didn't seem to
matter as much. Somehow he'd grown used to Laura's place.

Laura. Maybe he would go and see her. But no, he shouldn't drive—didn't want to be one of those idiots who killed other people. Leaning back against the couch, he closed his eyes and floated.

Damn you, Jessamyn, I'd like to screw you, he thought, then he grimaced. Not in the physical sense, he wouldn't. Not anymore. What he wanted now was to get even with her, to send her reeling as he was reeling now. He wanted to see her old and ugly and most of all stripped of her power.

There was no chance, though. She was too damn clever. The only way he could retaliate for this trick she'd pulled was by managing to survive it, and at the moment his brain was too foggy to think of a way.

Some day . . . some day, he promised silently, and he thought of Laura. He was starting to understand now. He could comprehend her distrust of Jessamyn. He'd been so smart and condescending and all along it was Laura who had known her mother's true colors. He understood that wistful look in her eyes, that tautness in her voice. Jesus, what that bitch must have done to her when she was a kid!

It hadn't stopped there either. He was sure now that Jessamyn had had something to do with the folding of *Wentworth*. She'd dragged him to that party knowing Laura would be there too, and he'd played right into her hands.

"I wish I could pay her back, babe—for both of us—for a lot of things," he said softly. "I may have deserved what I got, but you never did. I'm sure of it."

Thinking of Laura made him want to reach out to her, to protect her, and it made him hate Jessamyn all the more. Jessamyn was jealous, he realized through the curtain of liquor descending upon him. Jessamyn was jealous of Laura. That was why she had shown such interest in him—part of the reason, at least, why she was determined to take him to bed. It was spite. Viciousness. Hell, maybe vanity.

Slowly, in disbelief at the fuzzy thought teetering on the fringes of his mind, he shook his head. Maybe he was drunker than he'd realized. But as he sat staring, he knew he held in his hand the perfect revenge on Jessamyn Friday, not only for himself, but for Laura too.

I'm not going to let her hurt you anymore, babe. I'm going to show her. We're both going to show her.

Rising he made for the bathroom, stumbling once. He sent

handfuls of water crashing over his head. He would go to Laura's office. No, *Wentworth* had folded. She was working at home, on a movie. He would go there.

On his way, in the back of a cab, he felt one momentary twinge of conscience because he might be using Laura. Then he told himself it would be okay. Laura loved him. He saw it in her eyes, he felt it when she touched him. Maybe he loved her too, and though he'd said it enough, he'd just realized that fact. Yeah, he loved her. Surely that was what had kept him after her for all these months.

Love. That meant people married, they reproduced, they split and paid alimony.

A cold, sober part of him whispered that wasn't what Laura meant by the word. And him. What did he mean? What did he want? It had all gotten blurred for him since meeting Laura.

Turner pushed the thoughts far down inside him and promised himself he would make it all work—for Laura's sake—as he savored the brilliance of his coming revenge.

When Laura opened the door to her apartment, she looked owly. Owly and welcoming. How could she make him feel so damn good about just showing up? The room beyond floated.

"Hi there," he said. "What's wrong with your eyes?"

"Guess I lost track of the time—didn't have any lights on except my desk lamp." Her typewriter still purred softly. "Why didn't you use your key?"

"Didn't think about it."

She cocked her head. "Ah-hah. And you've been having a few."

"Yeah." Turner began to feel sheepish as he grinned at her. "To get my nerve up."

"What for?"

"You'll see in a minute."

He could sense her happiness just at having him here. It made him feel wonderful. Catching her around the waist, he led the way unsteadily toward the fireplace.

"I've been assessing the direction of my life, babe. I know I'm not making this sound quite like it should, but I want to marry you."

She didn't speak, just stared, and for a long moment he was puzzled. Then he saw in her unguarded eyes all the hurt of a lifetime of belonging with no one, all the slow dawning joy, all her disbelief—still—that she had really heard what he was saying.

"Well, what's the matter? I thought you might kind of like the idea."

He tried for jauntiness, but the words lumped in his throat. Her reaction wrenched at him. It humbled him. It told him how much this meant to her and made him want to shelter her. It also made him uneasy—but why?

"Laura?"

He was scared now and starting to sober, until he recognized that she was crying. She dug her fingers into his chest and turned her head aside to hide it from him.

"Yes, Jake. Oh, *yes!* It's just that I never—I didn't think you'd ever want to make a commitment—"

He kissed at her tears, his aim faulty.

"I'll ask you again when I'm sober," he said. "Make a better job of it."

"Oh, no!" There was laughter in the tears now. "You might change your mind."

"Not a chance of it, babe. This is the only way I can think of to keep you from taking up with Greenberg or someone else like him when I'm out of town." He kissed her again. "You know what? We're going to make one hell of a team."

"Will you still serve dessert in the buff?"

"Yeah, sure, and take you to tacky theatres."

She threw herself into the firmness of his arms, and he staggered slightly. They laughed together.

"I think I'd better put you to bed," she said.

He brushed back her hair. A jubilation filled him. He had made her happy, and that knowledge touched something in him that he couldn't quite name.

"Sorry, love, but I've got to hole up at my place tonight. There are some loose ends left from work I want to take care of."

"But, Jake, you're not in any condition—"

"Don't worry. I'm not driving." He grinned again and traced the line of her lips. "Crazy, huh? Coming over here in this condition and leaving ten minutes later. This hasn't been the best of days for me, but it did get me thinking. I love you, Laura."

"I love you, Jake."

"I'll call tomorrow. We'll get you a ring and do this up right."

In the back of the cab, as lights flew by, blinding him, Turner thought of the joy in Laura's eyes and vowed he'd try and give her the sort of marriage she deserved. He'd try not to hurt her. He'd try to do right by her. He had a strange sense of wanting to live up to her expectations.

He was damn lucky, he decided. Damn lucky.

Back in his apartment, he poured himself one last drink to cap the evening. He drank half of it and then picked up the phone. Slowly, carefully, he dialed Jessamyn, her private number. It rang five times.

"Hello?"

Yes, that was Jessamyn herself, he thought.

"Ma? Hiya, Ma," he said cheerfully.

He could hear the icy silence, the disgust. He figured in another moment she'd slam the receiver so he spoke quickly, depriving her of the chance to think this was a wrong number.

"Jess? It's Jake," he said. "Just wanted to call you up so you could celebrate a little."

There was frost on her voice as well as caution. "Will you please tell me what the hell you're talking about?"

"Sure thing." He nodded, enjoying himself. "Laura's just agreed to marry me. I figure that makes you my mother-in-law."

He held the phone away from his ear, prepared for a crash on the other end. "Give me a year or so and I'll make you a grandmother too."

Eighteen

Jessamyn paced without seeing, ignoring the two white dogs that trailed at her heels. *Turner was lying!* He was making this up. He wouldn't really do this.

Or would he?

In the middle of her mirrored bedroom she halted, not knowing which way to go. Her heart was racing, indexing a confusion she rarely felt. She felt stunned and threatened.

She thought quickly, frantically. It was not often she made a misstep, but maybe this time she had. Perhaps she had overplayed her hand. Perhaps she had underestimated Turner. Could she finally have encountered a man too strong to knuckle under to her? Or was he lying?

Impatiently she shoved away the dogs that were begging for chocolates. She had no time for them. The first thing she must do was determine whether there was any truth in this, whether Turner was merely attempting to annoy her—as he damn well had!

From directory assistance she got Laura's number. Turner had sounded three sheets to the wind. Even if he was seeing Laura, Jessamyn didn't think he'd been calling from there.

"Darling?" This was going to surpass any Oscar performance she'd ever given, she thought drily as Laura answered. She made her voice light and happy. "Jake just called me to tell me the good news about the two of you. I'm so thrilled!"

In the silence on the other end, she read surprise. But what was the source of it? She held her breath.

"Thanks." Laura's voice sounded guarded. "Thanks, Jessamyn."

Jessamyn frowned. So it was so.

"Have you set a date?" she asked.

"No, not yet."

"Well, let me know when you do. It's so exciting."

As she hung up, her mouth settled in a line she rarely allowed herself, one which brought the danger of traces of age. It wasn't fair, she thought. Laura wasn't even pretty. Laura was plain— plain like the despised aunt who had raised Jessamyn. Plain like the cousin Jessamyn's age who'd gotten all the attention when they were girls.

Everyone had made such a fuss over that whey-faced cousin. Just because she played the piano in Sunday school and sat around smiling at white-haired old ladies, being a puppet. They'd ignored *her* there in that little Iowa town where she'd been sent to live when her father died. Instead of the velvets and satins her Daddy had dressed her in, her aunt had made her wear cottons and hand-me-downs and told her, "pretty is as pretty does."

One of the dogs whined, returning her to the present. Jessamyn shuddered and scooped him up.

Of course Jake Turner wasn't really interested in Laura. He was only doing this to get back at her.

For a moment Jessamyn's face clouded, and she thought how unjustly she'd been penalized for having a child. She hadn't known when she planned it that it would turn out this way. She hadn't known that people would be forever inquiring about this Other, as though Jessamyn Friday had ceased to have an existence of her own. She hadn't known that some men would become so entranced with a toddler they'd all but forget *she* was in the room! Laura should be forgotten, out of Jessamyn's life now, but instead she was back making trouble.

Well, Laura wasn't going to have Jake Turner.

Flinging open her closet, Jessamyn began to dress. She had no need of Deidre to help her, and she would drive her white Mercedes herself. She'd made a little mistake with Turner over cocktails, but she was going to set it straight right now.

At Turner's apartment building the security guard recognized her—not because she'd been there before, but because of her pictures. Jessamyn gave him her most radiant smile.

"Will you have someone take care of my car for me?" she asked, pressing a tip into his hand. "Mr. Turner is expecting me."

Like that she was admitted, uncontested.

She used the bell three times, four times, and there was no answer. Surely the guard would have told her if Turner was out. It was only just midnight. Then she heard sounds. The door opened. Turner stood there, leaning heavily, his eyes barely focused. He was bare to the waist, and though he was not as sloppy about it as most men were, Jessamyn recognized he was very, very drunk.

"I've come to apologize," she said, making the words sound small and contrite. "May I come in?"

"Sure, Jess." He swung aside. "Always glad to welcome my mother-in-law."

A wave of fury seethed through her, but she controlled it. She had to tread carefully, she reminded herself.

"I guess I deserve that," she murmured, taking care to keep

her voice humble. "What I did—walking out on the project—
was inexcusable. It—I wanted to control you, Jake. Don't you
see? Don't you understand? I've always controlled people,
Everyone. It . . . it was the only way I could be safe."

She let her eyes flutter anxiously up to his. He brushed past
her and sat down on the couch where by the empty glass on
the floor and a discarded shirt, she judged he'd been asleep.

"Jessamyn, I don't know what the hell you're talking about,"
he said.

She drew a silent breath. He was more sober than she'd
guessed, or more intelligent. He wasn't going to buy the scared
little girl act, so she changed direction.

"I'm telling you." Her voice was flat now. "I'm used to
getting what I want. I hated you when you wouldn't give it to
me. I wanted to show you how powerful I was—to teach you
a lesson." She spread her hands in a gesture of helplessness.
"But I guess I'm the one who learned something."

Turner looked at her, but he did not ask the question. Was
he immune to her? No, his responses were merely dulled by
liquor.

"I learned," she said, the words low in her throat, "how
much I want you." Her eyes faltered downward in embarrassment. She sat tentatively on the edge of the couch, taking care
not to touch him. "I've never wanted any man—I've never
been afraid of losing any man—the way I have this last half-
hour."

Slowly, earnestly, she raised her eyes to capture his. "We're
too much alike, Jake. We both love power. And when we don't
get it, we both catch at the best way to retaliate."

Jessamyn paused. She willed a nervous tremor to pass over
her lips. She *was* nervous! She was the tiniest bit uncertain of
Turner. The prospect of a man as strong-willed as she was
excited her. Once she aroused Turner, it would be like rape.

"That's why you proposed to Laura tonight, isn't it?" she
said. "You *knew* it would make me desperate! It's not really
a business deal we've been struggling over, it's the bedroom.
We're both used to being the one in power there, and that's
not possible. Well, all right. I'll—I'll give mine up. I've never
had to ask for a man before, but—" She let her voice grow
husky. "Don't you think it's time you took me to bed, Jake?"

Turner leaned back against the couch. He chuckled.

"Jesus, Jessamyn, you're something else!" he said. And then, more thickly, "I proposed to Laura because I wanted to."

Jessamyn froze, wondering if it was true.

"No. No, you didn't. You don't want Laura." Her hand slid to the inside of his thigh, and she was rewarded by his startled oath of awareness. "You'd be bored silly inside of a month. You couldn't stay faithful to her, and you know it. Laura doesn't have what it takes to keep your interest. A man like you needs . . . a challenge."

Turner had lifted himself from the cushions on his elbows. He stared at her. But he had not spoken, and she could tell by his eyes that he was hypnotized by what she was saying.

Jessamyn let her hand slide higher. "Tell me you've never wanted to make love to me," she whispered. He didn't answer. She thrust her face against his. "Kiss me!" She opened her mouth, and he kissed her clumsily, and beneath her fingers she felt his erection.

Then, as though he had been burned, Turner pushed away from her. His expression was one of driven wildness.

"My God, but you're degenerate!" he said hoarsely.

She smiled at him. "*We're* degenerate, darling. That's why we're going to bring each other such pleasure. No one who plays by the rules ever learns what pleasure is. You know it. I know it. You and I are two of a kind, Jake. We don't *need* rules!"

As she spoke, she unfastened the sash securing her wrap dress. With a fling of the shoulders she exposed her bare breasts.

Turner lurched to his feet, drawing her along with him. His flesh slid against hers, exciting her.

"Get out of here."

Jessamyn laughed, deep in her throat.

He tried to shove her, but stumbled, falling heavily on top of her, bringing them both to the floor. As if automatically his hand came up to explore the side of her breast.

Still laughing, Jessamyn shifted beneath him. She unzipped his pants and let him spring free.

"Damn you . . . Jessamyn . . . I ought to . . ."

He was panting and incoherent. He had half-rolled from her, and one hand held her throat as though to strangle her. But it had moved there with desire, too. Turner wasn't going to kill her; he was going to give her what she craved.

Jessamyn felt her openness beneath the brown silk garter-belt, her only undergarment. She ran eager hands up his chest, scratching his skin.

And then his lack of movement came through to her. Opening her eyes, she saw him lying there, his arm across her.

His eyes were closed. The hand that had been at her throat lay limp. As a slight snore sounded, Jessamyn realized he had passed out, and his lovely erection with him. Tears simmered in her eyes.

As she sat up, looking at him, a shocking realization bored its way through to her. Turner had not been interested in her. She had come to him sweetly, willing to abase herself as she had with few other men, *and he had not been interested in her*! Now she began to understand, as she had not in their earlier encounters, that his refusals to be pinned down were not the tricks she'd thought them, but the movements of a man who had not been brought under her spell.

In that moment Jessamyn understood she would never have him. Her eyelashes closed like the fringe of some underwater creature digesting its prey.

Staggering to her feet, she raised one needle-heeled shoe above his groin. But just before she started its downstroke, reason cut across her volcanic fury. There were ways she could revenge herself on Turner far better than by stomping his balls. She shrugged back into her dress, fastened it with meticulous care, and then just as deliberately began to contemplate Turner's future.

He had chosen Laura. Well, fine. When she stopped to think about it, the whole situation was rather amusing. It put her in an exquisite position for dealing with both of them. And poor Laura was so hopelessly jealous!

Her eyes flicked over Turner's half-dressed body. Even now it held a fascination for her, but she would never be such a fool as to act again on that fascination. No, she would lay other plans for Turner.

And poor little Laura . . . if only she knew how close this man she was going to marry had come to fucking Jessamyn. Yes, that was the truth of this encounter, and she and Turner both knew it. Perhaps he was not really so immune to her. He would have screwed her from instinct, from raging animal lust, if he had not passed out.

A smile, slow and smoldering, lighted Jessamyn's face.

Turner had been too drunk to perform. But he had also been too drunk to remember he hadn't. What had happened here tonight didn't really matter. She still had a perfect weapon in her possession!

"Jake, I'm terrified. Those people out there are expecting Jessamyn Friday. It's bad enough being an unknown, but when they're *expecting* her—"

"You're not an unknown, Kimberly. And you're a damn fine actress, aren't you?"

The wraithlike blonde who stood beside him managed a cheeky grin.

"Well, you seem to think so!"

Turner grinned back at her. "Yeah. I do."

They were in a small closet off the hotel conference room. Outside the door a small mob of reporters had descended on a table of free liquor and hors d'oeuvres, awaiting the announcement Turner had so confidently summoned them here for last week. Kimberly was right, too. They were expecting Jessamyn. He'd taken pains to see that rumors about his upcoming project had leaked out long ago.

Christ, what a mess. But he was still alive less than twenty-four hours after Jessamyn had dropped her bombshell. His head, even though it was throbbing, was still on his shoulders.

Lighting one last cigarette, Turner stole a glance at the woman who would play the lead in *Helen Somebody*. Wraithlike was still the best word he could use to describe her. There was something haunting about her large eyes and the strong, strangely mobile structure of her cheeks. Her hair was so light that at times it made all of her seem almost transparent. She didn't begin to equal Jessamyn's beauty, but visually she was very interesting.

More important, she was, as he'd told her, a damn fine actress. This morning when he'd awakened, hung over but already determined to salvage his project by filling the role abandoned by Jessamyn, Kimberly's name had been the first that sprang to mind. She'd always been somewhere on his list of second choices, but that morning her image had come into focus with sudden clarity.

Shamelessly he'd called and placed all his cards on the table.

"What it means is you save my ass," he'd told her bluntly. "And you get a crack at a good role in return. What do you say?"

After locking herself in her bedroom and reading the script he'd shoved at her, she'd said yes. Turner didn't know what might have happened if she hadn't—or if he hadn't been able to keep his network backing by taking a huge cut in money.

"Hey, I sold you to the network, didn't I?" he said to cheer them both.

There had been so much to do, so much to think about in the hours since then that he already was growing hazy about that hurried meeting with the network. Almost as hazy as he was about the things that had happened the night before. He remembered proposing to Laura, and he remembered Jessamyn coming to see him some time in the night. She had wanted something, but he couldn't remember what. He hadn't tried to remember, he hadn't thought about it, there hadn't been time.

"So let's get this over with," he said to Kimberly. "That's a real rich-bitch dress you're wearing. They'll figure I've paid through the teeth to get you for this part. They're going to love you."

Laura opened the door to the room Jake had reserved for his big announcement and slid toward a corner. By showing up here, she hoped to demonstrate that she had whatever it took to weather the weeks when he and Jessamyn would be working together. Besides, she thought with a smile, this was a big moment for him, and she wanted to share it.

On the other side of the room she saw Jake conferring with his director and another man she vaguely recognized as a network official. They must just now be grouping, gathering together to go through the forms of an announcement, though she was sure everyone in the room already knew what they would say. Jessamyn was conspicuously absent, no doubt preparing to make some dramatic entrance. Who was the blonde who was at Jake's side?

The three men and the blonde had started to move when Jake looked up and saw her. For a second she thought she saw irritation crackle through him. Had she done the wrong thing coming here? She had never before turned up where he was working, but this was different. This day was special, and several days ago, even before he'd asked her to marry him, he'd spoken as though he expected her here.

He excused himself from the others and came toward her.

"Hi there," he said, a trifle uncomfortably, and then he kissed her.

Laura was even more surprised than she was delighted as his lips brushed hers. He was not annoyed at all.

"Hi," she said, smiling. He looked as though he felt slightly foolish, and she wanted to laugh with joy that he had crossed the room to acknowledge a bond between them in the presence of everyone here. "Hope you don't mind, I came to cheer."

"Good. I can use it," he said with startling grimness. "Here's Saul. He'll keep you company."

Before she could speak, he had left her, and Saul Finer, sporting a new green suit for the occasion, was sticking a hand out in her direction.

"Hey, Laura, congratulations! I understand you've finally nailed him."

"Thanks, Saul. I don't believe that's how you're supposed to phrase it, but in this case you might be right."

Saul laughed. "Want something to drink?"

"No thank you." She liked Saul; he was funny and friendly. Laura nodded toward Jake and the others. "Aren't you going to join them for your share of glory?"

"Come on, Laura, you know where we writers rank in the scheme of things."

"Ummm, but you're one of the partners."

"It's still Jake's show, and God, does he deserve this moment in the spotlight!"

Jake was stepping forward now, turning his head to flash a wide smile back at the blonde.

"Who's the girl?" asked Laura, watching them. "Someone from the network?"

Saul had moved a platter of deviled eggs and was hoisting himself onto one corner of the buffet table. He stared at her, and his amazement was so palpable Laura looked back at him.

"That's Kimberly Curran. She's the star."

"The star! But I thought Jessamyn . . . ?"

Jake was starting to speak now. Her attention was divided. Yet some awareness brought the bulk of it to rest on Saul.

"You mean you don't know?" he said. "But of course! Jake probably hasn't even had the time to call you since it happened. Jessamyn walked out yesterday. Broke her contract. And she was so clever about it, it looks as though there's not a damn thing we can do."

The last of his words sounded in Laura's ears as if from a distance. Yesterday Jessamyn had dealt a blow to Jake's big project, and Jake had gotten drunk, and Jake had come to her in his drunkenness and asked her to marry him. She was not so blind that she could not see a revenge motif in the chain of events; each act was interconnected. But standing there in that room full of strangers, she would not let herself believe it was the one and only reason for Jake's proposal.

Nineteen

For three days now Laura had been strangely quiet. At first Turner had been too caught up in the high of getting his first big project off the ground even to notice. When he finally had, in bed the night before, he'd attributed it to her preoccupation with her own work. Now he was puzzled. She'd finished the treatment this morning and taken it to the producer, yet still she seemed withdrawn. And not the least euphoric at having conquered it, Turner thought. He listened to her move in the kitchen, creating something, alone and remote, and he frowned.

It was inconvenient having his life tied up with someone else's. He'd spent long weekends with plenty of women, but he'd never lived with any of them. Now, standing before the fireplace in Laura's living room, he was acutely aware of something out of balance. It made him feel on edge and slightly annoyed.

Lighting a cigarette, he smoked in silence, then went into the kitchen. She was at the sink, washing a large bowl.

"Nervous energy now that the treatment's in?" he asked.

She glanced up, then bent to her work again as if to avoid him.

"Yes, maybe that's it."

"Come in and have a glass of wine. I'll get you unwound."

He reached out to encircle her waist, but she turned away with perfect timing.

"Maybe later." She started past him with the now dry bowl.

He snagged the dish towel in her hand, detaining her. She was forced to look at him.

"Laura, what's wrong?"

For an instant he saw the imprint of unhappiness in her gaze. It worried him.

"Nothing's wrong." She sidestepped him to open a cabinet, and this time he did not reach for her.

Instead he spoke slowly to her rigid back.

"We've got to be honest if we want this to work, babe."

Hand against the cabinet door, she froze. When she finally turned, the unhappiness in her eyes had deepened visibly. She took a breath.

"Yes, that's true, so answer me this—did you ask me to marry you because you wanted to, or because you were mad at Jessamyn for walking out on your project?"

Turner felt his body gripping inward, assuming a protective tautness as he found himself on the defensive.

"Christ, Laura, that's a hell of a question to ask!"

"It's one that has to be answered. I've been trying to avoid it, but it can't be avoided if, as you put it, things are going to work."

He thought furiously, shamed by the gray eyes fixed on his, demanding honesty. Laura was so damned ethical. It made things hard. She wouldn't understand it if he told her there were shades of gray in any issue, but that in his own way, within the limits of his capabilities, he supposed he loved her. She'd be hurt if he acknowledged that Jessamyn had been a factor in his decision. He didn't want to hurt Laura. But he didn't know what was right by her in the long run.

"Hey," he said, holding out a hand to her. "Come here."

Reluctantly, uncertainly, she did, and he put his arms around her.

"I asked you to marry me because you're the first woman who's ever made me feel like doing that," he said. Maybe total honesty wasn't the best thing for two people after all.

She seemed to search his face for an answer he could not give her, and he saw in her expression traces of a doubt he had not dispelled. He kissed her quickly, seeking to sweep away the doubts for both of them.

"Forget about Jessamyn," he said roughly. "It's our life now. Yours and mine."

She pushed back and looked at him gravely.

"Jake . . . there's one more thing I have to know. Did you and Jessamyn—have you ever slept together?"

"Christ no, babe!"

Guilt trickled through him as he thought of how close they had come. Like a trap door opening beneath him, something shifted—a flash—a memory. He had not tried to recall that night with Jessamyn in his apartment, but now an image from it was there unbidden: Jessamyn on his couch, shrugging free of her dress to expose those magnificent breasts. And he had wanted them.

"God, Laura, don't even think it!"

Covering her eyes with kisses, he tried to quell the uneasiness rising in him.

He remembered an instant when rage and lust had combined at the sight of that nakedness. And drunk as he'd been, he'd had a hard-on. The only trouble was, that was *all* he remembered. Just those full breasts jutting at him, and his own fury.

But he hated Jessamyn. He would have thrown her out untouched for Laura's sake if not for his own. He wasn't entirely filthy. He had some morals. He couldn't have—wouldn't have—done what Jessamyn had been provoking him to do.

Or had he?

"I don't like it." Nel scowled at Eddie to warn him she didn't want any argument. She didn't want him trying to reassure her.

"Come on, Nel," he said, ignoring her authority in the matter. "Laura seems as happy as can be. And she's level-headed, not flighty. I think you've got a flea in your ear. You're worrying over nothing."

"Ha!" She flounced off the couch in her own apartment and poured herself another glass of sherry. Her hand was trembling a little bit. She frowned. Everything at once, she thought. She was sure that Laura was heading for heartache.

"If she's all that happy about it—and all that sure it's right— why has she waited five days to tell me about it?"

Eddie chuckled indulgently. "You're jealous."

Nel stalked across the room and back again, the trailing hem of her saffron robe whipping behind her like a panther's tail.

"I don't want Laura to be hurt," she said succinctly.

"You can't keep that from happening if it's in the cards, Nel."

"The hell I can't!" Setting her glass down with a crack, she stalked toward the bathroom. The trembling in her arm was getting worse—worse than she had ever felt it. Laura's visit seemed to have triggered it. She couldn't let Laura make this mistake, she thought fiercely.

She slammed the bathroom door, locking it behind her, and leaned against the sink. Her arm was twitching uncontrollably now, an alien creature lashing about with no relationship to her.

Eddie pounded on the other side of the door.

"What are you doing in there?"

"Just what did you think I'd be doing?"

"I know that sneaky look of yours when I see it. You're hiding from me."

"Yeah—so why not go away and save me the trouble?"

She heard a thump and figured he had leaned his shoulder against the door.

"Listen to me, Nellie. If you're fixing to meddle in Laura's affairs, it's just not ethical. I know you love her. I know you want to see her happy. But it's her life, Nel, just as yours is yours. Come out of there and let me talk to you. I'm not going to let you stir up trouble."

The spasms in her arm were growing stronger. She stared at it in horror. She gripped it in the other hand, but could not still it.

"I'll do what I want to, Eddie. You're not a cop now. You can't stop me." Still holding her arm in the opposite hand, she pressed it against her body, and all of her was now wracked by its tremors.

"Nellie . . ."

"And don't try wheedling either. It won't work."

The doorknob rattled.

"Damn you, Nel! I've got a good idea to break this door down."

"Yeah, but you won't." She was gasping now, but she kept the words steady. She sank to her knees, bending over the smooth brown limb that no longer belonged to her.

"Come out, Nel! What scheme are you hatching in there? What are you fixing to do?"

She heard the words from afar, her mind thick with the

proof of her own mortality. What could she do? What could she do?

I'll send my ghost back, she thought crazily. I'll haunt Jake Turner if he makes Laura unhappy.

Cold waters rushed at her, and time stood still.

"Nel? Are you okay?" called Eddie's voice.

With an anguished cry she heard the splintering of wood. Eddie was breaking down the door. Eddie was going to see her.

Jessamyn pushed the supper tray beside her away untouched. She rose to move restlessly through the small sitting room adjoining her bedroom.

It was stupid of Nel to injure herself. It was careless of her, and it showed thoughtlessness about her work. What if she wasn't here when she was *needed*?

Jessamyn nursed a grudge that Nel should have checked into a hospital without consulting her. It had all been so sudden. That stupid pulled muscle that Nel should have seen to weeks ago resurfacing this afternoon. Now the routine of the household had been disrupted. In spite of the other staff members the place seemed empty.

Nel should take better care of herself at her age, Jessamyn thought. She always had before. She'd never been sick. This was all because of that man Nel was seeing. She was getting too involved with him. She was losing her head.

Jessamyn sat down and then stood up again. She could not remember when she had not been accustomed to Nel's presence somewhere in the house, somewhere within call. She had grown to depend on it, and now she was edgy.

Deidre gave her timorous tap and opened the door.

"Miss Friday?"

She edged in as though expecting a blow.

"You have a visitor, Miss Friday. It's Mr. Greenberg. Harry said he thought you'd want to see him."

Jessamyn hadn't seen Van Greenberg since that birthday party she'd given Nel. She wondered now, with some annoyance, what he could want.

It didn't matter. She could do with company tonight. Maybe later she would go out, stay out late. Maybe Greenberg would take her.

"All right," she said, smoothing her pink knit slacks. "I'll see him. And bring me my dogs."

She ran a brush through her hair, then went into the living room.

"Van, darling," she sang out gaily. "What a surprise." Stopping with hands on her hips, she pulled an accusing smile. "But I don't know if I should welcome you or not. You've been wearing false colors. All this time I'd thought you were still with Columbia, and now I find you've been with ABC for at least two years."

"Five years, Jessamyn."

He sat down easily and looked at her. There had always been something chilling about those blue eyes of his.

"I suppose I'll forgive you," she said, tossing back her hair. "What will you have to drink?"

"Nothing, thank you."

"Harry, bring me a sherry then."

On Harry's heels Deidre came into the room. Jessamyn smiled as the dogs the maid released scampered pell-mell toward her. Who could fail to notice how they adored her? She reached into a china box for a morsel to reward the larger of the two, who had reached her first and was panting in expectation.

"Deidre! The chocolates need filling." Why was she cursed with such an inept staff?

Jessamyn sat down, and the dog at her feet, by grunting and wheezing, managed at last to heave itself onto the couch beside her.

"Well, Van," she said to Greenberg. "What brings you around?"

"I've been seeing Laura," he said.

She looked up abruptly from petting the white dog. So what, she wanted to say.

"She is your daughter, isn't she?" Greenberg pressed when she didn't respond.

Instinct told her not to let the aversion she was feeling show.

"Yes, so I'm told," she said, and she turned the edge on her voice to silk as she gave a slow smile.

Long, long ago—longer than she cared to remember—she had slept with Greenberg a time or two, captivated by that air of detachment, which he'd worn even then. Was he telling her now that he'd bedded her daughter? It filled her with fury. Him, Turner, Laura—they were laughing at her behind her back. They were all her enemies.

Jessamyn kneaded the ears of the dog beside her until it yelped.

"If you've come to ask for her hand, I'm afraid you're a bit late. She's marrying someone else."

"Yes, I know."

"Well, then?"

Lighting a cigarette, Greenberg settled back, completely unruffled. He took a studied draw on the cigarette before speaking again.

"I want her. And you, Jessamyn, are going to see that I get her."

The amber depths of Jessamyn's eyes filled with poison.

"Want her? How quaint! Why don't you and Turner just have a duel to see who walks her down the aisle then? For your information I don't give a damn about you and your love life!"

"I have no intention of marrying her." Greenberg smoked calmly. "I liked having her available. It soothed me. I'm not prepared to give that up."

Jessamyn snapped to her feet.

"Well, you're mad if you think I'm going to lift my little finger! Laura bores me. The subject bores me. Now can you find your way out, or shall I call Harry?"

The cigarette still glowing between his fingers, Greenberg's hand cracked smartly across her cheek as he stood up.

"Sit down and shut up. I have an appointment to get to and no time to waste watching you play crown princess. You're going to do exactly as I tell you, like it or not."

Jessamyn stared at him, holding her cheek. The pain hardly fazed her, but no one dared speak to her like that! She felt dizzy, as though something she needed desperately was slipping away. Against her will she remembered Laura's father and the way he'd treated her and his indifference—though he'd never struck her. She remembered the way he'd given her orders, and she'd been forced to obey. This conversation with Greenberg was bringing it all back. She swayed, unsteady with anger, furious with the present and furious at being made to remember the past when she'd had no power.

"Get out!" she hissed. "Get out of my house, or I'll ring for my men!"

Greenberg regarded her from eyes of transparent aquamarine.

"As soon as I'm sure you understand what I'm telling you, Jessamyn. Because if you don't do what I'm asking, I'm afraid you're going to find that movie you were supposed to start filming soon—a movie you need unless you want to find yourself called a has-been—has hit a snag. Right now one of the major backers is having second thoughts about you in the lead role. Thinking they should have someone . . . fresher, shall we say?"

She sucked in her breath. It wasn't true! She didn't *need* the movie, and she was nowhere close to being a has-been.

"I don't believe you! You don't have that kind of power."

"See for yourself. The number's two-one-two-one."

His calm was frightening her and out of that fright Jessamyn made quick and skillful decisions. Greenberg had made the mistake of aiming a blow at her entrails, at her career. She'd call his bluff. She'd give the bastard the sort of trouncing he'd never forget. She crossed the room and with flying fingers dialed the producer for her new movie.

"Lou—no bullshit—when do we start filming?"

On the other end of the line there was silence, then a too-soothing voice.

"Soon, Jess. I can't say exactly. The truth is we've had a little delay, a little problem with one of the backers . . ."

A shudder of panic ran through her, and across the receiver she saw the thin knife edge of Greenberg's smile.

Laura switched the ignition off and sighed deeply, trying to drown disappointment over what, after all, had not been unexpected. The network had not bought the package Richard Knox had put together. Her treatment would not go to script. With firm, swinging steps she started up the walk to her apartment. There was nothing to do now except start hunting something else.

Jake was at the dining table, papers spilling out around his briefcase, making notes with a felt marker on a yellow legal pad. He murmured a distracted greeting without looking up.

"Well, we were shot down before we got off the ground,"

she said, tossing her handbag toward the couch. "The treatment's not even going to first script."

"Too bad, babe. I'm sorry to hear it."

He glanced up with a quick smile, then bent to his work again. Laura felt disappointment nudging her. She had expected a little more interest, a little commiseration, just a sympathetic hug, perhaps.

"I thought maybe we could go out somewhere. Chase the blues."

"Sorry, babe, but Lucks and I decided we needed to work out some camera shots. These next few days were the only time he could fit in."

He stood as he spoke, and Laura realized he was in a sports jacket. His zippered garment bag lay over one chair.

She knew a producer's life was one of comings and goings, absences at the worst times possible, yet she felt let down.

"Oh. I see," she said.

The papers in Jake's hands cracked against the table. He thrust them irritably into the briefcase.

"From the tone of your voice, you don't at all."

"Yes, damn it, I do! It just happens that I'm feeling a little down right now."

"And you think I should be Mr. Nice and hold your hand? I'm sorry, I'd like to, Laura, but I haven't got time. I've got to catch a plane in an hour and twenty minutes." He glanced at her. "Frankly, I'm not sure the death of a project that hadn't even been sold merits that much mourning in any case. You knew the book you were working from wasn't so great. You said so yourself."

Laura stared at him, stung by his curtness.

"I don't need my hand held, though I must say it would be nice if you showed some empathy for my problems."

His head came up, and his eyes blazed. "Problems? You don't know what problems are, babe! What did you stand to lose on your script? Thirty, thirty-five thou, maybe? I've got almost three million bucks riding on my back—investors' money—and if I don't bring this film in on budget, if I don't do it brilliantly and to perfection, I'll never have a chance to do a decent film again! Instead of having the money and the reputation to take some well-crafted novel and turn it into something people will be touched by, I'll be stuck with doing hack work—garbage some network coke-head picks instead of me! I wish to Christ I had a few problems of your magnitude. It would be like a goddamn vacation!"

She wanted to strike at him for his arrogance. They glared at one another as he jerked up his garment bag and opened the door. Laura started to speak and didn't, feeling too incensed to put thoughts into words. She watched Jake shrug, heard the front door slam and the start of his car engine. Long after it faded, she still stood motionless in the empty room, until at last the telephone began to ring.

Twenty

Eddie slumped with relief in the hospital waiting room. Nel was going to be all right. Leaning back on the couch, he closed his eyes, feeling not pity but horror for Nel. Horror because she was a proud, strong woman, and he knew how she must hate her disability, how it must shame her.

When he'd seen her there on the bathroom floor, he'd been devastated, partly by her condition and partly by guilt because he'd recognized how much she must have wanted to hide it from him. Nel valued her privacy, and he'd intruded on it. But love accepted anything, even this. Somehow he would have to make her understand.

What if she refused to see him now? The thought left a gaping hole in his insides. Numb, hardly aware of what he was doing, he got up because visiting hours were ending now and he had to leave.

In the lobby he let himself be swept along as part of a crowd, moving while all the time his thoughts remained on Nel. He had driven some distance and stopped for a red light before his instinct for self-preservation kicked on. He glanced in the rearview mirror and almost automatically picked out a car that his subconscious told him had been there longer than chance dictated.

When the light changed, Eddie pulled away quickly. He

drove three blocks, turned left, then turned again. Increasingly tense he glanced in the mirror. The same car was still behind him in the distance.

Not now, he thought desperately. Not until I know about Nellie. Not until I know that things are okay between her and me.

Easing into the right lane, he accelerated. At the corner he swung right, killed his lights and pulled into an alley behind a dempster dumpster. Eyes straining against the dark, he looked over his shoulder. Seconds later he saw the car that had been behind him shoot past.

A damp sweat coated Eddie's forehead, and he breathed uncertainly. He thought he had lost them, but had he really?

Laura's lips were set in a firm line to hide her turmoil. Her elevator car glided toward the ground floor at Studio City. It was not thoughts of the recently concluded meeting that were disturbing her, it was thoughts of Jake. She could not forget his arrogance or the way he had dismissed her concerns as inconsequential, and she was miserable. Two days had passed since their clash. Even the new film project Richard Knox had called to offer her just minutes after it, which she had been discussing with Knox this morning, could not blot out the bitterness or the doubts.

Maybe she'd been deluding herself, thinking she and Jake could co-exist without destroying each other. She agonized at the thought. The extent of his self-centeredness had shocked her. She realized now that while she believed there were other things in life besides one's work, he apparently did not.

Then yesterday Lupita had called to say Nel had checked into the hospital for treatment of that pulled muscle. Although Laura knew it was silly, it worried her thinking of Nel in a hospital bed. Laura longed to kick something, but there was nothing to kick.

As she crossed the lobby, she saw a man with wiry white hair, consulting his wristwatch. It was Daniel Katz. He looked up and smiled.

"Laura. How are you?"

"Just fine—thanks in large part to you." His odd little smile was so warming that she found herself reflecting it. She liked Daniel Katz, though because of his high position, she was always a trifle uncertain how far to unbend. "I'm working on a treatment for Richard Knox," she said.

"Oh?" He sounded only mildly surprised.

"Yes, I didn't get the staff writing job you told me about, but Richard gave me a crack at a Movie of the Week they were putting together. It didn't turn out, but at least he's giving me another chance."

"Well, it sounds as though you have your foot in the door at any rate. He must like your work." Katz smiled again. "I was just standing here wondering whom I could collar to have lunch with me. Why don't you be the victim and tell me all about it?"

Standing there with him had taken her away, however briefly, from her disturbing thoughts.

"All right, I'd like that," she said.

He took her to a Chinese restaurant on San Pedro, and though she had thought she was not hungry, she found herself succumbing to more than a few of the tempting little dishes offered in the endless dim sum lunch. The restaurant did not serve liquor. Instead they both enjoyed its hot and delicate jasmine tea.

"So you're Jessamyn Friday's daughter," Katz commented after they had chatted for some time.

Laura looked up in surprise. His mild expression gave her no clue to what he was thinking or how she should respond.

"Yes, but don't hold it against me," she said, hoping it passed for humor.

Katz chuckled as though he found the answer immensely amusing. "I won't, I promise."

Laura felt uneasy. Had Jessamyn been poking around somewhere, preparing to make trouble?

"How did you find out anyway?"

Katz's gray eyes danced merrily.

"Oh, I always like to dig up some background on the people I hire or point toward a job. I knew all about you before I told you about the *Gauntley* opening."

Laura regarded him with fresh interest. He was not the pussycat he seemed. Of course one could not be and reach the level in the industry he had, but his manner lulled her into forgetting.

"That's how you knew Michael Townes then," he said. "He did a film with Jessamyn some years back."

A short laugh of disbelief escaped her.

"Do you have to keep track of *everything* when you're in programming?"

Chuckling, he refilled their cups with the pale, hot tea.

"No, I've just been around for a long time. I was directing back when your mother was making her first films. But television was becoming such an exciting venture that I couldn't resist, and somewhere along the line I got separated from the individual endeavor."

He stopped and shot her a look as innocent as it was penetrating.

"Does it bother you, my calling her your mother?"

Laura swallowed, wondering what emotions had shown on her face.

"No, I—it's just that Jessamyn and I have never been very close."

The clattering of dim sum trays filled the sudden gap in conversation.

"I'm sorry," he said gently. Then he smiled. "I hear you're going to marry Jake Turner, and I approve. I hope you're going to ask me to the wedding."

Laura blinked, refusing to give way to the dampness that threatened her eyes from the strange emotions inside her and this positive word that she'd needed to hear so badly.

"I can't think of anyone I'd rather have help us get through it," she said.

It was almost two when he dropped her off at the lot where she'd left her car. She drove home lighter in spirit. Dan Katz was an odd little man, but so kind. She was glad their paths had crossed again.

As soon as she walked in the door, she flipped on her answering machine to check for messages. There was only one, Van Greenberg's smooth voice asking her out tonight. A shiver of amazement, and something else, ran over her. Didn't Van take 'no' for an answer? She'd avoided him ever since that afternoon when he'd almost ruined things between her and Jake, and when he'd called last week, she'd told him she was getting married.

Provoked by his persistence, she snapped off the machine. She'd call Nel to tell her she planned to visit tonight. Then she'd settle down with the novel she was to adapt and begin to make notes for themes and scenes.

Before she had gotten very far, the phone disturbed her.

"Is this Laura Fitzgerald?" a voice asked. "This is Daniel Katz."

"Oh, no, thought Laura as anxiety struck her. Surely he wasn't going to ask her out! She'd assumed it was just a friendly gesture when he'd asked her to lunch—and he knew about Jake—but why else would he be calling?

"I know you're going to think this is silly of me," he said, "but I've been thinking. Back when I was a director, one of the most challenging scenes I ever had to stage was a wedding reception. I've always wondered if I could bring one off as well in real life. Would you and Jake consider letting me try yours—as my little present? I'm awfully fond of Jake, you know. Bernie Goldman and I go way back, so Jake's almost like a nephew. You're the bride, though, and I don't want to horn in if you have plans. What do you say?"

She leaned against the telephone table. A little present was hardly what he was suggesting! All at once she felt sad. Katz sounded so happy, and she was so miserable. She and Jake hadn't talked of plans at all, wordlessly relegating their marriage to the lowest priority in their lives in the weeks ahead.

"I don't know what to say," she admitted slowly.

"Why not agree then? I'd like to see if I still have the touch after all these years."

Still she wavered, caught off guard by this extraordinary offer.

"I think we'd both expected to keep it small . . . not make a fuss . . ."

"Of course. I understand. Just a cake and champagne somewhere, and you looking lovely in a long white dress. Those touches make it seem like something special—something lasting—don't you agree?"

Laura closed her eyes. Something lasting, that was what she wanted. Suddenly, desperately, she wanted to cling to what Daniel Katz was saying. But was she deluding herself, believing that those trappings could make any difference? The fact was she was scared, not only about the future but about the present too. Would Jake even come back after the bitter note they'd parted on? Did she even want him to, knowing how self-consumed he could sometimes be?

"I suppose you're right," she said. "But I don't know . . . Not that your offer isn't perfectly lovely, you understand. You're very kind, but—"

"Let's leave it to Jake then, shall we? Unless he disagrees, I'll take your answer for yes."

Laura found herself laughing weakly, wondering how much she'd been maneuvered by the seemingly innocent Katz.

"And," he added gravely, "I guarantee a first-rate production."

"I'm sure it will be. But you will keep it small, won't you? And simple?"

"Just let me know when and how many. I'll stick to whatever you like."

When they had said goodbye, she stood shaking her head. Until this moment she'd never pictured herself in the role of bride. At least she hadn't pictured it beyond a city hall ceremony and supper somewhere. Now her emotions wavered, delighted and hopeful one minute, bleak the next.

She was in the kitchen, getting out cheese for an early supper, when the doorbell rang. Frowning, she wiped her hands and went to answer. She didn't especially want to see anyone, and if it was Greenberg—

But it was Jake. He stood looking slightly unsure of himself, framed by the door.

"Hi," he said. He cleared his throat. "I seem to find it necessary to be apologizing to you a lot, so this time I decided to say it with flowers."

His eyes were serious, but the corners of his mouth were curving. He held out an enormous cone of green florist's paper to her.

Laura made no move to take it. She felt wary and incredibly brittle.

"I thought you and Lucks were going to be away a week at least. Why didn't you use your key?"

She understood the strain he'd been under, yet she could not forget the way he'd slighted her work nor help wondering whether that would always be his true assessment of it. Had the argument between them the day he left marked the start of an unraveling that could never be stopped?

"I thought you might have changed the lock," he said. "Wouldn't have blamed you if you had."

The humor had gone from his mouth. His words seemed stretched as tightly as her nerves. They seemed to reach for each other in the same instant.

"Ah, damn it, Laura, this isn't going to be easy," he said,

pressing his cheek against her hair.

"I know. I'm finding that out." She closed her eyes, leaning into his chest, trying to escape the fears fluttering about her.

"I want to make a go of it," he said.

She felt her doubts receding; she willed them away.

"That's all that matters then. We can."

But as she spoke, she wondered if it was enough at all. There were times when she wondered if she really knew Jake.

He slid his hands down over her shoulders, catching her by the elbows and holding her slightly away. He was grinning, happy.

"So aren't you going to look at your bouquet?" he asked. "I practically bought out the flower shop, after all."

She smiled at him and blinked away a tear. "You're crazy—" she began, then doubled with laughter as she opened the cone of tissue and saw the arrangement inside.

Dark clumps of broccoli nestled against bobbling bunches of beets, and parsley provided a feathery background. Three large white leeks adorned the center of the masterpiece.

"Oh, Jake, *where*—"

"A roadside market. Had to buy some daisies too, to get the paper, but I ate those on the way."

"I love you!"

She circled his neck with her arms, and a broccoli clump fell free.

"I'm glad," he said, his lips against hers. "Hate to think I'd wasted these romantic trappings." Raising her hand to his mouth, he half-kissed, half-nibbled it, one eyebrow rakishly cocked. "Eleven perfect cabbages, my dear, and you are the twelfth."

"Is this your way of telling me you're hungry?"

"Yeah, babe. But not for veggies." He took them from her and tossed them onto the couch. "Take me back?"

"Always."

Still pressed together they walked to the bedroom.

"A white dress, huh?"

Nel ruled from her hospital bed as though from a throne. She had seen that the pansies Laura brought her were placed exactly where she wanted them, and she had sent Eddie and Turner off for coffee so she could have a cozy chat with Laura. The invalid's role was not for her. She had finagled extra pillows from a nurse and sat bolt upright, her robe a deep carmine red dripping maribou at neck and sleeves.

"Well, kiddo, I'm glad this Katz has convinced you to go whole hog. I can't remember the last time I've been to a wedding. They're fun, and I wish you'd do it up big."

She lighted the cigarette in her holder and waved it grandly. Laura looked worried.

"Good heavens, Nellie, you're going to set yourself on fire with those floppy sleeves!"

"Not me. I'm steady as a rock," Nel said smugly. The tremors had been gone from her arm for twenty-four hours.

Not that it was anything the doctor had done. He'd made that clear. All the same, it pleased her. The awful weakness had gone from her right side too.

Laura, curled on the bed beside her in spite of hospital rules, squeezed her free hand. "Okay, now, Nellie, tell me what they've found out about your arm."

Meeting her eyes directly, Nel took a long draw on her cigarette.

"Exactly what I told you they'd find. I'd pulled a muscle. Oh, yes. And maybe I smoke too much."

Laura's head shook in exasperation. "I give up."

"Wouldn't do you any good if you didn't. Ask Eddie." Nel grinned. "I get out of this place tomorrow. So tell me more about the wedding."

Laura lifted a hand. "What's to tell? It'll probably be three months before we get to it. Jake's got to wrap up his film, and I've got to wrap up my script."

Nel snorted. "Some Romeo and Juliet the pair of you make. They cut Turner's shooting days when Jess backed out?"

"Yep—eighteen to fourteen. Cut the prep time too, though I'm not sure he minds that all that much, he's so hot to get started."

"You could get hitched during post-production."

It was occurring to Nel that if it were three months to the wedding, she might miss it.

"Uh-uh. I'm not going to spend my wedding night in a dubbing room."

"Wedding night! We're talking technicalities, aren't we?" Nel arched an eyebrow.

Laura smiled at her, and Nel felt the affection.

"So tell me about Jess's movie. She's going to win another Oscar with it, I suppose?"

"Yes, I suppose. There was some sort of snag a couple of days ago, I understand, and Jess has been in a mood like you wouldn't believe. But Stan dropped in to see me today. He says they start filming in eight weeks. It sounds like everything's just fine."

As though on cue the door opened. Jessamyn entered, smiling gaily.

"I must say, Nel, you seem to have your illnesses in fine style," she remarked across the roses in her arms. "Laura darling! What a lovely surprise to find you here. Now I can properly offer my congratulations."

Nel listened closely. Was there a too-throaty note when Jessamyn addressed her daughter? With utmost innocence Jessamyn had swept the pansies aside, filling their place with her own arrangement.

"Tell me all about it," she was gushing. "Where will the honeymoon be? Do you have a house?"

Laura looked wary. She slid from the bed, preparing to leave.

"Our plans are still pretty uncertain."

"Well, darling, do keep me posted. Perhaps I can have a little party for you. I know Jake likes parties. Why don't you give me a call next week? We'll have lunch together."

Nel could sense Laura's confusion. Nel herself was feeling it. She couldn't recall a single time when Jessamyn had dined with Laura voluntarily—certainly not as a twosome. Could this show of sweetness on Jessamyn's part be truly genuine?

There's a chance, but I wouldn't bet on it, she thought silently. If I were you, kiddo, I'd double my guard.

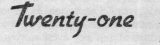

Twenty-one

The next two months were the most hectic of Laura's life. As she held her breath, the new script she was developing for Richard Knox was approved for one revision and then another, each one requiring two-and-a-half weeks of work and days of waiting. Then one day the phone rang, and she heard herself receiving the go-ahead for a final polish. The movie had made it out of the limbo of projects in development and would be produced.

"One out of twenty—good odds to beat," Knox told her as she laughed in disbelief.

"I know, I know!"

The amount of money spent in optioning books and paying writers to develop scripts that would never be produced would be regarded as clearly insane by anyone outside the business. Laura felt giddy that she had hit paydirt on only her second try. By the law of averages she could expect several failures before she hit again, but she knew she could succeed now, and that knowledge was enough to keep her going.

On the day she delivered her final revision, going sleepless for thirty-six hours to meet her deadline as half of her lines of dialogue suddenly seemed to displease her, Jake returned equally enervated from the end of his shoot. They made love, slept, and made love again. When daylight came, with curtains drawn and telephone answering machine on, they slept until noon.

"Christ, look at the time!" exclaimed Jake when he saw the clock. "They'll skin me alive if I don't get going."

He was out of the bed without pause, and Laura felt her lovely sense of tranquility rudely ended.

"Surely you're allowed to sleep in after working two weeks straight," she protested.

"Babe, you don't know the production end of this business." He made a face. "I was one day over budget, which they're mad about, and after raving about every set of dailies I sent back, they've decided they don't like any of them. My director and the studio editor don't see eye-to-eye on things, which need I say creates problems? I have to get over there before the first cut starts and with it World War III."

"All right." Laura sighed. "Good luck."

"Thanks, babe." He stooped to kiss her, already on his way out, dressed but not even shaven. "I'll try to get away for dinner. Want to stay here or go out?"

"Go out. I've spent so much time inside these last two days I feel like a bat."

But at four that afternoon Jake called to say he could not

get away for dinner. Two days passed before they saw each other again.

Laura was coming out of a conference room with two co-producers from Charring Cross Films when she looked up and saw him leaning against a wall at the end of the corridor, apparently waiting. Surprised, she excused herself as quickly as possible and went to meet him, not so hurriedly as to seem less than businesslike to the Charring Cross men, she hoped.

"Hi," she said. "What are you doing here?"

He was wearing jeans and a tweedy jacket, which made him seem younger than usual despite the lines beneath his eyes. Several days' growth of reddish-brown beard obscured the cleft in his chin.

He grinned at her.

"Waiting for some approachable-looking broad to come along. Want to audition?"

He twirled one finger through a tendril of hair and watched it curl. Laura, striking his hand away, glanced over her shoulder.

"Not right here I don't, you idiot! How'd you find me?"

"How does anyone find anyone in this town? I called your agent." Taking her discreetly by the elbow, he led her around the corner. "So you're into a new project, huh? Movie of the Week?"

"Yes, and Michael Townes is part of the package."

"That ought to sell it if it's not sold already."

"It's not. And I'm not so sure Michael will help. It's a wonderful role, but Michael?" She shook her head.

"No? What's the role?"

"A pro boxer turned teacher."

Jake laughed.

"Hey! What are you doing?" she protested as he opened a door and shoved her inside.

"Fixing to put the make on you." He leered. "One of the advantages of having once worked at this studio. I know all the dark little corners."

He kissed her, curling his tongue around hers with insistent playfulness until she succumbed.

Back toward them, a squat man sat pulling film through a Movieola while a sallow-faced gopher rewound it from huge plastic trash cans. The gopher gave them a dirty look. Laura,

avoiding his eyes, laughed breathlessly. She was slightly embarrassed but thoroughly captivated by Jake's high spirits. The
quickness of his shifts of humor still amazed her.

"Well, actually I don't have any more time for this," he
drawled, looking at his watch. "Just stopped by to tell you I'll
meet you back at your place at five. We're going to drive up
toward Oxnard to look at a house."

"Oxnard! Jake, you can't be serious!"

He wiggled his eyebrows. "Love among the rutabagas, my
dear. I got a line on one that's supposed to be as near a steal
as anything in southern California's likely to be."

"It's too far—a good hour's drive from Universal. And
that's with no traffic."

"The drive time's shorter than to Malibu. You miss the
bottlenecks on 405. Anyway, it's not really in Oxnard, just up
that direction. I kind of thought you'd like the idea."

She put her arms around his neck. "You know I do!"

Only when they were free of urban sprawl, winging their
way past acres of black soil lined with lettuces, did Laura
relinquish all fear of some postponement. She leaned back in
Jake's cherished twelve-year-old Mercedes and felt herself grow
as light as a cloud.

"It would be heaven out here," she murmured. "But would
we be crazy?"

"Probably." He grinned. "Let's wait and see the house before we decide. For myself, I like a drive at the end of the
day—helps me unwind. And what with you getting into movies
now, you won't have to make the trip every day, maybe just
once a week." Soberly he reached across the seat to take her
hand. "I think we need the chance to get away by ourselves."

Laura nodded slowly. She wanted what he was suggesting,
and she was reassured by his seeming interest in making things
work. But what if she wasn't able to make a steady go of
movies and special projects? What if she had to go back to a
staff writing job once again?

"Besides," Jake was saying, "we need somewhere where
we can entertain, babe. Those contacts are important for both
of us. A dollar will go father here than it will other places,
and we'll look better." He paused. "Sounds crass, I realize,
but the truth's the truth."

She flinched, wishing sometimes he would refrain from
spelling it all out and at the same time feeling guilty that she

should object when he was, as he had said, simply being truthful.

The house, reached by a drive that curved around the knobby trunks of enormous palm trees, was old. A rough upthrust of land gave it a castlelike perch, setting it apart from the condominiums and sleek new structures that were its neighbors. It was tall, with cool walls and a shaded white terrace overlooking steps that went down to the Pacific splashing directly below. The huge living room had a fireplace equally huge, one which the real estate woman who'd met them there insisted was ready for logs. Half an hour after entering the house, they'd signed the contract and had the keys.

"Oh, Jake! It's wonderful!" Laura whispered as they stood with arms entwined in the empty living room.

"A steal, and still awfully damned expensive," Jake said wryly.

"It's going to be worth it, Jake. In spite of our crazy schedules. In spite of everything. We're going to have a wonderful home, a real home, one where nothing can ever spoil our happiness."

Disengaging himself from her, he lighted a cigarette. He went to stand at the terrace door as though in thought.

Laura was motionless, aware of some tension, aware of something crowding between the two of them.

"Well." He turned abruptly. He was smiling at her, but the smile was forced. "This does make things seem awfully final, doesn't it? I guess we'd better tell Dan Katz when we want the wedding." He hesitated, and there was grimness in the line of his jaw. "You do still want to go ahead with this, I take it?"

Her throat hurt with anxiety. The question shocked her. She thought of this house, of the small room that would make a perfect nursery.

"I want to very much."

And you? she wanted to ask. But she couldn't. Jake was looking at her, and there was darkness in his eyes, a seeming torment that she could not comprehend.

Wordlessly he held his arm out to her. She went quickly to where she could see the steps leading down to the ocean, and she felt him cling to her as she clung to him.

"I love you," he said at last. "God, Laura, I really do love you!"

There was something desperate in the way his fingers traced

her cheek. It frightened her. He was no more certain they'd
make a go of this marriage than she was.

As suddenly as he'd caught her to him, he released her,
lacing her fingers with his own and kissing her hand.

"We ought to open some wine—drink a toast to the house,"
he said. "We can stop and get some cheese somewhere and
have a picnic."

In spite of the light tone, his eyes were still shadowed and
far away from the welcoming room they were turning their
backs on.

What was it? What was happening to the occasion that
should have been so happy? Laura wondered.

"See anything of Jessamyn while I was gone?" he asked
when they had reached the entry hall.

His voice sounded odd, almost too casual. She looked up
quickly.

"No. Nothing. Why?"

"Just wondered if you'd . . . talked or anything."

But Jessamyn's offer of lunch had proved just vacant formality. Laura had called twice and had not even been put
through to her.

"Jessamyn and I have never talked," she said moodily. "I
doubt there's any chance we'll start."

For an instant she thought she saw relief in his expression.

"Yes, of course. Just curious." He smiled.

Jessamyn flung the magazine she'd been reading from her
bed and rang for coffee. It was morning—half-past-six—and
she still had not slept. How dare Nel pull this? she thought in
fury. How dare Nel stay out all night like some oversexed
child? It was undignified. Ridiculous. And had Nel forgotten
she'd been in the hospital with a pulled muscle just two months
back?

Next to Jessamyn, amid the satin sheets, the white dogs
were snoring, their plump bodies making warm spots against
her thighs. *They* had fallen asleep long ago, she thought re-
sentfully. But it was Nel she resented and not them. Her doggies
loved her. They adored the rare treat of being allowed to stay
all night with her. She could trust her doggies. Everyone else
took advantage of her.

Impatiently she rang again for service. A sleepy-eyed Deidre
appeared at the door.

"I'm waiting for some coffee," Jessamyn said shortly.

"Yes, Miss Friday."

Jessamyn lay back in her satin pillows and let herself pout. She'd been unable to sleep last night for fear of The Dream, and that was all Nel's fault.

Nel had grown too cocky, coming and going at her pleasure. She'd been hired to be part of this household. Now she was presuming Jessamyn's good nature.

And these overnight absences had been going on for weeks, it seemed, even months. All the servants had known about it but had said nothing. Three night ago she'd had The Dream, that terrible nightmare, and Nel hadn't been there. *She'd come to depend on Nel, and Nel hadn't been there!*

On impulse she flew from the bed to stare in her mirror. An energy born of anger surged through her. Why should she depend on anyone? She didn't need to. She was going to prove that, and she was going to remind this town just how glorious Jessamyn Friday was.

"Put that down and draw my bath," she snapped as Deidre entered with a tray. "Lay out my clothes. And get out of that stupid robe before I throw something at you."

"But Miss Friday—" The maid was stammering like the imbecile she was. "Miss Friday, where could you possibly be going this time of morning?"

"I'm going to the Beverly Hills for breakfast and—" She cocked her head with a thought that pleased her. "Yes, and I'm taking my dogs."

The animals were so fond of her that they had no need for leashes as other pets did, she thought as she swept into the opulent hotel on Sunset Boulevard with them at her heels. Deidre walked several paces behind the dogs. She was gawking—why hadn't Jessamyn realized she would? Nel never had gawked, but then Jessamyn reminded herself she was annoyed with Nel.

At this early hour, the public rooms of the hotel were almost deserted. In a corner, however, a lone *paparazzi* was cooling his heels, waiting to see who was breakfasting in the Polo Lounge and if any small scandal could be made of guests taking early departures.

Jessamyn's eyes flicked over him as he aimed his camera. At the entrance to the Patio she scooped one fat dog into her arms.

"Deidre, you take Ying-Ying," she ordered, nodding.

As Deidre bent to the other dog, the photographer came nearer.

"Miss Friday—" He clicked away as he asked his question. "Mind telling me what you're doing out so early?"

"Taking my dogs to breakfast."

His finger almost faltered on the shutter.

"In *there*?"

"Of course. I love them."

She pretended to kiss the dog in her arms, and he licked her eagerly. The disgusting little photo monger was getting wonderful pictures. He was getting a wonderful story. By to-morrow—even today—thousands of people would see these pictures. Ravishing, whimsical Jessamyn Friday, indulging her dear little dogs. Why hadn't she thought of bringing them along with her before? They were the perfect foil for her. Her fans would love it. When she left here, she must pop into Cartier's and have some collars made up for Po and Ying-Ying, perhaps something with a few tiny sapphires, or plain gold with Cartier's recognizable clasp. If they were going to be photographed, her darlings must look their best.

The photographer was opening his mouth for another ques-tion, but the maitre d'—a woman—interrupted.

"I'm sorry, madam, but your dogs can't come in here. State law."

"Really? Just send the manager in, and I'm sure he'll tell you how sweet my doggies are." Jessamyn swept by her.

The entire staff of the outdoor dining nook was at her dis-posal. She was seated not in the shade of the giant pepper tree, but in warm morning sunlight. Coffee was before her before she could order it. The waiter and water boy called her by name.

"Orange juice with champagne and croissants for us," she said, flicking an eye at the gaping Deidre. "And bring some steak tartare for my doggies."

In a hotel that prided itself on not blinking at names, where kings and millionaires and anyone worth a piss in the film world had been seen, she heard the almost imperceptible rustle of staff gliding in for a glimpse of her. The *paparazzi*, having been barred from entering, was jumping and clicking, trying to get a shot of her.

"Oh, yes, and some chocolates too," she called to the waiter.

She was going to show those bastards who'd tried to back out of the movie she was making just how much publicity her name drew. She was going to remind them just how big a star she was. And she was going to show Van Greenberg how small his power was compared with hers.

At the thought of Greenberg, her eyes grew narrow with hate. He would pay for meddling with her affairs, but in good time. Just now she was playing a waiting game, laying her own plans for Laura and Jake. She preferred things her way. She always had. Afterward there would still be plenty of time to deal with Greenberg.

"Oh, Miss Friday!" Deidre was staring around her. "This is such a marvelous place! This is such fun! So this is where Miss Laura's reception's going to be."

"Laura's reception?" Half way through shrugging free of her short fur jacket, Jessamyn looked up. This little tidbit from her maid annoyed her. She could afford the luxuries of this hotel. She didn't like the thought that Laura could too. "Well, if it's here, it will cost her every cent she's earned this year," she said.

But Deidre was chattering on happily.

"Oh, she's not paying for it. It's going to be a present from some man named Katz. I heard Nel say."

Jessamyn's hand missed the cup it was reaching for, and china clattered.

"Katz!" she exhaled, leaning forward, taut as a fiddle bow. "Do you mean *Daniel* Katz?"

"But Laura's in the midst of a project. She'll be tied up at least another month, maybe six weeks."

"All right. Six weeks then," said Richard Knox.

Laura looked from Knox to her agent and frowned at their intensity.

"That gives her no breathing time," said Ben Webber. "It's too much pressure. I can't let her do it."

The noise of the restaurant where they were meeting seemed unnecessarily loud. Laura knew what Ben was doing. He was trying to buy time without losing the project. Knox, a slender man whose dark intensity made him spellbinding, gave a smile that was as charming as it was uncompromising.

"If the project with Charring Cross doesn't go all the way, she'll get a breather. And it's always nice to have something else on your plate when that happens. Besides, Laura's a fast writer. She won't be pressured. She's dynamite when she's meeting a deadline. We love her."

Ben sipped his drink and looked at her in question. He was waiting for her to make the decision.

"I do like the project," she said slowly and waited to see if Knox would compromise.

She thought of the things to be done in the next few weeks, the fittings for a wedding dress, supervising the moving of things from her apartment to the house near Oxnard and the arrival of new furniture. And the second draft of the Charring Cross script was coming due. . . .

On the other hand there might not be a third draft. If she let this project go, she might find herself with none in sight at all. She was wary of that possibility. She didn't want to begin the ordeal of waiting all over again. This would make the third project she'd done for Knox, the start, perhaps, of a reputation.

There was another consideration, too, and that was Jake. She had come to realize long ago that he worshipped success. She didn't want to seem less than gritty in her pursuit of it. She wanted him to see her in steady demand.

"I guess if it's got to be six weeks, then six weeks it is," she acquiesced.

It was well in the future. After the wedding. She'd just have to manage to have things in hand by then.

Ben Webber was giving a slight shake of the head, swirling his drink.

"All right, but she's got to have more up-front money under those terms."

"We're talking less bonus then."

"Agreed."

Laura listened, realizing that she as a person had ceased to exist. She had become merchandise, a contract item to be haggled over with little emotion. Knox, whom she had thought so charming, whose approach for this project had flattered her, regarded her as though examining a head of lettuce.

"Okay. Six weeks and we'll iron out the rest." He rose and tossed down the last of his drink. "Hey, have a good wedding."

Twenty-two

Eddie Brown gave critical study to the satin tie he had been attempting to adorn himself with for Laura's wedding. He always felt silly in a bow, but Nel would love it. To his annoyance, though, he was all thumbs. He'd been fiddling with the damn thing for fifteen minutes and still kept bungling it, but this time, he thought, the results looked promising.

The doorbell rang. Eddie swore in exasperation as the slippery satin eluded his fingers. Throwing down the tie, he stalked into the living room.

"Who is it?" he asked, punching the intercom.

"Maintenance, sir."

Just what he needed when he was due to pick Nel up in forty-five minutes. Suppressing impatience, he opened the door, admitted a short kid with curly ringlets, wearing a jacket marked "Ron," and started back to continue battle with the recalcitrant tie.

He was not sure what made him look over his shoulder. Perhaps he'd been waiting so long for them to find him. Perhaps it was an uneasy alertness left from his earliest days as a cop in Detroit.

As he turned, he saw only a blur of movement, the flash of an ice pick. Survival reactions, so deeply ingrained they'd never been lost, made him act.

Without even thinking, he struck at the ice pick. His other hand dealt a single strong blow to the neck of the phony maintenance man.

His assailant went down with a gurgling gasp, a death sound. Eddie stood with legs splayed, scarcely able to assimilate what had happened.

Stupidity, he thought. It was plain stupidity that had let this happen. He lived in a place with a uniformed guard in the lobby. He kept a snub-nosed Smith and Wesson in his bureau drawer. He'd taken precautions, knowing they'd come after him sooner or later. Yet all because of a necktie, he'd opened the door and let their man right in.

Then Eddie realized his left hand was bleeding. The ice pick had caught the edge of it and torn the flesh. Crazily, his first thought was that he must not stain the clothes he'd put on for the wedding. Next he remembered he must not leave any trace of it on the man who'd attacked him. He could call it self-defense, of course—the man on the floor would certainly be found to be a professional hit man. But doing that would mean time and publicity, and in the end it would be pointless anyway. If this one hadn't gotten him, another would. He didn't want the complications of explaining this dead man, especially not this afternoon.

Eddie wrapped the handkerchief in his pocket around his wound. He could dispose of it later in another part of town. Bending, he checked for the pulse he knew would be non-existent in the neck of the curly-haired killer.

In the bathroom, as he covered the cut on his hand with two Band Aids, he tried to think. This was a high-class apartment house with little coming and going in its halls. A maintenance man with a bundle would not likely be noticed even if anyone saw him. There was a package of new sheets still in their plastic package in his closet, white ones that Nel had razzed him about for being too plain for her taste. They'd do. They'd do just fine. Removing his jacket and putting on gloves, Eddie went to work.

The shortness of the body in the living room made it a good fit in the sheets, just as it made the green jacket with "Ron" on the pocket too skimpy on Eddie's long frame. But no one expected custodial help to be dressed right anyhow. He hunched up and dragged the bundle along behind him. To a passer-by it would look like a painter's dropcloth, furnace filters, anything.

The hallway was empty when he looked out. He dragged the bundle down toward a service elevator and propped it against the wall. He punched a button. The elevator doors slid open. He shoved the bundle inside, and with gloves still in place removed the green maintenance jacket, tossing it in too. As the elevator started gliding six floors downward, he walked slowly back to his apartment, a little depressed at how easy it all had been.

In the bathroom, as he stood ripping off his gloves, a strange mood overtook him. Eddie leaned his head against the wall. They knew where he was now; they knew what name he was using. He'd known he was living on borrowed time, but now that the prospect of death was becoming a fact instead of an idea, he resisted it.

He didn't want to die. Him, the cop who in his day had taken a hundred chances. Was he scared? He hadn't been when he'd decided to talk to the FBI and that house committee. He'd been resigned then, and angry—with himself most of all. But after that he had found Nel.

For a moment Eddie felt physically ill. The role of mouse in the cat-and-mouse game was a role for someone else, not him. It would be easier for someone who hadn't been a cop, who couldn't second guess, who was more unaware. He wanted to tell someone about that feeling of icy helplessness. He wanted to tell Nel.

Only he couldn't tell Nel unless he told her all of it. He'd have to tell her he'd been a fool—no, more than a fool. He'd been an innocent, a patsy, and finally much worse. She'd understand. Nel always understood. But he didn't want to tarnish himself in her eyes.

Resolutely he straightened and walked back into the bedroom. Slipping into the white dinner jacket, he buttoned it and tied a perfect bow.

"I feel like some damned mannequin, dolled up like this. Don't know why I let Laura talk me into it."

Nel plucked pettishly at the cymbidium orchids pinned to the shoulder of her silky yellow dress. They made her feel gorgeous, but why let anyone peg her as vain enough to admit it?

"You look beautiful," Eddie said.

All afternoon it had kept striking Nel that he seemed distracted. But now he beamed at her as they danced to a soft, romantic tune.

"Best-looking woman in the room, including the bride," he added.

"Hey, now! Any more talk like that and I'll tell them how much you really spent on that painting you gave them," she cautioned Eddie. "Found it in a junk shop and had it reframed, huh?" She rolled her eyes.

Eddie's hand moved closer around her waist and squeezed. "Come on, Nellie. You eat up that kind of talk."

"Hah! Well, right now I'm interested in eating up a piece of Laura's cake."

Nel glared at Eddie fiercely amid the lavishness that was to have been Laura's "small" reception. It was small enough, she acknowledged, despite the potted palms and sprays of white and yellow flowers, the trays of champagne, and the three-piece combo playing in one corner. Yet it was also tasteful, unmistakably elegant, the perfect setting for Laura herself.

Nel looked affectionately at the girl she had watched grow into a woman. Laura was smiling, standing between her husband and Saul Finer, who had been the fourth member of the bridal party in their brief chapel wedding. In her high-necked white dress and soft pompadour, she looked like a bride from some other era. And beautiful, Nel thought.

Laura's dress made Nel imagine something spun from a cloud. Yard upon yard of silk illusion had gone into the leg o' mutton sleeves with their deep, fitted cuffs. The lace that edged the Victorian neckline had been imported from Belgium. The small coronet of fresh water pearls riding the gleaming dark crest of Laura's hair in lieu of a veil had been a gift from Nel. And at her throat, suspended from two narrow gold bands, hung a five-carat heart-shaped diamond, which Turner had given her only last night.

Grudgingly, Nel admired his taste. The pure understated elegance of that necklace was a perfect reflection of Laura herself. Nel looked at Turner, handsome and, yes, happy-looking in his black tuxedo and let herself warm toward him—for Laura's sake.

Nel closed her eyes. She was tired, drained. Her legs felt as if she'd spent eight hours on them, rehearsing a new show, when in fact she'd lolled around her apartment most of the morning and done nothing more than stand by Laura's side for ten minutes during the wedding this afternoon.

At least she'd made the wedding, though, she told herself with satisfaction. And she was going to live it up at this reception. Opening her eyes, she looked around her again, relieved that Eddie had not returned yet and she could let down for a few minutes more.

An unusual mix of people filled the private party room at the Beverly Hills. There, hobnobbing with Hollywood-types accustomed to these surroundings, were the servants from Jessamyn's household. Those of longest standing—Maria, Lupita, Roberto—had been the only guests apart from Eddie at the actual ceremony. Only DeeDee, who'd have given her eye teeth to be here, was missing, poor thing, stuck on location with Jessamyn. Next to Harry, the houseman, Michael Townes was chattering madly to two men Nel didn't know who were patently gay.

Nel sighed and wondered how many of those in attendance would prove to be Laura's friends in bad times as well as good. Portero had come up from Mexico with a director named Avilas and some sultry fake blonde from the series Laura had written for there; Laura's agent was here as well as Jess's; there in that corner were some people from *Twenty-two Wentworth* and the producer Laura was currently working for; the blonde who'd been Jess's replacement in Turner's film was talking to Saul Finer's wife.

Laura seemed to bring out the best in people. Nel figured that half of those here were basically rats. She could only hope Laura never encountered their dark sides. She ran a hand idly up and down her arm.

"Here we go," said Eddie, returning.

Nel enjoyed a forkful of cake and watched the menagerie.

"Nice party," said Eddie. "I think they'll be happy."

"I hope they will."

Nel let a glob of frosting melt across her tongue. Damn Jessamyn, it wouldn't have killed her to come today. Las Vegas, where she was filming, was only a plane hop away, and it would have meant a hell of a lot to Laura. Why, after all these years, Laura should still be even slightly susceptible to Jessamyn's approval, or lack of it, was one of those mysteries she'd never solve, Nel supposed.

But, hell, maybe they should all be glad Jess hadn't come. The cynical side of Nel kept remembering that part of Sleeping Beauty where the bad fairy came to the party and with her anouncement set the course for future evil.

"Nellie."

Eddie took the empty cake plate from her hands and set it aside.

Nel looked up in surprise and saw that his face had become uncommonly serious.

"Listen, Nellie, I've been thinking. When this is over, let's you and me jump on a plane for Mexico, have a little time to ourselves. What do you say?"

This suggestion caught her unprepared. Usually it was marriage he was pushing.

"You got a preacher lined up there?" she asked suspiciously.

He laughed, but there was something strained about the sound of it.

"You're the hardest woman to get along with I've ever known. Here I'm offering you a trip to Acapulco, and you act like it's a scam." He waited. "Well? How about it?"

Nel looked at him shrewdly, trying to determine what was behind all this.

"I figure it's the perfect time," he said. "Jessamyn's away, you're free. You could take a vacation."

He sounded so earnest, almost urgent. Nel reached out and touched his cheek.

"I'll think about it, but right now I want to dance some more. I aim to wear the soles out of these hundred-dollar shoes!"

She waved to Laura, who was looking in her direction, and started for the dance floor, knowing Eddie would follow.

Happy past belief, Laura turned to her husband, about to urge him toward the dancing too. She could feel his fingers twining tightly around her own, feel the energy pouring back and forth between the two of them, and as they had done so frequently this last half-hour, they smiled at one another. There was something magic about the fact of marriage and it made no sense. They had slept together, lived together, and yet standing here amid this fuss and congratulations, they were welded together in some new and electric way. And looking into his eyes, she knew Jake felt the same.

He started to speak, in this their first split-second of privacy since leaving the chapel. But at that moment she saw Daniel Katz, who had been eluding her, and darted her free hand out to detain him.

"Dan—we've been trying to catch you ever since we arrived!" she laughed. "You keep slipping away."

His eyes twinkled at her from a face bathed in pleasure.

"I've been enjoying myself, and you looked busy."

"It's beautiful, Dan. Thank you so much," she said. Then, words seeming inadequate, she did not resist the impulse that told her to plant a kiss on the cheek of the odd little man who was beaming at her.

"Thank *you*," he replied. His eyes had misted. He took his glasses off and polished them. "We couldn't have cast a prettier bride, do you think, Jake? Ah. I see that Jessamyn's here."

Laura looked around, surprised by the calm announcement. She had not expected that her mother would come, even if she'd been in town instead of away on location. But Jessamyn had come, and Laura did not know exactly how she should feel.

She had wanted it—she could admit that now—and she wondered if there was a part of her that would always be a child under Jessamyn's spell. At the same time she felt wary. She watched the grand entrance, the silly white dogs in their Cartier collars, trailing their owner. Jessamyn was smiling, her gown of shimmering, salmon-colored lurex floating from an empire waist, huge opals surrounded by diamonds and coral glittering at her ears and throat. She was approaching them with both hands outstretched. What did it mean?

"Laura, darling! Aren't you simply glowing!"

To Jessamyn's credit she did not hug her. They both would have known that was phony, Laura thought. Instead her mother caught her hands and leaned back with a smile that almost looked sincere.

"Jake, darling, congratulations. Aren't you lucky?" She nodded carelessly to Katz. "Hello, Dan. I understand you're the one who's throwing this little affair."

Laura did not hear Katz's answer. Instead she looked at Jake, apprehensive of his anger now. Although he knew Jessamyn had been invited, he had not faced her since her vicious blow at his career. To Laura's puzzlement she perceived in him not the undiluted animosity she'd been expecting, but a wariness, a tautness that seemed uneasy. As though attempting to hide it from her, he smiled and squeezed her hand.

"Don't worry, I won't try to drown her in the punch bowl," he whispered.

In spite of the light note, Laura could feel his tension. Jessamyn flicked a glance toward him as if she too were aware of it and it pleased her.

"Look, darlings, I really can't stay." Jessamyn linked her arm through Laura's. "I just popped in to wish you well and to give you a little present I've worked up for you."

Raising her voice, she gestured for attention.

"Listen, everyone! I've got an announcement to make! I've thought and thought about what sort of present to give Jake and Laura, and it seemed to me that their own production company would be the perfect thing—assuming they won't mind too much having me as a silent partner. The money's in the bank, and the papers are all drawn up awaiting whatever name they choose for it. I do hope you'll all join me in wishing their venture great success."

There were gasps in the crowd as people realized the magnitude of what she was saying, then applause, more for Jessamyn's largess than for anything else, Laura felt sure. She was stunned, and she saw the same emotion reflected in Jake's face. If what Jessamyn said was true, she was talking of millions invested. Why?

This was Jessamyn's show now, completely so. Every eye in the room was fixed on her. Van Greenberg regarded her from a distance, blandly smoking. Daniel Katz's eyes had lost their twinkle. Saul Finer—poor Saul, who was about to be kicked out of his partnership with Jake, it seemed—looked thunder-struck. Why? Why this change of direction, Laura wondered again?

Like a tigress who knew no one would challenge the sweep of her claws, Jessamyn smiled, now at Daniel Katz and now at Van. It was not a pleasant smile. She turned to Laura again before there could be questions.

"Laura . . . Jake . . ." Her voice was intimate. "Let's the three of us bury the hatchet. What do you say? I know I haven't given either of you reason to like me. I'd like to do this as a means of atoning—I really would. It would free Jake to develop his considerable talents as a producer without the constant worry over finances. And Laura, I understand you're coming right along as a writer—"

"What's in it for you?" Jake's voice was sharp and welcome in Laura's ears as he cut in.

Jessamyn gave a slow and candid smile. "Money. Of course. I'm sinking a lot of it into this, and I expect to make lots more. I'm confident you'll put together spectacular films, Jake, and we've all got sense enough to know my name attached to this, even as a silent partner, is good for publicity."

She paused and took a glass of champagne from a passing waiter.

"Cold, hard business. I know you wouldn't believe any other reason. Still, I did hope the arrangement might appeal to you. It would give the two of you a lot of freedom, a little boost. We don't have to love each other to mutually benefit, do we? That's the ugly truth about what families exist for, I'm afraid, Laura darling."

Laura steeled herself against the irony in Jessamyn's voice and against the thought that perhaps it contained a germ of truth. She felt Jake's eyes seeking her own. They were troubled, uncertain. The wariness that she had sensed in him on Jessamyn's arrival was even clearer now, but something else was pushing through. Temptation? Eagerness? His dislike of Jessamyn, his distrust of her was there in his face, but Jessamyn's offer appealed to his weak spot, Laura realized. It gave him a chance to have power instead of courting it. It promised him success faster, and the opportunity to prove himself was Jake's greatest need.

"Whatever you want, Jake." The words stuck in Laura's throat as she answered his unspoken question.

He shook his head, but slowly. "No, Laura. It's up to you."

Laura knew it wasn't. Not really. He was willing now to defer to her no matter how much this meant to him, but she couldn't put herself between Jake and the chance this would give him. She couldn't even appear to. And meeting Jessamyn's gaze, Laura knew that Jessamyn knew it too.

"It's a wonderful offer. Thank you, Jessamyn," she said. She saw Jake grin.

Maybe I'm wrong to assume she's up to something, Laura thought as she watched her mother making her way back toward the door for her departure. Except I know I'm not wrong. I've been around her too long. I've hoped she'd be different too often. I've been too naive. Damn it, she's deliberately trapped me, springing this business partnership in public so I'd have no choice but to accept it!

"I want to dance," she said, turning abruptly to Jake.

"Me too," he said happily, but his arms were too tight around her, as though in spite of everything some worry still remained with him. "The first thing we'll do is hire a bodyguard and an accountant to make sure we survive with Jessamyn," he said.

"And then, Mrs. Turner, I'm going to lay the world at your feet."

Laura smiled, but deep in her throat she felt tears. Closing her eyes, she tried to lose herself in music and laughter. Ten minutes ago she had been so happy. Ten minutes ago her future with Jake seemed as fresh and unspotted as the white dress she wore. Now, unaccountably, it felt soiled. As she whirled in Jake's arms, she sensed she was playing some new game with Jessamyn—a game that she must win.

Nel glided contentedly in Eddie's arms, enjoying the growing gaiety of Laura's reception and riding the music, which always lifted her.

The next instant she did something she'd never done on a dance floor before, something she'd never done anywhere before in her life, in fact. She stumbled.

"You okay?" Eddie asked, catching her.

"Yeah, sure."

She'd been watching a waiter, wondering if he'd cut through the dancers and spill his tray of drinks. Maybe she'd unconsciously dodged and made a misstep. But the combo had not played many more bars before she did the same thing again, this time without a waiter in sight.

"Eddie, I've got to sit down," she gasped. She was suddenly dizzy.

"Nellie?" His eyes were frantic as he walked her to a chair and eased her into it.

Nel managed a grin. "Damn, I guess I'm snockered. Guess I'm getting too old to guzzle so much champagne and then try to hoof it."

"Want some coffee then? I'll get a waiter."

She shook her head. It wasn't champagne affecting her. She knew it. Eddie knew it.

"What I really want is for you to take me home. Will you do that, Eddie? Let's just slip out. I'd hate to spoil Laura's good time."

Eddie looked torn apart. She hoped he didn't press her.

"Are you sure, Nel? You're going to miss a lot of fun. You could just have that coffee. Then we could take a walk somewhere until you felt better."

Nel shook her head again. Coffee wouldn't help, and she was starting to feel desperate. She thought she was breathing, but the air didn't seem to reach her lungs. She had to get away. She didn't want to spoil things for Laura. Not now. Not here.

"Please. Just take me home," she said.

Twenty-three

In Jessamyn's house everything was deserted. It seemed strange to let herself in with a key, and Nel suffered pangs of jealousy as she thought of the rest of the household staff still enjoying themselves at the reception.

"Feeling any better?" asked Eddie as they walked through silent rooms.

Nel nodded.

Silent rooms. That was what she was becoming, her limbs a collection of spaces no longer occupied by sentient muscles.

"No coming in," she said at the door to her apartment. "I'm just going to sleep this off."

Ever since Jess had made that scene about her staying out all night a few weeks ago, Eddie had often spent the night here with her. But not tonight. She could feel a telltale trembling starting in her right arm.

"Let me stay with you, Nel."

Eddie's face was concerned — more concerned than it should be over her being a little bit tipsy.

"Go on, Eddie. I'll be all right." He didn't budge, so Nel pushed at him playfully, but her voice came out harsh and sharp. "I don't need a nursemaid, Eddie!"

She watched him struggle with the agony inside him and searched his eyes for any trace of pity. He had, after all, broken down that door and seen her gripped by her disease in all its ugliness.

But there was no pity. Reluctantly he turned away.

Nel loved him more then than she had ever loved him before, for allowing her her dignity, her vanity, even when it tore at his very entrails.

"Hey," she said in a husky voice, "we could just neck a little before you go."

He closed her eyes with his kisses and held her close.

"If you want me, Nellie, call," he said. "And think about that trip to Mexico, will you?"

Then he left.

Inside her sitting room Nel turned on every light. As she crossed the room to her chaise longue, she suddenly became aware of feeling nothing, nothing at all in her legs. They had ceased to exist except that they held her—they had not failed her completely yet. She eased herself down on the couch and waited as the spasm in her arm grew stronger.

This time she simply watched, mesmerized by her own helplessness. A mindless anger swept her. With both hands, she clumsily began to beat at her legs, wanting to hurt them, wanting to prove they were still alive. The orchid corsage wavered at the edge of her vision with every blow. Why couldn't she feel anything? Why? She could bear the loss of her arms, but not her legs.

No, she shouted inwardly, she would not be hysterical. She would control herself—even the trembling arm—by sheer force of will. Bending over double, resting forehead on knees, she instructed the arm to obey her. After a long time the tremors ceased, and it seemed to comply.

Now her familiar room seemed like a cage. Restlessly Nel walked out to the living room, turning on lights. She walked onto the patio, to the pool where she had spent so much time, where she had laughed. The stars were bright tonight, and their sparkle and the backlit greenery along one side of the pool made it seem like a stage.

The stage that was still the core of her. After all these years with Jess she still thought of herself as a dancer. Inside her head, music started to play.

Nel whirled and kicked a slender leg head-high, and then determinedly she kicked again. No. No, she could not believe that her dancing had ended tonight at Laura's party. She could not believe she would never depend on these legs again.

But the tempo increasing inside her was more than that of music. It was something else that pushed her, nudged at her, and all at once, down the long stretch of the deserted pool, she was moving, spinning, strutting, keeping time to the silent music of an old routine. Kick-turn-kick-turn-kick-turn-dip; kick-turn-kick-turn-kick-turn-dip. Swing it down the center now; make your smile wide. Tum-de-dah-de-tum-de-dah-de-dum-dum-dum.

Her arms described wide arcs. A fine sweat started around her hairline. She hurled herself around the entire perimeter of the pool, faster and faster, putting herself through the most demanding steps. She dropped to her knees and walked Jolson-style to the music, then backed up with a tushy thrust and danced again. Her pectoral muscles were taut, her hands poised gracefully on outstretched arms. Her legs were carrying her, but she could not feel.

Now she was gasping for breath. *Look at me! Look!* she wanted to cry. *Where is my defect?* She was pushing her legs, but they had not failed her.

A mystical happiness began to settle over her. Perhaps she would not dance after tonight, but for now the music was lifting her up and up, making her light, freeing her of the ground as she had not been since she was a girl. She was free . . . she was free . . . and nothing else mattered.

Her pointed toe reached for a star, and then on the downward swing it did not stop. She crumpled, collapsing on the coldness of the patio. Tears flowed from her without her volition, as all other parts moved without her now. She heard herself sobbing. Her fists ground the concrete, resisting it over and over until they bled.

Twenty-four

Laura washed down two aspirins with club soda and tried to ignore the din of the party going on around her. It was louder than most, the wake for a comedy series that had been can-celled, and Jake was having a fine time, his rusty head bent to intent conversation in the opposite corner of the room.

As of tonight they'd been married a month. She'd hoped

Jake would remember, maybe even suggest a small celebration. Instead they were here because Jessamyn knew a character actor from the moribund series would be hunting work now. He'd be great in a role in Jake's new project. His presence would practically guarantee it went to series, Jessamyn said.

This was the third night this week they'd been to a party because either Jake or Jessamyn thought the connections were right. Laura tried to expel resentment from her mind. Of course Jake had to contact people, but it seemed to Laura he'd managed that well enough working with Saul or with Bernie Goldman, and still had some time left for a private life.

If I had my own car, I could go on home, she thought. But her second-hand Chevy was in for repairs, and she'd ridden into the city with Jake today. Of course she had a key to his Mercedes, she could take it. Only then he'd be stranded. Anyway, though he pretended otherwise, she knew he died a thousand deaths at the thought of anyone else driving his cherished car.

Maybe it was just this lousy headache that was making her sulky, the product of relentless hours spent on her new project for Richard Knox. Or maybe she was still worrying over her lunch with Nel.

Laura eased herself onto a couch and wondered if Jake would be willing to leave when he'd finished his pitch.

Nel and Eddie had spent a month in Mexico, returning only when Jessamyn's location shooting ended. Laura had thought it was wonderful for them, but Nel had looked tired today. Too much dancing till dawn, she'd said in that breezy way of hers. Nevertheless, Laura felt concerned. At least Nel had given up smoking, which might explain part of that drained look. Withdrawal was making her shaky, Nel said.

"Hey. Do you like to mess around with married men?" asked a voice in her ear.

Jake had draped himself over the back of the couch and was grinning at her.

"If that's an invitation to your place, I do," she said with a smile.

"Takes too long to get to my place. I was thinking we could use the bathroom." He nodded toward a hallway, clearly teasing.

"Sorry, but I tried to use it about two minutes ago for other things and found it being used to divy up horse."

"Great. They won't notice us then." He kissed her neck stealthily. "Want to go? How's your head?"

"Don't ask."

"Okay. I'll just say goodbye to Parker and we'll duck out."

They stood up together, and Jake squeezed her hand. While he circled around to speak to the character actor, Laura walked toward the door.

A dark head, beautifully shaped, caught her attention. She smiled and waved.

"Hello, Michael. How are things going?"

As Michael Townes caught sight of her, he fairly bristled.

"They'd be going one hell of a lot better if it weren't for you," he snapped.

Nearby two men stopped talking and looked at him. Laura was stunned.

"I wanted that lousy Charring Cross picture," Michael continued, more vehemently. "I wanted the chance it would have given me to change directions. But no, it's down the tubes now, and all because of you!"

"Because of *me!*"

This was the first she knew that the Charring Cross film had been rejected, but then it wasn't uncommon for the writer not to hear. If a film went to production, they called and praised you; if it didn't, there was silence, likely as not.

"Michael, I don't know what you're talking about!"

"I'm talking about that damned script of yours. That's what sunk the project! The concept was wonderful, but you couldn't bring it off. You didn't have the expertise. You're too bloody new as a writer!"

Everyone around was listening now. Laura's face felt hot. She couldn't believe a friend of long standing was turning on her like this, and she was incensed by these gratuitous potshots at her skills.

"Well, you could have walked into those meetings with network, too, instead of swishing. That would be a big first step in changing direction!"

Someone snickered, and Michael started to color. Then Jake was at her side, his frown disapproving.

"Christ, Laura, what—?"

"Never mind. Let's go."

They broke free of the party and walked to their car in utter silence.

"I guess I made a scene," she said. She leaned her throbbing head against the seat.

"Yep. I guess you did." Jake wasn't condoning it.

She sat up, thoroughly angry, ignoring her head.

"Jake, he attacked me in front of all those people! The Charring Cross project's apparently off, and he said my script was to blame! He announced to everyone present that I'm too green to write a movie. Never mind my ego, what do you suppose that does when my name comes up for some project with someone who heard him?"

"Not a hell of a lot. You know how things are at parties. But it doesn't exactly help either of us for you to have called him a swisher."

"*Either* of us!" She didn't like what she was hearing. Clamping her jaws together, she settled back. "Yes, I'm aware what parties are like—and I'm sick of them."

"Stop sticking your head in the sand. They're essential."

"Oh, yes—so Jessamyn says."

Jake nodded darkly, letting the car leap forward with frightening speed.

"So now we're back to your jealousy over Jessamyn, are we? I wondered how long it was going to take before that surfaced."

"I'm not jealous." Laura's words were so tight she could hardly release them. "I'm just surprised you let yourself be manipulated, that's all."

Jake's voice was only barely controlled.

"You're a damned idealist, Laura. I was too, once. Do you think you're the only one who ever wanted to stay pure and undefiled in this business? Sure, I'd like to be free of Jessamyn's influence, but I'm not. Go easy on the virtue. You're integrity hasn't been tested yet."

After a long silence, he reached over and took her hand.

"Look, let's not quarrel, shall we? But to give the devil her due, Jess does have a good head for business. I think we'll be able to promise Parker Gordon as part of this package, so I think tonight was worth it, what do you say? Tomorrow night will be just ours, I promise. We'll build a fire. Laze around. Got an anniversary to celebrate, as I recall."

He squeezed her hand. "Okay?"

Laura held herself rigid against him, then gave in.

"Okay."

* * *

The following day it was almost eight when Jake came home. Laura was on the terrace, standing at the top of the long flight of steps leading down to the ocean, watching a small dog run up the beach, snapping at waves.

"Hi," Jake said, coming out through the open terrace doors to embrace her.

"Hi."

They nuzzled each other.

"See you're in your working uniform," he said, grinning at her jeans and loosely tied shirt. "Black and white for business and jeans for working."

"Oh, Jake! I'm not *that* bad am I?"

"You're great. Gorgeous both ways. Besides, it gives me a clue to what you've been up to."

"Come on, I've got a surprise for you." She caught his hand and pulled him back toward the house.

"Let me guess. You've adopted a St. Bernard. My God, we'll never be able to keep it in chocolates!"

Laura laughed. "In the kitchen, silly. Where do you usually get your surprises?"

He wiggled his eyebrows. "Sometimes in bed. Ummm! Fresh mushrooms. He tossed a handful toward his mouth like popcorn and lifted the lid of a skillet. "This it?"

"Yep. Veal marsala."

"I'm drooling already. Want to help me take a shower before we eat?"

Afterwards they dressed, touching often. While Jake built the fire, Laura put the veal on plates, glad for the day help who would come in tomorrow and tidy the kitchen.

They ate by firelight. When the last of the wine was gone, Jake pulled her down in his arms and they lay on the softness of carpet covered by a white bearskin rug.

"Going to be hell if we ever get a live-in housekeeper," he teased. "Cramp my style."

"I doubt it." She flicked at his chest.

Laughing softly, he stroked her hair.

"I like this." The fire on the raised hearth above them made dancing shadows of gold in his eyes. "I like *you*, Ms. Turner." Tucking one arm beneath his head, he let his gaze rove over the room, taking in the glass-and-chrome tables and the modern slinged-bottomed sofa upholstered in tan suede that had been their greatest extravagance. "Hell of a lot different from the place I grew up in. And a hell of a far cry from the way things were with my parents."

Laura nestled his cheek against her hand. He always looked grim when he spoke of the past, and there was a flash of that same ill-at-ease uncertainty she'd seen in his eyes the first time they met. That was why he drove himself so. That was why he needed success. They had never spoken of it, just as they never spoke of her years with Jessamyn. They were both trying to make a separate reality here in the present.

When we have children, we'll really have succeeded, Laura thought. We'll be our own complete unit, looking ahead instead of backward.

Inside her an eagerness stirred, which she had felt more and more of late. Allowing herself to love Jake, with all the risks attendant on love, had unlocked all the most guarded of her hopes. Of course the time would have to be right for having a child, and Jake would have to agree, but she longed to add this dimension to her life. A child, wanted and treasured, would somehow free her from Jessamyn, connecting her firmly to the future.

"Hey. Let's keep next weekend free and have it all to ourselves," Jake said. "We'll turn on the answering machine and pretend we're not home. I'll pick up some mettwurst at a place I know, and we can cook on the beach. I've noticed that stable up the way rents horses. We can try riding—and if you tell me you already know how, I'll pinch you."

The completeness of his plans set her laughing again.

"Pinch then 'cause I had lessons as a kid and I'm pretty great!"

"Umm, I should have guessed." He rolled her over on top of him and spread her legs, urging her to a kneeling position. "All that natural talent I've been noticing . . ."

He moved enticingly beneath her, and Laura felt her body reaching out to his. His hands slipped up the front of her thighs to her waist, and he undid her zipper.

"God, but I love the feel of you!" he whispered.

Shoulders lifted off the floor, he kissed her. They were wedged together, and their tongues met greedily. Jake's hand shoved into her pants, exploring her moistness.

The doorbell rang.

He cursed.

"God damn it, who's that?" he said as it rang again insistently. They looked at each other, wrenched from completeness, and finally with a groan, he rose.

Moments later from the front hall Laura heard Jessamyn's voice.

". . . Hope I didn't disturb you," she was saying. "I was just on my way to a party at Marty Q's and thought I'd swing up this way first. There are some business things we should talk over."

Laura stuffed her shirt back into her jeans and fastened them, immediately angry with herself for reacting like a guilty teenager caught on the couch. It was Jessamyn who was in the wrong, not her. Marty Quinlan's house was in Malibu and nowhere near here. She did not seriously try to hide the fact she was out of sorts as Jessamyn swept in.

"Hello, Jessamyn. Where are the dogs?"

"Oh, I don't take them out at night. They need their beauty sleep." Jessamyn's gaze skipped over the empty dishes on the hearth. "Supper by firelight. Isn't that fun."

To Laura the words spoiled the act they claimed to approve.

"Darling, do you suppose you could fetch me some iced tea?" Jessamyn asked now. "I'm simply parched."

Jake was settling into an armchair.

"Of course." Laura matched Jessamyn's dripping honey with her own and hoped that Jessamyn recognized it as equally false.

In the kitchen she tried to control her temper. Iced tea, for God's sake. It would have to be made hot and then poured over ice. Furthermore, it was assumed by the others that she'd be the one to make it. Leaning an elbow on top of the microwave, she breathed deeply. Calling her part of the newly formed production company had been pure farce.

From the living room she heard the drone of voices, but the sound of it wasn't loud enough to drown her own thoughts. If Jessamyn hadn't wished this production company on them, their house would still be inviolate. Their evenings alone wouldn't be invaded—at least not by her. If it hadn't been for the bloody company, Jessamyn would have been well out of her life by now.

She tried to keep me from getting work, Laura thought; she tried every trick to come between Jake and me. And I know this latest phase—the business—is some sort of trick. Why can't I tell her off, tell her I'm wise to her, tell her to get her own tea? Why can't I bring myself to break with her once and for all?

Laura pushed down resentment, dropped ice into a glass, and carried the freshly made tea into the living room. She felt a sudden urge to pour it on Jessamyn's head.

"Money is no object," Jessamyn was saying. "If he likes the role and you think he's right for it, then we'll have him. And that, I should think, pretty much takes care of the project you're working on now—except of course for selling it. Now them—" She interrupted herself to take the tea with a smile and set it aside untouched. "That brings us to one of the things I really wanted to talk about."

She crossed her legs. They were slim and attractive against the hem of her silky cream dress.

"You've got this project all but wrapped up," she said. "And another in gestation. Now we've really got to start going after the people to sell them to—and the critics. I think FFT ought to have a party, get cozy. Wait, Jake, I'm aware that you know some of the network people, but not enough. Hy Weinstein's new at CBS, I believe, and rumored to have a soft spot for westerns. Who better to hear about your *nouveau* oater, I ask you? And Robin Sells would mention us nicely in that damned syndicated column of hers if she came. She owes me one."

For one who had never dirtied herself with the TV scene, Jessamyn had learned an amazing amount in a short time, Laura acknowledged. Jessamyn was intelligent. That was what made her so dangerous.

"Well, we can work that out in a minute," she was saying. "More pressing, I think, is Kimberly Curran. She's a fine actress, Jake, and she wants to work with us—with you. If *Helen Somebody* is a smash, as the network is saying it will be, we could do worse than to throw her at people again while her name's still hot. I think we ought to start looking seriously for a property for her. What do you say?"

Good God, how Jessamyn could turn things to her own favor! In the past month she had become as thick as thieves with the blond actress who had stepped into the role conceived for Jessamyn herself.

Jake was frowning slightly. "I don't know. The idea's good, but the timing isn't. Juggling two projects is one thing; three's quite another. I don't want to overcommit myself."

Jessamyn's eyebrows raised. "Darling, hire an associate

producer then. Let him handle the legwork. Let him handle the location problems. It's putting together the packages that's fun anyway, isn't it? Free yourself up."

Neither of them was even going through the motions of asking her opinion, Laura noted.

"I'll be thinking of something for Kimberly, but on a low level," Jake said. "I don't like the thought of giving up control on the other projects. As far as the party goes..."

He paused to look in her direction, and Laura smiled woodenly. She mustn't speak her mind. She mustn't show vexation with Jessamyn, or Jake would be accusing her of jealousy again. More and more she was certain she and Jessamyn were playing a game for very high stakes. At risk was not just a business partnership, but her marriage itself!

"Good," said Jessamyn, rising. "I thought next Saturday might be a good time."

"All right. Next Saturday then." Jake nodded.

"And it would throw more attention on you if we had it here instead of at my place. Unless you don't feel up to entertaining on that scale yet, Laura darling."

"I'm up to it. No problem, Jessamyn."

So much for mettwurst on the beach, she thought.

Already Jake was showing her mother out, the two of them intent on whatever they were saying. Laura picked up the empty supper dishes and Jessamyn's untouched tea and walked into the kitchen. No jealousy, no resentment. She repeated the self-admonition like a litany.

Jake strolled into the room, hands in his pocket.

"Well, I guess that kills next weekend," he said ruefully.

"I guess."

And Jessamyn's visit had spoiled this evening too, she thought. The romantic mood that had held them by the fire was gone, evaporated. This nearly limitless chance to create fine films was as tantalizing to Jake as chocolates were to Jessamyn's fat white dogs.

"It won't be like this forever," he said as if to convince himself as well as her. He came forward a few steps and put an arm around her. "Once we get rolling, things'll get smoother, and we'll have more time to ourselves. You'll see."

She held at bay the tears that wanted to burn her eyes, the dimming picture of the future.

"I hope so. I don't relish the thought of trying to raise a

family the way things are now."

Behind her she felt him stiffen.

"Is that an announcement?"

His voice was guarded, the voice of a stranger. Laura pulled away to look at him, as upset by what she heard there as by the rest of the evening.

"No—but would it be so terrible if it were?"

He shook his head slowly. "Christ, Laura, it would be the end of your career. Don't you know that?"

"I can't see how my being pregnant could possibly matter a damn. I assume those network veeps in their blow-dried hair know people fuck."

"Sure they do—and they know that's different from setting yourself up to play Mama. Try that before you've gotten good and established, and they're not going to take you seriously as a writer. If that's what you want, fine. But those are the facts."

Laura stared at him, put off by this unexpected coldness.

"Is that your opinion, or is it Jessamyn's?" she asked and stalked from the room.

"Hey, Laura. Nice party."

"Thanks."

Laura smiled at her departing guest and watched Jake dangling Hy Weinstein's wife on his arm as he had been for fifteen minutes. The woman must be a nymphomaniac, Laura thought, judging by the way she'd cast herself on various men throughout the evening. Or maybe, just as the life of a network official was more demanding than that of a producer, the life of a network official's wife was more difficult too. Who could say? Maybe Weinstein was so constantly caught up in projects that he was never home to satisfy even the most basic cravings.

She looked around and was pleased again with the ambiance she'd created for this party. Everywhere she looked she could see white Lenox vases filled with orchids, their delicate white petals spread to expose magenta dappling, their waxy green leaves and unopened buds giving everything in the vast living room the feeling of a tropical paradise.

Her dress too was a deep, glossy green, a long, fluid Halston creation wrapped on one side and secured at the waist by a silkened scarf. It's low, unstructured top was held up by one narrow strap. There had been no thought of wearing anything but panties beneath it. The dress had come through the evening in splendid shape and so had she—even though that creep of a character actor Jake was wooing had pinched her bottom.

She congratulated herself on her own planning. The caviar iced in silver dishes had not run out, and the rumnaki, the pickled mushrooms, the chilled asparagus tips, and bite-sized quiches had been in good supply. All in all she thought she had been a success.

Other guests were leaving. The party was breaking up at last, thank God. Now the Weinsteins took their departure—it was the first time they'd been together all evening—and Jessamyn, the last to go, made her way toward the door with one arm tucked through Jake's. She was laughing softly, and as they reached the hallway, she glanced back toward Laura with an unreadable smile.

In anyone else's eyes it would be mere comraderie, this clinging to Jake, Laura thought. Even she herself did not believe it was real flirtation, only the trappings of it, designed, she would bet, to needle her. She dumped the contents of the ashtrays in the trash and filled them with water.

Jake wandered into the kitchen, looking pleased with himself.

"Well, did we sell Weinstein?" she asked.

"Yeah, I think so. I've got an appointment to see him first thing Monday." He stood lost in thought while she went out and came back with two more ashtrays. "Don't bother straightening up," he said. "Tish will do it."

"Tish doesn't come till Monday. I don't want to have to smell these things all day tomorrow."

"We should have live-in help."

She shook her head. "We manage just fine."

"Weinstein was appalled we didn't," Jake said, dwelling on this point, which had never captured his interest before. "He couldn't believe we didn't have anyone here to help out tonight."

Laura tossed a dish towel onto the counter, turned off by his willingness to dance to Weinstein's tune.

"Well, I don't happen to think we did so damn badly, but if you do, then maybe we should borrow one of Jessamyn's spares the next time. Maybe we should borrow the dogs too, so we can really make a good impression!"

Turning her back on him, she walked into the living room.

Damn it, what was happening to them? What did it matter what kind of help they had?

The fire was dying. She knelt to punch the last of it into a pile and watched new flames leap into being where heat was concentrated. Behind her, she was aware of Jake, though she had not heard him.

"Hey, babe. The party was fine," he said.

He placed light hands on her shoulders, but she did not respond.

"I just want to give you better," he said, his voice halting. "I want you to have what other women around here have."

"I have what I want. My God, Jake, don't you see how affluent we'd look by other standards? And that's not what matters anyway. What matters is us—and whether we're happy."

She was facing him now, wanting desperately to get through to him. Surely he wouldn't be drawn into this sort of material competition. Sometimes she thought she caught glimpses of a less certain Jake, not quite so confident, not quite so wise as he pretended to be. Why didn't he turn to her? Why was he so easily influenced by someone like Weinstein when those weren't his standards? It made her uneasy.

He stretched out full-length in front of the fire. His face was a reflection of its restless energy.

"But don't you see, Laura? There are no more frontiers left to conquer—and pushing out, overcoming hard odds, that's always been part of the human impulse. These days the only way a man can test himself or prove himself—to anyone—is by making a bundle."

Reaching out, he took her hand, twirling her wedding set slowly around and around her finger.

"I want to look around me and have the satisfaction of knowing I've made it. I want to know I've done something with my life. I want to know I'm worth something. Damn it, I don't want to be like my old man."

Laura didn't understand. Yet she knew he was revealing some private part of himself to her, and she spoke softly.

"Your father had a drinking problem, Jake, and he was a bully. You're nothing like that. You never will be."

He smiled uncertainly. "Not if I have you to believe in me, I won't."

They watched the fire together. He spoke again.

"I ran into Saul at lunch today. He ignored me. Pretended not to see me. Guess he's still sore about the arrangement with Jessamyn."

"I'm sorry to hear that, Jake. I liked Saul."

"Yeah. So did I. He's so open. Not macho. I always felt I could be—oh, well." He shrugged. He eased her down so they lay facing each other. "Just as long as you're still my friend, babe."

Laura arched one eyebrow, teasing him. "In spite of Mrs. Weinstein, you mean?"

A pale amusement lightened his somberness. "Christ, wasn't she something?" He paused. "Not jealous, I hope."

Enjoying herself immensely, Laura folded one arm beneath her head and lay back.

"Not in the least." From under her lashes, she watched his surprise. "If you'd headed for a closet, I'd have had to negotiate—her or the wonderful property I've found for Kimberly Curran. Never marry a man whose price you don't know, that's my motto."

He grinned now. "Are you serious?"

"Yep. A novel that was published last year. I'd never heard of it, but the cover made it sound interesting. I started reading it just for fun, and fifty pages into it, it hit me."

"You're right. You know my price. Hey, what's the title?"

He was eager, and that special chemistry was there between them.

"Tell you tomorrow—if you ask me nicely."

"Uh-uh." He lunged on her, restraining her arms with his own. "Tomorrow I have plans for you. I've been reading this really great book too, see, and it's given me ideas. First I'm going to tie your hands and feet to the bedposts. Then—"

She was laughing now, and she pulled an elbow free to dig at his ribs.

"Oh, shove it, Turner!"

He recaptured her arm and stretched it high above her head, bringing them together.

"That's exactly what I'm telling you I've got in mind—Turner."

Suddenly, at one in the morning, the telephone rang. With a groan Jake rolled over and answered it.

"Oh," he said an instant later. His voice had chilled.
He handed her the phone.
"It's for you. It's Greenberg."

Twenty-five 🐦

"Are you happy, Laura? Are you glad you married him?"

Laura looked up from her salad, surprised as usual by Van's candor.

"I'm very happy. I love him," she said simply.

Greenberg took a cigarette from his case and tapped it thoughtfully, looking out across the crowded restaurant.

"I do hope I didn't cause any bad feelings, calling you."

"No, of course not." She could hardly admit that Jake had stalked upstairs in pointed silence, and that after those overtures to each other in front of the fire, they'd fallen asleep on opposite sides of the bed. "It was one hell of an hour, though," she acknowledged. The rest of the weekend had been strained, and the week that followed improved only by its focus on business.

Now it was Monday again. Laura looked at her watch, thinking of the meeting Jake had insisted she come to this afternoon. She'd have to get a cab. Her car was in the shop again. She wanted to get a new one, but Jake was being virtuous over money just now. Oh well, in a few hours she'd find a cab and learn whether Jessamyn shared Jake's enthusiasm for the novel she'd found. She hoped her St. Laurent suit, with its crisp, white jacket, trimmed by gold buttons at the waist and cuff, didn't wilt in the meantime.

"This producer you thought I should meet is awfully late," she said. "Either he's forgotten, or he's decided he doesn't have time for novice screenwriters."

Greenberg's blue eyes rested on her calmly.

"He won't be coming. There was no producer. I wanted to see you, and I doubted there was any other way."

Laura leaned back. She found herself tensing, annoyed and uncomfortable now.

"I suppose I'm not a very gracious loser," Greenberg continued. "I didn't like having you vanish from my life. In fact I even went to Jessamyn before you were married. I tried to persuade her to help me. I'd had it in mind that she might lie for me, tell you she was carrying Turner's child." He paused and brought the cigarette to his mouth. "You know, of course, that they were intimate."

A coldness welled through her. Greenberg was frigntening. His innuendo was frightening.

"So much for confession," he said wryly. "Jessamyn wouldn't help me obviously, and you say you're happy. I suppose I had to see you and hear for myself. That's all."

He gave a slight smile. The eyes holding hers were bottomless. Laura felt threatened and shocked by her misjudgment of Van Greenberg.

He isn't even apologizing for what he tried, she thought. And it was ghastly. Mad. She had not believed—still could not believe—that Van cared for her enough to try such an outrageous thing. More likely, and more appalling, he had gone to such lengths—or simply brought her here and invented the story—out of the merest whim.

He reached across the table and covered her hand with his own. She drew back quickly.

"I won't bother you again. I promise, Laura."

She nodded, unable to shut out thoughts that his words had sparked. He'd been wrong about Jake and Jessamyn, of course. Jake had assured her.

"Look, I—I'd better go now, Van." She rose. "Frankly I think this was rotten of you, and it's upset me."

Why hadn't Jessamyn gone along with what Van wanted? The fact that she hadn't touched Laura with surprised relief.

Van was standing now too, still smiling.

"I understand. I'm sorry," he said. "But Laura . . ."

She looked back over her shoulder, already turning away.

"If you ever need anything . . . if Jake ever needs anything . . . I'm here."

Barely able to concentrate on the words he was speaking, she nodded. Two hours remained until her meeting with Jake and Jessamyn, and by then she supposed she would feel more composed. Yet there boiled inside her one unhappy conviction: This conversation had added a new and unwanted element to her life.

Outside on the curb she was edged out for the only cab in sight. Her resentment climbed. Why shouldn't something go right? Why did Van have to say what he did about Jake and Jessamyn? Why should she have to endure such doubts when Jake had none, and why, in this city reliant on automobiles, should she be stranded here like some child?

Her mouth took on a stubborn look. She pushed back her hair. Nothing like the thought in her mind had ever occurred to her, but suddenly she was tired of being sensible and patient and ultimately submissive.

Going back inside, she called a cab and took it to a foreign car showroom. One hour later she wrote out a check for a new green Audi.

She drove it along La Jolla to Jake's office. The building where she stopped was small but sleek. FFT Productions occupied the whole fourth floor. Here there were no studio editors with whom to haggle. Jake had his own editing room, and as soon as he began to shoot another film, he would have his own hand-picked editor. The services of a nearby sound studio were at his disposal. He could now deliver to a studio—or network—a product bearing no one's stamp but his own.

Laura had not really known the extent of her mother's wealth. Now, looking around her, she marveled. Jessamyn must really believe in Jake to foot these bills. Drawing a deep breath, she opened the door to the conference room.

It was long with bittersweet carpeting, paneled in teak. At one end a retractable projection screen hid in the ceiling. A cabinet at the other end housed the projector, and next to it there stood a small but well-stocked bar.

Her suit hadn't wilted, and Laura felt glad now at having splurged on one in the new shorter length. She shook her head to the drink Jake offered and crossed the room, her flared black skirt brushing encouragement against her knees. At the oiled teak conference table Jessamyn and Kimberly were laughing about some outrageous sight they'd seen as they left Sak's.

Laura took a chair, and Jake sat down comfortably at the head of the table. There still were places around it for seven more people.

"Well," Jake began with a look that said he was confident.

"What do you ladies think about the novel we've found?"

Kimberly laughed giddily. She was high on something, booze or powder, Laura thought. And the neckline of her blue dress was outrageously low. She looked vaguely declassé sitting so near to Jessamyn.

Jessamyn for her part wore an expression that was immediately businesslike. Was it an act? No, of course she was really interested in view of her investment.

"Jake, you know it's fantastic—touching, moving, everything that makes a good movie."

She leaned forward intently, excluding Kimberly, excluding Laura. Her eyes were smoldering. Jake was smiling.

You know, of course, that they were intimate, Van had said. But he'd been wrong.

Laura pushed the thought from her mind and tried to concentrate. She longed to reach out and take Jake's hand, but he would rebel. He'd known she was lunching with Van today. He hadn't liked it. No, damn it, she refused to fall prey to doubts.

Jake's smile was widening now, shifting to her.

"That's exactly what Laura said when she read it—and I agree. Laura says it adapts well as a telescript, too."

What's more, I want to do it, Laura added silently. Out of stubbornness she'd refused to raise the subject with Jake, waiting to see whether it occurred to him that out of courtesy, if nothing else, the project should be offered to her. Naturally it hadn't. Sitting here now, she felt not a grain of guilt about the check she'd written for her new car.

"What luck for us," said Jessamyn. "When shall we start working on it then?"

Jake hesitated. "I guess I can hire some help on the oater, and I'll backburner the other project."

He gave Laura a sideways look that was boyishly sheepish. Her mood eased up, and she basked in his unspoken praise. He liked the novel she'd found. He really did like it! Until this moment she hadn't known how much, but there had been pride in that glance. He approved her judgment. He was willing to give over a project he'd hatched to someone else so he could work on this one.

"Well, darling, since you're the one who unearthed this, do you want to have a crack at writing it?" asked Jessamyn brightly.

Laura caught her breath. She looked quickly at Jake. She'd

wanted this, but it was the last thing she'd expected. After being ignored in all other business dealings, she'd supposed that Jessamyn would cut her out of this one from sheer spite. And what if Jake didn't want to work with her?

But Jake was grinning.

"I think you could do a terrific job of it, babe. What do you say?"

Jessamyn was watching her with that bright look, incredibly innocent, incredibly friendly.

But there's not a drop of innocence in her, Laura thought. Why is she offering me this?

It clicked into place. Her mother meant to hand her a challenge she couldn't handle. Something surged through her blood. A fighting response. She knew she could do a dazzling script with such a wonderful story line from which to work. She also knew she'd be a fool to try it. Anything she did was sure to be picked apart by Jessamyn's skilled fingers. Well, then, she'd just have to turn out a script that was unpickable!

"I'd love it," she said. "If Stan agrees and we pay his commission, naturally."

This was one round that she intended to win from Jessamyn. I will win it too, she thought grimly. I'll make you admit that I'm a good writer before we're through.

Another thought hovered in her consciousness, but she would not acknowledge it. Maybe, for once in her life, she could really please Jessamyn with something she did.

Laura sat lost in her own thoughts as the talk turned to Kimberly's cut. In spite of the lunch with Van this had been a very good day. Her latest project for Richard Knox would be wrapped up in a week or ten days. Then she had this to look forward to. She felt like celebrating and decided to stop and get a huge stuffed animal to take home to her housekeeper's daughter.

Then Jake was consulting his watch and rising. The meeting was over.

"What say we all adjourn someplace and celebrate?" he suggested.

With a vetoing smile, Jessamyn shook her head.

"I don't believe we'd better. Kimberly had a touch too much plum wine at lunch by the looks of it. I'll see her home."

"Oh, now, Jessamyn, don't get down on me!" Kimberly

protested almost pitiably. "I was scared to death about this meeting! You know I was."

"That's all right, darling." Jessamyn patted her arm. "I won't throw you over."

Jessamyn never offered me that kind of comfort, Laura thought. She looked away.

Now Jake was also reassuring Kimberly, teasing her and resting one arm on her shoulder. They led the way slowly out through the reception room and toward the elevator.

"You're awfully quiet," Jessamyn observed. "Having second thoughts about tackling such a big script?"

Laura's hands moved toward her skirt, but it had no sheltering pockets.

"No. No, as a matter of fact I was just thinking." They were a few steps behind the others. She looked at Jessamyn candidly. "I had lunch with Van today. He told me he'd been to see you before Jake and I were married. Thanks, Jessamyn."

The amber eyes she'd tried all her life to reach stared back at her, and there was a rare surprise in them, a rare defenselessness.

For an instant—just an instant—Laura thought they connected. Then Jessamyn shook back her lush hair and laughed.

"Of course, darling. No thanks necessary. I wouldn't have suggested you for this script if I hadn't thought you'd do a beautiful job."

Nel sat in an easy chair and swung one crossed leg lazily.

"Jess, we've got to talk," she said. "I want an assistant. I need one. I can't keep up the pace like I used to, especially now that you're producing pictures as well as being courted for damn near every big-budget film that's being considered for the next three years. I'll do the interviewing myself. There'll be no time involved for you. What do you say?"

Jessamyn jerked her hand away from the manicurist as the woman wailed over smeared work. She leaned over one arm of her fur-covered lounge, and her eyes were steely.

"Just what the hell are you talking about? What do you mean?"

Why couldn't she just tell Jess the truth? Nel wondered. It would be a lot easier than this scene she sensed brewing. Maybe she was afraid of being turned out at a time when she most needed to cling to the identity of this job. Or maybe she had some soft-headed thought that Jess would panic and just couldn't face it.

Lord, there've been so many tempests lately, and right when I want them all behind me, she thought. It had been so hard telling Eddie and reconciling him to the thought of it all from time to time. And maybe she'd have to tell Laura too. She didn't know. It seemed graceless to her, announcing to people that you were going to die. Eddie said she had to tell Laura. She just couldn't face going through it with Jess too.

"The work load's getting heavier," she said. "And while you don't get any older, I do. This arm's still bothering me. I'd like a little more time to myself."

"More time to spend with that blackamoor lover of yours, don't you mean?" sneered Jessamyn.

Nel felt her spine straighten. By God, there were lines even Jessamyn didn't have the right to cross, and she had just stepped over one in tone and language.

"What are you doing, fixing to quit?" her employer continued angrily.

Sitting forward, Nel matched Jessamyn's pose with her own.

"If working conditions don't improve a little, I might do just that. Your head's getting just as big as those tits you're so proud of flaunting."

Here she'd intended to spare Jess some trouble by having someone trained to fill her shoes when they fell empty, and this was the sort of thanks she was going to get.

Jessamyn glared at her.

"All right. Do whatever you like. I'm sure I don't care." Her hand swept the manicure tray, up-ending bottles. "Get this off me! And find another color. This one's old."

An actress to the core, Jess swept out grandly. The dismayed manicurist ran at her heels like one of the dogs.

Nel sat for long minutes, staring into space, the bonds of half a lifetime snapping inside her. Damn you, Jess, you've never cared about anything but yourself and your own convenience, she thought slowly. And I've humored you—pitied you—never wanted anything of my own enough to lock horns with you. That's the essence of our friendship. That's the only reason we've managed to get along all these years, isn't it?

"I've chuckled at your tantrums and your dirty dealings

because they never touched *me*," she said to the empty room. Her open palms smacked the arms of her chair as she stood up. "Damn my butt, I've chosen to be as blind to what you are in my way as Laura is in hers!"

The thought of Laura caused a frown to cross Nel's face. Jess hated the girl. There was no telling what she'd try to pull in the years ahead.

And I won't be here. Even if you catch on to her, what kind of match will you be for her when she's schemed and plotted all her life?

Resolve hardened in Nel's heart.

She had never been less than loyal to anyone in her life, but she'd be damned if she'd go to her grave without leaving Laura protected.

Looking out, she made sure Jess was still on the patio with the manicurist. She walked quickly into the bedroom, swung back a painting, and began to twist the dial of a safe that Jessamyn thought no one in the household knew existed. No one did—except Nel. She'd come into the room unexpectedly years ago and caught Jess turning away from the wall with a guilty look. Later she'd snooped. One day when she was pissed at Jess, she'd spied from the next room and thought she had a good idea of the combination.

It took three tries with different numbers, and Nel was growing nervous before the safe clicked open. With surprise she shoved aside a diamond necklace she'd never seen, hunting for the item of greater value that she thought must be there.

Yes, here it was, Jess's damn diary—names, dates, and details of all the men she'd slept with through the years. Even as she drew it out, Nel wondered if Jessamyn kept it out of insatiable vanity, because she intended to shock the world with it someday, or—

But with the leather-bound diary there was a packet. Letters. Nel read two hastily.

There was no question now. Jess kept her journal for blackmail. And these letters . . . love letters from powerful men, names signed . . . letters Jess could use as leverage. What power did Jess have that she could make sane men take leave of their senses?

Well, whatever power it was, the fruits of it would no longer be in Jessamyn's hands. They would be in Laura's. Nel would make her see what they were worth, how they need never even be used, so long as Jess knew Laura had them.

Best of all, there's nothing Jess can do to stop me, Nel thought with satisfaction. Even if she tries to get even, what can she do to me? Not much, except maybe send me to jail for the rest of my days.

Jessamyn searched wildly in the safe. *They weren't there! Her diary and the letters weren't there!* Heedless of her sculptured nails, she clawed at every inch of the hole in the wall again and yet again.

Fear surged in her. She'd been robbed! And for some stupid reason, whoever had broken in had taken—

But reason cut across her rage like a cooling stream.

Stepping backward, Jessamyn looked at the safe, eyes narrowing. Her diamonds were there, the ones that she'd chosen not to declare on this year's taxes. How silly of her to have missed that glaring fact. She hadn't been robbed at all, not in the classic sense. She knew who had her letters. And she had no doubt at all of getting them back.

First she went to her desk and scribbled an address. Then she called her newest houseman and gave him his instructions. Her newest employees were always the ones most eager to please. They obeyed without question. And in this case the man had not been around long enough to develop any inconvenient loyalty to Nel.

Jessamyn walked lightly down the hall. She turned the doorknob to Nel's apartment without knocking.

"Planning a little trip, Nel?" she purred, surveying the suitcases open on Nel's bed.

Nel glanced up warily.

"That's right."

Nel was shrewd, thought Jessamyn smiling with pleasure. She'd always liked that, Nel being almost as clever as she was herself.

Almost, but not quite.

"I wouldn't count on getting far until you give back my letters," she said, still in that throaty purr.

Nel straightened and stared at her levelly. It satisfied Jessamyn to see uneasiness touch Nel's eyes. Nel had always been too smart for her own good. Too smart and too smug, as though she couldn't be touched by Jessamyn's power. It would be such fun to see her squirm . . . and then be rid of her.

Nel stretched and patted back a yawn.

"Afraid you're a little late for the letters, Jess. They've already gone."

Shit, she thought as she said it. *If only they had!*

They lay like a hijacked canister of plutonium right there in her purse. She'd counted on having at least a few hours to make her getaway. Now she cursed her own carelessness. Yet even while lambasting herself, she was talking.

"You don't figure I'd let a little treasure trove like that stay around where you might get it back, do you, Jess? Fat chance. When Roberto left for the day, I gave him a package to drop off for me—not that he has any notion of what's in it. Planning's one of the things I do best, Jess. Don't you remember? I knew there was a chance you'd open that safe before I cleared out. This way, even if you nail my hide to the wall, you won't get those letters."

Jessamyn's face had gone white with fury.

"What have you done with them?"

Yes, she's falling for it, Nel thought with relief. Thank God, I saw Roberto leaving and listened to him grumbling about his dental appointment. If Jess grabs up the phone and calls to check, he won't be home. And Lupita...if she calls Lupita in from the kitchen and questions her, Lupita will play along. I can raise an eyebrow, and she'll know something's up. That's how Lupita is.

Jessamyn moved toward her now, and Nel could see her trembling. It was not the trembling of fear. Jess's amber eyes sizzled.

"You fool! You've always been such a fool, Nel. Do you suppose I've trusted you all these years—let you know as much as you know—without some teeny insurance? *Where are those letters?"*

"Where you'll never get them, Jess."

Nel grinned cynically. She had never been and was not even now afraid of Jessamyn Friday.

Slowly, unnervingly, Jessamyn laughed. She spun in a childlike motion, her hair a fiery curtain, and with head thrown back, still laughing in mockery, she faced Nel.

"Oh, yes, I will. I get everything I want. You should know that. I'll have them within the hour—you're going to see that I do. And if not, Nel—"

She hugged herself, looking triumphant. Her lips were curved in a smile, but her eyes held malice.

"If not, Nel, how do you think that boyfriend of yours will like that blue movie you were in before I met you? Oh, he may be broad-minded. He may be able to live with most of it. But there are about five minutes I think he'll find ver-ry interesting. Or has he watched you make love to a woman before?"

The words thundered at Nel. Her head, her heart, her mid-section, all staggered under the blow. That movie, the one dumb thing she'd done in her life because she was starving! She'd tried to buy back the reel of it years ago and was told it was in the hands of a private collector. Was Jess lying? No. *Jess* was the collector! How had she learned—?

But Nel knew it didn't matter.

The room had swayed around her and was just now steadying itself. Jessamyn's face was out of focus, her words indistinct. "...so you see, if you want to trade, Nel, it's really quite simple. Get me my letters, and Eddie doesn't get the private screening I arranged for him about five minutes ago."

No wonder Laura has never accepted what you really are, Nel thought. Look at me, just look at what a chump I've been! I've seen you scheme; I've seen the evil in you. Yet I never thought you'd hurt *me*. Maybe it's because you're so damn beautiful, Jess. It makes it too hard to believe you're what you are.

Nel's mouth felt dry. She fought the impulse to betray it by wetting her lips.

"You're crazy if you think Eddie will care. Hell, he knows all about my career in porn," she said with effort.

Jessamyn's lips were curving more certainly now.

"You're bluffing, Nel."

She was trapped. God, how that movie would look in Eddie's eyes—her face and her body the very age he remembered! And Eddie was so damned moral. He'd probably never compromised in his life. He'd hated trash movies back in Detroit, thought the people who made them and the people who showed them were scum. If she defied Jessamyn now, she'd face Eddie's contempt.

But if she caved in, she'd leave Laura helpless. Didn't this very moment, this very experience, prove how much Laura might need the safety of those letters in the years ahead?

Her safety—maybe—or Laura's. It came down to that. And Laura hadn't had her fair share of happiness yet.

"I reckon you'd better roll the film then. You won't get the letters."

Ignoring Jessamyn, she bent and began to pack more quickly.

Twenty-six

Laura tried to make sense of the tumble of Eddie's words on the telephone. Nel had packed up . . . she was gone . . . she was upset, thinking he'd be mad about something, only he wasn't . . . damn that woman Jessamyn, she ought to be shot!

"She's not here, Eddie," Laura said for a second time, aware he hadn't heard the first time in his agitation. His alarm was getting to her now. What was this all about? Could Nel actually have left Jessamyn the way he was making it sound? But surely . . . surely Nel didn't mean to vanish. Laura hugged herself against the thought.

"Look, if she shows up here—if I hear from her—I'll let you know. Okay, Eddie?"

She hung up and pinched at her lower lip thoughtfully. What was happening? This didn't sound like Nel. Poor Eddie. He'd said he thought Nel was running away from him, but that didn't make sense. She wished Jake were home with her tonight instead of at a meeting. She was worried.

When the doorbell rang twenty minutes later, she hurried down from her study. With relief, she looked through the security hole in the door and saw Nel.

The words "Well, there you are!" formed on her tongue as she opened the door, but intuition stayed them. Maybe it was better to feel her way through this. Find out what was happening.

"Well!" she said, stepping aside to let Nel in. "What are you doing out in the country?"

Nel held a package firmly in one hand. Her eyes were tense.

"Look, kiddo. We've got to talk. I'm taking off for parts unknown, and there's something here I think you ought to have." She shook the package. "Damn it, Laura, you *need* this whether you like it or not. So sit down and listen. And how about a drink?"

Laura made instantaneous decisions. Something was wrong. Nel was acting and sounding as though she really did mean to give Eddie and everyone else the slip. But there'd been some giant mistake—Eddie had said so. She *loved* Nel. Eddie loved Nel. She had to set this straight.

"Help yourself to a drink," she said. "I'm afraid I'm in the midst of a call with Richard Knox. Just let me tie things up with him, and I'll be with you."

She hurried up to her study and then, pausing just long enough to listen for Nel's movements at the bar, called Eddie.

"Nel's here," she said in a low voice. "I'll stall her as long as I can. Come over."

She didn't wait to hear his answer; there was no need. Dialing the time-and-temperature number, she let it give its spiel, then called down to Nel.

"Nel, I'm trapped. Make me a drink and come on up, why don't you?"

This way there'd be no chance of Nel getting bored or curious and picking up the living room phone. Laura swallowed and thought furiously, mentally writing what seemed to be the most important dialogue of her career.

For twenty minutes, after Nel appeared in her study, Laura pretended to carry on a conversation with Richard Knox about a recently completed script. She was silent at times and rolled her eyes often, hoping the acts suggested an argument and some sort of stupidity on the other end.

"Okay, Richard, if you think they want it in, I'll put it in," she said at last, eyeing the clock on one wall.

Nel was starting to fidget. She'd risen and was pacing. How long would it take Eddie to get here? Laura had no idea. Her mind began to turn to other delaying tactics she could use.

"That man will be the death of me yet," she said, standing up and shaking her head. "Hey, I'm glad to see you, Nellie. I'm all by my lonesome, as you can see, and was feeling sorry for myself over supper alone. How about if I put on two plates, and we'll make it a gala occasion?"

Nel shook her head impatiently.

"No, kiddo. There's no time for that. I . . . I want to get away for a little while. I'm in a hurry."

Laura frowned. "I don't understand. Are you and Eddie taking off on another trip? You don't sound very eager—"

"Laura, *please*. I'm in no mood to explain. Damn it, why should I have to? Oh, hell, kid. I know I sound bitchy, and I don't mean to—not with you. Just listen to what I've got to say and don't keep interrupting. I haven't laid many lectures on you through the years. I'm entitled to one."

Laura smiled. "Okay. But I do seem to remember a doozy of a lecture you gave me once on what I should and shouldn't do with boys."

Despite the tension on her face, Nel grinned.

"Didn't want you to wind up too much like Jess."

"Oh, is *that* what you had in mind. At the time I thought maybe you were preparing me to join a convent." She linked her arm through Nel's. "Come on, let's go downstairs and get comfortable then. You've really got my curiosity stirred up now."

In the living room Nel put her lighter to a cigarette. She looked so elegant sitting there with those slim legs crossed, thought Laura. *What was this about? What had happened between Nel and Jessamyn?*

"I did something today that I shouldn't have," Nel began abruptly. "Not that I'm feeling any guilt, mind you. You've always been too naive about Jess, Laura. I wouldn't trust her in the workplace, I wouldn't trust her where you and Jake were concerned."

Laura's mouth twisted. "Neither would I."

Nel nodded slightly.

"Good. Maybe the scales are dropping off your eyes then. But don't underestimate her. I did. I've brought you this ammo to fight her in case she ever crosses you. I want you to use it."

Laura looked at the small package Nel tossed onto the couch beside her.

"It's her diary. And a lot of letters from male admirers. You don't have to read them—probably make you sick. But every man in there would do you a favor to get his letters back. Remember that if she ever tries to back you into a corner."

Laura stared at the package, then brought her gaze up slowly to meet Nel's. Blackmail. It sounded so sordid. And yet. . . .

"You stole these? You did this for me, Nel? But why?"

Nel made a gesture of grand dismissal.

"Nah, it wasn't for you. What kind of sentimental slob do

you think I am? It was just my way of settling a feud between Jess and me—just sheer malice." She pointed imperiously with the finger holding her cigarette. "But you use them, damn you. Let her know you have them at least. I'm serious, Laura. She doesn't play fair, and you can't afford to either. Not if you ever hope to hold your own against her."

The air around them was wordless now. Laura swallowed. She couldn't pretend not to see the weapon placed in her hands. She couldn't pretend not to think it would be handy one day either.

But why had Nel done this? It wasn't like her. Malice, she'd said—but Nel wasn't a malicious person. What—?

"Oh," Laura said with relief as the doorbell rang. "Let me see who that is."

Eddie knew as soon as he saw Laura's face that he was in time. He heaved a great breath, the first he'd really taken in an hour or more. Before he'd even seen the end of that filthy movie, it had shot into his mind what Nel was likely to do. He'd raced to the phone, but she was already gone. When Laura had called, he'd cursed the cleverness that had led him to trade cars this morning—buying time, outwitting his pursuers a little longer. He hadn't had the feel of this new one. The trip here had seemed to take forever.

Nel was rising indignantly, angrily at the sight of him.

"Damn you, Laura!"

Laura's look was a trifle guilty. Her eyes pleaded with Eddie as she started toward the stairs.

"I think I'll leave you two alone. Yell if you need anything."

Nel, bustling, refusing to meet his gaze, snatched up her purse and started past. Eddie caught her arm.

"Let me go. You'll hurt my arm, Eddie."

"Huh-uh, Nel. It's you who's going to hurt it if you try and pull away."

He could see the shame in her face—and her stubborn pride.

"What kind of craziness is this anyway, Nel? Do you think I give a damn about that movie? Oh, I'm mad okay, but only at that—" The words he used made Nel's eyes widen. "—Jessamyn. What the hell kind of monster is she anyway? Why have you put up with her all these years?"

Nel looked surprised now and a little uncertain. He saw her lips push together as she fought against tears.

"You don't have to pretend, Eddie. Don't have to chase around hunting me like a madman either, just because you know I'm sick and—"

"*Damn* you, woman!"

Eddie flung her arm free in exasperation.

"Can't you give me credit for anything? Why can't you accept the fact that just maybe I love you? Maybe . . . maybe once in my life I would have condemned you, Nel. But not now. We all do what we have to do. Sure I was shocked seeing you—seeing you do things like that. I just figure you had a good reason—"

"I was *starving*, Eddie!"

Her lips trembled once. They stood squared off like two fighting cats.

Eddie sighed.

"Don't want you to starve, Nel. Don't want you to ever want for anything again," he said softly.

Slowly her head bowed. She shielded her face with one hand.

"Shit, Eddie. I'm so ashamed."

"Of what? It's that woman you were a friend to all these years who ought to be ashamed, humiliating you like that. But then maybe I ought to thank her. Maybe now you'll move in with me, hmmm?"

A moment passed. Then she grinned with a trace of her old cockiness, his Nel.

"Reckon I'll have to. Reckon I'm a little old to count on picking up my career as a porn queen to pay the rent."

"Queen!" Eddie sniffed. "You weren't even the star of that thing."

He started edging her toward the door. One part of him felt light. He'd take care of Nel now. He'd take care of her to her dying day.

Another part of him worried, almost reluctantly, whether he was wrong. If he made Nel part and parcel of his daily life, would he make her a target for the men who were after him?

Twenty-seven

Jessamyn slid out of the sleek little gold Mercedes, which was her toy. She slammed the door and looked with relish at the tall white house above the beach. It had taken months of waiting, weeks of contemplating this project for Kimberly, but at last she had Turner and Laura exactly where she wanted them. And after teaching Nel the lesson she had three days ago, she was no longer worried that Nel might try any smart tricks with those letters. Nel had probably left town—wouldn't dare show her face again. All in all she was enormously looking forward to this evening.

A smile curved Jessamyn's lips as she walked toward the door. No one stood in her way, not now, not ever. The fan magazines were full of her pictures because of this latest film, and though it was still months away from the tedious interviews with small-town reporters, which were part of the publicity grind for any release, the studio and Stan himself were already being deluged with requests for them.

Her asking price for her next film would be spectacular, she thought smugly. The money she'd sunk in this farce of a production company would be recouped. Perhaps she'd form another company, a real one. She had a natural capacity for this side of the business, and there was never enough between roles to keep her occupied. Besides, it was a very provocative property they'd optioned for Kimberly. As she rang the bell, Jessamyn reflected that Kimberly really could be molded quite nicely to her own tastes.

"Hello, darlings," she said and was pleased that her voice was suitably subdued, almost indiscernibly so, just enough so that in retrospect they would recognize that quality had been there.

Laura was wearing a blue-green blouse, and her eyes seemed greener and larger than Jessamyn remembered. Jessamyn smiled inwardly, knowing part of that look was caused by hopefulness. But then Laura spoke, and there was uncharacteristic crispness in her voice.

"Hello, Jessamyn. Could I get you something to drink? Coffee? Some iced tea?"

Beneath the words Jessamyn heard the sound of one alert, almost to the point of battle readiness. Would Laura ever do battle with her? She doubted it.

"No, thank you, I really can't stay. But we did agree to get together tonight to discuss how *Shadows* is shaping up, didn't we?"

They had moved into the living room as they talked. She lowered herself with easy grace into a chair and looked from Laura to Jake. Neither of them sat down, which told her they were tense and that she automatically controlled the situation.

"I've been in Vegas, catching up on some fun I missed while we were shooting there," she said. "I just got back a couple of hours ago. You'll have to give me a précis of things. Has Andrew Benjamin decided yet if he's free to direct?"

"He is, and Petronelli will be the cinematographer, assuming we're ready to go to production before the first of the year. Petronelli's good, Jess—even when there's not a budget to consider."

"Well, then. It sounds as though we're in good shape. First pick of every crew chief, a new star, fine story . . . there's only one problem. Kimberly thinks the script we've got just doesn't come off—and I agree with her. I'm sorry, darling."

She fluttered a look of concerned apology in Laura's direction, enjoying the moment of total silence that followed. She watched as Laura's eyes swung to her husband, clearly expecting him to speak in her behalf. He didn't speak, and Jessamyn enjoyed the expression of outraged hurt that swept Laura's face.

Turner looked shaken, as Jessamyn had known he would. But he had not yet perceived that he was now locked into this project while Laura was, or soon would be, locked out. All in all, she had slipped the wedge between them rather neatly.

"All right, Jessamyn."

Her daughter's voice startled her.

Jessamyn had expected anger, or the sort of mute acceptance in Laura's nature that would drive the wedge she had planted deeper and deeper. What she had not expected at all was this tone, this movement of jaw that reminded her of the uncompromising man who had been Laura's father.

"If there's a problem, I'm sure we can fix it, Jessamyn. Exactly what do you think is wrong with the script?"

Incredibly, Jessamyn felt herself challenged. She hid her irritation behind a laugh.

"Darling, really—"

She felt a script shoved into her lap.

"Come on, Jessamyn. This is a rare chance for me to learn. You're supposed to be a very good judge of scripts. Let's go through, oh, the first five pages, and you can point out the flaws."

Hate made a paralyzed mess of Jessamyn's vocal cords. She could think of reasons, invent them, but she was too furious. Her lips drew back in a smile.

"I don't really have time to discuss it line by line, but of course if you want to tear it apart on your own and try again, and Jake wants to wait—"

Laura snatched back the script.

"Since you seem so vague about what the problem is, I think I'll spare myself. As a matter of fact this frees me to pick up a pilot offer I'd nearly turned down."

Her coldness was almost convincing as she left the room. But the anger and disappointment was there, thought Jessamyn—and so were the problems.

She put a hand to her forehead and sank back. She had won.

"Was I too harsh, do you think? I didn't really—"

"You're wrong, Jessamyn." Turner's hands were curled into fists of frustration, and he was glowering. "It's a good script, a damned good script. And well it should be. Laura's worked on it, thought of it, day and night for weeks. She's turned herself inside out trying to capture that book."

"Well, she hasn't succeeded. You'll have to find someone else."

He shook his head slowly.

"No. I just had to see how far you'd push this. I had to see how much you'd mix spite with business. That isn't going to happen on my turf, Jessamyn. I'll bow out of this project before I replace Laura."

Jessamyn stood up. She liked the sense of victory in this moment.

"Do you really expect me to believe you'd turn your back on everything that you have now to spare Laura's feelings over one rejection? Forgive me, darling, but I know you too well for that! You seem to forget..." She fluttered her lashes and let her gaze flick lightly over him. "I'm in a better position to judge your moral fiber than most."

His expression was angry now.

"Listen, Jessamyn—"

"No, you listen. I want that film. You've made commitments, and you're going to see them through. Seeing how devoted you are to Laura—or how devoted she *thinks* you are—I'm sure you wouldn't want her to know about that night I came to your apartment. I believe that's known as incest, darling. How do you suppose she'd like learning you'd poked around inside her very own mother?"

Beneath his russet hair his face was void of color. He stood helpless with fists half-curled, staring dumbly at her like some great ape encountering something he could not comprehend.

"God damn it, Jessamyn—that's a lie," he said hoarsely.

But there was enough uncertainty in his voice to make her smile.

"Not that it was that great," she added. "Frankly, darling, I'd thought all along that you'd be much better. Still, my loss on that one was also my gain, it seems."

He looked sick. Positively gray. And Jessamyn knew he must be in turmoil. Gathering up her small suede handbag, she spoke again.

"Let me know in the next few days who's doing the new script. Don't bother seeing me to the door. I know my way."

Laura's fingers punched at phone buttons in her silent study. *Damn* it. She'd been wrong about the nature of Jessamyn's ploy in offering her the *Shadows* script, and now look at the corner into which she'd painted herself.

She'd thought Jessamyn meant this script to be a project she couldn't handle, something that would make her look foolish in her failure. But Jessamyn's actions downstairs just now made her realize Jessamyn would have faulted any script she'd turned in. No, Jessamyn's real game wasn't just to sandbag Laura with an impossible project. It was to create trouble between her and Jake, leaving him in the midst of the project and her on the outside with feelings hurt.

Only it won't work, Laura thought fiercely. I recognize the scheme now.

Yet she *was* hurt.

She'd turned in a fine script, and what had made her happiest about it was that Jake had told her so. He'd said all the things she already knew, that it was dramatic, sensitive, each turning point played out just perfectly. Then, when Jessamyn attacked it, he'd said not one word in its defense.

Why not? Because of what Van had said about Jake and Jessamyn?

"Ben? It's Laura," she said with a tight throat as her agent answered. "Ben, I want you to find me a pilot. I don't care what it's about or who it's for, but I want a pilot!"

She could hear amazement in his speechlessness. And he didn't have half an inkling how desperate she was.

She'd really set herself up with that grand announcement about a pilot offer. It had been a line, and if Ben couldn't pull off a miracle, she'd face the added humiliation of having Jessamyn know. At the moment it hadn't mattered, she'd been so furious. Now she felt weak with the full force of her folly.

"Laura . . ."

Good Ben. Wonderful Ben! He wasn't even going to ask her why!

"Laura, the only possible thing I've heard about is with Hugh Archer—not really quite a pilot, but a first-week episode for something inspired by a movie CBS ran a few months back. I don't know if it's been filled, and the terms—"

"I want it, Ben!" She brushed angrily at her tears and kept them from wetting her cheeks. Wouldn't you know it would be with Archer, she thought bitterly.

"As I recall, you met Archer once and didn't like him. And I'm not sure of the chances for this series. Give me a few days. Let me see—"

"No, Ben. Get on this. Tonight. Please." She made herself laugh. "I'm not the innocent I used to be. I don't have to love the people I work with, do I?"

"No, but it doesn't help to have bad blood between you either," he answered. "All right. I'll contact him and let you know."

As she hung up, she heard the front door close. Jessamyn was leaving.

Why, Jessamyn? Why did you do this? a part of her cried. Is it because you wanted Jake?

But it wouldn't be that. It was something deeper. It was something that had always been there, between the two of them. Yet only now could Laura perceive the full force of her mother's animosity.

She wrang out a washcloth and pressed it against her burning cheeks. She wanted to go downstairs composed, able to show Jake she harbored no anger. Would he have seen through Jessamyn now? she wondered.

He was sitting on the edge of the couch. Just sitting there, staring straight ahead.

"Jake?" she said softly.

He recoiled as though she had struck him.

"I heard Jess leave . . ." she began, then stopped. Something had changed in the way he was looking at her, and it made a terrible tightness rise to choke her. Had it mattered so much to him whether or not she could bring off a script or . . . Again she found herself remembering what Van had said.

His eyes were hollow with pain. They silently, relentlessly, avoided her own.

"Did you get things worked out?" she asked around the tightness. "Is everything okay?"

Jake exploded from the couch, face twisted with anger.

"Christ, do you always have to be Mary Sunshine? It's like living with a saint. It's like a chain around my neck! You're so damn virtuous, you're so damn understanding—are you really that big a doormat, or are you just trying to make the rest of us feel guilty because we're not like you?"

"Now just a damned minute, Jake! That's not fair!"

"It sure as hell isn't!"

"I was just being civil—"

"Do you think that's the be-all and end-all, being civil? Christ, I'm sick of talking about it. Of course things aren't all right!"

Turning on his heel, he walked swiftly toward his study. Laura stood for a moment with heart pounding in anger and fear.

When she reached the study door, he was shoving assorted papers into his briefcase.

"Do you want me to tell you I'm pissed?" she demanded,

shaking with dismay at his confrontation. "All right—I'm pissed!
There wasn't a thing wrong with my script, and we both know
it."

"Why didn't you fight for it then?"

"Why didn't you?"

"It's your bloody script!"

"What did you expect me to do, make a scene with Jessamyn? Oh, no! Because the minute I did that, you would have
thrown it in my face that I was jealous of her!"

"Maybe you should have done it anyway. Maybe it would
have been better."

His voice was bitter. His eyes snapped at her, meeting hers
directly for the first time since she'd come down the stairs.

Then the instant of contact was over. His gaze seemed to
wince from hers as from something he could no longer bear to
view, and fell away.

Could a script really matter so much to him? she wondered
again. Anguish tore out her words, froze her in place.

Jake snapped his briefcase closed. The sound was like a
shot, like the deliberate breaking of something strong. He started
out of the room without a word.

"Where are you going?" asked Laura as he brushed past. A
terrible fear was beating inside her.

He looked back once but did not stop.

"Out. I'm going out."

Twenty-eight

Eddie frowned as he rang Laura's doorbell. He had a hunch
he knew why she'd asked him here without Nel this morning,
and he wasn't sure what he'd say.

A young woman in a blouse and skirt let him in. She was
pleasant. The housekeeper, Eddie guessed. He sat down, and
she went out, and a few minutes later Laura came down from
her study. She looked . . . not exactly older, but more grown

up than she had when he first met her, and that made him sad. There seemed to be a set to her mouth and a darkness to her eyes that he didn't remember from the other night. But then she smiled at him.

"Hi, Eddie. Thanks for coming. How's Nel?"

He nodded, sitting down again as she did.

"Busy rearranging my place. Rearranging my life."

Laura laughed, and he heard the affection in her voice. Yes, he liked this girl. He understood why Nel had done what she had done for her. This morning, though, under the smile and the laughter he sensed something deeply unhappy. That troubled him.

"I don't quite understand why you wanted to see me without Nel," he said.

Laura locked her fingers together and looked very briefly toward the terrace.

"Oh, don't you, Eddie?"

Her back had straightened. There was dignity in her bearing. Eddie started to wonder if Laura weren't a little wiser, maybe even a littler grittier than Nel had realized.

"Because." Her eyes came back to his like an arrow finding its target. She was unflinching. Only those fingers, locking more tightly together, betrayed an anger, a tension—he didn't know what. "I have to know about my mother. I have to confront something I've been avoiding too long."

Hands parting into fists of determination, she sprang up and rounded the couch as she spoke.

"Somehow—somehow when it's me involved, I've kept making excuses. I've practically made a career of excuses. Well, I've run out now. I know the kind of person she is. But I need to know everything, Eddie. I need to know it isn't just me. What did she do to Nel to make her leave? Tell me, Eddie. I need to know."

Her fists had come to rest on the back of the couch. Her knuckles were white. The strain was evident in every part of her body as she leaned toward him.

Eddie considered. He traced two fingers of his left hand over the crown of the hat on the table beside him.

"Yes, I guess maybe you do," he said at last. "I'm going to tell you anyway."

He kept the hate from his voice as he told her about the houseman showing up with that movie. worming his way in on Jessamyn's orders, setting it up, and saying it was a surprise from Nel.

Laura's face was so pale when he finished that Eddie was afraid she might collapse. She wasn't a woman who was used to rage. That made her good, but it also made it hard on her.

"You know right now—right this minute—I'd use those letters to hurt Jess if I could," she said in a near whisper.

Eddie studied her.

"But you won't," he said at last, relieved at the assessment.

Her smile was thin.

"You're right. Because then I'd be too much like her, and I never want to be like her, Eddie. I'm me. And that's okay. And if I can't make it on my terms, well, then I'll sink."

Eddie stood up, put on his hat, and smoothed the brim.

"Sometimes you can't win against dirty people without being dirty yourself," he said. "But I'm glad some people try."

He wondered if he was giving her bad advice.

Even though he hoped she'd never use them, he hoped she'd take good care of those letters.

Twenty-nine

"Hey, Jake honey! I'm having a party tonight. Why don't you come? No one's seen much of you since you set yourself up as a big time producer."

Turner grinned at the telephone.

"Thanks, Celeste, but I'm a married man these days. Hadn't you heard?"

"Sure, honey. I heard. But that doesn't mean you're dead and buried, does it? Not in this town." There was a pause, then a sly laugh on the other end of the line. "Anyway, Kimberly Curran tells me you're staying alone at your old apartment. It sounded to me like you could use some fun."

Now Turner was mildly annoyed. Who the hell had given

Kimberly permission to blab where he was staying? What right did she have to speculate on what that meant? He'd had to talk to her about her role in *Shadows*—he was stuck in the project, so he was going to damn well make it good. And he'd been down, and one thing had led to another. He'd invited Kimberly over for a lousy drink.

"Our house is way out. We kept the apartment in case one of us was working long hours on something—which I am now," he said. "Sorry. I won't be able to make your party."

He hung up and sipped at the Scotch sitting by his telephone. It was his third since lunch, and he was a little bit high. Four days since he'd left Laura, and he'd spent the nights drinking, the days immersed in business, trying every hour to avoid the guilt that made him feel like slime.

Four days. Christ. What was he ever going to do?

The door to his office opened, and the assistant producer he'd hired to take over the western for him waved a sheaf of papers.

"Need you to take a gander at these," he said. "Shooting schedule. Hope to hell we don't have to waste more time on that chicken coop scene than I've blocked out for it. I've got a feeling we'll shitcan it anyway once we start to edit."

Turner opened his mouth to speak, to tell this man who was taking over his film that the chicken coop scene had bloody well better stay in and be as funny as he had envisioned it. But the assistant was already ducking out again, and his phone was ringing. More out of habit than a willingness to forego an argument about the scene in question, Turner answered it.

"Jake, it's Nico Christodoulou," said his secretary. "Do you want to take it?"

"Yeah. Sure."

As associate v.p. at Columbia, Christodoulou had turned down a project Turner had been pitching before getting sidetracked on the current one for Kimberly. Turner wondered now what he could want.

"Hey, Jake-o!" he said with so much cheer it was suspicious. "Are you still trying to peddle that thing about the dyke minister in the inner city?"

"Not exactly." Turner was cautious. "I've put it on hold. Have a new film going for Kimberly Curran. Why the sudden interest? Want to reconsider?"

Christodoulou laughed. "Something like that. Columbia and I have parted company. I'm at Universal now, and they're hot for something socially relevant. I figured your idea might fill the bill."

"It might." Turner didn't like the callous way Christodoulou summed up the story. That story touched Jake. But the prospect of getting it into production—spoken for ahead of time—was too much to resist. Three good projects nailed down in as many months, he thought with a grin. Not so long ago he'd been the one who had to go out selling. Now, it seemed, the buyers were coming to him.

"How about lunch tomorrow?" the voice on the phone suggested. "We could talk about the licensing fee, Jake-o. Kick the thing around."

"Can't make it for lunch," Turner said. He didn't like being called Jake-o either.

"Breakfast then?" asked Christodoulou.

"Okay. Breakfast."

When they'd concluded their conversation, Turner reached for his drink and finished it. The silence of the room came out to smother him.

He'd slept with Jessamyn. Christ. How could he have? It was Laura he cared for, Laura he wanted to be worthy of, and now he never could be.

For a moment he caught at a shaft of anger that she should be so unreproachable. Then he felt the long slump into depression.

Laura would never forgive him if she knew. But that didn't matter—he couldn't forgive himself. *Would Jessamyn tell her?* He didn't know. For the time being Jessamyn meant to hold it over him, taunt him, use it to get what she wanted and to amuse herself. After that, he didn't know.

Another telephone call. It was Saul Finer, cool and distant. Thanks but no thanks, he didn't want to do the *Shadows* script. It was too difficult a book to capture, too many shades of meaning to bring off well. Goodbye.

Turner's mouth felt dry. He rubbed the stubble of beard on his face and then was surprised to discover it. Had he been so hungover he'd forgotten to shave this morning? He couldn't go on like this. He had to patch things up with Laura. He had to make her understand. He had to ask her forgiveness.

*   *   *

Tish, the housekeeper they had retained, was dusting in the living room when he came in. She looked up at him in surprise. A little hostile, he thought.

"Where's my wife?" he asked.

"In her study, working."

There was no greeting, no friendly word, just information.

Less confident with every step, he climbed the stairs. She'd be glad to see him, and he wouldn't try to get by with humor this time. He'd just tell her how damn sorry he'd been for turning on her and hope to God she didn't ask for explanations.

The door to her study was open. Once it had been a sun porch, and she stood silhouetted against the last light of day pouring in through the windows. Her back was toward him as she spoke into the telephone.

"I do appreciate the offer, Richard, but I seem to be tied up with a series just now . . ."

He ached to step forward and touch that delicate hair. He ached just to hold her.

But he could not hold her—not forever—not without deserving it. That was what had fascinated him about this woman and what filled him now with sudden despair.

You're a coward and a fake, he told himself bitterly. You know if you come back, there'll have to be explanations. You'll have to tell Laura about what happened with Jessamyn, *and you can't face that*! She believed in you. She looked under the smile and the slickness and found the other parts of you—the ones you were afraid to share because they were flawed and uncertain. She tried to reach out to those parts, but you screwed it all up, didn't you, Jake old boy?

"Yes, of course it could fall through, but I don't think it will . . ."

Her voice was gentle and sad, and panic gripped him.

He couldn't face her!

On noiseless feet he turned and walked back down the stairs.

Laura sat alone in the darkness of her study, her unseeing eyes focused on the nothingness that lay beyond. Four days had passed since Jake left. He wasn't coming back. Why couldn't she accept it? Why couldn't she have seen it long ago?

She'd tried to build something out of dreams. She'd wanted so much to have stability and to know the closeness of sharing her life with another human being that she had closed her eyes, her ears, even her logic to all signs that she and Jake simply were not suited, in temperament or any other way, to make a go of things together.

Had there been no bond at all between them? Had she tried to create a relationship, whole cloth, where none existed? No, she believed Jake had loved her; she had to believe it. Maybe just not enough—or maybe they'd been too different.

Like an intruder in the dark, the telephone rang. She jumped, disoriented in familiar surroundings. Again it rang, and again. Putting her hand out, she switched on a light.

Could it be Jake? Hope fluttered in her throat, but she put it aside. She answered cautiously.

"Hello?"

"Hi, Laura. Hugh Archer. When are you going to get that bloody treatment to me?"

She passed a hand in front of her eyes, which stung from the light. Her mind was elsewhere, and her tongue had trouble functioning.

"It's getting there," she said. Thoughts struggled into shape. It was strange that Archer was calling. She still had another week to finish the treatment for the first episode of his proposed *Anne of Green Gables* series.

"Getting there?" Archer pressed. "What does that mean? Can you give me some idea?"

From her eyes, her hand moved on to her hair, dismantling it. Her whole life was coming apart, and now when she wanted to be left alone, Archer was checking on her, addressing her with an abrasiveness to which she was not accustomed.

"I don't know. I've got the last act left." She knew she sounded hostile. What time was it? She squinted at a clock.

"Look, lady, if we're going to nail down this project, we need to do it. I mean *now*. There's a rumor that Shrugman's going to split from CBS, and he's the one who's interested in doing this series. If I don't get it to him in a day or two, it may be too late."

There was a pause, then he added in a pained tone, "What's the matter? I'd been promised you were a fast writer."

"Nothing's the matter," she said sharply. Did people know Jake had walked out on her? "I'm not used to being nagged about something that's not due for days, for one thing. And in case you need another thing, you seem to have stretched the truth just a little when you told Ben and me what would be involved in pulling together this segment. Just a few minor changes from the original movie, you said—and then when I started to write, you began to spell that out as new conflict line, new characters. What you really wanted was the guts for a whole damn new pilot! All right. You're getting it. But if you wanted it in less time, you should fucking well have contracted for less time—and paid!"

She slammed down the phone.

For an instant the violence inside her was so strong that she stared at the slim white instrument, fighting the urge to rip it from the wall. She wanted to grab its curly tail between her hands and straighten it. She wanted to destroy.

Her hands were shaking. She stood and paced the room with tight, short steps. This was ridiculous. What was the point of just letting this build inside her? She and Jake had to talk this out rationally. They had to look with brutal clarity at whatever options might remain to them. It was their only hope.

Quickly, before this cool stream of reason left her, she dialed his apartment. She didn't want him coming here. They could meet tomorrow. They could talk in some place that was less emotionally charged. She was free of Jessamyn's spell. She knew what Jessamyn had done. There was just the barest hope some sort of life remained for her and Jake—not perfect, but worth keeping in spite of its flaws.

On the other end, the receiver went up. A laughing voice answered, a woman's voice.

"Hello?"

Laura's hand went out to the phone's umbilical cord, yanking it, ripping it, and in that moment she knew the final fury of being cheated as she realized she had only succeeded in wrenching it free of its jack.

"You got to tell her, Nel."

Eddie held her hand between his own, trying to communicate by touch and tone the urgency of what he was saying. They were in his apartment, and she had forsaken the chaise lounge he'd bought for her for a plushy club chair with its matching ottoman. He supposed it was psychological, this more upright position. She was fighting it, his Nellie. There were times when fighting wasn't enough, though, and he could see she was going downhill.

Her eyes still had their sass and spark, but the rest of her looked tired. She *was* tired. Every day a little more energy crept out of her. Damn that white bitch Jessamyn. What she'd done had taken days—weeks—off Nel's life. He could see it.

"Oh, Eddie, don't scold me tonight," she pleaded. "Why don't you just fix us a drink? I wonder if Jake's going to tag along with Laura?"

Eddie's back was toward her. He measured his voice as carefully as he measured the liquor he was pouring.

"Oh, I think he knows the two of you like to be alone. I'll run along too when she gets here."

So Nel hadn't seen the article, he thought. It was in the same cheap tabloid that had Jessamyn and her dogs splashed on the front. He wouldn't have seen it either if the damn thing hadn't fallen off Nel's table. Jake and that actress out together. He couldn't believe it. He couldn't understand. Eddie shook his head.

"No, don't leave," Nel said as he sat down on the ottoman and gave her a glass. "Laura said she wouldn't stay long, just in and out."

"Nellie, that girl loves you. You got to tell her," he said gently.

Stubbornly Nel shook her head. "I could be run down crossing the street, I could be in some fancy hotel when the roof caved in. Why make her grieve any longer than she has to?"

These days Eddie could not grow as exasperated with her as he once had. He merely looked at her.

"Because of fairness, Nel. She has a right to know. You've shared a lot. You'll hurt her if you don't share this."

A ghost of anger rose to fill Nel's eyes.

"What about me? What about me being hurt? You don't understand, Eddie. You don't know what it's like to be afraid, to want to tell somebody something and yet not be one-hundred percent sure how they'll react."

"Oh, don't I? Listen to me, Nel." Eddie set down his glass and leaned forward. "There's something I've wanted to tell you for months—ever since I got here—but I've been afraid you wouldn't understand. Afraid . . . you wouldn't think the same of me."

She was staring at him in amazement, and Eddie knew now there was no turning back.

"Eddie Brown, if you're going to tell me you've got a wife stashed away somewhere, I swear I'll kill you!" she whispered.

Eddie felt the smallest of smiles.

"No, Nellie, not that. Never that. You're the only woman who ever caught my fancy."

"Then what—"

"Okay." He took a breath. "Do you know how I first got elected, Nel? I got in because folks knew I was squeaky clean. I never accepted a bottle of booze, or even a drink. I never knocked off a free piece with the girls on the street, though I've got to tell you, Nellie, I got offers enough."

For a moment he could not keep the devilment from his voice, and Nel, hearing it, snorted in answer. Eddie rubbed his hands together. He felt suddenly old now, and weighted down, and he had the sudden flashing premonition that in telling it, he was bringing it all to an end.

"Eddie Brown, the straight cop, that was me. And I felt good about that, Nel. I felt good about never once bending the rules to help myself. I even felt good about raiding that club of yours until you skipped." He smiled at her gently. "People trusted me. And when Jonas Jones and Lewis Keeton came to me and asked me to run for the state legislature, I was flattered."

Nel made an impatient movement.

"Eddie, I don't see what this has to do—"

"You will, Nel." Eddie paused, trying to sort it out for himself as well as for her. It was so confused and yet so terribly simple. "I got so much done—the new women's prison there in the city in reach of families, the new free clinic. I was helping my people, Nel, and I wasn't shaking hands with anyone under the table to get it done!" His voice had fallen to an outraged rasp.

It took a moment before he could continue. When he did, his voice was normal again.

"After that it was to Washington. Housing projects. Block grants. Renovations. I went after a lot, and I got it, and I figured I was helping not only the people who used those buildings, but the people who built them. More construction, less welfare. It all looked so nice.

"About two years ago I learned—and no matter how—that of all the construction projects I've gotten taxpayers' funds for these last fifteen years, Jones or Keeton or both were unlisted partners in corporations somehow involved in at least a third of them."

Nel didn't react at first. Then her forehead wrinkled. "You

mean they were using you, Eddie?"

"Yeah. They were using me."

The words were bitter.

Jones, a minority lawyer, kingpin in the city's Democractic machine. Keeton, a restaurant owner always getting his picture in the paper for charity work. He'd thought they wanted the same thing he did. He'd consulted them time and again. Would the voters go for a prison or subsidized housing? Would the free clinic reach more people located here or here? Grass roots all the way, he'd done his own studies and then turned to them for more input as men close to the people, but Jones's cousin was part-owner of a big development corporation, and Keeton's wife's brother-in-law had made a killing in slum real estate.

It had all been so tidy. No one who bought or sold a piece of property or signed a development bid had been connected in any way to Eddie Brown. Later he'd learned there'd been kickbacks too, all the graft and greed that he hated and that he'd thought he'd kept the taxpayers free of because he was an honest politician.

What a chump he'd been not to suspect. All those years he'd flattered himself that he'd been given his start because Jones and Keeton believed in him and in their city. In fact he'd been picked to be their patsy.

"You thought I might hold that against you?" Nel asked in tender tones. "It wasn't your fault, Eddie, and hell, we all have blind spots." Reaching out, she patted his hand consolingly.

But she didn't know the worst of it. Eddie gathered his courage.

"There's more," he said. "When I found out, I was so damn mad I confronted them. And they talked. Oh, how they talked! If I spilled the beans, I'd have mud on me, they said. I'd get turned out of Congress. And if that happened, what kind of help would the people in my poor little district have left? Who'd get them the federal funds for that Senior Citizens' center? If I kept my mouth shut, I'd help a lot of people, they said. If I talked, well, a lot of people would lose."

Nel was looking at him in horror now. He bowed his head.

"I lived in their pocket for a year, Nel. I let them get away with it."

Her next question was a whisper. "And then?"

Slowly he began to rub his hands again.

"I had my eyes open then. I began to see more. I found out

Jones and Keeton were just part of it, low boys in the scheme. They held hands with a federal judge, and with another congressman more savvy than I. Then I found out Keeton was dealing in more than real estate. He was also running drugs.

"That was too much to swallow. That meant I'd been protecting scum. Just before I found you, I went to an FBI man I prayed was straight. A secret grand jury was called. I gave a deposition. A few indictments have come down already. A few more may come. I went to a closed meeting of the House Ethics Committee and told what I knew. Then I resigned."

Nel's eyes were shining with tears.

"And that's why you've been using a different name," she said. "You're going to be a witness, and you don't want any publicity."

"Something like that," he said. There was no point in telling her that the men he'd fingered didn't want him around as a witness. Why, when the days of her life were so few, should he upset her?

"Oh, Eddie!" she said, and in those two words he heard love. It cleansed him and lifted him and made what had been and what was to come inconsequential. Nel opened her arms. Eddie buried his head in her lap.

At the door a light tap sounded.

"Nel? It's me," said Laura.

The caress of Nel's arms flowed over him like soothing waters as he straightened. They sat looking at one another, entwined, and Eddie knew it was for all time.

"You've done a lot of good. More than any man's share," Nel said.

He stood, straightened, and opened the door to Laura.

Eddie watched the two of them as though they were distant pictures on some TV screen. He felt as though all the loose ends of his life had been tied up. For the first time in a long time, he felt at peace.

"So how are you? How's Jake?" Nel was asking.

"Fine. Just fine."

Eddie was becoming aware of things again, and he saw Laura's eyes fall away as she answered. Was Turner cheating on her? Somehow Eddie had expected more from the man than that. He was starting to understand Nel's strong determination to protect Laura. He'd grown attached to her. He wished there were something—any small thing—he could do.

They were chatting now, and Laura was making Nel laugh. She'd finished some script and said the producer was pushy.

"I thought you were doing the script for Jake's new project," Nel said.

"Not anymore, by mutual consent. This one might go to series, Nellie. Make me lots of money. And none of the head-aches of working with relatives."

Nel didn't seem to hear the hollow note behind the cheer-fulness. That in itself showed she was slipping, Eddie thought.

Laura was on her feet now. She smiled at him, and he saw the unhappiness in her eyes.

"Behave yourself now, Nellie. Eddie, you take care of her."

"I try my best," he teased as she brushed his cheek.

Maybe Nel was right. Maybe Laura had worries enough without the added one of learning she'd lose Nel. Laura was a fine girl. She deserved a break. Eddie found himself hoping to hell she hadn't seen that gossip item.

Laura had taken a new way back from Nel's, a way not so fraught with memories. The passing sights might give her some-thing to fix her mind on, however briefly. But now a red light held her captive in front of a newsstand, and on a long line of tabloids, laughing at her, were Jessamyn and the dogs.

She gazed at them dully. The lighting was poor, but the images were there in her consciousness, large and clear. They seemed to be omnipresent. They jeered at her. Two women stopped to buy one of the papers, then bent their heads in avid fascination as they moved on.

The light turned green. Pressing her foot on the gas, she leapt ahead. They would read about Jessamyn, and then if they worked their way through, they would come to the bit of gossip about Jake and Kimberly.

It hurt, that article. It hurt more than the fights, the sepa-ration. She didn't even ask herself whether it was true or not. She knew it was.

Oh, Nellie, I need you tonight, she cried silently.

But Nel had looked tired, too tired to burden with troubles that were a product of Laura's own making. As she drove toward the empty house on the beach, Laura knew that tonight she was all alone.

Thirty

Jake Turner hurled the script he'd read for the third time over his desk. The bile of irritation filled his mouth. He rose to stride the length of his office and stand scowling out, his hands curled into fists that ached to break a hole in something.

The *Shadows* script—the new one—stank. Should he call Jessamyn and say he was walking out on the production company?

He beat one fist lightly against the wall as he tried to decide. The script was flat, predictable, lacking the sensitivity that Laura's had promised. But the package had been sold to the network on the basis of the story and on Kimberly Curran. If he didn't make the film, someone else would.

Turner turned to look at the leather couch and paneled walls of his office. He felt trapped. Beyond that door was his own editing room. Beyond that door was the sort of financial backing he'd never had before. Was he willing to kiss it all goodbye over one inferior piece of writing?

His conscience stirred uneasily. Jessamyn had said he wasn't one to stand on principles. She'd been right, damn her. He wanted to be strong; he wanted to have the kind of integrity people respected, even while they were bitching about your stubbornness. With an aspirate sound of anger, he stalked back across the room.

It was late afternoon, and he hadn't had a drink all day. He considered one, then vetoed the thought. He didn't need booze. He wasn't the weakling his father had been.

The hell you're not. You're falling apart, screwing Kimberly because you're so damn lonely and so damn afraid.

Through his own weakness, he'd lost Laura, and in losing Laura, he'd lost himself. Now he knew why he'd been drawn to her, why he'd known in his gut his fate had to be bound up with hers. He'd needed Laura because Laura knew there was more to life than bigger and bigger deals, more than your own super-stardom. He'd known it too, but he'd been afraid because without those trimmings there might be so little to him. If he couldn't prove himself through success, how *could* he prove himself? What, beyond achievements, did he have to offer Laura?

Fleeing the thought, he blundered from the room. As the door closed, he found himself standing awkwardly in the editing room. Christ, what excuse could he give old Woody for this agitation, for being here?

Then he knew no excuse was necessary. Not for the old man rewinding film from plastic trash cans. Woody's mind was so rotted by gin that he was aware of little else except being once more where he longed to be. Once he had been one of LA's greatest editors, part of the union that was the industry's most elite. Now his hands shook, and his mouth hung slightly ajar. He had come here begging for work as a janitor, odd jobs, anything, and Jake, unable to see a man who had been so brilliant humiliated, had created this busy work and paid the old man's wages from his own pocket, never telling Jessamyn.

Now, in a cold sweat, Turner stared at him. Am I going to end up that way? he wondered.

Woody looked up, and a smile of vague recognition lit his face.

"Oh, hello, Jake. How are things?"

"Fine, Woody. Fine. I have some raw footage I'd like you to take a look at one of these days."

"I'll do that, Jake. Just as soon as my mind starts perking a little better."

It was a fiction in which they both indulged. Woody would never edit a frame of film again.

What happened to you? Turner wanted to shout. Is it happening to me? Am I going to end up with someone letting me live my pitiful fantasies? Then, mercifully, he heard his phone begin to ring.

When he answered, it was Nico Christodoulou.

"Hey, Jake-o, you've sold yourself a movie," he said. "Universal loves it. ABC loves it. In fact they're talking maybe going backdoor to series if the numbers look decent."

Turner listened with growing amazement. The decision had been swift. He knew the reason for it; now was the time when projects were being sold or not sold for the fall season. As the facts soaked in, he began to congratulate himself on his own good luck.

Meanwhile Christodoulou was talking away.

"The honchos at the network are huddling about the series outlook right now. They want to give you a call if they decide they want a bible. Are you going to be where you are for another hour or so, Jake-o?"

For once Turner found he could tolerate the inane extra syllable appended to his name in the guise of chumminess.

"Sure. I'll be here," he said.

When he'd gone through the requisite round of mutual congratulations and ego-stroking, he hung up. Damn, he thought, he was proving himself to be one hell of a hot producer. A few days ago he'd pitched an idea of his to the west coast series people at NBC, and they'd been interested. One of the two was sure to pan out. He started to grin.

He went to his personal liquor cabinet and poured himself a drink. His mood was lighter than it had been just moments ago. Selling a project was always the hard part. Once he did that, he had unlimited confidence in his ability to bring it off. What the hell, even *Shadows* might not turn out so badly. He'd have total control himself, not farm any decisions out to that asshole assistant of his. And the trades and *TV Guide* were carrying promos for *Helen Somebody* next week. The critics were going to rave about Kimberly in that role. . . .

Sure. He could turn *Shadows* into a good little pic—not great, but good. He'd work around the script. And meanwhile he might have a bloody little series in his hands. Maybe even two of them. Not bad for a poor boy. Not bad at all. Turner drank to himself and to his own successes.

With a sudden impulse he returned to his desk. He put a phone call through to Christodoulou.

"Say, listen, Nico, if ABC wants me, tell them to catch me at home," he said. "I'll give you the number."

Smug with the knowledge of his own greatness, he finished his drink. He was tired of hiding out like some criminal over his misstep with Jessamyn. He'd been drunk. It hadn't been his fault. And the affair he'd started with Kimberly this past week, well, Laura had all but pushed him into that with that temper of hers.

He was going home, and not with his tail between his legs

either. Laura would just have to bend a little, understand things weren't always a fairy tale. He had a right to the comforts of his own home, a right to her company. He'd warned her he wasn't perfect. And she was, after all, his wife.

Laura was on the floor, pretending to be a lion with Tish's four-year-old daughter. It was an enchanted world, a perfect world in which their pretenses were real, and the adult realm of contracts and failures and carefully chosen language was pretense by comparison.

The smaller lion pounced on an aardvark disguised as a sofa cushion. They both laughed merrily.

I knew this was how it would be with a child, Laura thought. I wanted this, the chance to play and love someone the way that Jessamyn never loved me. Of course, if I were more like Jessamyn, I could have it. I could just sleep around and let nature take its course. But I'm not like Jessamyn, and I never will be, and I don't even give a damn about that anymore. Except I wish I could have had this.

"Now let's catch a snake," she said, and she heard the door open.

Hair falling over her shoulder, she looked up and saw Jake standing there. He was the very image of Beverly Hills success: white slacks, blue and white striped shirt, a cream-colored sweater knotted casually around his shoulders.

"You're back," she said, and the words were guarded. Had he come to pick up his things? To tell her his lawyer would call her? His arrival surprised her, and she clamped down viselike on all emotion. Was he here to stay, and if so, did she even want him to?

He'd adopted a swaggering pose, thumbs hooked in his belt. "Yeah, I decided we'd both been behaving like a couple of kids," he said carelessly. But behind the carelessness she thought she glimpsed for a minute something lost and haunted. "We have to work harder at living together, I guess. Who's this?"

"Tish's daughter. Her name's Jamie."

Laura got to her feet. She gave Jamie a gentle nudge. "Run find your mom." As the child ran out, Laura found it easier for her eyes to follow the child than to turn and face this near-stranger standing in the room with her. "Tish is full-time now. She lives here," she said abruptly. "She and Jamie have the two rooms off the kitchen."

She heard his silence. Then he shrugged.

"Why not?" he said, moving toward the bar. "We can afford it. Things are looking up for us."

She wanted to tell him there was no additional cost since Tish and the child were getting their rent and utilities free. Instead she simply stared at him. No apology, she thought. None at all. Not that she wanted him to crawl, but he'd simply walked back in with no acknowledgment of the rift between them. He spoke, he moved with something near to arrogance.

With a sinking feeling, Laura realized that very element in him once had attracted her. Once she had liked his relentless self-assurance, been delighted by the brashness that she'd thought masked a core of vulnerability. Now she was no longer sure what the inner Jake Turner was like, and she was repelled by this outward conceit.

She opened her mouth for a bitter response, but the telephone rang.

"That'll be for me," Jake said.

He smiled at her, and she knew a desperate outrage. Why had he come back? Why? He expected to walk back into this house—into her life—as though he had never been gone. He expected to instantly turn it into his domain. He expected all calls to be his.

He was laughing now, and taking a long pull from the drink in his hand as he hung up the phone.

"Well, there you are!" he said with a look of triumph. "ABC wants me to develop a series for them. Not bad for the new boy on the block, huh? I've got something cooking at NBC West Coast too. Think I'll call them right now and see if it's come to a boil. What's new with you?"

Shock at his behavior—at his assumptions—still immobilized her. She watched him move, half-listened as he was put through to the proper official and carefully dropped word of his already pending series, wheeling and dealing, pushing for another decision.

He could drink, make deals, parade his importance in other places where it would be fawned over. Why had he come back here, where she was?

Slowly, with an effort of will that tore at her physically, she closed her mind against the question. If she did not, she would soon be persuading herself what wasn't true was true. She would be explaining away all Jake's behavior, all their misunderstandings. She would be deceiving herself again, believing that he loved her.

He was hanging up for a second time, and she had neither words nor heart for further conversation. Picking up the reading glasses she had discarded to play with Jamie, she started from the room.

As she walked past, Jake touched her hair.

"I've missed you," he said as though it were an afterthought.

Laura felt words catch in her throat and a sharp, searing pain. Inside her something was tearing free and shriveling. Something was about to be lost for good.

She had loved him; perhaps she still did. Yet at the same time she now felt disgust and anger. Was he really so shallow? Did he really live for himself and for success? She could not find it in her heart to hate him for that weakness; she only knew she could not live his kind of life.

No, she corrected, it was not a question of being able, but of whether or not she wanted to, and she didn't.

Jake's hand moved on her shoulder, skillful and certain.

"Why don't we go upstairs?" he said.

She turned in her astonishment to look at him. In a moment of unwelcome insight, she realized it had never occurred to him that she might be the one to call their marriage quits. He supposed she would welcome him always, on any terms, drunk or sober, short-tempered or smiling, fresh from the bed of Kimberly Curran or anyone else he chose.

Perhaps she had given him reason enough to suppose she would, she realized bitterly. Slowly, with a hardness she hadn't known she possessed, she nodded. If Jake believed she was willing to continue this charade of a marriage, then she would— for her own purposes.

Regardless of what anyone said, regardless of logic, she wanted a child. Jake, without even knowing, could give her that much at least. For years, for her whole life it seemed, she'd given and given. Now, just for once, she was going to take.

Jake stared at his wife, at this woman he thought he knew, the woman he thought was shy and predictable. She had turned to him there in the living room not two minutes ago, unbuttoning her blouse with a brazenness that had surprised him.

"Come on," she'd said.

He'd been caught off guard. He hadn't been prepared for her to look so willing . . . so beautiful. Oh, he'd expected to make love to her, but not this easily. He'd thought it would take persuasion; he'd seen the anger snap in those clear eyes of hers.

Now in their bedroom she already stood completely naked, her head thrown back with a lack of restraint, an inhibition, that baffled even as it aroused him.

"God, Laura, I'm sorry," he said thickly, unzipping his pants.

"I know." She turned with an almost mysterious toss of those magnificent black curls and turned down the bed.

Turner quivered with eagerness, something clawing at the back of his mind that he tried to ignore. He pulled her to him ravenously, washing himself in the coolness of her skin, and her laugh was bewitching. It inflamed him, confused him. He didn't know this side of Laura existed.

Maybe it was just his presence. Maybe she had missed him. Yeah, that was the secret, he thought, confidence flooding him.

Her lips pressed his, cool and demanding. My God, she was a she-devil. Was this the woman who once had seemed so shy, almost reserved? Her overtures were like a hefty shot of vodka. Urgency overtook him. He moved inside her quickly, desperate to capture this wildness, this—this sizzling abandon such as he'd never seen in any woman.

She was laughing softly, laughing as though she gloried in this act. Her eyes were shimmering. Her hands roved over him, touching him everywhere, controlling him. He kissed her savagely again and again, and she returned his kisses. He felt himself shooting into her. She laughed again.

This time it unnerved him somewhat. Panting from his own exertions, he looked into her eyes and saw something foreign there, an insatiability.

"Make love to me again, Jake," she whispered. "I'm hungry."

The narrow tips of her nails scratched circles around his flat nipples until they hardened.

"Christ, Laura . . ."

His mind was excited, but he was appalled to find himself spent. He *wanted* her. God, how he wanted her. . . .

Laura's lips nuzzled down. She became the aggressor. Her tongue found his still soft flesh, coaxed it, played with it, drew

it into her mouth. With each rhythmic motion he was restored
to full manhood. He began to swell, to burst with his own
need. She was eager for pleasure. Eager to give it.

"Now," she said, lying back with sudden command. "Make
love to me."

Dazed by his own desire, he was quick to accommodate.
He kissed her breasts in a worshipful frenzy. Laura . . . Laura
was so perfect for him. He'd never tell her what he'd done
with Jessamyn.

And he knew, he *knew* he couldn't have felt like this with
Jessamyn. He exploded, gasping.

Sure Luara had missed him. They were great together. He
grinned and looked into her eyes, and what he saw there made
him suddenly desperate to make love to her again and again.

That wild look was still there, undiminished. It challenged
him. And even as it aroused him, it sent a vague uneasiness
trickling through him. For something in it suggested that Laura
was in control now, in a way he did not understand. Something
had changed behind those green-gray eyes staring back at him.

"Damn it! *Damn it!* Just think of the money we've lost!"

Ben Webber scuffed his shoe against his desk like a woebe-
gone child.

Laura, listening, tried to share her agent's outrage. He'd
just gotten word from Hugh Archer, who'd gotten it from the
network. The word was no-go on the *Green Gables* series.

"They say it costs too much to mount a period piece," Ben
fumed. "What utter crap! As rightly as I recall, it was a period
piece two weeks back when they were crazy about it. Archer
must've been right. It must've been Shrugman who was pulling
for it, and now he's out."

His expression was half-I-told-you-so and half-dejection.
He'd had his own reservations about this project, Laura remembered, but it had grown on him.

"Come on. I'll buy you a drink somewhere," he said.

Laura shook her head and stood up. She knew she should
be thinking of the thousands of dollars a week a series would
have meant for her, but before coming to this meeting in Ben's
office, she'd gotten another bit of news that made it seem
unimportant. The doctor's lab report was back. She was definitely pregnant.

"Thanks, but you've got other headaches to manage, I'm

sure. I'll give you a call tomorrow to find out what else is on the horizon to keep me employed."

I've got to scurry and get a new project right away, she thought. I've got what's-its-name to provide for now as well as myself.

She allowed herself one small second of humor. When since she first set out to make it in this game, hadn't she been scurrying? At first it had been to establish herself. Then it was to prove herself to Jake. Now it had become a question of simple economics.

Though, come to think of it, she had not been married to Jake long enough ever to grow financially dependent on him. Laura winced inwardly at the fresh proof of her failure. Not until now had she had such a clear view of her marriage's brevity.

When she was alone in her car, she drew a long breath. Only now could she finally feel anger over losing *Green Gables*. It was such a fine story—no sex, no gimmicks, just the warm and funny account of an imaginative orphan girl cast into the household of an elderly bachelor and his straitlaced sister. The two fine old veterans who'd played in the pilot adored the series idea—and had even said some nice things about her writing. Manuel Martin, who could have his pick of male leads in half a dozen other series, had expressed a serious interest in the project. Now because of the loss of one man at the network, everything was out the window.

Maybe next time, Little One, Laura promised the life inside her. To her surprise, her pride made her fiercely eager for that "next time." Then she drove along in an increasingly somber mood, for now, though she had tried to avoid the thought of it by filling her mind with other things, the time had come when she had told herself that she would part with Jake.

From her perspective, these last few weeks had only proved the futility of trying to maintain their marriage. They spoke but did not talk, Jake parading his importance, drinking, telephoning, dashing off to the office, watching warily, like a caged wild creature, whenever they were in a room together. They made love with . . . not abandon . . . not even hunger. She supposed she would have to call it driven determination.

Driven. That was the key word to describing Jake now. He was not happy, and neither was she.

Yet as she pulled into the parking garage below his building, a faint hope flickered. Jake had changed. She honestly believed he had changed from what he once had been into this man corrupted by success and lost to her. But could he change back? Was it worth another risk, another gamble?

She walked with haste, almost running. Somewhere, in these next instants, she had to decide.

Jake's secretary was not at her desk. Laura checked the appointment book lying open on the desk, and it told her she would find him alone. What was she going to say? What she had rehearsed or something else that might bridge the gap that had opened between them? Rapping lightly, she opened the door to his office. There on the couch Jake knelt beside an attractive brunette dressed in blue.

"Oh, Jake, you're too funny about all this!" the woman was protesting, bent with laughter. Jake, laughing too, was draping one strand of her long hair up, enjoying himself.

"Hello."

Laura spoke the single word and waited. They both turned, looking sheepish.

"Do you suppose I could speak to you for a few minutes, Jake? It's rather important."

As though he sensed the coming clash, Jake rose and ushered the brunette out, speaking in low tones. Laura moved toward Jake's desk to make her stand, supporting herself with one hand against her trembling anger.

"I'd always supposed you were above the casting couch," she said mildly.

The door had closed. Jake was scowling.

"Now just a damn minute! It's not what you think, and you might just remember that this is my office. If you hadn't come barging in unannounced—"

"No, *you* wait a minute! Stop trying to make yourself out to be the injured party. That's your favorite trick, isn't it, Jake? God, maybe you really believe—"

"What the hell are you ranting about? Do you plan to go off like a firecracker every time you see me with a pretty woman? It's part of my job, and I'm sure as hell not going to apologize for it! Get used to it. Stop acting like a jealous brat. Grow up!"

Laura could feel her knuckles press the insensitive wood beneath them. How wasted that final moment of hope had been. She laughed at the irony of many things, shaking her head.

"You're telling me to grow up, Jake? That's priceless! You

can't even face up to your own weaknesses, can you? To Kimberly Curran or this little trick, or turning your back on a friend like you did on Saul Finer when it meant profit for you! Whenever you look less than perfect, you make excuses like some sulky child. And when you get a whiff of success because of a break most people would give their eyes for, you take all the credit and parade around as if you're God's gift to the world!"

"My, what a witch's tongue my sweet wife has! This sounds, Laura love, like sour grapes. I'm pulling ahead of the pack, and you're standing still!"

The words lashed at her like a cruel whip, after the loss of her series.

"Maybe I am . . . but at least I got where I am on my own merits! I didn't have Jessamyn's name and Jessamyn's charisma opening doors for me."

She knew she had struck deep. His eyes were razors. His voice grew uncomfortably soft.

"Did you now? Get there on your own, I mean. Don't you suppose Daniel Katz being your father had just the tiniest bit to do with your getting hired for *Twenty-two Wentworth*?"

Daniel Katz. It wasn't true.

She stared at Jake, wondering, and yet certain of one still more painful fact. He had wanted to hurt her with this accusation. He had deliberately wanted to hurt her.

Her lips moved, but just barely.

"You've had your say, now I'll have mine. I'm through with you. As it so happens, what I walked in on here today was just an appropriate curtain scene. I came to tell you and to give you the extra key to your precious car!"

She flung it at him, the symbol of affluence that he treasured, of his pretense of sharing when he never meant to.

"I'll see your things are sent. Don't come back to my house— not ever!"

His face was dark with fury. "Like hell I won't! You can't—"

"I can! I am. You want so badly to play the stud—I suppose it's the only role you're really equipped for—well, you've played it splendidly! I'm pregnant, and that's all I ever wanted from you. Did you suppose I'd marry you for any other reason, knowing how shallow you are?"

The words that had flown between them had filled her with

adrenalin. She crossed the room with head held high and threw
open the door, bumping him aside.

"See? You don't really have exclusive rights on walking
out," she said and slammed the door.

Jessamyn laughed, enjoying the lapping waters of her swimming pool, enjoying her own nakedness and that of the man
beside her. She felt immensely sensuous, eternally young, filled
with a simmering vitality and a sense of her own power.

She should have indulged herself like this more often, Jessamyn thought. In the warm dusk of evening she splashed and
turned, brushing her body against her companion's. Yes, she
should have tossed convention to the winds long ago. She had
been held down by Nel, always acting her conscience, always
making her feel guilty, always treating her like a child.

But yesterday Nel had checked into the UCLA Med Center.
Jessamyn had heard, but she didn't care. She'd grown tired of
having someone sitting in judgment over her long before she
sacked Nel. She didn't really *need* the woman; had only kept
her out of charity. In fact, she should have fired Nel years ago
and enjoyed herself.

"You're beautiful!" the man beside her whispered.

Jessamyn smiled lazily.

He was richer than she herself was, his presence here would
cause a furor if it were known, and the sorry son-of-a-bitch
had no idea at all that she was using him.

Not that he didn't deserve it! This was the big investor
whom Van Greenberg had almost persuaded to cancel his
backing for her latest movie. Jessamyn had taken pains to
learn which man it had been, and at a recent party celebrating
the film's predestined success, she'd taken almost equal pains
to meet him.

After that it had all been so easy.

She had pulled her serious act and some smoldering gazes.
He'd fallen over himself to take her to bed. Later, with a sigh,
she'd casually mentioned how near she had come to losing her
part in his movie—and this chance to know *him*—all because
of Van Greenberg. Flustered and contrite, a little surprised that
she knew so much, the unsuspecting fool had confessed that
he was the one swayed by Greenberg.

Jessamyn had pretended amazement. "But couldn't you
guess?" she'd gasped. "Didn't it even occur to you that it was
all a vendetta against me? Darling, what Van Greenberg likes

to do with women—well, I'm not exactly a Brownie Scout, but I don't do *that*! When I refused him, he said he'd see me thrown out of the picture."

The balding tycoon who had been Greenberg's pawn willingly became hers.

"Let's go inside," he said now urgently.

His erection was large and long, and as she slid it between her legs, the buoyancy of the water allowed her to bob up and down on it as though on a diving board, pleasuring herself, exciting him.

"No. Here."

She fixed her amber eyes on his.

She liked being screwed in the water, feeling the slippery wetness all around. He shoved it in, and Jessamyn lay back, gripping the edge of the pool. Things worked out so well, she thought, breathing faster. Soon she would see Greenberg get exactly what he deserved. She would—

"Miss Friday!"

Deidre's puny voice intruded on their romp.

With a curse Jessamyn felt the man on top of her thrash and start to sink, distracted. They both looked up.

The maid, red-faced even from a distance, had ventured but a few steps from the patio doors. She bent forward anxiously, caught between embarrassment and concern.

"Miss Friday, Mr. Turner's here! He insists on seeing you."

"Oh, does he!" Jessamyn had rolled onto her belly, her round breasts floating before her as she held the pool's edge. Beside her the man who had wrenched himself from her groaned in pain. "Well, you tell Mr. Turner I'm occupied at the moment. If he wants to see me, he can damn well make an appointment—"

Her jaw fell slack as she saw Turner shoulder his way past Deidre, shaking Harry from one arm as the houseman tried to detain him.

"Didn't know I needed an appointment to see a relative, Jessamyn."

His voice was loud as it rolled across the concrete of the patio. Jessamyn could see that he'd been drinking, but he was still a good long way from being drunk.

In a fury at his impertinence, she rose from the pool to stand dripping before him. She shook back her hair, then reached for a towel, taking her time as she stood before him in glistening skin.

"All right, you don't," she said coldly. "What is it you want? I'll give you five minutes."

He grinned and let her close the distance between them as Deidre and Harry made their exit.

"Just thought you'd like to know, Jess—I've made you a grandma. You will be anyway, in about nine months."

Pure hate flowed through her veins, and she saw it reflected back at her from the black planes of his eyes. It couldn't be. It wasn't right. They'd done this on purpose—just to spite her—and everyone was going to know!

She raised her hand to strike him, but her rage immobilized her.

"What's the matter, Jessamyn? Don't you like the idea? Do you know what that makes you, Jessamyn? That makes you *old*!"

"You, you—"

She swung at him now, but he caught her hand, laughing wildly.

"If there's a baby, you're sure as hell not the father!" she shrieked. "Not as often as you're drunk! Not the way you perform—or don't perform when you are! You couldn't get it up enough to impregnate a cat. When you tried to fuck me, you couldn't even keep it up long enough to—"

She broke off, hearing too late what she was saying. Then Jessamyn realized that she still held control.

Far from gloating, Turner was staring at her like a man just made aware that he was dying. His grip had grown nerveless.

"You lying bitch!" he said hoarsely with new understanding. "I've never screwed you."

Smartly, smugly, she broke free.

"That's right. You never did."

All at once Turner knew it didn't matter. He'd wanted to, would have, because he'd been weak and stupid. The fact that he hadn't didn't alter what he was at all.

He'd used what he'd believed he'd done as an excuse, a justification for living up—or down—to the safe, low expectations he'd always had for himself. Being friend/lover/person was harder than carving a name in the industry. If he gave Laura reason to hate him, it was easier on the ego than if he'd tried and failed.

"You wanted this," he heard himself shouting. "You wanted to ruin my marriage!"

But he knew he'd been the one who'd ruined it, and the world was empty of everything but the mocking sound of Jessamyn's laughter.

Thirty-one

Yesterday Jake, today Jessamyn. Laura looked at the telephone with hard resolve. She was going to get her life on track. She was going to snip her way free of the threads that had too often tripped her. Then she could begin to carve out a future that was sane—no more games, no more pretenses, no more people taking advantage of her because they perceived her as weak.

"I want to speak to Jessamyn Friday," she said. "This is her daughter."

She smiled, imagining the ripple those words would cause in the sleek, exclusive hairdressing salon where Jessamyn could be found invariably this day of the week. It was likely that no one in the place even knew Jessamyn had a daughter.

Of course the clientele of Philippe-Claude never had their privacy interrupted for a phone call when they were in his hands or those of his shampooists.

"Tell her to come immediately, that it's about some important personal letters of hers," she said, so firmly that the voice on the other end did not even demur.

Laura drew a breath as she waited. She felt slightly guilty. She also felt immense anticipation.

Just for once, Jessamyn, I'm going to have my satisfaction. Just for once, we're going to lay our cards on the table.

"Laura?" The voice springing into life on the other end of the wire was hushed but furious. "Just what the hell is this all about?"

A smile crossed Laura's face. Good, she was nervous then. If Jessamyn didn't want those letters as badly as Nel had thought, she'd never have come to the phone.

"I thought it was time we had lunch together," Laura said

mildly. "Nel gave me some letters of yours a while back. I thought you might want their contents for posterity."

Her smile grew into a grin as she heard only silence. She had the upper hand. Jessamyn couldn't shriek, couldn't even have the satisfaction of swearing there, amid the glass and chrome and foamy beige carpeting of Philippe-Claude's gossip-hungry salon.

"All—all right," Jessamyn's voice said tersely. "Tell me what it is you want, damn it."

Incredible that even Jessamyn could be manipulated, Laura thought, slightly dazed by her own power. There were so many things she could extract from Jessamyn with these letters: A gala baby shower written up in the movie magazines—that would probably be the worst humiliation Jessamyn could endure. Or money. Or favors from network officials. Anything.

But as she'd told Eddie, she'd never stoop to using those letters in that way. She'd never use them again. All she wanted was this.

"All I want is lunch with you," she said sweetly. "We can talk then."

"All right. Tomorrow. I have a standing table at Scandia—"

"I have a table at La Scala, Jessamyn. Today at one."

She envisioned Jessamyn, her hair limp with shampoo or the tint she must use now or maybe sticky from one of the oil treatments that she favored. She would be in one of her lesser outfits, too, and no matter how she rushed she wouldn't be able to remedy that situation, not as late as Laura was calling. On the other end of the phone, she heard an outraged sputter.

"Oh, very well!" snapped Jessamyn. "I'll see if I can make it by half past. You do have to be reasonable, Laura."

"Don't be late, Jessamyn. I have other things to do."

Laura hung up and cocked her head at the bedroom mirror, inspecting the woman reflected there, already done up for her luncheon appointment.

She had departed from her usual black and white to wear a neat little Castleberry suit in hot, vibrant pink. Its unstructured jacket swung open, revealing the long rope of finger-thick gold at her neck. Her nails and lips were polished to match the hue of the suit; her hair was swept up with elegant discipline. Heads turned to watch as Laura entered the restaurant.

She had asked for the table where she had sat with Nel and Eddie the day she landed her job on *Wentworth*. Across the way attention was being lavished on a party of six that included an eternally debonair Dean Martin. When Jessamyn entered he would be upstaged, and Laura liked the thought of it—not because she disliked the actor but because she liked the thought of all attention being fixed on Jessamyn for what came next.

The brandy snifter on the table held roses and baby's breath. Laura, admiring them, ordered wine and waited. At fifteen past one, a bustle at the entrance announced the arrival of Jessamyn.

Damn, thought Laura. *She's managed to get her hair done after all!*

Then she realized that Jessamyn must be wearing a wig. It lacked the rippling radiance of Jess's own hair. Her mother looked out of breath, too. She walked toward the table with quick, jerky steps, not smiling at those she passed. She was, Laura realized with satisfaction, trying to attract as little attention as possible, for while she had not been forced to come in a turban, she'd not been able to get home and change. Her one-piece black jumpsuit was almost too simple for La Scala, her makeup was faint, and the simple gold earrings she wore would hardly excite the envy of any upper-middle-class working woman.

"All right," she said, sliding into her seat. "Let's get this over. What is it you want?"

"How about some iced tea, Jessamyn?" Laura asked, enjoying her revenge. Of course Jessamyn wouldn't remember that night she'd demanded iced tea but never touched it.

Jessamyn looked ready to explode.

"Why the hell would I want iced tea? I'll have a—a martini."

The hovering waiter bowed and started away, obviously knowing that Jessamyn Friday drank her martinis up. Laura smiled inwardly, wondering if that gave her mother a false sense of satisfaction.

"Are you sure you wouldn't like iced tea too?" she persisted. "I'm sure it's nice and fresh here—"

"*No!*"

"Oh, all right. A martini then, and another glass of wine for me and—bring Miss Friday a glass of iced tea too. No, make it a pitcher. I really think she's going to change her mind."

Jessamyn looked at her shrewdly. Her mouth was pinched. "You wouldn't really do anything with those damned letters," she said. "You wouldn't have the guts. You're weak. You've always been weak. You want people to love you. And you don't have the skill to use them without getting burned. So give them to me, Laura. It'll be easier in the long run. I might just let you off unharmed."

Laura sat back, laughing at the amazing nerve of the woman across from her.

"Oh might you, Jessamyn? Well, isn't that big of you?"

Their drinks arrived. Laura waited, pushed hers aside untouched. She leaned forward, fingertips poised lightly on the edge of the table.

"Don't ever make the mistake of thinking I'm weak, Jessamyn. I'm not. I promise you. I'm not like you—thank God! But never think I'm not strong. Just because I don't lie and cheat and manipulate people like you do doesn't mean that. You've meddled in my work, you've broken up my marriage— but if you *ever* try to cross me again—if you ever try to touch any aspect of my life again, you'll regret it. I swear it."

Jessamyn moistened her lips. She was no longer sure of herself, Laura thought with satisfaction. Slowly Laura lifted her glass and sipped at the wine, while Jessamyn, as though reluctantly, followed suit with her martini.

"What is it you want from me, then?" she said flatly. "A pledge?"

"I want you to know I'm your equal in every way, Jessamyn."

It was almost time.

Reaching for her purse, Laura drew out a fat, brown manila envelope. She watched Jessamyn's eyes light greedily.

"I'd hate for you not to have the memories of all those lovers—for your old age," she added, and allowed the words to taunt.

Like talons, Jessamyn's fingers seized the envelope.

If Nel were watching this scene, she'd die, Laura thought. *At least she'd say I was crazy.*

"I know how you really want this iced tea, Jessamyn," she said, rising.

Picking up the pitcher, she stood and upended it over Jessamyn, wig and all, pausing just long enough to reach deftly out and flick back the wig, revealing Jessamyn's limp, shapeless hair, which she also drenched with tea. A camera zinged. The photographer to whom Laura had promised a good picture was at a nearby table. He'd collected his trophy.

"You—you—"

Jessamyn swung at her, then clutched wildly at the wig, trying hastily to fit it on her head as rivulets of brown ran down her face.

"I'll *ruin* you for this! I'll close every door in this town— every door on this *continent* to you!"

She was shrieking, out of control, as Laura had never heard her. Laura sat down.

"I doubt it, Jessamyn. The letters in that envelope are photocopies—good memories, but not credit in the bank. I still have the originals. I can ruin you without hesitation. I know how many people you've tortured over the years. I can call in a lot of favors."

Jessamyn sputtered inarticulately. She was staring, like a child. Her stance was even slightly pigeon-toed.

"I'll get even. I *will*!"

But the words sounded petulant. Fumbling for dark glasses, holding the envelope up to shield her face, she turned and fled the restaurant.

"I think I'll have the crab cannelloni," Laura said serenely to the distraught waiter who was running up to stop the scene. "And some asparagus. And would you send someone to change this tablecloth, please? It's really a mess."

Thirty-two

Nel had been in the hospital three days. Why hadn't someone told her? Laura hurried the length of the corridor, clutching a nosegay of pansies. It frightened her to think of Nel sick, to think of ever losing her. And Eddie had sounded so vague on the phone, so kind and cautious. What was the matter?

She rapped on the half-open door marked with Nel's number, poked her head around with a joke on her tongue, then stopped.

"Nellie?" she asked when she could find her voice.

The woman in the bed had Nel's face, but she seemed older. Her hair, always sleek and shiny, lay in a lackluster frizz.

"Yeah, it's me," said Nel, her humor weak. "Looking just like a Brillo pad. Some glamour, huh?"

Laura came to the bedside and gripped her hand tightly. Nel's fingers felt weak inside her own.

"Nel, what—"

"Sit down, kiddo. Are those for me?"

Laura glanced mechanically at the pansies. "Yes. Of course."

"Hey, I'm going to have to do this more often. I love the attention!"

The room was filled with flowers—two sprays of brilliant yellow roses and one of red, a small mixed arrangement, a rose bowl. . . .

"Nel, what are you *here* for? It can't be your shoulder again. And why not St. John's?"

Nel glanced at Eddie, who stirred and moved toward the door.

"I'll see you ladies later," he said.

When he had gone, the room was silent. Laura felt apprehensive.

Nel sighed and patted the side of the bed.

"Sit down, kiddo. We've got to talk."

Nel was frightening her. There was pain in those shrewd, wise eyes that Laura loved. She was afraid of causing Nel discomfort, afraid of jarring the bed. Looking around blindly, she found a chair and drew it up close. There was sympathy in Nel's expression. And affection.

"It's not good, is it, Nellie?" Her words were a whisper. She prayed she was wrong, but they knew each other too well not to read each other. Already her throat was tightening, already she was telling herself she must be brave for Nel.

Nel looked toward the ceiling. She was not sitting upright, but lay propped on pillows, and even the small arc of her eyes seemed slow.

"No, it's not, and there's no good way to say it. I've got amyotrophic lateral sclerosis—folks call it Lou Gehrig's disease. I figure you'll keep trotting in to see me, so you'd guess sooner or later. These wicked old bones aren't long for this world, but believe me, they've enjoyed one hell of a time while they were around!"

Utter stillness. They looked for a moment into each other's souls.

"But, Nel, there *must* be something they can do!" she heard herself crying in horror in spite of all those good intentions to stay calm.

"Sure, they can make me comfortable, keep me breathing a while longer, a few weeks, maybe. But I've already beaten the odds. I've already lived longer than most do after the diagnosis. I'm one tough lady. So no waterworks, okay now? I wouldn't have spilled all this except that Eddie made me think I ought to tell you while . . . well, while we could still say . . . hell, I don't know what."

Laura held Nel's hand between both of hers now. She knew what she wanted to say.

Don't die, Nel, please! Don't leave my life. I need you, Nel! Those were the words she wanted to pour out.

But she knew that would make things harder for Nel, and the only thing in her small power she could do for Nel was to make things easier. The only thing she could do was to show a scrap of Nel's own toughness, learned by example. Courage . . . determination . . . God, what a lot she'd learned from Nel!

She bowed her cheek and pressed it to Nel's hand, sneaking the tears off on her own cuff first so they didn't betray her.

"I'm going to miss you," she said simply.

"Yeah, well, I'm glad to hear it. Beneath this unspoiled exterior lies one big streak of vanity."

Laura righted herself.

"Nel, you know that's not true! You're good and unselfish and—"

"Shit, cut it out. If you have to paint me bigger than life, do it in some TV play. 'Girl from Detroit makes good'—or is it 'good make'? I never could re—"

"Nel, stop it!" Laura's words were raw with pain.

"Sorry, kiddo. Guess I get carried away with the jokes sometimes."

Nel's voice was gentle. She started to speak again, but something seemed to afflict her breathing. She caught at her throat, fear in her eyes, gasping for breath.

"No—don't—" she managed as Laura reached for the nurse-call button.

After an agony of waiting, the storm subsided.

"But, Laura, there's one thing I want you to know," Nel said, as though their conversation had never been suspended. "It's been good for me—all of it, really, but especially since Eddie found me . . ."

She seemed to let the thought slide from her. She looked tired now. With a great force of will, Laura rose and patted her hand.

"I'd better let you rest. I've got to go meet Ben now. He's hustling a job for me."

Eddie, as if waiting outside, returned to the room. Nel nodded slowly.

"How's Jake?" she asked, and her eyes, penetrating again for an instant, held a question.

Laura returned her gaze without wavering. She would not burden Nel with worry for her sake. She would not even let Nel suspect what she seemed to suspect.

"He's fine. Better than fine. In fact—" She took a breath. "We're going to have a baby."

A slow smile spread over Nel's weary face.

"Kiddo . . . that's wonderful!"

Laura hesitated, unwilling to end the sweetness of their mutual being. Finally, haltingly, she spoke again. "I love you, Nel, and I've always known that you—you're the one who—"

Her voice broke. She was unable to finish.

Laura followed the carpeting in her agent's tall glass building. In offices along the way other agents were talking contract, making deals, packaging next season's hit show, next year's big movie, and none of it—not any of it—mattered half a damn compared with Nel's life.

"Hi, Laura. Ben's waiting for you."

She was in Ben's outer office, looking at his secretary. Long, slick-tawny nails; blond hair permed and then caught back in unset curls; mouth perfectly painted and glossy, always curving in a bright look of professional cheer. Packaged. And alive—as Nel soon wouldn't be. Laura nodded without feeling and went inside.

The visit to the hospital had left her so splintered she did not register the presence of Hugh Archer in the room at first, in fact not until both he and Ben were on their feet, welcoming her with the hearty, there's-never-a-bomb-in-our-business voices, which people in the industry always used. From behind the fifteenth-century library table that served as his desk, Ben caught her eye to signal he understood her confusion.

"I've put our other appointment on hold," he told her as they sat down. "Hugh called here hunting you, and I told him he might as well meet you here."

Archer was leaning forward, the intensity of his eyes penetrating even the numbness she was feeling because of Nel.

"*Green Gables* is *on!*" he said triumphantly.

It took a moment for the words to reach her, and then she did not understand.

"Oh—you mean—?"

"Yes. As a series! For next season. We need a first-week script based on your treatment. Do you want to do it?"

She brushed back a strand of hair, more bewildered than ever. The series idea had been nixed only two days ago.

"Because of the shake-up," Ben prompted. He was frowning slightly, as though perplexed at her slowness. "Didn't you hear about Brughenheim's speech? My God, haven't you seen today's papers?"

"No. I—I've had a crashing headache."

She could hardly tell them she'd spent yesterday cloistered, soul-searching, and that this morning she'd been to see her lawyer to file for divorce. Those were personal problems, which you didn't hint of in the marketplace. That was why women weren't hired, why they didn't get ahead, because they had the audacity to live life on more than one plane. She couldn't afford to admit having any kind of problems. She had to provide for herself and her unborn child. As she sifted through all the thoughts bombarding her, Laura didn't know whether to cry or laugh.

". . . his speech to the affiliates after network announced he was taking over," Archer was saying.

So that was it. The network axe had fallen at the highest level. Brughenheim, it appeared, was the new president of giant CBS.

"He promised more wholesome family entertainment, said he'd give viewers what they claimed they wanted," Archer told her. "Didn't you hear?"

Why did they both have to keep asking that?

"By yesterday every hope of a family show the network had ever thought of was on his desk." Archer was animated. "He thought *Green Gables* filled the bill. So what do you say? Are you in for the project?"

The two men waited.

Green Gables was the kind of show she wanted to be with, she thought slowly. The kind she was good at—if she was really good at anything and her whole career wasn't due to the fluke of being Dan Katz's daughter.

But maybe Jake had been wrong about that, or maybe he made it up. She'd called Katz, determined to know, but he was away on business. And a series... a regular income, at least for the near future... it seemed like a godsend.

Only no longer was she dewy-eyed. She no longer believed that clouds always had silver linings. She'd known it long ago really, but had clung to the fiction, seeking... she didn't know what. Now she knew that no matter what your own values were, this world was dog-eat-dog.

Hugh Archer wasn't any sort of a nice guy either. With a presence and intensity that she hoped matched his own, she sat forward.

"Yes, I'll do the script. I'd love to. But only if it's in my contract that I do four segments a year."

Jake Turner sat in the commissary at Universal, staring at the ashtrays on the red tablecloth. He was the only one at the table who was not smoking. He longed for the taste of a cigarette, but he kept thinking that Laura had begged him to give them up for the sake of his health.

The absurdity of his thoughts caught up with him, and he grimaced, looking at Nico Christodoulou, some limp-wristed v.p. from programming, and the man who might direct his new series. Without interest he wondered what the hell the three of them were talking about. Why the hell did he balk at smoking after everything else he'd done to Laura?

The fact of it was that he was no damn better than his father. The beatings he'd administered to Laura were verbal instead of physical, that was the only difference.

And throwing that at her about being Katz's daughter when he'd brought the two of them together out of love, because he'd known how much finding a link like that would mean to Laura, because he'd wanted in the beginning to do something right for her. Hell. He was a monster.

From the start he'd had that nagging feeling of being unworthy of her, and when he'd thought he'd screwed Jessamyn, he'd set out to prove how unworthy he was by screwing Kimberly Curran and anything else that happened along.

Now what, he wondered. He figured Jessamyn was biding her time, waiting to fire him. He supposed he should walk out, act first, something. Trouble was, he didn't care. Without Laura, nothing mattered. And he didn't seem to know what to do.

Directed by the hostess, the man they'd been waiting for came into view. Another vice president. Christ, the woodwork was crawling with them, and as far as Turner could see, their only function was to get in the way. Why didn't they plaster the back wall with vice presidents instead of the lighted, larger-than-life-size pictures of the current crop of stars from Universal's films and TV shows?

"Glad I caught up with you," crowed the newcomer squeezing into the comfortable booth. "Hey, have you heard the big news from ABC? Their financial whiz Greenberg just got nailed for supplying coke. The network's fired him."

"Sacrificial lamb. Everybody knows a network's got to have someone dealing in favors like that if they want contracts."

"Yeah, but someone so high up? Pretty strange. I wonder who fingered him."

"Someone on the board of directors, so I heard. He'll have a shit hard time getting hired as a doorman anywhere now."

Christodoulou grinned over his wine. "You're wrong about one thing—Greenberg wasn't any sort of a lamb. Hey, Jake-o, isn't that your wife?"

He looked up and saw her. She was entering the room, looking around in search of someone, and as she started purposefully forward, a manila envelope tucked under her arm, Turner realized how totally in her element she was.

She saw him at that instant too. Her face took on a terrible hardness as she looked down. Turner felt as though a wrecking ball had hit his belly.

"Ex-wife soon—she threw me out a week ago. She's filed for divorce." He made a joke of it.

The limp-wrist from programming nudged his ribs. "Whasamatter, you try to keep too many chicky-poos on the string, Jake? I hear tell the lady's a real straight arrow."

Turner wanted to strangle the grinning bastard. How dare he presume to know anything about Laura?

"Yeah, she's decent," he snapped. "You even know the meaning of that word?"

Flinging down his napkin, he walked out of the dining room, wondering what the boothful of self-righteous bigwigs would make of his display of temper.

Nearly blind with rage, he plunged out into the falling rain, drawing up in confusion as it soaked into his collar and pelted his head. A tenuous thought seeped into him with the wetness. He stood there, rain-drenched, ignored by people coming and going beneath umbrellas. Yes. He had to try it.

There was a pay phone downstairs by the men's room. He went back inside and ran down the stairs.

"Jake Turner for Mr. Finer," he said when he'd rung the office where Saul now was writing for some lousy cop drama. He put a cheer he didn't feel into his voice, although the prospect of talking to Saul did make him feel somewhat better. "Hey, Saul. How you doing? Listen, I was wondering if you might be able to get away and have a drink with me this afternoon. I'm thinking of trying something, and I wondered— look, I know I was a heel when I broke up the company, Saul, and it's presumptuous as hell of me to even come crawling to you like this . . . but I would like to talk."

Saul Finer's voice was even cheerier than his own.

"Sorry, Jake. No can do."

Turner's spirits slumped again. He felt oddly isolated.

"Oh," he said. "Bad time? Well, maybe—"

"Nope. Not a bad time at all," Saul cut in brightly. "It's just that you're a schmuck, Jake . . . and a pretty damn small one at that!"

His fingers leaden and cold with the rain that had soaked them, Turner clung to the receiver, which had gone dead on the other end. Slowly he shook his head. He knew Saul was right, and he knew he had no right to, but he was going to fight for Laura. Even if she scorned him and called him everything he was. Even if he fell flat on his face in utter failure. He had failed without trying, and now nothing could add to the bleakness of his existence. Laura was what mattered to him—not the business, not his puffed up ego. He fished change from his pocket and began to dial Saul's number a second time.

* * *

Laura's mouth felt parched. She gripped her envelope. Hugh Archer and an exec from Universal were going through the usual pleasantries with her, but she felt wooden. The impact of seeing Jake here had been much harder than she'd expected.

"No, I'll have a cup of soup, please," she said as a waitress asked about wine.

She needed nourishment for the baby inside her, and to keep her going after the schedule she'd been on.

"Here's the script," she said, shoving the folder across the table to Archer. She'd done it in eight days, a minor miracle but one that was entirely necessary if the show was to air next season. Not only had she lost five pounds, but she was exhausted. At least the big push was done now. She could relax, catch up on sleep, take good care of the life-to-be that was at the moment her only glimmer of happiness.

She'd been to see Nel today, but Nel had been sleeping, sporting the smart wig Laura had picked out for her the day after Nel's revelation.

She was going to lose Nel soon. She knew it.

"Hey, you're one hell of a pro, you know it?" Archer was saying.

"Thanks." She thought he looked tense. "What's happened? Why the meeting today?" She'd been scheduled to drop the script off at his office tomorrow morning.

Archer was nodding, impatient and tightly strung. All at once she felt a terrible foreboding.

"*Green Gables* is going on as a replacement series," he said. "It airs in six weeks."

Thirty-three

"*You fucking asshole*, she's got tits! There's no way in God's green earth she could pass for eleven years old!"

"The hell she can't! She's childlike—utterly childlike. Anyway, the script calls for her to grow up, doesn't it? Let wardrobe worry about her tits for the time being. Christ, Hugh, she's perfect for the part! She *wants* to do it! And who the hell else have you seen who even comes close?"

Laura sank into a canvas chair and waited, wondering when this argument between Hugh Archer and his director, Brian Bernstein, would end. It was insane. More than insane. The shooting of *Anne of Green Gables* started tomorrow, and the title role still had not been cast. Everything about this project was spelling disaster because of the grossly insufficient lead time. Set people still were painting walls in the country kitchen; props were being wheeled in; costume fitters were working in one corner, relocated here within sight of Archer because he could not run all over the back lot, answering questions. There was a growing mountain of sleeping bags used by the crew members who were working twenty hours a day and sleeping on the set. And on top of everything Bernstein was insisting his girlfriend, a sixteen-year-old more than young enough to be his daughter, get the lead role. The same fight had been staged every hour of every day this week.

"Childlike!" Archer was steaming, harassed and rabid-looking. "That's some fucking joke, considering she's been in your bed for almost a year! I've seen hookers in this town who looked more childlike!"

"Then you can fucking get one of them to direct your series, because I quit!"

Bernstein stalked off.

Archer watched with murderous eyes, then turned to the jeans-and-blazer-clad girl who was his production assistant.

"Keep that lousy son-of-a-bitch out of my way for the rest of the day. I don't want to see him."

"Right, Hugh. Shall I try to line up—"

"Why? He knows he can't quit. The union would have his balls." He turned to Laura. "You need something?"

She raised a hand and nodded to Maxy, who now sat beside her. Thank God the former script editor from *Twenty-two Wentworth* had been Archer's choice for the same job here.

"We've got a problem," said Laura. "Eulah Beth and Andrew keep rewriting their lines, and we can't stop them—"

"Excuse me, Hugh—"

The line producer in charge of business details for the production came up, interrupting her. His hand was on Archer's shoulder.

"We've got a problem."

Already Archer, glancing at his watch, was turning away.

Maxy gave a dry shrug and nudged a sugarless mint from the roll in her hand.

"Looks like we tackle the two old dears again ourselves," she said. "Hey, Laura, you okay? You look mighty pale."

Laura hadn't told anyone she was pregnant. Did she look as drained as she felt? The schedule she'd been on was bad enough. It didn't help that she woke up in the hours she should have been sleeping to lie awake for long stretches, wondering what—if anything—could have made things work between her and Jake.

"Just a product of this rarefied atmosphere," she said. The doctor had told her she'd feel tired during this first trimester. She managed a smile.

Adam, recruited because she and Maxy knew his work from the *Wentworth* days and because Archer had seen the advantage of teaming people already used to working together, sauntered up to join them. His expression was as out of sorts as ever.

To wrest order from the bedlam of having no scripts ready, the network was putting him and Laura up at the nearby Sheraton-Universal. Writing around the clock, Laura had produced another segment, and Adam now tossed Maxy a folder, which Laura surmised held Week Three.

"Well, mama editor, there it is. This ought to be enough to hold us until we're cancelled."

The joke was so close to the truth none of them laughed.

"Just because we go up against a show that's made the top ten for two years running?" said Maxy. "Such a pessimist!"

"Shit," said Adam, draping himself on the bare floor and lying back wearily. "You know—we all know by now—that it's going to fail."

"We'll go six weeks at least. Long enough for the net to have figures showing that nobody's watching us," Maxy predicted with cynical wisdom.

But we all believe it's doomed no matter what we do, thought Laura.

The network had given *Green Gables* a big publicity splash, but not the reams of articles and more importantly the weeks of hype that would have the audience looking for a show before it even hit the air. Maxy was right. Throw it on without adequate preparation, against competition that would murder it anyway, and in spite of a wonderful cast and wonderful scripts, it was going to sink.

Ta-dah, the network would have done its best. Bring on the sleazy sitcoms.

"Hey, Laura, have I told you today that I love my part?" Manuel Martin, who would play the schoolmaster, upgraded to a more important role for television, came up beaming to perch on the edge of her chair. He was lean and pantherlike with beautiful, heart-stopping eyes, and Laura was sure he sincerely loved the whole story-concept as much as he seemed to.

"I read your second week's script last night," he continued, and though he was still smiling, he was serious now. "It's so fine, Laura. And it's so fine to be part of something with the quality this series has."

She'd heard Eulah Beth and Andrew, also cast in continuing roles, saying much the same thing to one another. They meant it, too, she thought. But were they turning a blind eye to the facts? Surely the writers weren't the only ones who expected the series to flop.

"Hey, don't look so glum," Manuel urged as she murmured polite words of thanks. "This mess will get straightened out by tomorrow. We might even have someone for Anne—or we can dye Maxy's hair red and let her play the part."

Maxy snorted and took her leave. Manuel caught Laura's hand.

"Come on. Let's go somewhere and get a sandwich. We'll even go outside the studio—no, we'll be really daring and go clear down to Sunset."

The warmth of his hand was an unexpected spark of sanity. Through the chaos around them, there came the definite sound of small objects scattering. A voice rose, shrill with frustration.

"How can I tell what it's going to look like when I don't have anyone to fit it on?" demanded the costume fitter, who had heaved a box of pins. "*If* they have an Anne tomorrow, she'll have to be pinned into everything she wears, right down to her bloomers!"

"I'll take you up on the sandwich, but not on Sunset," said Laura. After lunch she was going to steal the time to visit Nel.

But Nel was asleep, as she had been on Laura's previous visit. Her breath came sporadically, sometimes ceasing so long that Laura's heart caught.

"Oh, God, Eddie! Can't they do something?" she whispered. "Use oxygen? A respirator?"

He shook his head.

"Nel says it won't do any good—she'd rather have her cigarettes."

In the past week he had aged years. There were lines at his eyes.

"Has Jessamyn—does she know?"

His mouth grew hard. "She hasn't been in—just sends lots of flowers. Nel doesn't mind."

"Doesn't *know*? Laura wondered. No, Nel was lucid. That was the horror of it. She slid her arm through Eddie's, and they stood a moment in silent comradeship. It was so quiet here . . . so peaceful. This was the real world, and the one she'd left a few hours ago was only pretend.

"I'll come back tonight," she said at last. *Somehow*, she added silently.

Back at Soundstage Twelve, she ate a boiled egg, though she didn't want it. She was so tired . . . *so* tired, but she had to keep going. And the doctor really thought she could work in two naps a day, she thought with glum amusement.

"Where've you been hiding? I've been hunting all over for you!" Maxy pounced on her, sounding testy. "Network doesn't like the teapot scene. They want it oomphed up."

"By four o'clock?" Laura didn't try to hide her sarcasm as the Second Week script was shoved toward her. Just yesterday they'd loved the teapot scene.

"No," said Maxy. "At half-past-three."

Laura started toward the cubbyhole made for her with portable walls. What had taken her long, grueling days to produce had been read and dissected by someone, somewhere—not any of the network people they were actually working with, but some assistant who needed to justify his salary, more than likely—in possibly twenty minutes.

And the changes that pleased that unknown person would have Archer in a tailspin, she thought. It was too typical.

At three-fifteen she emerged with the changes made and eyes and body stiff. Where was Maxy, and was there time to let her skim the replacement scene? Laura looked around at the same confusion she'd left. What was happening? Did they have an Anne yet?

As soon as she began to walk, she had her answer. At the

other end of the soundstage Bernstein was dogging Archer while Archer's female assistant tried to intervene.

"She can *dye* her hair red! Let me call her agent and tell him she has the part, Hugh."

"Casting's sending me two more girls. Will you just let me get to them?"

No program, not even the worst of them, had ever been this close to shooting without a main part cast. It was insane. But now Archer caught sight of her, and he was scowling.

"Jesus, it's about time! Were you writing it out in cuneiform? You've just missed Fairchild. He's on his way over to squeeze ass at makeup. Get that to him and meet me at six. We'll decide what we really want to do with that scene."

Laura clamped down on her temper. Everyone was edgy, brusque. She made her way outside, hoping to find a shuttle to take her to makeup. There were none in sight, so with a sigh she set off at a pace just short of trotting. Once she had delivered her substitute scene to the network liaison, perhaps she could get back to her hotel and steal a few hours' sleep.

But she went through the red door of the makeup department only to find that Fairchild was on his way back to Soundstage Twelve. Probably in the only available shuttle too, she thought bitterly.

Outside again she pressed a hand to her head to push back the tiredness. If she called for a shuttle, she might have to wait ten minutes for it. Common sense told her she could have the revisions in Fairchild's hands by then.

I can't force myself to do it, she thought, looking back up a gray line of buildings. She wanted coffee, five minutes' rest, anything. Instead she beagn to walk mechanically once again.

The lights of the soundstage were dreamlike now as she stepped in. Noise and confusion droned disconcertingly in her ears. Archer, with Fairchild, was on her at once.

"God damn it, where have you been?"

"At makeup hunting—"

The revisions were ripped from her hands and shoved at Fairchild.

"Here, look this over," said Archer, ignoring her presence as he would a TV with the sound turned down.

Fairchild thumbed blandly through the revisions. "I'll see you both at eight. We'll have dinner sent in. If there are any more changes in this one, let's iron them out tonight. Otherwise we'll get Laura going on the treatment for Episode Four."

"Episode Four!" Laura exploded, ragged with surprise and anger.

Archer, plainly peeved that she was mixing in, glanced at her.

"Yes, and by the way there's someone from *TV Guide* waiting in my office to interview you. For God's sake, bluff if he asks you who we've got for Anne."

A messenger from casting was loping toward them.

"Hu—"

"I don't give a *damn* who's waiting for me!" Laura spoke so vehemently that all of them looked at her. "You promised Adam and me another writer. You said we'd get a breather after Episode Three!"

"I haven't had time to find another writer!" snapped Archer. "And you're the one who wanted it in your contract you'd do three more segments."

Her head spun as she tried to digest what he was saying. She wanted to sleep . . . she wanted to see Nel . . . and now frail, white-haired, tyrannical Eulah Beth was bearing down on her. . . .

"Laura sweet, I just can't speak these lines in this last scene with Matthew. They don't seem quite *right*. So Andrew and I have changed . . ."

Eulah Beth's wrinkled face wobbled, an image on water. Laura tried not to cry out, tried to keep herself from falling, but as her knees gave way, darkness rushed over her, and she had, for the briefest instant, the sense of being back with Nel.

"Eddie . . . a cigarette."

Nel's voice was a whisper, shallow, inaudible. Eddie lighted the cigarette and held it to Nel's lips. For a long time now he'd been holding them for her, ever since he'd realized she'd given up this pleasure not to prolong her days, but because her weakening arm—and her pride—no longer allowed it.

Now her lips could scarcely hold the cigarette tightly enough to inhale. Every time he lit up for her, he prayed it would kill her. Nel would like that, controlling her death as she had controlled her life. He was in agony, watching her helpless.

But Nel never so much as choked, just lay there peacefully. In Eddie's eyes she still was beautiful. The sleek black wig Laura had bought her was not really Nel, and yet it was—Nel as she wanted to be.

He was glad Laura hadn't seen her awake, wouldn't know the last stages. Someone at the studio had called less than an hour ago and told him of Laura's collapse.

They'd found this number in Laura's pocket, the caller had said. They were taking her to St. John's. He'd given them the number of her home and felt sorry there would be no one there to care about her except the housekeeper.

Naturally he would not tell Nel.

"Laura came in while you were sleeping," he said. "Said she'd try to get back sometime, but she's pretty busy."

Nel had finished the cigarette. She spoke again.

". . . no . . . damn . . . good."

He knew Nel meant she herself wasn't. Leaning forward he winked suggestively.

"Hey, there, Nellie, I'd say you're pretty good at a lot of things. When you get out of here, you and I are going to have ourselves one fine trip."

The corners of her mouth twitched. Eddie told himself she was trying to smile.

The trip they would take was a daily game now, and every day he changed the location.

"I've been thinking we might try Amsterdam," he said. "All those girls in cages . . ."

Her eyes blinked. She struggled to speak.

"Eddie . . . I don't *want* this . . ."

Something pooled in her eyes—tears from his Nellie who he'd never seen cry. She was pleading with him, and he'd never failed her. He knew what he had to do. He'd get the stuff.

It was morning. Or maybe it was afternoon. Laura didn't know. She looked at the whiteness around her, the comforting sheets, and for a moment was grateful merely to lie there, not pushing herself when she was exhausted, not having to keep up appearances that all was well.

Tears overflowed her eyes and ran down her cheeks. She struck them back angrily. She was raw with the grief of losing Jake, and nobody knew, nobody gave a damn. Here she no longer had to pretend. Let's face it, I don't have the energy to pretend, she thought wearily. But I'm not licked. I'll rest—for the baby's sake and for my own. I'll bounce back. I'm going to make it just fine on my own. Nothing's going to stop me.

They had brought her here yesterday, and when she first had awakened and realized what had happened, her only thought had been an instinctive fear about the baby. But the baby was all right. The doctor had promised her that three times.

They were allowing her no visitors. Nervous as well as physical exhaustion, they said. Well, who was there to see her? Nel was across town in a bed like this one, and Jake was gone. That left Maxy, Ben, maybe Archer slipping a script to her to fix. She grimaced. Already she could feel herself growing impatient at lying here. But if rest was what was needed, then she'd rest. Whatever the price, she meant to survive.

Her door edged open. She turned her head without enthusiasm, expecting a nurse.

Instead Daniel Katz cleared his throat.

"Hello. How are you feeling?"

She tried to find the energy to be surprised.

"How did you get in?" she asked. "They're not letting anyone see me."

His face crinkled in a smile, and he came toward the bed.

"Just walked in. When you act like you know what you're doing, people never question it. If you don't feel up to it, I'll leave, of course."

"No. It's perfectly lovely."

They looked at each other, and the moment seemed curiously awkward.

"I'm sorry," Katz said gently. "About you and Jake too, I mean. You must have been under terrible pressure this last month."

Laura didn't answer, and tears came from nowhere to threaten her. The gears in her head seemed to mesh so slowly. *Are you my father?* she wanted to ask. She looked at his disarrayed hair, the kind gray eyes. She'd tried to see so many links where none existed—between her and Jessamyn, between her and Jake. Even if she knew, this one might prove just as disappointing.

"There's been one good thing," she said. "I've learned I'm going to have a baby." She stopped, realizing how odd the comment must sound. "I don't know why I said that—it must be whatever they're giving me here. I haven't exactly been broadcasting the news."

But she did know why, didn't she?

"Oh," Katz said. He regarded her in a moment of sheer bewilderment before a smile broke through. "Well, that's wonderful! It really is. In fact it makes what I came here to see you about seem even more sensible."

He spoke with calm, but he seemed to be floundering. Laura felt the weak beat of her pulse grow faster. Was it true? Was he going to tell her?

Daniel Katz cleared his throat.

"I just got back from Rome, you know, and when I heard about you and Jake . . . it just seemed to me that when you leave here you shouldn't go home alone to an empty house and unhappy memories. I've got an awfully nice couple that looks after my place. Let me take you there. Let the three of us take care of you for a while."

Perhaps he was no more willing to acknowledge her than Jessamyn was. But she was stronger now than she had been once. She pressed the question anyway.

"Why?"

He blinked. His gaze avoided hers.

"Jake said you were my father. Is that true?"

A gusty sigh escaped him. He rumpled a hand through his fringe of hair.

"I'm not sure," he said, and his face looked sad. "I think it's very likely. I lived with Jessamyn for about four months around the time when you'd have been conceived, and in those days she wasn't—I don't believe she was sleeping with anyone else." He sighed again. "Jake must have guessed, considering your age and who Jessamyn was working with then, and taken it on himself to bring us together."

Because Jake cared, thought Laura. Damn it, Jake had *cared*! A pity time couldn't turn back on itself—but time never could.

She rubbed at her forehead, which was starting to feel annoyingly thick.

"I'm sorry. I shouldn't have asked you," she said, thinking how kind Katz had been to her.

His tense expression gave way to glowing brightness.

"Oh no—I've wanted to tell you." He caught her hand, squeezed it shyly, and smiled. "I'm afraid I just didn't know how you'd react . . . all those years when you were growing up with no one to care. And I had no idea. And I can't make it up to you." He paused, and the brightness dimmed for a moment. "We'll never know for sure, of course. Jessamyn would never give either of us that satisfaction. But I'd like to believe you're my daughter, Laura. I'd like to start from now and be your father."

She smiled and knew that the proof didn't matter.

"I'd like that too."

Katz polished his glasses and stood up.

"I've tired you out. I hope my coming here hasn't upset you."

She shook her head from side to side against the pillow. So many questions danced in her mind. Had he pulled any strings to get her the *Wentworth* job? To help her in any way?

"Dan? How did it happen? You and Jessamyn are so . . . different."

He turned from the door, his smile as rueful now as it was kindly.

"Oh, I was young and eager to make my mark on the world, and Jessamyn was very beautiful." He rumpled his hair. "Even then, though, it was apparent how vicious she'd become if she ever had power. So beautiful . . . and so corrupt."

The door popped open, almost flattening him. The charge nurse, starchy and short, bustled in and stopped, staring at his presence indignantly. Katz, his eyes twinkling with mischief, smiled at her.

"I'm Dr. Katz, just in consulting with Miss Fitzgerald about megavitamin therapy. Has she been resting well?"

The nurse snorted what was probably her opinion of vitamins.

"Yes, Dr. Morton's been seeing to that." She turned to Laura. "Miss Fitzgerald, there's a man at the nurses' station insisting he's your husband. He was out here yesterday, too, but we understood . . . do you want to see him?"

For an instant Laura's heart leaped, with longing and with a love not yet completely laid to rest. Then, curling her hands into fists of hard resolve, she shook her head.

"Are you sure, Laura?" Katz asked softly as the nurse whipped out again. "I don't know what the differences were between you, and I'm aware Jake's been on a sort of power trip of late. But sometimes it's awfully hard for people in our business to sort out values. I'm not sure Jake's any different from how I was once—confused about what really matters."

Laura smiled, not quite certain of what she was feeling.

"I'm not sure of anything much these days—but no, I don't want to see him."

Katz nodded.

"Take care of my grandchild," he said, and let himself out.

Eddie watched the heroin hit Nel's system. Her body did not convulse like some he'd seen. When enough time had passed for her heart to stop, he felt for her pulse. She lay tranquil now. Truly tranquil. Nellie had departed on that trip.

He dropped the spoon and the needle into the trash can, still clutching Nel's lighter that he had used to heat the stuff. It was nighttime. Eddie went to stand at the window.

He could not believe she was really gone. Her vital presence still seemed to fill the room, wisecracking, badgering him, giving him the same loving hard time as always.

He'd gotten the stuff last night, after seeing Nel's tears. This morning, though, she had seemed so much better. She'd even managed to smile at him. He'd known it couldn't last, that it was one of those good days before the end that folks talked about. Still he couldn't bring himself to snuff out her brightness then.

This afternoon the suffering had returned, the terrible struggle for every breath of air. Nel wasn't meant to endure that sort of humiliation. He'd chosen the evening visiting hours because there was little chance of interruption by nurses or anyone else.

For a moment, just as when he'd left that dead man in the elevator, Eddie thought how easy it all had been. Killing someone, finding a source of smack, giving it, all seemed like child's play. It made his years as a cop look bitterly futile.

Eddie passed a hand in front of his eyes. He could see Detroit as though it were yesterday. That had been the reality of his life—that and these months with Nel. In between everything was cobwebby. Had his entire life been wasted?

Walking back to Nel's bed he put on his hat, cocking it down slightly the way she liked it.

"I'm ready for our trip now too," he said, the words caressing her. "You didn't think I'd plan it and then run out on you, did you, Nellie?"

He thought carefully as he walked down the hall and joined a group of visitors and white-clad interns in an elevator. He could not let his guard down yet, not here so close to so many doctors and life-saving gadgets. Therefore he did as he'd done every time he left the hospital; waited until a cluster of people headed for the parking lot and then left in the midst of them.

As he started his car, he wondered why the men who were following him hadn't simply wired the ignition, blown him to smithereens. Maybe it wasn't their style. Maybe they were tidy.

They did not keep a single car after him as he drove. Yes, they were tidy. A block behind him he saw a blue Cadillac, a yellow Lincoln, a small and dark Ferrari. Which would it be?

He drove to a part of the city where streets were deserted. He got out and did not look back. There was a streetlight on the corner. Eddie walked toward it. He heard the sound of the shot and in its echo knew that he and Nel would never be apart again.

"More!" demanded the greedy mouth to her left.

Hair tumbling back over her shoulders, naked, Jessamyn laughed.

She stood on her knees in her heart-shaped bed. A muscled young man reclined on her left; Giorgio, her Italian count, on her right. In her hand she held a bottle of champagne that she tipped slightly, now on this side of her, now on the other, and as the delectable liquid slid down her breasts the two men lapped it from her nipples like nursing twins.

She swayed herself above them, exultant, glorying in the frenzy to which she was driving them. They had started this party three days ago, celebrating Tico's twenty-fourth birthday.

The Italian, Giorgio, had long ago started to bore her, but Tico, who had a small part in the new picture she had just signed for, was inexhaustible. An animal. Even now he shoved the other man aside, threw Jessamyn down, and rammed his way in.

"Jesus, Jessamyn honey, I sure like your games!" he grunted.

A sound of satisfaction purred in her throat. She trailed one hand over his hard, raw body. Tico wasn't especially smart, but he pleased her enormously. And he couldn't get enough of her. He'd made that quite clear.

Her own breathing quickened. She eased her pointed nails in and out of his flesh.

"How'd you like to do this every night, hmmm, Tico?"

His circumference increased, nearly splitting her. She laughed wildly. A few—a very few people—had made the mistake of thinking Jess Friday was growing older. She'd proved them wrong. She'd never been more popular than she was right now. Or richer. Or more powerful. 'I want Van Greenberg's head,' she'd told the balding tycoon who'd shared her swimming pool. And he'd seen to it that the two-bit actress O.D.'d at Greenberg's apartment, and that a stash that Greenberg didn't know existed was found there.

She locked her fingers in Tico's tousled black hair, moaning and smiling. She would take Tico in. She'd teach him. She'd mold him to suit her, and his wonderful animal body and urges would be all hers.

On the stand by her bed the phone rang, but she ignored it. One of the servants would answer. She'd left strict orders not to be disturbed.

There were no bad dreams left in her world now. She must tell Nel. Yes, she thought smiling at her own generosity, she'd bury the hatchet. Tomorrow she'd make it a point to go see Nel.

Thirty-four 🦅

Yesterday, after Dan Katz left, she had made them let her sit up. Today Laura was determined to read. But as she lay amid the comforting white pillows, she found herself wondering what was happening back on the *Green Gables* set. Had they chosen an Anne? Had they started to shoot her first script today, right on schedule? Would she still be able to write at least one more episode by the time she got out of this bed?

Suddenly, for the first time in weeks, she laughed.

"Oh, no! I've become an addict just like the rest of them!" she confessed to the walls.

My father's daughter, she thought, *and in my own right a darned good writer. Dan didn't pull any strings for me. He's not that type. Whatever I've gotten, I've gotten on my own.*

Outside in the hall she heard the rattle of buckets. She liked the daily cleaning. It reminded her of the small hotel in Mexico, and Portero's endless jokes and going for beer. Nice things. Small things. Yes, she was definitely a person who liked small things.

A foot and a mop wedged her door open, as the ponderous black woman who cleaned her room started in. But the rest of the woman was still outside, talking to a co-worker in the hall.

"Whatcha think of that fancy funeral they're giving her? Ah, you're just too young to remember, then. I can still see her in that movie where she danced in the spangly red dress. Wanted to be just like her, yes ma'am!"

Humming vigorously, playing to her unseen audience in the hall, the cleaning woman backed into the room. Her expansive rear was turned toward the ceiling as, with hands on knees, she waggled it in her version of an admired dance step, to a rhythm only she could hear, then straightened and lifted sausagelike legs in what were supposed to be pert kicks.

She was dreamy-eyed as she turned and saw Laura watching her.

"How you doin' this morning, honey? You lookin' better."

Still humming, still filled with life, she reached for her mop.

But Laura was looking at her, fingers holding tightly to the sheets. She did not remember the tune or the steps, but once she had seen an old movie where Nel had danced in a spangly red dress.

"You—who were you talking about?" she asked. "Who danced like that? Was it Nel Simmons?"

The cleaning woman's face broke into a delighted smile.

"You heard of her, have you? She was a long time back. Don't know what happened to her all these years. My, but she was one classy lady!"

As she splashed her mop into the bucket, the woman who had spoken executed a few light-footed steps.

The shock of it slammed against Laura like an enormous wave and then with equal speed receded. It was not so unexpected. Nel had prepared her for it. But learning like this . . . from a stranger . . . and the cruelest part was being isolated here, cut off, and having no part of the end of Nel's life.

She brushed angrily at the tears that were flooding her. Nel had suffered; she was glad that suffering had ended. And a part of her, whispering, knew already what she must do. Nel deserved a better tribute than tears.

Laura sat on the beach below the rambling white house she had shared with Jake, watching shallow waves bring fresh-washed grains of sand toward her and lift others away.

Like life, she thought.

It was almost evening.

She had thrown the hospital into pandemonium by walking out without a discharge. She had sent her own housekeeper into a tizzy by showing up unannounced. And for what? To see that headline. To know Eddie was dead too. She felt so numb inside. So empty.

But she'd done what she knew she had to the moment she realized she'd never see Nel again. Tomorrow she was going to Nel's funeral. There was nothing to be won lying there in that hospital bed. What fitting tribute could she give to Nel, who had believed in her, except the one of picking up and going on with life?

The stone step where she sat was slightly chilly. Her old shirt and jeans were comforting, like her own skin. Above the low splash of the waves she heard a sound. She turned. Jake was standing halfway down the stairs, the fire of the setting sun brindled in his hair.

"They told me at the hospital you'd gone home. I'll leave if you ask—but please, Laura, let me have five minutes."

For a moment she felt they were part of a painting, frozen, with Jake above and the sea below. Slowly she looked back toward the water, emotions already too overloaded by the loss of Nel to feel.

"I don't believe there's anything left to say, Jake."

She waited but she did not hear his footsteps moving away.

"I've got to try."

He came a few steps toward her. His voice was clear and rich and urgent.

"Once I thought—maybe even said—you had no guts, Laura. That you were soft, that you wouldn't survive. Now I know I had it all backward. You're the strong one. Kind and caring, yes, but with your own kind of courage. The courage to do what you believe.

"And me?" He laughed unhappily. "I was willing to sell

my soul—and our marriage too, I guess—for a whiff of success, maybe because deep down I wasn't sure I could ever be the brilliant producer I wanted to be. When I thought I'd done—something unforgivable—that I'd—that I'd slept with Jessamyn but was too drunk to remember . . . I didn't even have nerve enough to come to you and be honest and hope to God you loved me enough to understand. So I made it worse. I tried to throw all the blame on you. I ran around with Kimberly to prove—I don't know what. That I didn't need you? Or that I was certifiably no damn good."

"I'm sorry for you, Jake. I really am."

Her throat ached for him. She hoped this confession would ease the despair she heard in his words.

Again he came a few steps down. He stood level with her shoulders now.

"That isn't what I came to tell you, Laura. I came to tell you that—" He swallowed awkwardly. "I'm on the wagon. In terms of wheeling and dealing as well as booze. I'm finished with Jessamyn's company. I'm finished with the series I was going to do for ABC. In fact it's going to take a hell of a lot of work for me not to be finished period. But I mean to do it. I mean to get up the ladder again. Only this time I want to know I've done it on my own. If I can do that, Laura—prove myself—would you let me come back? Let me have one last chance?"

She did not allow herself to hear all he was saying. The numbness over Nel, over Eddie, over many losses was a welcome barrier between them.

"Please, Laura! Without you, nothing I do or am will ever have meaning!"

There was anguish in his voice. He dropped to one knee on the stone step above her.

"I love you, Laura. When I first said those words to you, I had no idea what they really meant—what love really was. Now I do."

Each word was a caress filled with longing. She trembled in response. There were lines on his face that hadn't been there before, across his forehead, at the corners of his mouth. Her fingers ached with the need to reach out and smooth them away.

"Laura, I—there's never been another woman who's touched what's inside of me. There never will be." His darkened eyes swept hers. "I can give something of myself in return now,

Laura. I understand that part of it. I don't want to lose you, even though I've been selfish and arrogant and I deserve to. Please—I'll do anything, anything you ask to make things right. I want what there is—what there was once between us—to work again."

Echoes of other chances given rang in her thoughts. She buried her head in her hands. She had thought herself strong. She had thought herself impervious to this man, and yet now she felt herself battered by a despair and a yearning even deeper than grief.

"I want it to work too, Jake. I think . . ." She fought to keep her voice steady. ". . . you'll always be the only man I love. But I don't know if it can work. I think it's too late. I think we're too different."

Raising her head, she met his eyes. They reached for her, wild, lonely, desolate, and the interlocking of their gazes wrenched at her. Heart and sinews seemed to rip apart within her and leave her bleeding. A silent cry of pain rose in her throat. This look . . . this look was pulling at her as violently as the crashing waves behind her pulled at the sand. With a blink against tears, she turned back toward the sea and heard him leave.

The door to the Forest Lawn funeral home in Hollywood Hills opened to her. Laura, in her soft gray dress with billowing sleeves, stood suddenly in a crowd, a crush, a room full of people. Through the hushed discreetness reserved for such occasions wove a faint hum, an unmistakable thread of life continuing. Laura could not decide whether the atmosphere was glib—an insult—or whether its energy was exactly right for Nel.

She saw the closed casket, black and gleaming and raised above the mounds of flowers that spread on either side of it for several yards. White sprays, red sprays, crosses and wreaths, one cheeky arrangement gay with tiger lillies. Beyond the casket Jessamyn stood, the perfect picture of mourning. She wore a black Chanel suit and a storybook hat that rode the rippling waves of her hair, accenting its radiance and giving her a look of eternal youthfulness. On one arm she carried a fat white dog collared in black.

"Oh, she was my best friend. My very best friend. We were *so* close!" she was declaring.

She had thrown this funeral for Nel. The papers had mentioned it. What a hypocrite, Laura thought.

Jessamyn's coterie had never been larger. The heads of two major movie studios were with her, and her agent of course; stars and directors, a publicist, a handsome young man who hovered around her like a current lover, and—like her dearest of all chums—Kimberly Curran.

At least Jake wouldn't be here, Laura thought dully. She'd believed him yesterday when he'd said Jessamyn meant nothing to him—Kimberly meant nothing to him.

She had tried to be inconspicuous, but as she moved into the room people spoke to her. The room was so crowded, not only with big names but also with the people Nel had loved.

"*Lauracita!*" Lupita pushed through to take her arm. "What are you doing here? Every day I am checking the hospital, and they say you'll be staying there some days *más*."

Laura smiled and brushed a kiss on her cheek. She was swept onward.

"Laura!" A white-haired soundman she'd known only by name before he signed on with *Green Gables* was holding her hand. Laura knew he must have sneaked away from work to come here. "You okay?" he was asking. "You sure scared the hell out of all of us."

"I'm fine now. Fine . . ."

A producer was offering condolences, saying he remembered bouncing her on his knee. All she wanted was to be free of them. All she wanted was to stand for a moment with Nel.

Now Jessamyn was sashaying toward her, all bright falseness. She held out a jewel-clad hand.

"Laura, darling! I'm *so* glad you're here. You've given us all such a worry!"

Laura looked at the beautiful face she'd longed to touch as a child, at the amber eyes where she'd sought so desperately to spark some pleased acknowledgment of their kinship. Suddenly she knew that the old fascination was gone. She felt nothing toward this woman—no longing, no wistfulness, not even sadness.

Go to hell, Jessamyn. Have you told these people with you how you threw Nel out when she was sick and dying?

High among the roses and baskets of glads and tiger lilies lay the one who had been in the truest sense her mother, Laura realized. Mentor, friend, source of wisdom—how many things Nel had been to her! Together they had formed their own generations, their own kind of family. She had been drawn here today by bonds that went deeper than blood.

Ignoring Jessamyn's outstretched hand, Laura skirted her with the same distaste she would feel toward any other stranger who intruded upon such private mourning. Then, at last, she was standing by the mountain of flowers erected to Nel.

A thought flashed before her, a memory of the day Nel told her she was dying. There had been that terrible interval when Nel fought for breath. But afterward, when Nel spoke again, it had seemed to Laura that they shared communication so complete it had never been interrupted.

Now it never would be, Laura thought.

The scent of the flowers was much too sweet in the crowded room. Yet as she stared at them, thinking how pleased Nel would have been at all this evidence of admiration, she found herself regretting that in her return home yesterday she'd not thought to order an offering of her own. She would have sent . . . but here, at her feet and almost hidden, she caught the purple of pansies. She knelt, touched that someone else had remembered Nel's simple favorites.

Her finger sought the card and turned it over. She saw the words.

From Laura

In Jake's hand.

Pressing knuckles against her mouth, she felt the sudden searing of some insight mixed with pain. The pansies told her so much about Jake. About them.

Yesterday she'd been afraid to hope . . . afraid to believe. Now she knew he loved her. She knew he had changed. Blindly she looked up, seeking him.

He stood on the other side of the room, apart from the crowd. His eyes were on her, but he held himself immobile. As they looked at one another, Laura could admit to herself how much she really loved him, really needed him.

She tried to rise but couldn't. Her knees had lost their strength. His face had been uncertain but now, like an advancing swordsman, he began to shoulder his way toward her, clearing passage through the crowd. He knelt but did not lift her.

"Laura?"

His hand closed over hers, and Laura saw her anguish and longing mirrored in him.

"I'm all right."

"I ordered them when I thought you were still in the hospital," he said simply. "I thought you'd want it."

People were noticing them, assuming she'd collapsed again, and giving them space. Laura felt herself being lifted gently to her feet.

"You shouldn't have put yourself through this," Jake said roughly. His face was ravaged. "You ought to be resting. And you—you're going to have that baby."

He said it so uncertainly, so awkwardly, that for a moment Laura remembered him as he had been the night they met in Jessamyn's study. Then, looking into his eyes, she knew he was that same man, torn and tested and made stronger by his fate as she'd been by hers.

"I'm going to have *our* baby," she corrected in a whisper. "Do you care about that?"

As though unable to restrain himself, he touched her face. His jaw moved unsteadily.

"Christ, Laura, I care about *you* more than anything in this world. I love you so much. If you want our baby, for whatever reason, I care about that."

For the first time Laura had the sense of looking directly into his soul. There was no more facade. As they stared at each other, helpless to move, she felt herself in the presence of something elusive, the beginning of family ties born not of blood but of loving and giving and working to nurture them.

The child inside her was hers because she loved it, not the other way around. That was the truth of things. The truth of what there had been between her and Nel. The truth, perhaps, of generations.

"I love you too. So very much," she said.

She slid her arms around Jake's neck.

A second of disbelief passed before he lowered his mouth to hers. There in the midst of the crowd, in the midst of Nel's funeral, they kissed each other, over and over. Jake's hands held her face with tenderness never known before; they sheltered each other. And as their lips moved, expressing what words never could, Laura felt the slow-dawning wonder of bonds that could not be broken.

"Let's go home," she said, and slipped her hand in his.

Jake nodded.

From somewhere distant, Laura felt the warm approval of Nel's smile.

Jessamyn watched the little scene with foaming jealousy. That bastard Turner fawning over the wife who was supposed to be divorcing him—and everyone watching them! Why the fuss?

"Gee, who was that?" asked Tico, as the couple with their arms wound tightly around each other took their exit. "The girl's sure got some pretty face."

Jessamyn fixed him with a scathing look. He shrugged and moved away to stand by Deidre. Sulking at the ingratitude of those around her, Jessamyn reached down to pet the doggie resting in her arms.

But her doggie didn't respond to her. He didn't even raise his head. Jessamyn shook his plump little body to rouse him from his lethargy. Then, as comprehension reached her, she cast him from her with a cry. Ying-Ying thumped to the floor at her feet and lay unmoving.

"Deidre! Deidre!" she shrieked.

Tico, the simmering human animal who shared her bed and kept The Dream away, had disappeared. Where was Deidre? Where was her dull little maid? She turned, stumbled, her storybook hat came askew. There was Po, her other white dog, hopping at the knee of a kneeling Tico. She called for Po, but the dog was licking greedily at Tico's hand, gobbling something.

"Aw, the little buggers love anybody who stuffs them with chocolates." Tico's voice floated to her. "Regular little junkies Jess has made of them."

Jessamyn felt tears, and a horrible panic, start to rise.

Her dogs were gone.

Nel was gone.

She was alone.

About the Author

With her two previous LOVE & LIFE novels, A PRIVATE MATTER and INSIGHTS, and her historical romance, CAPTAIN'S PLEASURE, Mary Ruth Myers has touched the hearts and imaginations of readers from coast to coast. She writes of relationships—of human ties forged and tested in new ways, as contemporary men and women struggle to meet timeless needs.

A graduate of the University of Missouri School of Journalism, Ms. Myers wrote for newspapers in Michigan and Ohio before turning to fiction. She lives amid an eclectic mixture of modern furniture and pre-Colombian art with her husband, Henry, who owns a clock shop, their young daughter Jessica, and two cats. Their house, in the small Ohio village of Yellow Springs, is on the edge of a nature preserve. Ms. Myers likes to walk in the woods each morning before settling down to work in front of her new word processor.